Symphony
of Secrets

ALSO BY BRENDAN SLOCUMB

The Violin Conspiracy

Symphony
of Secrets

Brendan Slocumb

ANCHOR BOOKS
A Division of Penguin Random House LLC
New York

AN ANCHOR BOOKS ORIGINAL 2023

The Library of Congress has cataloged the Anchor Books edition as follows:
Names: Slocumb, Brendan, author.
Title: Symphony of secrets / Brendan Slocumb.
Description: First edition. | New York : Anchor Books, a division of
    Penguin Random House, LLC, 2023.
Identifiers: LCCN 2022058719
Subjects: GSAFD: Novels.
Classification: LCC PS3619.L645 S96 2023 | DDC 813/.6—dc23
LC record available at https://lccn.loc.gov/2022058719

Anchor Books Hardcover ISBN: 978-0-593-31544-6
eBook ISBN: 978-0-593-31546-0

Book design by Nicholas Alguire

anchorbooks.com

Printed in the United States of America
10   9   8   7   6   5   4   3   2   1

This is for anyone whose voice was muted; for those who didn't have the chance to be heard—or for those who, like my brother Kevin, had their voices taken far too soon.

OVERTURE

1936

SIXTEEN HOURS BEFORE HIS DEATH, Frederic Delaney realized that he'd left his Hutchinson champagne stopper at home. It had always accompanied him to a debut performance. Always. What would its absence, now, mean on this night of all nights?

The rumble of the crowd beat against his dressing room door. A moment ago, he'd welcomed it like a quilt tucked around his shoulders, but now he felt the pressure of the audience's expectations enshrouding him, a white torrent against his chest.

He tried to convince himself that all would be well. He'd order a second bottle of champagne. It would be on hand by the end of the performance.

Besides, this was a brand-new moment in his life, a fresh start. Maybe it was time for a new ritual anyway. A second bottle to symbolize his second chance.

Tonight was, without question, that chance. Finishing this last opera had been an arduous journey (he imagined telling Edward

Kastenmeier, the *Times*'s head music critic, "Be sure to use the word *arduous*."), but now, looking back with perspective and distance, he could admit that the writing, and the rewriting, was well worth the agony. This, he told himself again, was his greatest creation, and it was, in a word, *glorious*. He knew it in his bones.

He mouthed the word to himself: *glorious*. He imagined how the word would look in print.

This was the music—this magnificent opera—that would relaunch his career. He would bestow a sardonic smile upon Kastenmeier when they next saw each other. "Has-been," Kastenmeier had called him, along with "washed-up" and "ridiculous." Tomorrow Kastenmeier would be whistling a tune replete with remorse, apology, and just a tiny bit of envy. Frederic only wished he could be there to watch Kastenmeier eat crow.

Frederic patted his trouser pockets again, still hunting for that errant stopper.

Until tonight, the ritual had always been the same: Pour out two glasses of champagne. The toast. Cork the bottle. The performance itself. The applause. The return to his dressing room. Then: Emptying out the final two glasses. The second toast. That was how it had gone for years now, years beyond counting. Beyond what he wanted to count.

He'd always brought a champagne stopper with him; a few years ago, in those heady days that would soon be his again, he used to leave it in his tuxedo pocket, because he'd have premieres several nights of the week, all in different theaters. Tonight a ballet uptown, tomorrow a Broadway musical, the next night a medley in a vaudeville house, and then the premiere for a film score. Champagne every night of the week: pour out two glasses before the performance, two glasses after, and the rest of the bottle—if any drops were left—a sacrifice to the gods.

No stopper in the little basket next to the refrigerator. He patted down his pockets a final time, as if a cork would magically manifest inside one.

So he'd throw away the rest of the champagne. For a moment he considered drinking it—that would be one way of making it gone—but of course that was absurd. He needed to have his wits about him during the performance.

Time to begin the ritual. The beginning of a new life.

He retrieved the two glasses from where they glowed upon a shelf, their wide bowls open to the night.

Then he slid the photograph out of his breast pocket. He propped it on a stack of books.

Uncorking the champagne, he poured out the two glasses, lifted one in a toast. The warmth of the liquor smashed against the back of his throat like a wave of joy, unexpected and familiar.

"Here we go, kiddo," he said, tilting the glass toward the photograph before taking a second sip. He sat back, closed his eyes briefly, and then opened them. If only he could cork up the champagne again, hold the trapped air in its bubbles tight inside the bottle for just a little longer.

The knock came at the door. "Mr. Delaney? Five minutes."

It was time.

He gulped down the rest of the glass's contents, barely tasting it, and set it down empty next to its still-full twin. He stood for a moment, resting the full weight of his palms on the desk, looking down at the glasses and the bottle and the photograph. Then he tucked the photograph back in his breast pocket.

When he opened the door, the crowd's murmur instantly expanded, nearly swallowing him in its roar.

With fewer than sixteen hours to live, Frederic Delaney stepped into the backstage corridor on his way to the lights and the applause and the accolades that he was certain would soon be his.

He passed a colored custodian. "Hattie," he told her, "have a fresh bottle of champagne waiting for me when I come back. And that half bottle on my desk—get rid of it. But leave the champagne in the glass."

ACT 1

Bern

1

The Extra K

Bern

PROFESSOR BERN HENDRICKS WAS LATE to class when the sound of an incoming email pinged in his inbox. He'd put on his favorite blue pinstripe, short-sleeve, but nobody would notice under his jacket and, wouldn't you know, there was a wrinkle right under the pocket. The jacket didn't completely cover it. So he'd had to haul out the ironing board and heat up the iron, and that took longer than it should have. Now he was running a good ten minutes late. But with the *Quicksilver* symphony flooding his earbuds, how could he hurry? The students could wait a few more minutes.

Maybe he should just skip class altogether, he thought. The *Quicksilver* was the obvious excuse. Delaney's *Quicksilver*—so-called because of the extraordinary melding of alto and tenor saxes layered over French horns—was one of Bern's absolute favorites. Bizet had effectively used an alto sax in his *L'Arlésienne* Suite, but Delaney's *Quicksilver* took it to an entirely different level. Every time Bern listened to the allegro moderato movement, it was as if a hole suddenly opened up in his chest and music cascaded in. No matter how many times he heard it, the melody rippled across his spine and he shivered under its impact. "That was double good," he mumbled to himself.

No wonder Frederic Delaney was the hands-down best composer—not just in America, Bern would argue, but in the entire world.

So there he was, seriously considering missing a class in only his second week of teaching just to listen to a symphony he'd heard hundreds of times before—when his email chimed.

He stared at his phone, hit PAUSE on the music.

Even without Delaney's music playing, it seemed as if Frederic Delaney were, right then, communicating directly with Bern from beyond the grave. The email was from the executive director of the Delaney Foundation. What were the odds that he'd get a message right when he was listening to—

He opened the email.

Dear Bern:

I hope you have been well since we last met.

I'm reaching out with a time-sensitive matter regarding Frederick Delaney.

I know that the school year has just started and you must be quite busy, but would you contact me as soon as you get this? Please call the number below, no matter the hour, from a location where you can speak freely. Someone will always be monitoring this line.

Sincerely,
Mallory Delaney Roberts
Executive Director
The Delaney Foundation

Right then he was halfway across the grounds of the University of Virginia, minutes from class. In the shadow of the ancient oak trees, the lushness of the early autumn grass glowed around him. He took a breath, and then another. Students played Frisbee on the terraces.

He wasn't aware of any of them, even when a Frisbee sailed past his left cheek, so close that he felt its breeze.

The email was some kind of scam. It had to be. Mallory Delaney Roberts wouldn't be writing to *him*. He doubted she even remembered who he was. She'd met him only a handful of times. Last month he'd seen an article in *Time* announcing a partnership between the Delaney Foundation and the Vatican for new musical outreach to Eastern Europe. And this woman was calling him Bern? The words glowed on the screen.

I'm reaching out with a time-sensitive matter regarding Frederick Delaney.

He'd paused right before his favorite section in the *Quicksilver*: the French horns' epic battle with the trombones, when the horns fought for supremacy but the trombones would, in just a second, kick their asses. "Sorry, horns," he mumbled as he logged out of his playlist. He googled the Foundation and clicked the link to the website, where Mallory's thumbnail photo smiled serenely at him. A bouffant helmet of too-dark dyed hair, pearl earrings, and a pearl choker.

The most memorable and last time they'd met, she had clasped his hands with both of hers and said, "Congratulations" and "I'm so sorry for your loss." He'd shaken her hands and said, "Thank you," and when he'd met her eyes, he had seen the gleam of tears to match his own.

By then, a month after their adviser, Jacques Simon, had passed away, there had been just two PhD students left in the program: Julie Ertl, who was already making plans to quit academia and go into advertising, and Bern. The ceremony—the unveiling, the signing of the books, the presentation of the first printed copy to the Delaney

Foundation—had seemed empty and all too silent without Jacques, who'd revered Frederic Delaney almost as much as Bern did. Almost.

He was about to be fifteen minutes late—the cutoff for how long students had to wait for a professor. They'd probably already be packing up. They might as well get a head start on the weekend, he decided. And this matter was *time sensitive*.

He'd explain and apologize to the kids next time.

Instead of heading up to the lecture hall, he dashed down to his office in the bowels of Old Cabell Hall. It had been built at the turn of the century, with typical Greek Revival architecture of red brick behind white columns—nothing like Columbia's chaos of golden stone and modern glass. Here the hallways and classrooms smelled musty and of distant mice.

Bern locked the door to his tiny broom closet of an office, sat down, and dialed Mallory's number.

The phone rang only once before a brisk woman's voice answered. "Delaney Foundation. Hello, Professor Hendricks. Hold, please, and let me put you through."

The phone clicked, and then another woman's voice, smoother, slipped through the phone line. "Bern. I'm so glad you reached out as quickly as you did."

He recognized her voice: old money, the most expensive prep schools in Connecticut or Rhode Island. "Of course," he said. "It's a pleasure to speak with you, Ms. Delaney."

"Bern, please. We've been through this before. It's Mallory, remember?"

"I know," he said, "it's just—" He didn't know how to complete the sentence. He was speaking to royalty. This was a woman who probably had the president of the United States in her "favorite contacts" list. And she knew who he was: Bern Hendricks, a poor kid from Milwaukee who used to eat bologna three times a week because his family couldn't afford anything else. Again—involuntarily—a wave of gratitude for Frederic Delaney, for all that Delaney had given him, washed over Bern.

"Are you someplace you can talk?" she was saying.

"I'm in my office."

"Are you alone?"

"Yes," he said, sitting up straighter. Had he done something wrong? Had the Foundation discovered some error or discrepancy with his work on the Quintet? He'd gone over those footnotes dozens of times. He, Jacques, and Julie had all triple-checked one another's work. What was the problem? "Is there something I can help you with?"

"As a matter of fact, there is. Something urgent has come up." She paused. "We found some original documentation from my uncle, and we wondered if you'd be interested in an opportunity to assess it."

"Documentation? What kind of documentation? Music? Letters?" Adrenaline and relief shot through him, a cold rush of blood from the top of his head to his feet and back. She probably wanted him for something small and meaningless, he told himself. Frederic Delaney had been one of the twentieth century's most prolific composers; he'd known everyone, so new letters often surfaced at auction houses or estate sales. Some letters—the ones with great signatures and substantive text—sold for tens of thousands of dollars.

"We found something that requires someone with a specific skill set. And of course I thought immediately of you."

"Okay," he said, thrilled to help. "Can you email it over? I can look right now. What is it?"

"I'd rather discuss this in person, if you have the inclination. There's also a nondisclosure agreement that we'd need you to sign."

"A nondisclosure agreement?" Bern repeated. His brain was churning. "What did you find?"

"Again, I'd—"

"Are you here?" he asked. "In Charlottesville?"

"No," she said, "I was rather hoping I could lure you up to our offices." He could hear her smile. "We're on the top floor of the Foundation, as you may remember. Quite near Juilliard."

She wasn't going to tell him what they'd found, that much was clear. But he wanted more information. He tried a different tactic. "What kind of skill set are you looking for?"

"Partially it's your work on the *Rings Quintet*," she said slowly. "And you probably know more about Frederic Delaney than almost everyone. Including me, and I'm related to him." Again, he could hear that smile through the telephone.

"Let me look at my schedule." He checked his calendar. "I could possibly fly up Friday afternoon, if I can get a flight out. I'm teaching all this week. But this feels like quite a haul for some documentation. Are you sure you can't just scan it and send it to me via email? I'm happy to sign your nondisclosure electronically."

"We'd rather show you. We haven't allowed scans yet of the—of the—documents."

Something about the way she hesitated over that last word sent Bern's head spinning. What kind of document would she be reluctant to scan? Was it so fragile?

"You must have found something really special," he said. A diary? Delaney had kept no journals, although he did use an office calendar that he never fully updated. Could it be a letter discussing the genesis of the Quintet? That would be life changing—Delaney had rarely mentioned his inspirations for the opera cycle, which was why Jacques Simon had created the annotated Quintet in the first place: all those painstaking scholarly attributions for all of Delaney's musical influences had taken them eight years to compile.

Another pause. "It is. It's—" She didn't finish the sentence.

"Did you find an undiscovered piece of music?"

One of Delaney's compositions turned up now and then. The most recent time one was found and played—the *Domino Winds* overture—the New York Philharmonic had premiered to a packed auditorium and received a seven-minute standing ovation, and the audience had shouted, "Again! Again! Again!" until the Philharmonic encored the overture, in true Delaney fashion.

"I really can't discuss it over the phone," she said.

So it *was* an undiscovered piece of music. It had to be.

Of course.

He said slowly: "You found it, didn't you?"

"I beg your pardon? We—"

"You found it. You found a piece of *RED*. You found the original. How much? The overture? An aria?"

A very long pause, during which Bern tried to assess what it would mean, finding even a page of the original *RED*. His head swam.

"Bern, please. I—I think this would be better discussed in person, in the proper setting," she said, stumbling over her words, sounding on edge. "Can you be here once you're done teaching for the week?"

"Just tell me this. How much did you find? Is it more than a page? Do you have a whole act?"

"Bern, I—"

Her hesitation was enough. "I'll be there tonight," he said. Before Mallory could respond, he was already on his laptop, emailing the head of the Music Department to say that due to an emergency he would need to cancel all his classes for the rest of the week—could a graduate student take over?

"That's wonderful news," Mallory said. "We'll send our plane to pick you up. When can you be ready?"

It was actually happening. A piece of *RED*—the elusive, mysterious, impossible *RED*—had been found.

And out of everyone on the planet, Bern himself—a poor bologna-sandwich-eating kid with a beat-up French horn—was going to actually see it. Be one of the very first people to touch it, to decipher Frederic Delaney's distinctive handwriting.

"Give me an hour," he said.

2

Olympic Glory

Bern

ON THE DELANEY FOUNDATION'S PRIVATE PLANE, Bern kept glancing down at his pin-striped shirt—he was glad now that he'd ironed it—and pinching the armrest in the glove-leather recliner that cradled him. His parents had had a La-Z-Boy with a wooden paddle that broke after a couple of years, leaving a jagged spear on one side; that was his only experience with a recliner. This one, caramel colored, was softer than a baseball glove, conforming to him. It looked like it would be more appropriate in a British pub than an airplane. The flight attendant asked if he wanted wine, champagne, or a cocktail, and he shook his head, asked for seltzer water. He wished he could iron his jeans.

In the meantime, he spent the flight to New York City reviewing everything he could on his laptop—but he knew it all, since he'd spent eight years living with it.

In 1920, the first year the Olympics were held after World War I, the modern Olympic flag debuted. On a white background, the five interlocking rings symbolized the world's five continents united by the Olympics: blue for Europe, yellow for Asia, black for Africa, green for Oceania, and red for the Americas. A young Frederic Delaney, whose immensely popular, singable music had already outsold that of all other contemporary composers, had been tapped to write five operas, one for each colored ring.

Over the next sixteen years, Delaney worked on the *Five Rings of Olympia*, an ode to the energy and passion of a new world, celebrating the rebirth of hope after the Great War. In the first opera, the Olympic torch disappears. The swiftest, most decorated runner of the five continents must hunt it down. Throughout each opera, Mikhail—his nationality is never specified—journeys around the globe to retrieve the lost torch. Along the way he battles demonic monsters and accomplishes herculean tasks: in *BLUE*, he rescues the lost princess; in *YELLOW*, he performs sacrifices to find the true path to the torch; in *BLACK*, he outsmarts the trickster spider god; in *GREEN*, he overcomes the Pacific Islands' mythical sea monsters; and then, finally, in *RED*, he recovers the torch.

In 1921, the first opera, *The Theft of Europa: The Blue Ring of Olympia*, created a major sensation. Opera had never been so popular, so accessible, so beautiful. New fashions based on the characters' costumes sprang up worldwide, and the melodies and arias were reworked into popular ballads and classical adaptations. Three operas followed over the next five years: *The Asian Prophesy* (*YELLOW*, 1923), *The Dark African Heart* (*BLACK*, 1924, and a nod to Joseph Conrad), *Ocean Odyssey* (*GREEN*, 1926). Today, when the operas were performed for modern audiences, a note in the playbill discussed the use of colors to represent various nationalities: what was acceptable in the 1920s is no longer tolerable. But Delaney's music remained as compelling as ever—transcending race, color, and creed.

Everything was on track to perform the full Quintet in the days leading up to the Olympic Games in 1928, once the final opera had been finished.

That final opera, *Triumph of the Americas: The Red Ring of Olympia*, would be an ode to Americas' first peoples, as well as to the immigrants who came after, and who lent their stories and their music to North, Central, and South Americas. It would utilize grand swaths of folk, jazz, Latin, Indigenous, and other musical elements to tell how Mikhail finally recovers the Olympic torch.

In multiple interviews, Frederic Delaney promised that, true to its name, the opera's debut would indeed be a triumph. Opening night was eagerly, even hysterically, anticipated. Tickets sold out immediately, and throngs filled the sidewalks outside the theater, many dressed as their favorite characters. Everyone wanted to know what happened to Mikhail and how he recovered the torch; but even more, they wanted to hear Delaney's new music. For the past decade, Delaney's affection for Black culture and Black music had helped bring together people of all colors and nationalities. *RED* was reputed to provide an entirely new means of integrating classical, jazz, blues, and folk.

The year 1927 came and went, and no *RED*. Slowly word began to leak out that Delaney had lost the only full copy of the opera. How was this possible? Opera scores were enormous, thick volumes written on large sheets of foolscap. This wasn't a folded napkin abandoned in a trouser pocket.

No sketches. No documentation. Delaney was a bit like Mozart, scribing a first draft, copying it almost verbatim into the final, and destroying the original. He'd lost the only draft of *RED*.

Some people accused him of never writing a note; they said he was too burned-out or drugged up.

Delaney's story continued to shift: He'd left it on a train or in a taxi. It had been lost in a fire. A rival stole it. Bern and Julie used to joke that Delaney should have named his dog Figaro after eating and farting out an entire opera.

The lost opera became both a cause célèbre and a joke. In 1931, a radio play with a detective purporting to hunt down the errant pages ran for eight months. *As lost as a Delaney opera* found its way into the lexicon. *Doing a Delaney* became common parlance for losing something or for, eventually, just a boneheaded move.

But the bottom line was that *RED* had disappeared, probably in early 1926. Delaney spent the next ten years laboriously rewriting *RED* from memory. He finished it in late 1935.

In 1936, the *Rings Quintet of Olympia* was to be staged for the first time all together at the Olympic Games in Berlin, but Delaney prohibited the performance. Like many in the international community, he refused to further Hitler's propaganda machine and did not want his *Rings* to be seen as endorsing the Nazi regime. Plus his *Rings* would have too closely mimicked Wagner's own *Ring* cycle; Hitler loved him some Wagner.

So, instead, on July 15, 1936, and running for the next five consecutive nights, the *Rings* debuted at the Met in New York City. Tickets were the most difficult to procure for any concert in recent memory. Thousands of people attended the weeklong celebration. Millions more listened over the radio. Everything culminated in the grand debut of *Triumph of the Americas: The Red Ring of Olympia.*

It was to be Frederic Delaney's glorious victory, his retribution for all the mockery, for all the petty insults.

Instead, *RED* fizzled.

The story was strong. Mikhail recovered the torch and all was well. But the music was not what Delaney had promised. Instead of invention, there was repetition. Instead of synthesis and heartrending melodies, there were hackneyed tunes.

The morning after *RED*'s premiere, the critics were vicious.

Frederic Delaney's valet found him on a couch in his living room. He'd killed himself with a mixture of pills and alcohol. He left no suicide note.

The plane touched down, and there was no security, just a few steps across the tarmac to the terminal's glass doors. A man in a black suit and a chauffeur's cap met him inside and escorted him to a town car. Now Bern really wished he'd re-ironed his pants.

Throughout the drive into the city, he tried to imagine what this discovery would mean—to him and to the world. Finding some evidence of the original *RED* could be life changing. It might transform how Delaney was studied, played, immortalized. Despite Delaney's triumphs, primarily for the Quintet and for his earlier work, Delaney had died a laughingstock. "Repugnant and uninspired," the critics had called him and his later compositions. "A hack who should just brick himself up with his money and never come out again." Only the Delaney Foundation, created a few years before his death, redeemed his image and transformed him into the beloved composer the world knew him as today.

But what if this piece of *RED* was all Delaney had promised it would be? What if it truly was a work of genius?

Bern might have the opportunity to correct history—to give back to Delaney a little of what Delaney's Foundation had given Bern. Perhaps Bern could be part of the team that would fully and finally restore Delaney to the pinnacle of American composers. Where he truly belonged.

In Midtown Manhattan, a block west of Juilliard and Lincoln Center, lettering a foot high spelled out THE DELANEY FOUNDATION on a cream-colored modern building. Sliding glass doors sighed open on Bern's approach, and his footsteps rang out in the vast lobby. Over the past dozen years, he'd been here several times—for performances, events, cocktail parties.

Some evidence of the original *RED* was inside. His chance to set the record straight was inside.

The doors closed behind him.

Five minutes later Bern was being ushered into the presence of

Mallory Delaney Roberts, Frederic Delaney's great-niece and one of only two surviving members of the Delaney family. He'd met her a handful of times. Thank goodness he'd re-ironed his shirt—even if it was now covered by his best sweater-vest and a blazer. And his pants didn't look too bad, he told himself.

He wanted to bow, or to salute. What was appropriate in the presence of American royalty? Licking her hand?

Before he had the chance to make a fool out of himself, she was coming around her desk to clasp his hand with both of hers. Instead of her trademark pearls, she wore only a silver chain and small silver earrings. Her hair seemed darker than he remembered, an oily jet-black, as if she'd coated it with shoe polish. Her yellow skirt and matching yellow blazer with a very white blouse seemed to beam at him almost as much as her smile. "Bern, so wonderful to see you again. Thank you so much for coming," she said.

"Thank you for asking me," he said, returning her handshake. "I can't believe I'm actually here again."

"You're always welcome," she said. "We really appreciate you dropping everything for this."

A bookcase took up an entire wall, packed with reference works about Frederic Delaney. With some satisfaction, he noted a first edition of the five-volume *The Rings of Olympus, Annotated Version*, by Jacques Simon, Kevin Bernard Hendricks, and Julie Ertl.

"Of course," he said. "We are talking about *RED*, right? How much of it did you find?"

She laughed again. "Eager as ever, I see. Let me introduce you to Stanford Whitman, our chief in-house counsel."

He'd barely noticed the stocky bald man in the gray suit sitting in an armchair near the desk, but now shook his hand as well.

"Nice to meet you," Bern said. "Can I see it now?"

Whitman gestured to the desk behind them, where lay a few printed sheets titled *Confidentiality and Nondisclosure Agreement.*

Bern signed both copies without reading. He folded one copy and put it in his pocket. "Okay, now where is it?" he repeated.

"I'll need your cell phone, please," Whitman said, shrugging. "Just temporarily."

"So I don't take secret pictures?" He wasn't sure whether to be insulted or amused.

"Don't be offended," Mallory said, laying a hand on his arm. "It's policy. No phones. We don't even have ours."

Bern handed over his phone, which Whitman carried out of the room.

When he'd gone, Bern said, "I've been going over and over this and what it could possibly be. What did you find? Is it a piece from *RED*? The original *RED*? Is it in his own handwriting? I'd recognize it anywhere."

"You really don't disappoint," Mallory said, her eyes alight. "I can see we made the right call." She slipped out of her office, Bern at her heels. Whitman met them in the hall, and the three of them trooped down to a door. She unlocked it—a dead bolt and a finger-print reader—and led them into a windowless office that looked like it could have been in any upscale hotel: impersonal but comfortable. A desk with a monitor hulked on one side; on the other, a cream-colored couch and three beige chairs huddled around a narrow glass coffee table. She gestured for him to take a seat on the couch; she sat across from him, and Whitman hovered over her shoulder.

"If this is what I think it is," Bern said, "I'm glad I'm sitting down."

She didn't answer, gesturing with her chin to Whitman, and eyed a file cabinet next to the desk. Wordless, he took two strides to the cabinet, pressed his thumb against a keypad on one side.

"That sure is a lot of security for one piece of music," Bern said, trying for humor. Neither of them laughed.

A moment later Whitman turned, holding a thick sheaf of bound papers.

"No way," Bern said steadily, eyes on the manuscript. He tried to breathe. The pages enveloped his vision: ten inches wide and four-teen inches long, bright white, a huge manuscript. "Don't tell me you found *all* of it? You found *RED*. The whole thing."

"Yes," Mallory said.

Whitman handed him the bound folio. Bern hesitated a second before he could curl his fingers around it. It was heavy, and somehow warmer than he'd expected.

ORIGINAL *RED: DO NOT PHOTOCOPY OR DISTRIBUTE.* COPY #3 emblazoned the top of every page, with a CONFIDENTIAL watermark in the middle. The paper was white, fresh. This was a scanned copy.

He opened it at random: Delaney's unmistakable handwriting, musical notation, and lyrics—*And here I sing with thee, swift of feet I am, returning like a rising tide to . . .* —and an oboe and violin duet soaring over a cello and bassoon accompaniment. It was evocative of the version that Bern knew of *RED*, but this version was very dif-ferent: the melody, the rhythm, the instrumentation. He remem-bered an awkward trombone solo in this passage and had actually wondered why Delaney stuffed a trombone in to represent Mikhail here, of all places. "I can't believe this," he said, and realized that he'd repeated the phrase several times already. He turned to the next page.

"Maybe you should start at the beginning," Mallory suggested gently.

He was already turning to the beginning of the score. There was no cover: just a scanned blank white page. The scan had picked up every crease and fold, the edges of the original clearly visible. Gray patterns that must have been watermarks spotted part of one border. He turned to the next page and his heart hammered against his ribs as if he'd been punched from inside. He'd recognize Delaney's hand-writing anywhere, but couldn't honestly believe that he was looking at the words: *Triumph of the Americas: The Red Ring of Olympia.*

"Where did you find it?"

"We'll get to that," Mallory said. "Please take some time to read this, and then let's discuss it."

He clenched his fingers around the pages. The entire evening felt surreal, as if he were under water.

"Thank you," he said. "Thank you so much. I can't believe I'm holding this." He studied the top blank white page again, looking for some clue as to its location for the past hundred years. *Hi, if you're reading this, it means that you've found me in a shoebox in Frederic Delaney's attic.*

"You've got a lot of reading to do," Mallory said. "You'll need a few days with this, of course."

"A few days?" Bern asked, dumbfounded. "I'll have it done tomorrow."

"You're going to read it all right now?"

"Of course I am. I've been waiting all my life for this."

"I'll leave you to it."

But Bern didn't respond; he was already flipping the opening page, starting to read.

3

The Exuberance of RED

Bern

THE ORIGINAL, newly discovered version of *RED* began like the other: with the elusive sound of a flute spiraling above Mikhail, recently arrived in the Americas. That night he dreams of a woodpecker who offers to help him find the lost Olympic torch. Until Bern had begun researching the Quintet, he'd always thought the flute was a nod to Mozart's *Magic Flute*, but he discovered that Delaney had actually paid homage to a Native American tribe's love flute myth. Many of *RED*'s story lines came from Indigenous peoples.

He turned the oversize page, which took up much of the coffee table. This was definitely a Delaney manuscript. Bern recognized the firm, elegant handwriting, the trailing tails of the *p* and the *y*, how his slanting *f* resembled a violin's f-hole.

Even more noticeable were the "Doodles"—Delaney's own secret system of describing how the music should be played. All composers annotated their scores, indicating where musicians should speed up or slow down, get louder or softer, and so forth. Some composers used traditional symbols like arrows pointing up or down; others made up their own.

Frederic Delaney was one of the latter. Random patterns often danced down the margins of the page: hexagons, crosshatching, intricate swirls. On rare occasions, a Delaney score resembled an illustrated manuscript. Most of his annotations had never been fully understood nor translated.

Over the past sixty years, no less than fourteen dissertations—from the first, *The Triangle Motif in the Early Works of Frederic Delaney* (George Marshall, PhD, San Diego State University, 1951), to the most recent, *From Author to Artist: How Frederic Delaney's So Called Doodles Illustrate and Illuminate his Musical Genius* (Gwendolyn McManus, PhD, Bowling Green State University, 2018)—had been written about the Doodles. Scholars laboriously copied each image and the original page of its location, trying to tie the symbol with what was happening musically. All the dissertations had been procured, scanned, and filed in the Delaney Foundation's archive, and Bern had read them back in grad school, when he was working on the Quintet.

In a typical opera, the composer writes every note, from overture to finale. Often a librettist is brought in to write the words and the story, and the two—librettist and composer—collaborate to create the full work. The composer's music propels the narrative forward, bringing the words to life. Part of Delaney's genius was that he was both a successful composer and his own librettist, able to match dazzling, clever lyrics with extraordinary, memorable melodies.

Bern recognized the first four bars of *RED*, but on the fifth bar the original *RED* transformed: a flute carried the staccato solo line; an English horn swelled in the middle of a clarinet trio. The B-flat trumpet parts and the bass trombone sections echoed each other, twisting like birds in an updraft, spinning around like leaves. The woodpecker's aria made him tear up. What would it be like to actually hear the flute soar?

This original *RED* was everything that Delaney had promised the world. Scholars—Bern included—had long tried to figure out what had happened to Delaney's composing abilities in the late 1920s and early 1930s, coinciding with the Great Depression. How could someone that prolific descend so quickly? Depression? Stress? Drugs? He was a musician, after all: frequenting parties with Duke Ellington and Count Basie, the back rooms heaped with cocaine and heroin. Bern had thought that, by the early 1930s, Delaney's drug of choice was opium. Had Delaney, like Hector Berlioz before him, dreamed awake in a narcotic stew for the final years of his life?

Jacques Simon had been convinced that stress had done him in: so much pressure, at such a young age, had eaten away at Delaney's supreme confidence until he, quite literally, collapsed under the weight of it. He'd died at age forty and had written most of his most famous music before he turned twenty-seven.

Bern wondered again whether Delaney's celebrity had left him isolated those last few years. Was there anyone he could have turned to?

A small minority of scholars believed that Delaney had been undone by a relationship gone wrong. Delaney had never married; he'd dated glamorous show girls, but never seemed to hold a lasting relationship.

Mysteriously, in the late 1920s he'd developed the habit of asking for a bottle of champagne and two champagne glasses before a performance. At the end of the night, after he left, the stage managers would find his dressing room empty and both glasses drained. Scholars speculated that Delaney brought in his secret lover to drink with him before the show, but no one backstage ever admitted to seeing anyone else. Was she his secret muse, like Shakespeare's Dark Lady? No one knew.

Bern focused on the task at hand, as the original *RED* unfolded before him, brilliant and evocative: Mikhail's dance with the woodpecker, the purification scene in the sweat lodge, the prayer to the gods.

After the oboe cadenza's high C signaled the completion of act 1, he sighed and sat back, his inner ears ringing. The handwritten music was slightly difficult to decipher in act 2. Sometimes gray patches partially obscured it, as if the original had been stained or faded. He thumbed through the enormous crisp sheets, wondering what the original looked like, what those gray patches were. Where had the manuscript been hidden all this time?

Hours later—he'd totally lost track of time without his phone—he'd finished sight-reading the full score. His skull trumpeted with the flutes' echoes, the woodwinds' sweeping lines reminiscent of what Prokofiev would imitate a few years after this RED had been written. The Olympic torch had been recaptured, but with this new music, stronger harmonies, and crisper lyrics, Mikhail's triumph sung out in joy and glory—so much more believable, honest, painfully hard-won. The original RED now resounded in a world broken from the Great War and the Spanish flu. But this world would rise again, build itself up into something better and more meaningful than before.

The Olympic torch was restored to its glory, and the aria of the "Hymn to Apollo" poured down. On the score's final page, the last measure contained that resplendent E-flat chord, the way it had in the reconstructed RED, but now the chord, in Bern's imagination, resounded in a way that the reconstructed RED had not. Bern rubbed his hand across the page, brushed the first violin part, the four ledger lines marking the high G. He imagined Delaney's pen forming every note. The final section of the manuscript seemed to have more annotations and Delaney Doodles than the first half.

He flipped to the next sheet, and then to the next: all blank, with a few small splotches. Mildew? Water stains? He'd noted several empty sheets interspersed throughout the score. The scanner had faithfully reproduced every page—recto and verso—of the manuscript.

Bern sat back on the couch, let the folio fall onto the polished tabletop. The harmonies slowly faded from his mind. Far down the hall, or perhaps on another floor entirely, a vacuum cleaner hummed.

He hadn't noticed before. What time was it? Eight? Nine? Mallory still had his phone, and no clock hung in the room. He collected the manuscript, made his way back to her office. A warm glow poured from the half-open door.

He knocked, entered. She looked up with a tired smile and gestured for him to have a seat. "What did you think?"

"It's everything he promised it would be," Bern said, pacing toward her desk. "This is the man at his peak. It's double good." He closed his eyes for a moment, eardrums still reverberating to music that only he could hear. He spun, paced to the wall and back. "His use of counterpoint in the *Indian Elder* trio is exquisite. I've never seen that kind of counterpoint since Bach—so effortless. So totally precise. It's nothing like the *RED* we all know. This will change everything. All of music history."

"That's what we think, too," she said, watching him stride around the room.

He was in front of her desk again. "I'd have thought your own experts would have told you this already."

"They have. But you worked with Jacques Simon." She glanced down at the paperwork in front of her, then met his eyes again.

"There are other people who've studied the Quintet—"

"Professor Simon's work was head and shoulders above everyone else's. No one ever studied the Quintet the way that he—and you—did. So yes, I'd say your professional opinion means something."

"Where was it? Where did you find it?" Any scholar would naturally ask this.

"We were doing some renovation work, and it was hidden behind a panel," she said.

"What renovation work?" he asked her. "What panel?"

Maddeningly, she gestured to one of the chocolate leather armchairs across from her desk. "Please, sit down."

He sat—on the edge.

"We have a proposition for you," she told him, holding his eyes.

"We want you to get *RED* performance ready. Like Frederic Delaney himself would have, if the score hadn't disappeared. You know Delaney's handwriting and notations in the Quintet better than anyone else in the world. And we like the idea of an outside scholar of your caliber preparing the score for performance."

"You want an outside stamp of approval to confirm its legitimacy," Bern said. He was still holding the bound score; he wondered if he would ever be willing to let it go. Could he take a shower with it, stuff it under his pillow?

"Yes," she said. "We want you to create a brand-new score based on this manuscript. You'll have to compare it against the other version, the rewritten version, but the new manuscript is the basis for everything. For the world premiere, and for how *RED* will be performed and listened to from now on. What do you think?"

"I think that sounds pretty sick," he said, and then immediately, "Not *sick* in the 'sick' sense. I mean it sounds incredible. Thank you for the opportunity. I'd love to do it." He was kicking himself for stumbling—but, to be fair, it was probably the middle of the night by now, and he was exhausted and overwhelmed with everything that had happened.

She didn't seem to hold it against him. Instead she laughed and said, "We'll make arrangements with UVA for a leave of absence. This is too important to wait."

This was it. His chance. Under Bern's thoughtful watch, Frederic Delaney would be redeemed. No more "hack." No more *doing a Delaney.* No more *the dog ate my opera.*

"Can I ask why me?" he said, feeling undeserving, feeling the lack of Jacques Simon and Julie. Being the scholar who validated *RED* would elevate him to rock star status in the music world. "Frederic Delaney has been researched ad nauseum by every major music historian alive today. Plus there are other people who've studied the Quintet—"

"Don't you think that the music scholar who created the definitive *Rings Quintet* would be the best authority to do that? We very much want you to head up the work. You're the best man for the job, and you're also a DF Kid. I can't tell you how much it means to me, and to the Foundation, to know that a DF Kid would be the one who brought Frederic Delaney's lost manuscript back into the world."

In the early 1930s, after Delaney's star had dimmed but before the *RED* debacle and his subsequent suicide, he'd established the Delaney Foundation, which was still run by his descendants. One of the Foundation's key initiatives, the "Dream A Song" program, gave musical instruments to middle schoolers who couldn't afford instruments but desperately wanted to play.

Bern, growing up in Milwaukee, would never forget the day his own French horn arrived. He'd never seen anything so beautiful, so shiny. And it was all his. He didn't have to share it with his siblings—not that they were interested in music, but up till then he'd had to share everything with them: bedroom, clothes, even shoes. This had been all his, as long as he'd kept a B average and stayed out of trouble. He'd been so proud to be chosen.

Ask any DF Kid and they'd probably tell you the same thing: Being a DF Kid was life changing. It gave you an identity, a sense of purpose. You were on your way to becoming someone special. Now he had something to work for, to aspire to. Now he wasn't just another poor kid, eating bologna sandwiches three times a week for dinner and kicking his heels in detention: he was an aspiring musician, a performer. The Delaney Foundation thought he was something special. He would show them that he was worthy of their investment and belief in him.

He never grew bored with the endless musical practice. What began as a fumbling attempt at "Hot Cross Buns" led inexorably to Bozza, and then to Rosetti, to Mozart, to Delaney.

But he wasn't just playing the music. He'd fallen in love with it. Playing Schubert took him out of himself. These weren't just notes on the page—this was a blueprint for an entire emotional experience that he had never even dreamed existed. He was amazed that he could play the same piece two different ways and have two different experiences. And playing those pieces soon evolved into listening differently to those pieces. He'd hear a Delaney symphony from the New York Philharmonic, and then hear the exact same piece from the Chicago Symphony Orchestra—and could instantly tell the differences between the two, the subtle changes in dynamics or the conductor's interpretation.

It was as if he'd learned a new language and discovered that language was everywhere. Classical music, yes; but also rock, hip-hop, bluegrass: the genre of the music wasn't important—only that it *was* music. The Foundation had invited him into a stunningly beautiful world lurking everywhere, and he'd never had the senses to perceive it before.

While his friends were spray-painting graffiti and using windows of abandoned houses as target practice, he was practicing Dvořák and Mozart. Some of his schoolmates were in prison now, and Bern was convinced that he would have gone down that route, too, if the French horn had never found him. If the Delaney Foundation hadn't seen something in him, lifted him up to be something more.

He'd performed on that French horn for the next five years, until he left for Columbia to pursue a degree in musicology, focusing on early-twentieth-century composers—primarily the works of Frederic Delaney.

Thousands of DF Kids now populated the music world. Bern had once heard that, on Broadway alone, 75 percent of all theater personnel had a DF connection: not just the performers and musicians, but stagehands, producers, managers, lighting technicians, and so forth. Now expand Delaney's influence to classical, jazz, hip-hop, rock, country, and bluegrass genres, as well as radio, television, and film scores. No wonder the Delaney Foundation was one of the most beloved organizations worldwide, its name and logo as recognizable as Walt Disney's.

Yes. Bern would do this for the Foundation. He would do it for Delaney, whose music he loved more than any other composer. He was light-headed: Is this what it felt like when your dreams came true?

"I'd love to," he said. "When can I get started?"

"As soon as possible."

"Great," he said. "I can do that."

"We'd actually like the manuscript completed by March fifteenth."

"What's happening on March fifteenth?"

"The premiere is already scheduled for May fifteenth. Of course," she said.

Why May fifteenth? he started to say, but stopped himself. This was Delaney's birthday. What could be a more perfect tribute to resuscitate his memory?

"We've already planned a world premiere event that's going to livestream across the globe," Mallory was saying. "The logistics are still being worked out—it's all preliminary. We'll of course keep you posted as things develop. It's all very complicated, since nobody knows about *RED* yet."

"March," he repeated. "Six months." It had taken the Simon team almost nine years to analyze all five *Ring* operas—Bern had begun working on the *Rings* when he was an undergrad at Columbia. Two years—easily—per opera, with a team of grad and undergrad students.

But that had been a much more complicated task—annotating, researching, cross-checking. This job would be a lot simpler: just confirming and cross-checking. Plus he was already very familiar with Delaney's handwriting. Given how much time he'd spent with the Quintet, Bern already knew Delaney better than most people, even other academics. And certainly he knew the Quintet better than anyone.

Pondering, he opened the folio at random, onto a violin solo in the fourth aria, written in the Dorian mode, which then effortlessly switched to an eerie and dark-sounding Aeolian mode. This was Delaney's genius—there'd never been anything remotely reminiscent of this type of musicality, except perhaps in certain Appalachian regions in Kentucky or West Virginia. He remembered the reconstructed *RED*; the violin solo stayed in the key of G. No modal changes. No musical gymnastics that ended in a perfect dismount.

"You have my word that I will do everything I can to make sure that the world knows the real Frederic Delaney," he said. "We're going to make it slap."

"Oh," she said tentatively, as if assuming this was a good thing. "Obviously the score can't leave the building, so we've taken the liberty of preparing an office for you downstairs, in the archive."

"Is this mine?" he asked, holding up the score, which he was thinking he might want to have surgically attached to his body.

"At this juncture there are only three copies. We have two in the vault. You have number three. You're the only one who's going to use this copy, and you can write all over it."

"Will I be able to see the original?" Bern said.

"Yes, of course. We're preserving it right now, so you won't be able to see it until the team is finished." She led him over to the elevator bank, pressed *SB2* for, he gathered, subbasement two. He followed her, holding the score against his chest, stroking it absently, like a kitten.

The elevator doors opened. "We've set up a space for you down here," she said. They passed a security station, now unmanned so late in the evening. "For obvious reasons, we can't allow the score to leave the building."

Bern wasn't convinced he would ever be able to let go of the manuscript. Would they call in a SWAT team to pry loose his fingers? *Put your hands on your head and step away from the manuscript. Back up very, very slowly. We don't want to hurt you.*

"We thought that you'd be more comfortable down here. Plus

it's near all the source materials." The Delaney Foundation archive, housed on several underground levels, were legendary: Bern had used them regularly with Jacques Simon. The archive held all of Frederic Delaney's original compositions—songs, concertos, operas, musicals, quartets, quintets, and every other -*tet* he wrote—but those were really only the barest beginnings of the Delaney holdings. Rare manuscripts and memorabilia of jazz, folk, blues, hip-hop, and dozens of other genres all abided in climate-controlled splendor.

"Which panel?" he asked. "Which panel were you restoring? Where was it? Can I see it?"

"One of the Delaney properties." She headed down the hall and he hurried to catch up. He was about to ask a follow-up question when she stopped in front of an unmarked door, looked into a retinal scanner to unlock it. She ushered him into a room easily as large as her office, with a round conference table and a couch on one side and, on the other, a mahogany desk, a brass banker's lamp, and two walls of reference works—including the definitive Quintet.

He wondered again what time it was, wished he had a watch.

"You've scanned the score in, obviously," he said. "I'm going to need access to the digital file, so I can make notes directly on it. That'll save a lot of time."

She grinned at him. This was going to be fun.

Tomorrow, she promised, she'd set him up on the server and give him all the access he'd need, with fingerprint and retinal scans, as well as keys to the file cabinets.

For a moment he laid the score, facedown, on his new desk. In the raking light from the desk lamp, he noted a faint square shadow on that final blank sheet, as if another page had once pressed next to it, marking it. "Hey," he said. "Were there more pages with the manuscript? Looks like there were. See?" he showed her the white shadow.

"Yes, there were a few more papers. Notes and some other documents."

"I'll need to see them, too."

"I'll have them sent over to you tomorrow morning."

"Double good," he said. He slid the folio into his new file cabinet and pocketed the keys.

They returned upstairs to Mallory's office. She handed back his phone. "It's almost midnight," she said. He checked: 11:49. He'd been there for seven hours. He'd forgotten about dinner. Thank goodness New York had all-night pizza joints.

As they left together, he patted the file cabinet keys in his pocket to reassure himself.

The rest of the night was a blur. The Foundation had made a reservation for him at the Plaza Hotel, a few blocks away. "The Plaza? For real?" he asked her.

"Only the best for you, Bern," she said.

He could get used to this.

With the coolness of the autumn breeze on his face, he walked the width of Central Park South, the swish of taxis brushing by. Delaney's well-known "Singing Down the Stars" was floating through his headphones, a romantic melody for acoustic guitar, clarinet, and cello with a hypnotic repetitive chorus that he knew he'd be humming in his sleep. He matched his pace to the music. "Singing Down the Stars" was right. The melody engulfed him. Bern could have a major role in securing the legacy of one of the most important figures—not only of the twentieth century, but in Bern's own life.

The stars were, suddenly, everywhere, and he would soon be among them.

4

Sorrow Is Everything Here

Bern

BY EIGHT THE NEXT MORNING he was ensconced in his new office. He'd brought only one change of clothes from Charlottesville, and this was it: a short-sleeved polo that he'd ironed and yesterday's blazer, which hid the polo's short sleeves. He'd ironed the jeans, but they were still jeans. How could he wear jeans in front of Mallory Delaney Roberts? Stores weren't open yet, and it seemed more important to get to the Foundation than to get a new pair of dress slacks.

So there he was, seriously underdressed, retina screened, and fingerprinted, and now sitting in his very expensive desk chair, the original *RED* eyeing him up and down, no doubt also disapproving of what he was wearing. And there was that opening page, written in Delaney's distinctive handwriting: *Triumph of the Americas: The Red Ring of Olympia*. He wished he could put on a suit and a tie, maybe even a tux, if he was going to be working on this manuscript.

What a tremendous undertaking. He'd need two monitors, with

the handwritten version on one screen and the digital score on the other. On the second, he'd add his annotations where possible. A full opera, 811 pages, to be completed in five months. Which meant—he pulled out his calculator—about five pages per day.

He'd need to go back to Charlottesville, get his clothes. Or could he just stay here, buy clothes online, and have the Delaney Foundation take charge of shutting up his apartment? He needed an assistant to help with everything. Later that morning, when Mallory and the rest of the Delaney staff arrived, he'd ask someone for help.

But before he had the chance, at nine fifteen came a knock on the door, and Mallory entered with a very short woman carrying a tablet, who Mallory introduced as his new assistant, Stephanie. "Just let her know how she can help. She'll be out in the main library archive, but she's here for you."

"It's a pleasure to meet you, Dr. Hendricks," the woman said. Her voice was high and nasal, and she wore dark round glasses. She smiled after every sentence, as if it were delicious. "Your work on the Quintet is legendary."

"Uh—thanks," Bern said modestly. Legendary to whom? he wondered. He caught Stephanie eyeing his jeans. Well, at least they were ironed. "So first off, I need electronic access. And I need to see all other documents that were found alongside the score. And I want to see where the score was hidden. And I'm going to need help getting my stuff up from Charlottesville and finding a place to stay."

"I can handle all that," Stephanie said, smiling again. Her lips were bubblegum pink—exactly the same color as Bubblicious but almost too small for her face. "We usually put visiting scholars in the town house on Sixty-Third Street, but we have some other properties that are more comfortable. Just give me your contacts and I'll get right on it." Smile. "In the meantime, you already have access to the files. Let me show you where they are."

She leaned in, explained the electronic folder structure, how he'd have access to the full Delaney archive—to anything actually written by or about Frederic Delaney. He'd had such access when working on the *Rings Quintet*, so it was all familiar. He'd use the same system that Jacques Simon had drilled into him.

A few hours later, after he'd begun setting up a long-term system for the manuscript analysis, he was just getting hungry for lunch and wondering what the cafeteria on the second floor served when the additional pages arrived. He'd asked Mallory for them last night and, as she'd promised, here they were, again in another oversize folder, sealed, with the DF logo prominent upon it.

Bern went over to the couch, opened the folder on the coffee table. These were scanned, reprinted copies, too, not the originals. Eighteen sheets, more than a dozen of which were blank. One seemed to be a paper napkin, crinkle-cut ridges clearly defined, carefully spread out.

The last six pages—three sheets, front and back—gave him pause.

The first seemed to be a claim ticket, number 367, for luggage left at Pennsylvania Station. On the bottom, scrawled hastily, he deciphered: *5 st trks*. Street tricks? Saint trucks? He set it aside.

The second was a full page, front and back, of Delaney Doodles. This was unusual. Delaney always annotated the music directly on the page instead of creating a separate page of notations. This page was densely packed, top to bottom, with whirls and geometric shapes. Also, uncharacteristically, there was a word—*JaR*—on the top right corner, surrounded by what looked like wings or leaves.

He put it down, looked at it, adjusted his collar, brushed at his shirt, and picked up the page again—as if these Doodles, these first full pages of Delaney's direct communication with him, would make more sense if he were more presentable.

JaR—the *J* and the *R* capitalized, and the *a* lowercase. What did it mean?

He then forgot all about the other sheets as he turned to the final page.

He'd struck gold. He felt like he was in the presence of royalty. It was a good thing he'd ironed his shirt.

Frederic Delaney's handwriting, no question, transcribing a section of act 3 of the newly found original score. In the scene, which was inspired by tales of conjure women, Mikhail is lost in a forest where the trees are spirits of escaped slaves hiding from their enslavers. He must play the woodpecker's flute for them to speak to him. They recount their sorrows and their hopes for a better world. The singing trees' chorus was one of Bern's all-time favorite melodies—the original *RED*'s version was immediately miles above the one he'd grown up listening to—more sonorous and more heartrending, better constructed and better orchestrated, the bass line a C-minor drone with an alternating E-flat arpeggiated line. Whoa.

He pulled up the lyrics of the original *RED*:

I come to you for a chance to change what makes me who I am.
It will be better. It will be true. I gave up long ago what I was.
What they took from me.
My sighs and wails fell deaf on my tormentor's ears.
She gave me that which was ripped away.
The pain is gone, the life long-lasting.

What was fascinating, what made Bern's heart pound, were both the different lyrics and the notations in the margin, in Delaney's hand: *Needs a bolder arpeggiated line. This is exactly what I wanted but still doesn't feel like enough. Divide upper strings for more sorrow? Sorrow is everything here.* The last line was underlined twice.

Here were the rewritten lyrics of the *RED* that the world knew:

We all must change who we are, what makes us who we are.
We all shall strive to be better in this darkened wood.
We gave up who we were in order to become what we became.
She took it all from us. She took it all.
Our sighs and wails broke deaf on her ears.

She taught us that all must be lost and taken away.
The pain is real, the life long-lasting.

This was the *only* example in existence of a Delaney working document. Delaney destroyed all his sketches and early versions of every piece of music he'd ever written—much like Mozart's wife had done with her husband's musical sketches. Delaney explained in interviews that he wanted to be remembered for the final music, not for early rough drafts and false starts. To date, no one had ever found a rough draft. And now Bern had come across an authentic Delaney sketch, with notes in Delaney's hand: *Sorrow is everything here.*

This was a major discovery—and one that Bern could get credit for.

Bern was too jittery to sit still, so he left the folder on the coffee table and took a break for lunch, picking up a sandwich from the cafeteria (at least it was free with his name badge) and eating at his desk. He intentionally didn't glance at the folder lurking on the table in front of the couch. He tried not to think about it right now. His stomach had clenched, and he couldn't even swallow the turkey on wheat. What would it mean—to Bern, to Delaney's memory, to the world—to publish a headlining treatise in the *Journal of Popular Music Studies* about it? Maybe even a book?

He'd focus on the working pages later that evening, he told himself, and—just to keep from getting tempted—locked them away in the file cabinet. Right now he had to get started with the comparison and annotations.

He began comparing the two scores—the original and the rewritten. In both, the opening four measures of the overture were identical, but after that everything shifted. Similar melodies possessed utterly different harmonies; timing changes and lyrics often seemed interchangeable at the outset, but the more he examined them, the more he realized the tiny changes led to wildly different results. The reconstructed *RED*'s orchestration was messier—and, compared to the original, seemed almost amateurish. Flutes played in the lower register. Trombones were written in bass clef when the original *RED* used alto clef, which would make it easier for musicians to read. The violas played higher than the first violins.

Had Delaney been on drugs? Had the opium induced a mental break? What had been so deeply, stunningly wrong with him to produce such a disaster the second time around?

Now Bern would usher Frederic Delaney's lost masterpiece back into the world. As always, when he thought of Delaney he felt a deep, unreasonable connection to him. They both were Midwesterners: Bern from Wisconsin and Delaney from Indiana. But it was vastly more than that. Delaney's Foundation had transformed him from a kid with no direction and little ambition into one of America's leading musical scholars, and Bern could never fully repay that debt.

Those were the reasons that he gave for his obsession with Frederic Delaney, which went far beyond playing Delaney's music and knowing how to properly spell Delaney's first name. Packed away in a storage unit in Charlottesville was a suit embroidered with *FCD* on the pocket, which supposedly had been worn by Delaney at a Louis Armstrong concert in 1934—he'd saved up to buy it from a private collector, instead of the car that he'd told his parents he'd been saving for. Up until today, that suit had been the closest thing Bern possessed of Frederic Delaney himself. Now, here in the basement of Delaney's Foundation, Bern had never been so close to the greatest master that America—or possibly the world—had ever produced.

Bern had read every biography, every piece of music that Delaney had written. During his senior year of high school, instead of the obligatory spring break trip to Fort Lauderdale, he pilgrimaged to Frederic Delaney's birthplace outside Bloomington, Indiana. The house was a museum now; Bern's knees had brushed the velvet ropes as he'd tried to commit to memory *The Table Where Frederick Had Eaten.* Or *The Bed He'd Slept In.* Bern had actually washed his hands in *The Sink That Frederick Had Brushed His Teeth At.* Back in 1910, he was called Freddy, but it felt too common for Bern to ever dream of thinking of him as a Freddy.

The reality that Bern was now working on Delaney's masterpiece began to slowly sink in. In many ways he was relieved that Delaney had written it—there could be no mistaking Delaney's familiar handwriting on the original *RED*. Some scholars believed the only logical explanation was that, near the end of his life, Delaney had actually enlisted someone else to write the music for the reconstructed *RED*. Bern knew that wasn't true; he'd lived intimately with Delaney's handwriting for the *Rings Quintet*, and the handwriting for the original *RED* staring at him was identical.

Something else—something terrible—had destroyed Delaney emotionally or intellectually.

Whatever it was, this was Bern's chance to rehabilitate Delaney's name, much as Delaney's Foundation had rescued him.

But Bern needed help. The differences in the score were almost frightening. Slowly he compared the versions on the screens. It would be tedious work and impossible to finish by Mallory's deadline.

He picked up his phone.

5

A Shout-Out to the Boogie Down

Bern

EBONI'S NUMBER WAS, of course, still in his contacts. These kinds of calls were always dicey: when people drift apart, and you're the first one to reach out after a long while, and you worry that the person on the other end of the phone, or the email, or the text, won't respond. That she'll think you contacted her only because you need something. It's one thing if you're just business associates, but if you were friends—okay, not great friends, but friends—and you haven't been in touch, maybe she won't even pick up. Or, on the other hand, maybe she'll pick up and things will start up again as if you'd talked to her yesterday. It's a crapshoot.

He hoped he'd roll a seven. He pressed SEND.

One ring and she picked up. "There's a new place in the East Village," she said. No "hello." No "Bern, it's good to hear from you after all this time." Instead she said, "Insane crust. Crispy *and* chewy. Good fresh sauce. They do something with it that makes it slightly sweet, but in a good way."

"Is that Baldino's?" he asked.

"Good guess," Eboni said. "It's actually a cousin or a stepmother or something. They split from Baldino's and opened their own shop. Brick-oven. Seriously worth trying."

He'd rolled a seven, he thought. Winner. "Let's go. I'm back in New York."

"Wait, you're here? I thought you got a job down in Virginia? You get fired from there already?" Her voice was the same as always: crisp, with unapologetic intonations of her native Bronx. *Thwaught. Fi-yaad.*

"No, not quite. Almost a promotion. But I'm on a leave of absence."

"You can't take a leave of absence yet. You just started there, right? Must be something big to get you back here."

"It is," he said. "And I could use your help."

"It's gonna cost you," she told him. "You'll have to buy the next couple slices. Maybe four." He could picture her, phone tucked against her ear, hair in tight braids battering her back. He wondered what color the braids were. Green, maybe. Or yellow.

"It's a deal," he said, "but if things go right with this, you'll be able to buy your own pizza shop."

"Brick or coal?"

"Brick *and* coal," he said. "And electric, just in case."

"I'm in," she said. "Should I start looking for restaurant space?"

For years, at Columbia, they'd gone to pizza shops together, on a quest to find the Best Pizza in New York City. They debated Neapolitan versus Sicilian versus classic crust, canned versus fresh sauce, wet versus dry mozzarella. And toppings: Were mushrooms too wet? Were potatoes too Roman? Let's discuss pineapple, even. Eboni had worked in a Bronx pizza shop during high school—as a delivery person and then sometimes making pizza—at the same shop where her aunt worked. Bern and Eboni used to joke about starting a pizza restaurant together, if Eboni's plans on computer security went south, and if Bern couldn't make it as a musicologist.

"I'm actually in the Delaney building. Again."

"What? Delaney? You serious? They're going to take out a restraining order on you," she told him.

"No, nothing like that. I'm at the Delaney Foundation, working on this major project."

"Every project is a major project to you. The operas again?"

"Well, yeah," he said. "Kind of."

Eboni Washington had been the Quintet's computer analyst: she'd written code specifically for Jacques Simon's team, analyzed the musical structures, knew those operas almost as intimately as they did. Eboni, a doctoral student with one more year before completing her PhD, had immediately bonded with Bern when Simon had brought him onto the team. They were both very driven and recognized this in each other—they both came from poor Black households and were uncomfortable in Columbia's rarefied world.

"Do you know I couldn't get that one song out of my head for a month? 'The Bamboo Reed Dance.' I almost turned it into my ringtone."

"Jay-Z did a rap version of it," Bern said. "You ever hear it? You must have. And McDonald's used it in a commercial. Allstate did, too."

"Yeah, only a million times in the past few years. What's the project?"

He took a breath. "Same kind of thing as before. Musical analysis and score comparison."

"Analysis of what? Comparison of what? We did all the *Rings*."

"I know this sounds crazy, but I can't tell you over the phone," Bern said. "They're asking for NDAs for anybody involved with this."

"NDAs? You serious?"

"As a heart attack," he said.

"You want me to sign an NDA to do some computer code on some music," Eboni repeated.

"Um, yeah. Pretty much."

"I didn't have to sign anything with the *Rings*," she said.

"Well, this is different."

"It's that important?"

He didn't respond, and after a moment she went on. "Okay then. You can send a car over to pick my ass up."

"What?" He turned to stare at the phone's screen like it could explain her better than her voice could. "I can't send a car over to you. I don't have any authority. Aren't you still in the Bronx?"

"You're talking about me opening a pizza shop and signing NDAs and you can't send a car for me? And yeah, I'm still in the Boogie Down. If you're working for Delaney, you can get a car over here. I'll text you the address, same place. I'm booked until four, though. If the car ain't here by then, I'll be sitting in Midtown traffic all night and nothing's getting signed or done."

"Okay," he said. "Let me see what I can do."

"Great," she said.

"I'm really glad to be back in touch," he said.

"Me too. Just tell me one thing. Did you iron your shirt?"

"What?"

"Your shirt. Did you iron it?" She always teased him about his penchant for well-ironed shirts.

"Well, yeah. It is the Delaney Foundation," he said.

"A crease in both sleeves?"

"Is there any other way?"

"Good," she said. "I'll see you soon. I guess you're buying the slices tonight."

Moments later they hung up, and he picked up his office phone, dialed six. Within a few moments, Stephanie poked her head in. "Dr. Hendricks? Is everything okay? Can I help with something?"

"As a matter of fact, you can," he said, and then, cautiously, "I need to hire someone. A computer person." He waited for Stephanie to shake her head. To say, *Anybody who doesn't have the self-respect to dress appropriately at the Delaney Foundation certainly doesn't have the authority to hire someone.* Instead she said, "Of course," with that smile of hers—almost a wince, but not quite. "If you'll open the file marked C-16, you'll see a list of Delaney Foundation employees who should—"

"No," Bern said, "I'd like a specific person. I worked with her before, with Jacques Simon. She did all the computer backend for the *Rings Quintet*, and having her involved will really speed up the process. She's in New York and is available at four today. Can we send a car to get her? I'll give you the address." He couldn't believe he was even saying this.

She nodded, already tapping on her tablet and speaking into her headset. In a moment she'd ordered the car service.

Damn. That was easy. He threw himself back into the work.

The afternoon flew by. He'd gotten the first page done and was starting on the second, the overture's sixty-fifth measure, when his desk phone buzzed and the lobby's security guard said, "Professor Hendricks, your guest is here. Miss Washington."

It was just before five p.m. He hit the TALK button. "Okay, great," he said. "Please send her down."

He turned off the computer monitors, stashed the printout of the original *RED* in his desk drawer, locked it, and headed out to meet her at the security guard's desk right in front of subbasement two's elevators. Before he left his office, he checked to make sure his shirt was still pressed. He sure wished he weren't wearing jeans, but that couldn't be helped.

He met her just after she'd gone through the security screeners: she gave him a hug, and he hugged her back. It had been a long time, but he would have recognized her anywhere. Her hair was meticulously cornrowed close to her scalp, with tight, beautifully maintained braids swept up in an elaborate style that framed her face and then hung halfway down her back.

"Thanks for coming over," he said.

"Okay, Mr. Big-Time Delaney Employee, what's the top-secret project?"

"I can't wait to tell you," he said. "You're not going to believe this."

Before she could follow him back, though, she had to relinquish her phone. No phones on the floor at all. Bern had to show her where his was stashed before she consented to parting with it.

Finally she made it down the hall and into his office. He closed the door, and she maneuvered over to the plush chair next to the couch. "Well, damn. This place is nice," she said. "You sure got yourself in good with these white folks. No windows, though. How come you're in a basement with no windows?"

He sat on the couch. Held her eye. "First, you can't say anything to anyone," he told her.

"I ain't gonna give out your secrets," she said.

"I'm serious. This is a life-changing, very important project. The real deal."

"You're really geeking out over this," she said. "What is it?"

"I need you to sign an NDA," he said, pushing across the papers that Stephanie had delivered to him earlier that afternoon.

"I need to know what I'm getting into before I sign anything," she said.

"Well, I can't tell you if you won't sign it. That's the point of an NDA."

"I'm not signing. If I care enough, we can get started. But you have to tell me first."

"They want you to sign it," he said, a little more desperately than he wanted to sound.

"What the ef do I care what they want? And who is this 'they' anyway?"

"'They' are the executive board of the Delaney Foundation. Mallory Delaney Roberts. Frederic Delaney's niece. You met her at the ceremony." Now that Eboni knew it was Mallory herself, surely she would sign.

Instead, Eboni rolled her eyes. "Oh yeah. I remember her. She still wear those Golden Girls outfits?"

He decided to take the high road and ignore her. She'd never revered the Foundation the way he did. "They found something and they're keeping it under wraps. They want me to work on it and I'd like you to work on it with me. It's a pretty big deal." He thought for a moment. "You want me to sign it on your behalf?"

She just looked at him, her cornrows catching the light.

"You really can't tell anybody about this," he warned her.

She rolled her eyes.

That was the best he was going to get, he knew. And he also knew that a piece of paper was only as good as the person who signed it. The bottom line was that he trusted Eboni Michelle Washington. And—let's face it—he owed her for all the times she'd saved his ass, when Jacques Simon was chewing him out for forgetting to log in proper information or keep track of a musical source. Eboni always had a backup. She should have been a Girl Scout—she was always prepared.

So now Bern would sign her name to the NDA and hope nobody noticed.

Most people would look at her and jump to conclusions, and the conclusions were almost always wrong. If you saw her on the street you'd think she was a hood rat working on her next hustle. If you talked to her for ten minutes, you'd realize that she possessed one of the fastest minds you'd ever encounter. But if you got to know her, she might—*might*—let down her guard and reveal the warm, compassionate woman who hid beneath the tough-talking South Bronx persona.

He explained what he wanted from her: to start with a comparison of the reconstructed *RED* and the scan of the original *RED*, and then, in a week or two, when he had enough of his own transcription done, to continue to double-check his work.

She patted her pockets, exaggeratedly, for her phone. "Where's my phone? Oh, right, it was confiscated. How can I keep track of anything without my phone?" She thought a moment. "It's Tuesday," she said. "I can probably have a copy back to you by Thursday. Friday, at the latest."

"They're not going to want a copy of the original *RED* on your server," he said.

"Have your people call my people. My server's more secure than theirs, anyway. I guarantee it. I do this for a living, remember?"

"Okay," he said. "I'll have them call you tomorrow, first thing."

"Hold up, slick." She blinked at him. "Before you get all hot and bothered, we need to get one thing straight."

Bern knew it had to be too good to be true.

"My fee is nonnegotiable. Make sure you tell that to your Delaney friends. Don't let them think that because we go way back, they can take advantage of me. That shit ain't gonna fly."

"I don't think it's about money for them," he said.

"It better not be, that's what I'm saying. I know the Delaney Foundation. They only hire the best and, yes, I know because I turned down a position with them, thank you very much."

Bern had almost forgotten that Delaney's tech division had tried relentlessly to recruit Eboni during the *Rings Quintet* research. She couldn't stop going on about it. Eventually she'd turned down a serious six-figure salary to start her own company. She wanted to keep her business in her own neighborhood to help revitalize the area.

Eboni was brilliant—and at Columbia he'd encountered many very smart people. She told him once that she'd tested off the charts for spatial intelligence, which, in its simplest form, meant she was able to visualize shapes in three dimensions. She never got lost and could read a map at a glance. More important, she was able to detect patterns quickly and deftly, in ways that left him stuttering with amazement: once they'd gone to Central Park and she'd ambled across Sheep Meadow with him, stopping every few feet to pluck a piece of grass and then continuing on. She'd kept up with him the whole time—he hadn't been walking quickly, but he'd definitely been moving forward. After maybe the fifth or sixth instance, he'd asked what she was doing. She'd opened her palm and showed six perfect four-leaf clovers. She'd found eight more before they reached the other end of the field, and she hadn't even paused to search for them. That was Eboni in a nutshell: casually brilliant, able to detect configurations that mere mortals could not.

And yet he'd heard that her work designing cutting-edge computer security systems had not been going as well as people had predicted—meaning she hadn't yet sold her company for billions of dollars to a megacorporation. She'd hired a team of people, but everyone had thought she would have sold her company to Amazon or Google by now. She did many things brilliantly, but assimilating, giving in, or compromising was not in her playbook. He didn't doubt that she'd ruffled many feathers.

If she didn't alienate people, she often flew under their radars. Most underestimated her or wrote her off entirely. "That Eboni?" Bern had heard Columbia students say. "She's a lightweight. Total poser. Can't believe she's still here." They usually said this right before she obliterated them on an exam or a presentation. She was five steps ahead, or almost at the finish line, before her opponents even put on their shoes.

Now, he said, "I'll tell them that they should pay you what you want. You're the best at what you do, and I don't have time to train someone new. We can see what they say."

"Just talk to whatever stuffed shirt is in charge and tell them to authorize it. That's the only way you're getting me."

"Okay," he said, extending his hand to shake hers.

Instead she hugged him. "Boom. Now where is it?" she said, meaning the original *RED*.

"I have the scanned files here." He moved over to his desk, switched on the monitors.

"You seen the original?"

"No. Not yet."

"Mmm-hmmm. Where did they find it?"

"They haven't told me specifically," he said. "It was behind a panel or something."

She blinked at him again, elbowed him out of the way, and sat down in his desk chair. Typed a few keys. "It's encrypted pretty good," she said. "And the security is top-of-the-line. You go talk to your bosses and have the IT guys contact me first thing tomorrow so I can get a copy of the file."

"Any chance I can have them contact you now? Everybody's still working here, and I was kind of hoping—"

"It's after five," she told him. "There ain't no way I'm starting on this tonight. Like I said, I'll have it for you by Friday. And yes, I'll be available for you during normal business hours if you need something redone." She stood, grabbed a couple of Delaney Foundation pens from the cup on his desk. "Where are you taking me tonight? You want to hit that East Village place I told you about?"

"Nope, work comes first," he said. "When you get me the files on Friday, you'll get whatever slices you want. Even if they are Sicilian." He wasn't a fan of the thick-crusted Sicilian pizza.

"You got yourself a deal," she told him.

6

Jar *versus* Pot

Bern

BERN HAD TO TAP-DANCE with Mallory and the Delaney Foundation crew, but eventually Eboni managed to demonstrate that her server was more secure than the Foundation's, and that she'd put protocols into place to restrict additional copying of or access to *RED*. Reluctantly they sent over the file, encrypted and security protected, with a deadline of Friday for her to return the new files to them and purge her servers of all traces of it.

In the intervening days, he smoothed things over with his dean at the University of Virginia, who was surprisingly accepting of Bern's absence and coordinated with another associate professor and a few grad students to take over Bern's classes. Bern suspected that a call from Mallory and, no doubt, a thoughtful "donation" from the Foundation hadn't hurt matters. In any case, once word of *RED* got out, UVA would be fighting to keep him.

Friday evening at 5:34 p.m., true to her word, Eboni emailed him the compared files, via a secure data link. Until then he'd been work-ing manually: a laborious task that made his eyes ache.

To celebrate, Bern was true to *his* promise and that evening took Eboni out for pizza in the East Village. Eboni had her own very clear views of what Good Pizza consisted of (a crisp but chewy crust that could hold toppings and not sag, for instance). The students working on the Quintet could spend only a certain number of hours at work before their ears turned to mush and their analytical abilities got fuzzy, so sometime in Bern's second year of grad school they'd started a quest to find the Best Pizza in New York City. That meant all five boroughs—from Staten Island's notoriously thin crust to the thick and chewy ("Cake!" Eboni would scoff. "This ain't crust, it's cake!") Sicilian. The pizza was scored based on its crust, sauce, cheese, and toppings. Thus far the clear winner was Papa's Three, a tiny take-out joint on the Upper West Side, but all such crowns were temporary and in constant need of testing.

Bern had spent the week transcribing Delaney's music by hand, and fragments of *RED*'s phrasing buzzed in his ears and winged past his temples. He needed a break, needed to get Delaney out of his head in order to keep Delaney in his head tomorrow.

He packed up for the night, stashed *RED* back in its file cabinet, and headed out into the cool October night.

At the Foundation he'd been listening to A$AP Rocky's "Wild for the Night," but as he headed down into the Lincoln Center sub-way, with relief, he switched on Delaney's *Quicksilver*. He tried not to listen to Delaney's music while he was working. Once, in grad school, listening to Delaney's Trio for Two Oboes and Cello, he'd somehow rearranged the soprano solo at the beginning of *BLUE*'s act 2—transforming it into another trio. Jacques Simon likely would have been impressed if he weren't so furious. It had cost them two days of work to correct Bern's blunder.

Bern had learned his lesson: no more Delaney while transcribing.

It always transported him to a different place spiritually and emotionally. So during work hours he listened to 311, Geppetto's Wüd, and a host of other eclectic rock bands and classical artists. Bach and Schubert were standard favorites, but none compared to Frederic Delaney, of course.

Baranocchi's Pizza was a hot little hole-in-the-wall just off Tompkins Square Park: a narrow pizza counter on the right, with barely enough room in front of it to stand and order. The pizza oven—wood-burning, enormous, and seemingly Italian—consumed the entire back corner, and the heat poured over the counter and into the rest of the space. Three tables lined the left wall, but if you sat there, you'd have all the patrons' butts in your face as you tried to eat. Most people seemed to be eating at park benches nearby.

Eboni was waiting for Bern outside. "Delaney's love child finally shows up," she said when she saw him.

"I'm starving," he told her. He'd checked out the reviews of the place on the subway—very high marks, so he was psyched. "You want two?"

"Of course," she said. "And beer."

"The usual?"

In order to determine the Best Pizza in New York, they'd established a two-slice minimum: a baseline cheese on the pizzeria's best-known crust, as well as another slice, which could be exotic or intriguing or perhaps the pizzeria's calling card.

"I'll do the margherita and then the *cacio e pepe* on the Neapolitan crust," she told him. "I had the marg last time and it was good. Great seasoning balance on the sauce."

"Fresh?" Bern asked. Some sauces were made from fresh tomatoes; others from canned. Both had their pros and cons, but Eboni was a fresh sauce kind of girl.

They stood in line, ordered, and eventually carried the pizza, in two flimsy cardboard boxes, out to a bench in Tompkins Square Park. They kept their bottles of beer in paper bags.

Until then they'd just caught up with friendly banter—no talking shop: how Eboni's aunt was doing, how her older sister was out of rehab, how she'd hired three people for the company she was building. Now, though, as they sat on the bench and Bern bit into the baseline marg slice, he noticed Eboni giving him the side-eye. "What do you think?"

"Good crust," he said. "I think the sauce is a little too sweet. Wish it had more spice to it."

"The cheese balance work for you?" she said.

"Yeah, cheese is pretty good." He chewed thoughtfully. "Really good, actually. It's just the sauce that feels a little flimsy."

"What is it?" she said, and her tone had shifted. "What's on your mind?"

"Maybe there's a hint of too much olive oil," he said. "It seems a little bitter." He wiped his lips.

"Kevin, seriously, what is it?" Eboni said. No smile. No chewing.

"Um," Bern started. Eboni had only called Bern by his first name, Kevin, a handful of times, when she was being serious.

"No, I'm really glad I could bring you in on this project," he said, as if she'd objected to something.

"I'm sure you are, hotshot," she told him. "But what's going on? Is something wrong? You got your files from me. You can work all weekend now."

He took a breath. "So, I saw something on one of the scans that I'm not sure about."

"What?" Eboni finished her first slice, dug around in the box for her second—this one with double pecorino, vodka sauce, banana peppers, and Impossible Meatballs. "And don't say it's nothing."

Bern thought a moment, put down his slice, wiped his hands with thirty of the skimpy napkins that pizza parlors always provide. He made a mental note, yet again, to bring his own paper towels or wet wipes. "Something about one of those pages had been bugging me."

"Bugging you how? And you missed a spot." She pointed to sauce on the edge of Bern's sleeve.

"I'm not totally sure, but there was a word—*jar*—on one of the pages. No idea why he would have written *jar*, and it's been bugging me."

"Wait," Eboni said mid-chew. "You're wigging out over a jar?"

"No. Yes. I don't know!" Bern said. "It just doesn't make sense. No reason for *jar* to be written anywhere. It's actually on a page of his Doodles, not on a page of the score. I didn't send it over to you because there's nothing to compare it to, plus the Foundation doesn't want it to get out at all, I'm sure. I've never seen it before. On anything he's done. It doesn't seem to correspond to anything in any of his works. The closest thing I can think of is in *YELLOW*, when the warlord requests the jars of mountain honey. But that doesn't seem like it should matter, and it came long before *RED* was ever even written, anyway."

"Please don't go all Scooby-Doo on me," Eboni said, snapping her fingers in his face. "You probably have it halfway figured out by now, don't you?"

Bern smiled, shook his head. "I don't. Not this one. It's weird."

"When can I see it?" she asked.

"You'll probably have it all figured out the first time you look at it," he said. "You're the queen of crosswords, right?"

"I'm just 'the queen' to you," she said. "And you know something? I'm gonna get me a slice to go. Tomorrow's lunch. I haven't told you about this woman I hired, Colleen. Nosey as hell. Tries to figure out where I've been by checking out what I bring in for lunch. Then she tells me about her imaginary boyfriend, Luis—maybe he's real, but he sure seems like a figment of her imagination—taking her to that same spot. Always trying to outdo me. I can't wait to rub this one in her face."

Bern knew that she was taking his mind off work. "I'll get an extra slice for Colleen," he said. "The Foundation's treat." He maneuvered his way back inside. What was it about this *jar* that was so unusual? Did it have something to do with the reason the original *RED* had disappeared? Was Bern fixating on nothing, or was there something here? He didn't know, but knew the word *jar* would, again, keep him up late tonight.

Saturday morning, back at the Delaney Foundation with Eboni's compared files, he dug in. The days spun on, one after another, with Bern coding and analyzing a minimum of five pages a day, seven days a week. Sometimes he got seven pages done, but usually he struggled to finish just five pages by the end of the day. The process was laborious and meticulous, but every page became more thrilling than the one before: going so deep into the music, comparing every note, every annotation, and every phrase made it feel as if he were plunging deeper into the genius that had been Frederic Delaney. It was as if Delaney were communicating with Bern, solely and singly, across the span of a century.

In the meantime, the folder of those extra pages that weren't part of the original *RED* score still clamored in the top drawer of the locked file cabinet. He pulled them out every so often, reread that tantalizing sentence from the conjure woman character's "Song of the Trees": *Sorrow is everything here.* He couldn't wait to dig deeper into the research. Decoding the secret of the Delaney Doodles had the potential to be game-changing.

A few days after Eboni delivered the files, he took a midafternoon break and leaned into Stephanie's office, a few doors down from his own. He suspected she didn't like being in the basement, but she didn't say anything to him about it. She looked up when she saw him in the doorway, smiled that awkward smile of hers. It seemed a little more forced than it usually did.

"Hey," he said, "I was wondering . . . Any news from the tech team about that Doodle page? The one with *jar* on it? Mallory told me to talk to Julie Akers, but Julie wouldn't give me any details. I'd really like to get this sorted out in case it impacts the work I'm doing on *RED*."

Stephanie angled toward her keyboard, typed something. Then she said, "It looks like IT is doing a complete search for any mention of *jar* or *jars* in the entire Delaney archive, which is fully digitized and searchable." She added, "The mandate's been given. This is top priority."

"Fully searchable?"

She shrugged. "Well, as fully searchable as we can make it. Everything has been OCR'd, but of course the scanning is imperfect. We're doing our best to fill in the holes."

Optical character recognition software recognized text, allowing computer programs to find an actual word within a digital image. So, theoretically, if the letters *J*, *A*, and *R* appeared anywhere in that order in any of the Delaney materials, they should be findable at the click of a button. In practice, however, OCR technology, no matter how advanced, could still miss recognizing a letter or misread an *R* as a *B*, for instance.

"Can you keep me posted if you find anything?" he said.

"Of course. For future reference, the subset of anything other than the score can be found in folder G-17."

"You're not just looking for *jar*, though, right? You're looking for—oh, I don't know—*bottle* and *tub* and *pot*?"

She explained that the IT team was hunting for any kind of *jar* references: from mugs to vessels, bottles to bins. Two dozen eyes were scrutinizing any time that Frederic Delaney even thought about any receptacle.

But that was just the beginning. They'd hired two Fellows at the Metropolitan Museum of Art who specialized in the '20s and '30s, to see if Delaney had utilized the geometric motifs from expressionism and art deco on the Doodles.

Finally, they'd reached out to Columbia's legendary Lomax Cuellar, one of the top linguistic authorities in the world. Jacques Simon had worked with Cuellar on the Quintet, which also had a few scattered Doodles. Cuellar hadn't had any luck decoding them, but hopefully now that he had two full pages of Doodles, he'd make more headway in deciphering their purpose.

In the meantime, Bern confirmed that Eboni, too, could be hired to cross-check any *jar* references, since she could reload the original *RED* back onto her server, plus the other four *Rings* from her time with Jacques Simon.

Mallory wrote him an email approving Eboni's additional work. Immediately he texted Eboni.

BERN: Hey I have another job for you.

EBONI: With the same people? Gonna cost you a few more slices

BERN: Deal. Upside Down pizza in Jersey?

EBONI: Too far. 5 boros. New place in Brooklyn

BERN: Tell me when. Can you come to the DF?

EBONI: Not done til 6 tonight but will be down in Chelsea. I'll send address, get a car to pick me up

Eboni arrived a few minutes after six thirty, after most of the DF staff had left for the day. He showed her the Doodles page with *JAR* on it.

She remembered the Doodles from the Quintet—it had frustrated her then, that she couldn't figure out their meaning. "Remind me again when they first appeared?" she asked. "I always say you got to start at the beginning."

Bern checked his files. "1923. We have them on the original manuscript of the *Spider Web Waltz*. Just two little Doodles."

"Show me," she said.

He pulled them up from the DF archive: the musical score of the *Spider Web Waltz*, which was originally written for a Broadway revue. On the right side of the second page, near the paper's edge, hung three triangles, interconnected, with a series of wavy lines on the left side.

"What about his earlier stuff? When did he start composing?"

"In 1918," Bern said. "He was working for a music publisher, plugging songs, and wrote one that was a hit."

"But no Doodles?"

"Nope."

"What was special about *Spider-Man Waltz*?" she said. "What made him put them on that one?"

"John Sloan at Purdue wrote a three-hundred-page dissertation about it in the 1970s," Bern said. "I can get you a copy if you need some light afternoon reading. He has a theory that they're dynamic references, but that still doesn't make much sense to me. Why draw all that stuff when you can just put a *P* or an *F* when you want to make the music softer or louder? That's how he always did it."

"All right, chief, let me see what I can come up with," Eboni said, staring hard at the Doodle pages.

"That's it? *The* Eboni Michelle Washington is stumped? Can't figure out a pattern?"

She shot him another side-eye. "Yet. I just got it two minutes ago. I'll have it decoded by tomorrow."

"Despite hundreds of scholars not being able to figure it out?"

"Hundreds of scholars weren't Eboni Michelle Washington," she told him. "Amateur hour is over. Time for the pros."

But she had no more luck than the DF IT team decoding the meaning of *JaR*: there were altogether over five thousand references to *jar*, *basin*, *bottle*, *can*, *flask*, *jug*, *chalice*, *crock*, *cruet*, *decanter*, *ewer*, and so forth. And then the other dozens of spelling variations of *jar*, like *jab*, *job*, *ear*. None seemed to be associated with wings, or leaves, or whatever the trilobe symbol was, and no one could figure the way in.

Eboni, however, was up for a challenge.

7

Wearing Gloves

Bern

THE FOLLOWING WEEK, Eboni stormed in unannounced. "I'm sick of this," she said, shrugging out of her coat—New York was in the middle of an unusual late October freeze—and throwing herself on the couch. "Let me see those Doodle pages with my own eyes. The originals. I don't care how good your scans are, I'm sure they missed something."

Bern had forgotten to charge his earbuds, and had left his headphones at the Foundation apartment that Stephanie had set him up in. So now his music was ringing through his basement office: Santana's "The Game of Love." He'd been singing along. Now he turned it down.

"Hey," he said. "Now's not the best time. What're you doing here in the middle of the afternoon anyway? I have a meeting with the executive director in, like, five minutes and—"

"Why's it taking so long to look at a hundred-year-old piece of paper? I'd get it if it were the Magna Carta, but jeez." She rubbed her eyes. "This is driving me nuts."

"You and me both," he said. "I keep asking. They say they're being preserved. But as soon as they're done they'll let us take a look."

"Who's this 'they'? What kind of preservation are 'they' doing? If you're meeting with the boss, then let's ask her personally."

"Ask who personally?" came Mallory's voice from the door. "I hope I'm not interrupting anything too important?"

"Not at all," Bern said. "This is—"

"This must be Ms. Washington. How do you do. I'm Mallory Delaney Roberts." Something about Mallory's tone—in the drawn-out way she said "Delaney"—made Bern immediately want to shoot Eboni a warning look not to go off on this woman. Eboni didn't do well around people who put on airs—and he knew she was frustrated with the delays and her inability to figure out *jar*. It wouldn't take much more to set her off.

"I've heard so much about you," Mallory gushed as she extended a well-manicured hand. "You're just a miracle worker. Thank you for all that you've done."

Eboni smiled even harder, her very white teeth glittering. "Hello, dear," she said. "It is positively thrilling to see you again."

"I believe you know my good friend Elon?" Mallory said. "He couldn't stop raving about you. We'd really love to lure you over here."

"Yes, well." Eboni shrugged. "I took him to a great pizza joint in Brooklyn. He needs to get out more. I told him that he might be able to buy and sell the entire planet, but a great slice is really priceless."

"Oh, really? I love pizza. You'll have to take me there some-time," Mallory said. Even Bern could tell that she had no intention of ever going. And then to Bern, she said, "If this isn't a good time to talk—"

"No, no, it's on the calendar," Bern said. "Eboni just stopped in to update me about—"

"*Jar*," Eboni interrupted.

"Excuse me?" Mallory said.

"*Jar*," Eboni repeated. "That Doodle page with *jar* on it? He tells me he's been asking your people for the original for weeks."

Mallory looked flabbergasted. "But he has the page. I authorized it myself."

"The original," Eboni said. "We've requested it on multiple occasions. To do a full and accurate analysis, I'm going to need to see the original."

"Well, as I mentioned to Bern, all in good time. The paper's very fragile, and we must make sure it's properly preserved. That's the top priority right now."

"It's been over a month," Eboni said. "How long does it take to preserve one sheet of paper? Especially since you've assured Dr. Hendricks that having him review it is also a top priority. What am I missing?"

"These things have to be done carefully," Mallory said. "We can't just have anybody—" She hesitated, cleared her throat, changed direction. "We'll let you know when it's ready, I assure you."

We can't just have anybody. That phrase—he recognized it. He'd been hearing variations of it all his life. In grad school, undergrad, high school. *I don't think you should audition for this group. We can't just have anybody playing the first horn part,* or *You don't need to audition for district band. We don't need anybody off the street coming in, thinking they can make the cut.* Since he'd heard it all his life, he should have been used to hearing it now.

But not here. Not from her. Not from Frederic Delaney's niece.

He wanted to speak, but the realization knocked him back.

Eboni was quicker. "Oh, okay. I get it," she said. "What is it? The hair? The nails? The makeup? Oh wait, I know. It's the fact that we're too Black for you."

Mallory pulled back, her lipsticked mouth in a thin line. "I didn't mean that the way it sounded. My hugest apologies if you took it that way—I just meant that the paper is very delicate and we're doing our best to make absolutely sure that it's preserved in its best—"

"I'm sure that's what you meant," Eboni said cheerfully. "On paper, I look great. We both do." She pointed at Bern. "In person, it's a whole new ball game. We're good enough to research and figure out everything that you people have going on up in here, but we can't see a piece of paper I know he's been asking you for since the day he walked in? Come on. What's the holdup? You think he's gonna steal it? You think he's going to get fried-chicken grease on it?"

"I am so sorry—you must understand that I didn't mean anything by that—if it came across that way, just know it wasn't my intention—I am so—so sorry—" Mallory was stuttering. She had gone very white, but two red spheres had appeared on her cheeks, as if they'd been dipped in rouge.

"I'm sure you are," Eboni told her, taking a step closer, looking Mallory up and down, absolutely cool. Bern could tell that Eboni was vibrating with fury. "And here's what you're going to do. You're going to get us access to the original pages of the Delaney Doodles and the original score to *RED*. None of this scanned business. You've been jerking us around long enough. When will you be making it happen?"

"These are better than the originals," Mallory said, still flustered. "That's what I've been trying to tell you. Everything has been scanned and copied, and digitally enhanced."

Eboni had been standing in Mallory's personal space, bristling with fury and indignation. Now her face softened and she rocked back slightly. "As I'm sure you're well aware, digitized scans can be extremely effective. Almost too effective. They can pick up details that a human eye can't. As you are also probably aware, the original design of most scanners is modeled after a bird's vision. Birds have many times more rods and cones than humans do. Computer scans produce an intimate, detailed rendering, but right now we don't need that. We don't want a bird's-eye view with three times the detail. We need a human perspective. Are you going to grant us access to these pages, or are you going to keep stalling us and delaying the process?"

A pause. Bern waited, chest tight, for an explosion from Mallory, but Mallory said only, "Well then, we've all learned something new today. It's been an absolute delight—and so educational—to meet you, Ms. Washington. I'm so very sorry for your misconstruing my meaning. I didn't mean to offend you. Let me just check on the scans and see where they are in the process."

"Certainly," Bern said. "Thank you."

"It was a pleasure to meet you, Ms. Washington," Mallory repeated.

"Charmed, I'm sure," Eboni said. Her lips didn't fit around all her large square teeth.

When Mallory had gone, Bern shout-whispered, "Holy shit! That's the executive director of the Delaney Foundation! Are you trying to get me fired?" The back of his neck was damp with sweat. He imagined security coming in to escort Eboni out.

What would his life be like without the possibility of *RED*? How could he be so stupid to let things escalate so uncomfortably between the two women?

"She ain't nobody," Eboni told him. "You are so obsessed with Delaney that you can't even see when somebody's jerking you around? It ain't got nothing to do with your degree or your experience and has everything to do with what you see in the mirror."

"I—"

"Haven't you figured out yet that they need us? Trust me. Ain't nobody getting fired anytime soon, and certainly not a Black man."

"I—" he started to say again, and then stopped. All his life he'd been navigating the dangerous waters of discrimination: white people discounting him and treating him like they couldn't see him, fellow students assuming the only reason he'd gotten into Columbia was to fill a quota. He knew he'd always be the token Black professor in a sea of lily-white faces.

Now the Delaney Foundation had a Black man, a former DF Kid, spearheading the most important project they'd ever had, written by one of the world's most beloved white composers. The optics would play well in the media. Especially since Delaney himself did so much to connect Black and white. Bern held more cards than he'd realized. Eboni had, as usual, known this all along. "Later for all that," he said. "Just try to keep it cordial, okay?"

"What are you talking about? She started it! Besides, you should be kissing my Black ass for lighting a fire under her to get you them pages."

The next day, he received an email from Mallory:

Hi, Bern, great news. The original is ready for you. Set up a time with Stephanie for a viewing. See you soon!

Eboni arrived two hours later, cutting short a scheduled meeting to see the page with her own human eyeballs. Moments after Eboni stalked into the office, Stephanie knocked and poked her head in. Her smile looked more and more like she was in pain or had gas. "Hi, you two. Ms. Roberts asked me to escort you over to A-11." Wince.

"A-11?" Bern asked.

"Where we're keeping the originals." Wince.

As Stephanie led the way upstairs, Eboni said, "I swear if she fake-smiles one more time at me I'm gonna snatch those glasses off her face and make her eat 'em." She kept her voice down. Bern cracked up.

Meanwhile Stephanie led them past the guard station and into the elevator, up a level to the main room of the archive, in subbasement one. Low lights gleamed overhead, blond tables were arranged around a central research desk with carrels lining the walls. Off to one side, and through another security checkpoint, Stephanie shuffled down the hall and into a small room far to the back. Two chairs flanked a desk. In the back corner, a closed-circuit TV camera glared down accusingly. Stephanie droned on about the importance of no skin-on-paper contact. Bern stopped counting the number of times

Eboni rolled her eyes. Did the Foundation honestly think he was in kindergarten?

Bern and Eboni took their seats, and then Stephanie closed the door behind her and disappeared. Neither spoke. Bern wondered how many hidden microphones and cameras had been installed and who was watching them.

One of the archivists tapped on the glass door, opened it. She held a thin, slightly oversize envelope with a string tie. She set it before them, pulled out its contents: a single sheet of paper encased in glassine. They couldn't touch the manuscript anyway. So why were Bern and Eboni wearing gloves? Bern shook his head.

The archivist left them alone, and they stared into the single sheet with its Doodles front and back. They peered first at the back of the sheet, where the right margin still remained unmarked, and then turned the sheet over very slowly.

It looked just the way it did on the scan. Now they could see the faint indentations of a pencil, actually marking the lines. Delaney's pencil. Delaney's fingerprints on the page. Bern wanted to take off the plastic and smell the paper. Would it smell like Frederic Delaney himself?

They stared at the page, eyes tracing the Doodles, for some time. Flipped to the other side, then back again. The marks stared back, uninterested.

Again he turned the page, spun it upside down, then right-side up again. He laid it on the desk, with the *JaR* side up in the middle of the surface.

"Well, guess this is a wild-goose chase," Eboni said after a while, pulling it closer.

Bern didn't hear her. At this slight angle, the page looked different.

He didn't say anything, just gestured with his chin. He could actually feel Eboni stop breathing as she stood next to him. Her shoe tapped his leg, just once. Bern said, probably too loud, "Sure is nice to see this in person, though, you know? I need to rack 'em up."

Rack 'em up. They hadn't used that code in years, but of course she must have remembered: it was what all the graduate students said when they were doing something and didn't want Jacques Simon to overhear. Like the time Julie spilled water on one of the Quintet's first editions and Bern had called out, "Hey, we should rack up these books." Eboni distracted Jacques while Bern ran for paper towels.

Until Bern figured out where he stood with the Foundation—especially in light of Mallory's comment the day before—he wanted to keep all discoveries to just himself and Eboni for now.

They stared, unseeing, down at the page. The designs blurred and danced. Five more minutes crawled by.

Finally Bern stood, went to the door. The archivist, who'd been hovering inconspicuously outside, approached immediately. "I think that will do it," Bern said. "Thank you."

Stephanie awaited them in the main research area. She was on her phone, and Bern wondered if she was texting Mallory. In the elevator down to the subbasement, Eboni brushed his sleeve, caught his eye.

Back in Bern's office, he pulled out a sticky notepad he found in the desk. He was suddenly worried that his office was bugged.

I need to tell them, he wrote.

She shook her head, almost imperceptibly.

They looked at each other and, as casually as possible, headed out of his office. They went through security, retrieved their phones, and went upstairs and out into a misty early November. Cars sizzled past on damp streets, and the wind stung his cheeks. They headed west, toward Central Park and the chaos of Midtown.

Finally, a block away, near Lincoln Center, he spoke. "How did they miss it?"

"No freakin' idea." She shook her head. "The same way we did, I guess."

"You saw it, too, right?"

"Of course I did," she said. "Probably before you did. Rods and cones, baby. Rods and cones. And maybe just the way the light hit it."

The letters did not spell *J-a-R* as the scans had seemed to indicate: the *a*, lowercase, was not an *a* at all. It was an *o*, also lowercase, that had a squiggle or a shadow or a crease in the paper that made the letter—if you didn't examine it closely—look like a lowercase *a*.

Everyone had been combing for the wrong letters all this time—looking for *J-a-R*, not *J-o-R*.

"I need to tell Mallory about this," Bern said.

"Unbelievable," she said, shaking her head. "Millions of dollars' worth of equipment and it can't even distinguish an *o* from an *a*."

"I don't think anybody looked at the original after they scanned it in and enhanced it," Bern said, ducking around a halal food stand. "It probably went into cryogenic freeze once the scan was done."

"Yeah," Eboni said, considering. "Maybe. Especially if they were in the process of preserving it. I mean, it is a hundred-year-old sheet of paper. Did you see how brown it was? And I wonder what the gray stuff was all over the corner."

"They got careless," Bern said. "That's how they missed it. Probably because they're in such a hurry. All the hands-off white-glove treatment. They must have the same mentality Mallory has—that a scan was all they needed. The only reason we saw it is because you're so pushy."

"You're welcome," she told him. They were almost to Central Park now, waiting to cross at the light. Taxis and cars flooded past. A woman biked uptown with a little girl strapped to a tiny carrier behind her.

"I don't know about you," Bern said, "but I had to look at it at least a dozen times to see that it was an *o*, not an *a*." He paused, thinking. "But still. I don't understand how their searches didn't turn up anything for *J-o-R*."

"Maybe they were looking for a single word," Eboni said thoughtfully. "Maybe *J-o-R* is two words. Like a name." They crossed the street, followed one of the paths into the park. "Maybe *J* and *oR*. Or *Jo* and *R*. Did your Foundation buddies search for those?"

"No clue," Bern said. They walked on in silence, both thinking hard. "And there's something else, too," he said after a few moments. The burn of excitement rippled across his shoulders, into his chest as he thought more about those mysterious letters. "I'll bet you a million bucks that that's not Delaney's handwriting. I don't know why I didn't think of it or how I missed it, but I'm sure of it now. He didn't write that."

"He didn't write *JoR*?"

"No fucking way he did. I know his handwriting. I know it."

"How come nobody else figured that out then? Doesn't the Foundation have handwriting experts?"

"I'm sure they must. But I'm an expert, too, you know? Seven years of looking at his handwriting has got to make me an expert. He didn't write it."

"Well, who did?" Eboni asked.

Bern stared at a tree as if it held the answer. The tree stared back, impassive. "We've got to tell them all this. We need them to help figure it all out."

"Wrong-a-rino," Eboni told him. "We ain't telling them shit. We're holding the cards for once. I'm not saying that it will amount to anything, but who knows, it very well could and if it does, boom! You get your name in another one of those fancy research journals you like to read so much and maybe I get something out of it, too. My vote is that we don't say anything until we know more."

Did Bern really want to bite the hand that was feeding him? The white hand that had been oh-so-reluctant to feed his Black mouth to begin with? Mallory still hadn't told him exactly where the original *RED* had been found. Why were they hiding this from him, too?

"Okay," he said. "Let's give it a few days and see if we can come up with something. You don't have access to the full Delaney archive from your computer, do you?"

"They said that they gave me access when you brought me in to look for *jar*. Now I wonder if there's stuff they've kept from me." She thought a minute. "But your computer taps directly into their mainframe, so I can get through their firewalls. I can even hide the keystrokes so they can't follow us."

"So you want to go back?"

"Yeah," she said. "But no talking in there, okay? I bet that place is bugged."

"Really? You think they'd go that far?"

"Is it worth taking the chance?"

They stared at each other a moment, and then headed back to the Foundation.

Back in his office, she took her seat behind the desk and he stood behind her, looking over her shoulder. "Are you sure that—"

"Would you please chill? Jeez. I know what I'm doing."

A blur of computer code poured across the monitor. He had no idea what he was looking for, or at. She did, though. She typed another string of letters and characters that meant nothing to him.

JoR. What could *JoR* mean?

Thumbnail images tiled across the screen. Eboni zeroed in on the top left one, expanded it. Bern leaned over her shoulder for a closer look. A 1963 invoice from *Jonathan Reece Electrical Supply*.

She shrunk it, expanded the next. *James and Rollins Fine Upholsterers* furnished several new armchairs for Mr. Delaney in 1935.

Julie Royce's engagement party in 1934.

All these were too late: the original *RED* had been written, and lost, supposedly between 1924 and 1926.

And then: another image: A list. A passenger manifest.

Frederic Delaney's first trip to Europe in 1920, on the *Queen Mary*. A roster of passengers.

Delaney Party

And then a series of eight names.

The final name: *Josephine Reed.*

Jo R, Bern mouthed. Jo Reed.

Who was Josephine Reed?

Could this be Delaney's mysterious Dark Lady? And what was her name doing on a sheet of Delaney's Doodles?

8

Delaney's Dark Lady

Bern

A SEARCH FOR "JOSEPHINE REED" in the Delaney archive pulled up eighteen hits. Most telling, she'd accompanied him on his first European tour, one of the retinue of employees on his payroll, who soon dropped off. No scholar had ever paid attention to her before. Researchers had always assumed she was a general servant.

That night Bern lay in bed, staring up at the ceiling. 3:11 a.m. Delaney had never mentioned Josephine Reed. None of the journalists who'd covered him had written of her, either. The name felt utterly new to him, yet familiar.

He played the *Quicksilver* symphony again. The scherzo movement always put him in a good mood. He'd first heard it as a thirteen-year-old in All-County Orchestra: those perfect saxophone and French horn lines called out like sirens to a lost ship. The symphony was more properly titled Delaney's Fourth Symphony—the conductor Herbert von Karajan had bestowed the *Quicksilver* name in the early thirties. Delaney and Bern both hated the reference because Karajan had ties to the Nazi Party.

Bern owned seven different recordings of the symphony. His favorite was the recording by the National Symphony Orchestra under the direction of Leonard Slatkin. Slatkin's interpretation was by far the cleanest and most energetic. Lying on his back, Bern started fingering the first French horn part, which mimicked both alto and tenor saxophone lines.

He was drifting into a restless, burning half slumber when a text pinged.

EBONI: You up? I know you are. What you listening to?

BERN: Delaney's 4th. What's up?

EBONI: What if she was his secret baby mama?

BERN: Now UR sounding crazy. No record of mixed child

EBONI: No record of Josephine Reed either smart azz. Go back to sleep. I think it might be real. I got a feeling

BERN: Night

It was comforting that she was awake, too. Knowing that she was just as obsessed made it possible for him to fall asleep, *Quicksilver* humming in his ears.

A few hours later, his phone chimed again, waking him from that half-asleep, half-dreaming state he'd fallen into after dropping off too late and then sleeping too deeply. He shot up in bed, heart pounding, grabbed the phone. Another text from her. He decided to ignore it and call.

"Hey," she said. "Are you at the office?"

"Just about to head over," he lied. "What's up?" It was nine thirty—he was already very late.

"I don't like to talk on the phone," she said.

"Is talking that much worse than texting?"

A pause. "As long as they can't overhear you."

"They can't, unless the apartment is bugged," he said.

"Okay," she said. "So. We know that Delaney knew her. And possibly romantically."

"Hold on. We don't know that they were together."

"They were together. I can feel it. No way this woman was everywhere he was and not with him."

"Wait a minute. 'Everywhere'? How do you know?"

"Because I ran a facial-recognition search last night. Found her in five photographs. Check it out."

His phone pinged multiple times. He put her on speakerphone as he examined the screen.

The first photo showed a young Frederic Delaney, wineglass in hand, partially turned away from the camera, looking over his shoulder. Several Black people stood in the shot. Three men were gesturing. One held a saxophone. Behind him, at a round table, with the remains of drinks still littering it, a woman looked out from the frame. The caption read: *F Delaney 1920, Alibi, with Eli Evans, Red Simmons, Joseph Reed?*

Eboni's search had picked up *Joseph Reed*, and she believed that this was actually a photograph of Josephine.

He tilted the phone to get a better glimpse. Shoulder-length hair framing a coffee complexion, high cheekbones, eyes enormous. She was looking off to the left of the photographer. Not arrestingly beautiful, but very pretty. Striking.

Eboni said, "You don't bring your cleaning lady to a club."

The other four photos weren't captioned. Eboni's facial-recognition software had picked them up. In each photo, at the back of a crowd or against a wall or half turned away, appeared a woman who looked very much like the woman in that first photo. In no photograph did Frederic Delaney acknowledge her or touch her, but Eboni was right. Would Delaney bring his cook to a jazz club or what looked like a private party?

"I want to come to the Foundation. Be sure that I'm searching their full archive. You want to send a car for me?"

"Get a cab," he said. "The Foundation can reimburse you."

By the time he showered and made it to the office, it was after ten a.m. He handed the security guard his phone. "'Bout time you showed," the man said. "Ms. Washington's been here for ten minutes waiting for you. I asked her to wait outside, but she said you wouldn't mind. She said it couldn't wait."

"I don't mind at all. Good looking out."

"No sweat," he said. "I got you, Doc."

Bern headed down the corridor, scanned himself into his office.

Eboni looked up from his computer. "Dang, it's about time you showed."

He closed the door. "How'd you get here so fast?"

"Superpowers," Eboni said. She passed him a sheet of paper that she must have brought with her. On it were the eighteen hits she'd found last night as well as info on the five photographs.

She pulled up a blank Word document on Bern's computer, made sure it wouldn't save to the server, typed: *All references from 1919 to 1920. Photos 1920 to 1923. Nothing after 1923.*

If the Foundation was listening in, they had to hear a conversation, Bern decided. So he asked, "Hey, what did Colleen think about the pizza?" and wrote: *So she couldn't have been his Dark Lady. He was in his prime till 1930+*

EBONI: Maybe by 1930 DF had learned to hide her. Early on he made mistakes. Got caught with his pants down. She got photographed. Boom.

"She was super jealous," Eboni said aloud. "And she said her boy-friend, Luis, had been there already. Typical." They kept a verbal discussion about pizza going as they wrote down their real conversation.

EBONI: What was the name of his first music publisher? Didn't
    FD work for someone till 1919? The Europe trip is 1920

BERN: Ditmars & Ross

Eboni searched, found a file in the Foundation archive for Dit-mars & Ross. After a moment of searching, she shook her head.

EBONI: Nothing about JoR. Would DF have copied ALL the
    D&R archive? Or just stuff about FD?

BERN: No idea

EBONI: What happened to D&R archive? There's not a lot in
    these files

BERN: Maybe the D&R papers are somewhere else? Maybe
    there's stuff on JoR there?

EBONI: If we can find them online, I can tap in

They spent the next hour trying to figure out what happened to the company, but it didn't seem that the Ditmars archive had been donated to any library or archival source. Ditmars & Ross had gone under during the Great Depression.

Eboni rechecked the first Ditmars documents in the Foundation archive. On an index scanned card at the end they found: *From the collection of Samantha Bell, 1977.*

"Okay," Eboni said, "Give me a second." In a few minutes the screen bloomed with names and images. Eboni typed: *Samantha Bell is granddaughter. No record of death. But here's address.* An address and phone number in Yonkers. *Go out and call her.*

Eboni and Bern trooped outside.

Bern dialed the number. In a moment a woman's thin voice answered.

"Hi, is this Ms. Bell?" Bern said. "My name is Dr. Bern Hendricks. I'm calling from the Delaney Foundation. I'm doing some research and I came across some papers that you donated to us several years ago. Is that correct?"

"Oh," she said. "Oh, goodness. Goodness me. How nice to hear from you, Dr. Hendricks. I donated my grandfather's papers a while ago. Back in the seventies or eighties, I think."

"Do you remember anything more about what you sent us?"

"Oh," she said slowly. "Not really. I'm sorry. Your people came asking for any documents about Mr. Delaney. Grandpa had a music publishing business for a while, quite successful, but he lost it all in the Depression."

"Are there other documents?" Bern asked. "Documents that you didn't give them?"

"Oh yes, there was quite a bit that they weren't interested in. Materials from before Mr. Delaney worked there. And after, of course. There's a lot about the bankruptcy."

"Where are the files? Do you still have them?"

"Yes, yes, I think so. Last time I checked, but it's been ages. There were several file boxes out in the garage. I always meant to donate them but I haven't gotten around to it."

"Are they still in your garage?" Bern asked. Eboni looked at him, grinned.

"They are," she said.

"And you're still in Yonkers?"

"I am," she said. "Would you like to see them for yourself?"

"I would," Bern said. "When would be convenient?"

"Oh, we could set something up for later this week, if you like?"

"Sure," he said. "Or any sooner? What are you doing this afternoon?"

"Goodness," she said, laughing. "I don't have any plans. Come for tea."

Rather than taking a Delaney town car that could be tracked, Bern and Eboni hailed a cab, which dropped them off in front of a modest detached home in Yonkers. The siding needed paint, but the lawn had been neatly trimmed and a gutter on the right side recently repaired. Bern knocked on the door. A few moments later a home nurse answered. Her name tag read DAHLIA. They introduced themselves, and she led them into the living room, where an elderly woman wearing an orange and gray housecoat was working through a crossword puzzle.

They traded pleasantries for a few moments. Bern explained that they were trying to track down additional information about Frederic Delaney during his early employment at Ditmars.

"Several people have been through the boxes over the years," Samantha Bell told them. Her thin, bluish hair barely covered her scalp, which was very pink. "I really should have donated the papers to a university."

"Would you be interested in donating them to the Delaney Foundation?" Eboni asked smoothly. "We have state-of-the-art archival space, all climate controlled. Your grandfather's papers would be beautifully preserved forever."

Samantha Bell looked at her, considering. She was still very sharp, no question.

"And obviously the Delaney Foundation would compensate you for them," Eboni went on. "We generally pay two thousand dollars per box, depending on the condition of the documents and amount of material in each box."

"There are five or six boxes," Samantha Bell said. She struggled up, grabbed her walker. "Do you want to see them?"

On the way to the garage Eboni hissed, "How much you got in your checking account?"

"I didn't bring my checkbook."

"We can get a cashier's check. How much you got?"

"Enough to buy these, if I need to."

"Good," Eboni said. "Go figure out where your bank is. Because we're gonna buy some files today."

Two hours later an SUV cab left Yonkers with the entire Ditmars archive—six Bankers Boxes—packed in the rear.

9

Pros & Cons

Bern

AN HOUR LATER they spread the contents of the Ditmars & Ross files across Eboni's bright white conference table. The six cardboard boxes had spent years on a back shelf of Samantha Bell's garage: mice had gnawed in and built nests in two of them; in another, a water leak had stained and cemented about half the files into a crumbling brown mass. Apart from dust and silverfish, the other three boxes seemed in good shape: faded cream-colored folders in no discernible order; pages of music; four oversize accounting ledgers; old electric bills; insurance forms; and dozens of other business records, mostly about the Ditmars bankruptcy.

They stacked up the folders around the room, quickly combed the files, looking for any mention of Josephine.

In the fifth box, they struck gold: EMPLOYEES MISC., which apparently held information for temporary or part-time employees. Among the sheets, they found that Josephine Reed worked for Ditmars & Ross from July 21, 1918, to May 19, 1919. Her employment records were scarce, but they learned that she was paid eight dollars per week to sweep floors and perform "other cleaning and tidying services."

She was born in Oxford, North Carolina. Her home address in New York was 143 West Seventy-Fourth Street, New York City.

"Search for 143 West Seventy-Fourth Street," Bern told Eboni.

"In the Delaney archive?"

He nodded. He wished he'd brought his laptop, still in the Delaney offices. Since she wasn't using the Delaney computers, it meant her tapping in on her own computer, which took about half an hour. It was easier, though, because she'd set up Bern's computer in the Foundation offices as a conduit into the system.

In the meantime, Bern kept looking through the files. He was paging through insurance forms from 1910 to 1929, hunting for any mention of her, when Eboni said, "Fuck me sideways." She leaned back in her chair, grinning at him.

"What? What is it?"

"That's Delaney's address. 143 West Seventy-Fourth Street, apartment 1G."

"What was her apartment number?"

"It doesn't have one listed," Eboni said.

"But she lived in his building," Bern said.

"She was his baby mama."

"He didn't have a baby."

"Not that you know of. But wanna make a bet about what happened to her? Why she disappeared? She got pregnant. I'll bet you."

They looked at each other without speaking.

"This changes everything we know about Delaney," Bern said. "Everything. No wonder he had such an affinity with the Black community. He had a secret Black mistress the whole time. No wonder he never got married. It was her, all along. Her."

"Bet she didn't tell him she was pregnant. She just up and left him. Or maybe he sent her away. A mulatto baby would have destroyed him. If people learned he was gettin' down with the Black chicks—"

Bern was spinning along on his own track, not even hearing Eboni. "And of course he couldn't sit in his box at the theater with her. Of course he couldn't take her to shows. So he snuck her in and out of the theater and drank champagne with her secretly. That's why there were always two glasses."

"Maybe she gave up the kid. I wonder if there are orphanage records. Mixed-race kids must have been put up for adoption all the time."

"There were two glasses at the Met on the night he died," Bern said. "He never sent her away, and she never left him. She was around his whole life. Maybe she's still alive?"

"How old would she be? There's no age listed on the form," Eboni said.

"Well, if she was a few years younger than Delaney, she'd still be well over a hundred."

"But she could have lived a long time," Eboni said. "There could be kids who remember her."

For another ten or fifteen minutes they threw out conjecture and ideas, one wilder than the last. By then it was after two in the morning, and it had been a very long day. Reluctantly Bern grabbed a cab and went back to his apartment, his thoughts churning.

Next morning, Eboni's text woke him up, summoning him to come back to her office. He emailed Mallory and told her that he'd be working off-site again today, then took the subway out to the Bronx.

Eboni was waiting for him in the glass-enclosed conference room, sitting at a table that, uncharacteristically for Eboni, looked like the Tasmanian devil had come through, leaving behind a whirlwind of legal pads, laptops, coffee mugs, and white deli bags. It was only nine o'clock; her three employees weren't even in yet.

"You sure took your sweet-ass time," she told him, looking refreshed and energized despite only a few hours of sleep.

"What's going on?"

"I googled Oxford, North Carolina, to track down any relatives who still live there."

"Wait. You dragged me all the way over here to tell me that? Girl, what's wrong with you?"

"Settle down, slick," she told him. She bit into a bagel that had been sitting on a deli napkin next to one of the laptops. "I called you all the way over here to tell you that Oxford, North Carolina, might not be New York City, but"—she glanced at her monitor—"the Granville County Library System is state-of-the-art. Most of the Granville County genealogical records are online."

"It's the South," Bern said. "Ancestry is a big deal. You find anything?" He leaned over her monitor to get a better look.

"I just got started. There are a bunch of Reeds in Oxford. Thought you could put that PhD to work to show me what a good reader you are." She nodded with her chin toward one of the other laptops. "I bought a couple more bagels. The everything with the scallion spread is good. You should try it."

Bern had to get working on *RED*, he told himself, not spend his time hunting down this elusive Josephine Reed.

Instead, he sat down across from Eboni, pulled the everything bagel from the bag, and opened the laptop.

Over the next three hours, they pieced together that several Reed families had owned property just south of Oxford, North Carolina. One family had six children—five girls and one boy, Howard—and the middle child was Josephine. Howard, who'd died in 1983, had two children: Earlene and Alice, both of whom had married. They'd been the last of the Reeds.

A few minutes later Eboni unearthed Howard Reed's last known address.

"You think his family is still there?" Bern asked.

"Not sure. It's now owned by a Charles Hill," she said. "I can't find a number for him."

They hunted for another thirty minutes, unearthing dozens of Hills, many of whom might be relatives of Charles. "You know what?" Eboni said, turning and staring wide-eyed at Bern.

"What?"

"The airport into Oxford is right outside town. Go get us a plane from your DF buddies."

"Are you joking? A plane?"

"Why not?" She grinned at him. "This is worth a field trip, don't you think? And it'd be a lot faster and easier if we were boots on the ground. Let's just do this."

He thought. "It's not far from Durham. I can say there's a specialist I want to consult."

"You do that. Go call up a plane, hotshot. We're going to North Carolina."

The next day, the Delaney Foundation plane touched down just out-side Oxford. Bern closed his personal laptop. It had all his original research about the Quintet on it but none of the new *RED*. Still, it was better than nothing, and he'd spent the trip hunting for references to Josephine Reed. What if Delaney wrote the Quintet for her? What if she was his inspiration? What if he wrote all his music for her? It could change everything that anyone had thought about him. After all, this woman had been around when Delaney was doing his early work, which many considered his best music.

They slid out of the tiny airport and called an Uber to take them into Oxford.

191 Regina Street was a run-down, gray clapboard house; a series of lean-to porches, set on cinder blocks, extended well into the back-yard. Several cars, the newest probably ten years old, slouched in the driveway. "Look," Eboni said. "Somebody's home."

"Let's hope it's Mr. Hill."

Bern's and Eboni's footsteps boomed on the front porch, rattling the handful of potted plants on the steps. Bern knocked. People were inside; he could see their shapes dimly through the sheer curtains. No one came to the door. Eboni rang the doorbell and knocked again.

Feet rustled inside, and whispers.

"Really?" Eboni said to Bern. "Do they think they're invisible?" And then, louder, "Hello? Is Mr. Charles Hill there?"

"Who is it?" a high-pitched voice, possibly a child's, called out.

"I'm Bern Hendricks. My friend and I are looking for Mr. Charles Hill. Is he home?"

"He ain't here. He's in the hospital."

"Oh." Bern looked at Eboni. "Is your mom home?"

"Mama!" Small feet clattered away into the house.

A few moments later, an attractive woman in her thirties opened the door. Three children peered out from behind her. "Can I help you?" she said.

Bern introduced himself and Eboni. "We know this is a little weird, but we're trying to track down the previous owner of this house. A man named Howard Reed. We know that Charles Hill bought it from him in the seventies."

She shook her head, shifting her weight as if ready to close the door in their faces. "I'm sorry. My father, Charles, is in a nursing home. He's been there for four years now. He has dementia and isn't up for any visitors."

"Oh, I'm so sorry to hear that," Eboni said.

Bern broke in, a little desperately, "We're actually trying to track down relatives of a woman named Josephine Reed." The woman stared back at them, apparently not recognizing the name. "We understand that she had a brother named Howard. Howard Reed."

"Howard had two kids, Alice and Earlene," Eboni said. "Do any of those names sound familiar?"

"Yeah," the woman said. "Howard Reed was my grandfather. Earlene is my mother."

Bern and Eboni shared a glance. Bern's heart was in his throat.

"Who is it?" came a voice from inside. "Does somebody need something?"

"It's fine, Mama," the woman called. "I'll just be a minute."

"Girl, who is it?" an elderly woman shuffled up, peering first at Bern and then at Eboni. She was wearing polyester pants, a loose white V-neck T-shirt, and fluffy brown slippers.

"Hello, ma'am," Bern said. "We're here looking for information about a relative of Howard Reed."

"Lord. You want to know about my daddy? I ain't heard that name in a hundred years. What's this for? Are y'all here for the clothes?"

"No ma'am," Eboni said, apparently calling on a faint Southern drawl that Bern noticed immediately. "We're here to find out about one of his family members. Anything you can tell us would be very helpful."

"Ain't nobody asked me about Daddy since I was—well, little girl, I don't even remember the last time anybody asked me. Come on in here, honey. Both of y'all."

The house was clean, with well-maintained furniture: a very nice gray sectional and matching armchair. Children's toys lay in front of the television, where they'd apparently been abandoned when Bern and Eboni had arrived. In one corner sat a box marked NOT FOR RESALE. The woman, who looked to be in her thirties, introduced herself as Geri and followed close behind them. She told the kids to go outside and play. Before they could complain, Geri shot them a look and said, "I won't repeat it." The kids ran out the back door.

"Now what do y'all want to know about Daddy?"

"Well, ma'am, my name is Bernard Hendricks. This is Eboni Washington. We're really looking for information on Howard's sister, Josephine Reed. We won't take much of your time Ms. . . . ?"

"Hill," the older lady said. "Earlene Hill."

"Hey, Ms. Earlene," Eboni said sweetly. "Did you know Josephine Reed? Who she was? Anything about her?"

The front door opened. "Hey, Mama. You got company?" A tall woman with an impeccable bob came in, and a moment later a full-figured woman followed her.

"Hey y'all," Earlene said. "Come on in here and sit down. This is Bernard and—I'm sorry, sugar, what's your name again?"

"It's Eboni, ma'am."

"Ain't that a pretty name. You are just a real pretty girl, ain't you?" Earlene smiled at Eboni.

The two women introduced themselves as Earlene's daughters, Myrtis and Sandra.

As the ladies stood chatting, Bern caught sight of an upright piano against the back wall, tall and magnificently polished. "Your piano is beautiful, Ms. Earlene," Bern said.

"That old thing. Ain't nobody played it since I was a little girl. You wanna buy it?"

Bern laughed and said, "No ma'am, but I am a musician. I play a little piano."

"Oh, that is so nice. You fancy, ain't you?" Earlene said, looking at Eboni. They both laughed. How had Eboni bonded so swiftly with the old woman?

Then Geri brought in several bottles of water on a tray, along with chips, salsa, and a jar of Old Bay Seasoning. Myrtis and Sandra followed her; and then two other younger women, who were introduced as Kay and Judy, and whose relationship to everyone else Bern gave up trying to figure out. The living room was suddenly very crowded.

Eboni seemed in her element. "Girl," she said to one of the women—Kay? Judy? Bern had lost track—"I know I just met y'all, but can you please tell me what kind of foundation you use? Your skin is gorgeous."

The woman Bern thought was Judy laughed a slow belly laugh. The other—Kay?—slid into one of the twin recliners flanking the coffee table.

"Thank you, honey," Judy said. "'Round here it's all Revlon."

"For real?" Eboni said.

"Mmm-hmm. We get samples every month. I got so much makeup, I can't even give it away," Kay said as she pointed at one of the boxes marked NOT FOR RESALE.

"I'll be happy to take some off your hands," Eboni said.

"Girl, your hair looks good. How long did it take?" Judy asked.

"Thank you. I had to sit for five hours for this. You like it?" Eboni rubbed her hair, cornrows swept neatly to one side.

"It's beautiful. And I know that's your real hair. You got some Indian in your family?" Kay asked, reaching for a bottle of water.

"Uh-uh. My grandma is Jamaican."

Bern figured they could probably go on forever about hair and makeup. Recipes would no doubt come next. And then baby pictures. "So as we were saying," he said, "we're here because we're trying to learn more about a relative of yours. A lady named Josephine Reed. Do any of you know anything about her?"

"Josephine?" Myrtis said. "Mama, ain't that one of your cousins? I think I remember you a long time ago talking about somebody named Jessie or Josie or something. Ain't that right?"

"I had a cousin named Jessie," Earlene said, thinking. "But I remember Daddy talking about one of his sisters. I think her name was Josephine. I don't rightly remember, though."

"The name Josephine sure sounds familiar," Judy said. "Josephine Reed. I swear I've seen it before."

"You sure you're not thinking of Claudette?" Kay said.

"You know what? I do remember," Earlene said, staring off into space. Myrtis opened a bottle of water for her as she spoke. "Daddy had six sisters. I only knew four of them. His sister Billie had passed away before I was born, and he said the one sister he had left went north. I think she was in New York or somewhere. Could be her name was Josephine."

Bern and Eboni exchanged glances.

"Do you know if the one that went north had any children?" Eboni asked.

"Child, I don't know," Earlene said.

"We wondered if it was possible that Josephine had a baby," Bern said.

Judy said, "I never heard nothing like that."

"Everybody always said all the crazy people are on Granddaddy's side of the family," Myrtis observed.

"Don't you talk like that," Judy said. "You can't call crazy people 'crazy.'"

"Well, not crazy," Myrtis said. "But you know that something wasn't right with some of them. Remember Cousin John-John? They had to put him away at that hospital outside Durham. Dorothea Dix. He was artistic."

"He wasn't *artistic*," Earlene said. "He was *autistic*. And he was a real nice boy. Very very nice."

"He rocked back and forth and couldn't even look at you," Myrtis said. "Just sat there rocking all day."

"And what about your cousin Blondelle, who used to call on birthdays?" Sandra said. "Remember she used to call on all our birthdays? 'Hi, Sandra, it's your cousin Blondelle. Today's your birthday. You're thirty-six today.' Like I needed her to tell me that."

"And John-John used to talk about—oh, you don't even want to know," Judy said.

"But none of them were Josephine?" Bern said. "Do any of you know what happened to Josephine? Is there any other relative we could ask who might remember?"

Earlene shook her head. "I'm the last one left."

"Do you remember anything else, Ms. Earlene?" Eboni asked.

"He always wanted me to be a teacher," Earlene said thoughtfully. "All his sisters were teachers, he told me. You know, back then things was different. Everybody went to the same school. Everybody was in everybody's business, too. Daddy said that he took piano lessons from his mama. She gave everybody piano lessons. He stopped playin', though. He said his sisters were real good. You know what, I think I got some of his old music from when he was a boy. San, run upstairs and look in them boxes in my closet."

"Mama, Karl put all that stuff in the sunroom, remember? Somebody was supposed to come and get it for Ms. McCoy's yard sale." Sandra sprinkled Old Bay on a tortilla chip, popped it in her mouth.

"Ain't nobody going to Geraldene's yard sale," Earlene said.

"Ms. Earlene," Eboni said slowly, but with a smile, "do you know if Howard's sister Josephine played piano, too?"

"Daddy said all his sisters played piano. They played in church every week. You know, back then the schoolkids learned piano, too. I think I remember him saying he never got to play a lot cause his sister was always at that piano. That's it right there, see."

Bern and Eboni both turned to the tall upright piano against the wall.

"Ain't nobody played it in years. I remember Daddy saying he had to go to New York one time for something. No, maybe it was that he went with his sister? Yeah. He went to New York with his sister."

"Was this the crazy sister? Didn't Granddaddy have a crazy sister?" Judy asked.

Earlene shook her head. "Child, I don't know."

"What exactly is this for?" Myrtis asked Bern.

Bern said, "Well, we think that a Josephine Reed may have worked with Frederic Delaney. We're trying to see if there's a connection."

"Delaney?" Sandra asked. "Who is he?"

"The music Delaney?" Geri said.

"You know that car commercial?" Eboni said. She hummed a few bars of Delaney's "Scarlet Buttercups," which he'd originally written for a musical review in 1927, and which had been adapted and re-adapted countless times, from Jay-Z to Judy Garland to Mariah Carey.

"Oh yeah," Myrtis said, "Delaney. Didn't he write that song?" She hummed another tune.

"Yeah, that's him," Bern said. "That's 'Daytime Gambit.'" But he wasn't sure they heard him since they were all humming the tune now. "Frederic Delaney is one of the most prolific composers America ever produced. You want to hear some of his music? Here's a recording of Ray McMillian playing his violin sonatas—"

"Oh, for real?" Myrtis interrupted, clearly not interested in listening to a sonata or two. "You're saying this Josephine knew this guy? The rich one?"

"It's possible," Eboni said, reaching into her purse. She pulled out the first photo that she'd found of the woman looking out at the camera. "We think this is a picture of her." Eboni handed it to Earlene.

"Child, I can't see nothin' without my glasses." Earlene passed the paper to Judy, who, in turn, passed it to Sandra.

"Yeah, she looks like our people, don't she?"

"Mmm-hmm. Yeah, she does. Look at them eyes."

"So, you think this could be Josephine?" Bern said.

"Well, she does resemble people in the family. It sounds about right," Kay said.

Judy said, "I remember now. What about that old trunk in the basement? Doesn't that say *Josephine* on it?"

"What old trunk?" Sandra asked, and then, "Oh yeah, the black one? The one that Karl was always going to do something with?"

"Didn't it have writing on it?" Judy said. "I swear it did. Remember we used to play down there when we was kids?"

"It was locked, though," Geri said.

"Maybe it was locked when you was little, but I'm pretty sure we broke it open when we was kids," Judy said. "It didn't have nothing in it, though. I don't think."

"So there's a trunk that has Josephine Reed's name on it in the basement?" Bern said. He could feel his pulse fluttering in his throat.

"Probably," Judy said. "Unless Karl got rid of it? Mama, didn't Karl get rid of it?"

"Didn't Karl throw that trunk out when we cleaned out the basement a couple years back?" Sandra said.

"I don't think so," Geri said. "Did he? I don't remember."

"Would it be too much trouble if we checked?" Bern asked.

"Judy, can you take Bernard down and see if the trunk is still there?" Earlene dipped a chip in the salsa.

Judy stood, saying, "It's this way. We don't go down there much. We've been bugging Mama to clean this place up, but she just won't get rid of anything. I think she's a hoarder." She opened a door next to the stairs.

"Girl," Eboni said, "my mama's the same way."

Bern knew that Eboni had been raised by her aunt and her mother was never in the picture.

In the meantime, the three of them—Judy, Bern, and Eboni—carefully felt their way down the narrow stairs, using the walls for balance. There was no railing. A cobweb brushed against Bern's cheek. He jumped back.

"I think Mama means it's under here," Judy said, gesturing. Below the stairs, in the stairwell, junk lay piled to the underside of the steps: paint cans, badminton nets, cardboard boxes rattling with Christmas ornaments.

Bern dove in, handed whatever box to Eboni, who gingerly placed it out of the way. Finally, deep in the back, at the farthest corner, they caught the gleam of an old steamer trunk. It had been there a long time; humidity had sealed it to the cement floor. Bern tugged repeatedly before it came loose with a sucking sound. He pulled it free, lifted it—it was fairly heavy—and placed it in an open space near the steps.

Beneath a thick layer of greasy dust, the trunk had once been painted black. Bern brushed at the top; it seemed the surface had white lettering, but he couldn't read it in the dim light.

He carried it up the stairs. "Yeah," Eboni said, following him. "Show off them guns. I know you're trying to impress everybody, but do you need some help?"

"A lot of help you'll be in those heels," he said, struggling.

Earlene appeared at the top of the stairs. "Where's Karl?" she said. "He can help you."

"He's still at work," Sandra said.

Bern put the trunk down in the middle of the living room floor. There in the light, the writing glowed faintly through the dirt:

TO: Miss Josephine Reed
   Regina Street
   Oxford NC

Without asking permission, Bern forced the lid. The musty smell of old paper wafted up. A mass of paper, yellowed and brittle, filled perhaps a third of the interior. Bern picked up the first page.

"What is it?" Miss Earlene peered down. "Oh. It ain't even in English."

A full page, front and back, of Delaney Doodles. Then another, then another.

"This trunk has been down there all this time and you never cleaned it out?" Geri said. "I could've used this trunk to store my makeup. Or the kids' toys."

Bern tried to stand, but his legs wouldn't work. He gripped the side of the trunk. Cleared his throat, staring at those pages, unable to look away.

"Are you all right, baby?" Miss Earlene asked him. "You need some water?"

He was trying to imagine what this was, what all these papers could mean, paper upon paper, all original, yellowed, scrawled with those

Doodles, and why they'd been packed into a trunk in North Carolina instead of displayed front and center at the Delaney Foundation.

"Yeah," he said, after a pause that might have gone on for years. He'd lost all track of time, and of himself. "Yeah, I'm okay. Can I get that glass of water?"

Next to him, Eboni said, her voice as quavering as he felt, "Miss Earlene, you got anything stronger?"

10

Newfound Sisters

Bern

DELANEY DOODLES: page after page of them. Some had *JoR* in one corner or another, but none had the winged symbols of the Doodle page in the archive. The symbols poured over scraps of paper, receipts, envelopes. Several danced along cocktail napkins with faded embossed names of clubs: The Black Cat. Hidey's. The Alibi. The trunk's contents were musty but perfectly readable.

Scarcely daring to breathe, they laid one sheet on top of another as Earlene and her family looked on.

"Why did she have his papers?" Bern said. "Why would she have his Doodles?"

"You think our girl had sticky fingers?"

He met Eboni's eyes. "What else could it be? Think about it. This is Josephine's trunk. Why would it be full of Delaney Doodles?"

"No idea." She reached in, pulled out a tiny faded notebook; the interior pages were covered with the symbols. "Maybe he gave it to her."

"He gave her a half-empty trunk of scribbles?" Bern said doubtfully.

"I thought you said these were annotations," Eboni said. "About how to play the music."

"I thought they were," Bern said, and then: "Ms. Earlene, I know this sounds kinda crazy, but can we give you a thousand dollars for this trunk?"

"Oh Lord. For that old thing?" Earlene popped another chip into her mouth.

From the trunk Bern pulled an envelope addressed to Josephine Reed, from Pennsylvania Station, New York City, New York. Inside was a typed form, the blank lines filled in with handwritten blue ink:

FEBRUARY 2, 1928
Josephine Reed
Regina Street
Oxford, NC

Dear _Josephine Reed_:

The Left-Luggage Office of the Pennsylvania Station has the following item which belongs to you:

   Steamer trunk

We have held this item since _May 12, 1924_. If you do not collect it by _February 28, 1928_ it shall be disposed of. Please bring a copy of your claim ticket and/or this letter to the above address by no later than the date listed above.

Sincerely,
Campbell Brown
Chief Porter
Pennsylvania Station

Bern and Eboni both read it, handed it up to Earlene and her family. "Well," Bern said, "this explains how you got it. She must have dropped it off in the left-luggage office and never claimed it. Your father must have gotten it down here."

"And saved the letter," Earlene said. "That's my daddy all over."

"Ms. Earlene," Bern said, "can we buy this trunk from you?"

"You know what, honey," Earlene said to both of them, "you can take that old thing. If you want to leave some money, I'm happy to take it. I like you. Both of you. Y'all look so cute together. I still don't know why y'all are so happy about that old trunk, but you take it."

Eboni hugged Earlene. Then she shook Earlene's hand and went around the room and tried to shake the hands of all the women. Each one opted to hug her instead.

"You know you're our other sister now, right?" Judy said as she wrapped her arms around Eboni.

"Girl, you may as well start callin' her Mama now!" Myrtis chuckled.

"Y'all are just so friendly. Makes me miss my family," Eboni said.

Bern tried to figure out if she was acting, but she sure looked utterly sincere. He wondered how much of the kick-ass ghetto attitude was an act.

"Honey, I know your mama is a good woman 'cause she sure did raise you right," Earlene said. "Where your people at?"

"New York, ma'am. The Bronx. Have you been to New York, Ms. Earlene?"

"Child, no. I ain't been past Raleigh. Kay, didn't you go to New York one time?"

"No, Mama, that was New Mexico for that convention," Kay said, and then to Eboni, "We had a Revlon convention a few years ago and my supervisor sent me. It was so nice."

"Well, all y'all got an open invitation to come to New York. I'll show you around. We gonna have us a good time."

Bern closed the trunk. The sound of the lid falling into place was louder than he expected. Eboni jumped back half a pace, shot him a side-eye.

Bern extended his hand to Earlene, and she—and her family—all hugged Bern instead. Bern wrote Earlene a check for $2,500.

It took another fifteen minutes of promises to stay in touch and planning a trip to New York before he managed to haul the greasy trunk outside, after the Uber had been sitting there for several minutes.

As soon as they were alone in the car Bern said, "Do you realize that we just made history? We're about to change everything that scholars thought they knew about Delaney. Everything."

"I'll give Oprah your number after she interviews me, but right now I'm wanting to figure out where the guy's baby mama has gone to. It's all just getting more confusing. Why would Josephine have a trunkful of his Doodles?"

"We'll figure that out," Bern said optimistically. "Look how far we've come already."

She shrugged. "Yeah, all the way to North Carolina, to get more questions."

"We really need to tell the Foundation."

"Don't start with that again. We ain't saying a word until we figure this out. I don't trust any of them."

During the whole flight back to New York, they looked at page after page of the Doodles: all inscrutable, all oddly beautiful.

How had a trunkful of Delaney's Doodles ended up in North Carolina?

Who was this Josephine Reed, and what had happened to her?

ACT 2

1918

11

Coming to NYC

Scherzo: Josephine Reed

THE ROARING MAW of the subway system belched Josephine Reed up onto a nondescript dusty street with white numbers *1*, *2*, and *5* hanging all in a row on a blue sign. The wind whistled in a wavering B-flat up to an F-sharp, around or perhaps through the enormous tan brick building quivering on her left; it seemed to sway slightly in the air currents. An automobile blared past her with a *chug-chug-chug* that she could feel in her jaw, and the slapping of shoes on cobblestones and brick tinted her vision aquamarine and made her elbow twitch. She mumbled under her breath, "Pink, blue, white."

Her destination's directions were written on a nice square piece of paper folded three times and tucked in her reticule, but for the moment her fingers in their stained white gloves could only clutch its handle, not even open the case. Her fingertips were slippery with sweat. She went to ask the elderly lady in the yellow tea dress if she knew where the—

—and then Josephine couldn't remember the name of the place she was looking for, and the yellow tea dress passed by with a rustle and a tap of a parasol (*Who still carries a parasol nowadays?*), and a mustachioed man in a bowler hat bore down on her so that she jumped back and stepped on the foot of a little girl holding an older woman's hand. The little girl's sudden scream made Josephine stiffen.

"Black and red," she whispered.

"Watch where you're going," the older woman said, clutching the child, and Josephine could hear their intakes of breath, felt their dislike of her like an orange moss upon her skin. She wondered if it would leave a scar. Out of reflex, she turned away from them and stumbled off the sidewalk and onto the street, her feet turning in her shoes and her heels hitting the pavement with taps that jarred her eardrums. "Blue," she said, identifying the squeaking wheel of the wheelbarrow that trundled past, a ropy tall man in a ragged shirt holding the handles. But blue wasn't right, was it? There was yellow shot through, and maybe a hint of brown. What color was that?

Back to the sidewalk she staggered, passing brooms that swept and a woman laughing too loud in the sunlight, a man hauling ice from his truck into a building. The *tink, tink* of the pincers rang out silver and cold as they grabbed the cubes—

—and then she turned another corner and from an open door, like mint in cool water or the smooth taste of fresh cream, the sound poured over her: a trombone, a clarinet, and then a trumpet lifting itself up like a benediction, blessing the air with a run of notes that Josephine breathed in like the smell of the earth after a spring rain.

And then, there it was: this was what she had come for, come all these miles and through all this terribleness—

—and as the trombone twined with the trumpet and the melody bathed her cheeks, everything—the sign, the parasol, the car, the wheelbarrow, the glittering subway tiles, and the roar that bubbled beneath all of Manhattan—everything, at last: at long last: all, finally, made sense.

12

Jamming with the Fellas

Freddy

FREDDY DELANEY would always remember the leaves in her hair the night that Josephine Reed changed his life.

Right then, Eli Evans, the upright bass player, was all up in Freddy's face, blocking out the lights, the club, and the handful of audience members swirling their glasses at the far end of the room. "Did you even look at the charts I made for you?" Eli said, his tiny mustache quivering with fury, nearly disappearing into his bottom lip. Freddy could smell the cigar that Eli had smoked several hours before. "I told you this would be a waste of time," Eli said to the group, and then to Freddy, "It's time for you to go, man. You did your best but you need to go."

Freddy couldn't believe he was hearing this. His bandmates—the band he had put together—were firing him? How was this even possible?

But Red Simmons was nodding, his head bobbing on the end of his neck like a baby bird's. Freddy thought that at least one of the jazz combo should stick up for him, but they stood there, eyes blinking back at him.

The lights in the Alibi Club beat down, seeming to underscore the pathos of a yet-again almost-empty house. Those lights were the reason that nobody had come, Freddy was sure of it: How could musicians try creating an atmosphere of mystique in this shabby, too-bright dump? This flophouse shouldn't be lit up like it was Saturday afternoon: it should be dark magic and serenading moonlight. Whiskey fresh out of straw-packed crates, not watered-down hooch.

"C'mon," Freddy said to Eli, "it was better than rehearsal." The cold tendrils of failure were sliding like sweat down his back.

"It's time for you to go, man," Eli repeated, louder this time, to the room at large. Eli was barely tall enough to play his bass without a stool, but now his baritone voice curled into the back corners of the club. Eli arranged the sets, called the rehearsals, and corrected Freddy—only Freddy—regularly. Freddy wanted to believe that he wasn't a failure, he was just unlucky to possess the wrong skin color. He needed them to understand that at least his musicality was true.

He wanted—all he'd ever wanted—was to play music. Jazz, classical, blues, whatever, it barely mattered. What mattered was the feeling he got when he was playing: that he was at once everywhere and nowhere. That his music was reaching down into the hearts and souls of the people who were listening, somehow changing them for the better.

"It was better than rehearsal," Bobby Roosevelt put in. The drum player, heavyset in a threadbare suit coat, had dark pockmarks on his cheeks and a soft spot for Fred. "This time he managed to get through the third change with only six mistakes. He's getting better."

"Nine," Eli said.

"Eleven," Freddy thought he heard. But who had spoken? An impenetrable ring of empty tabletops lay between the audience and the band members onstage. Only one person was close enough to have overheard, and she wasn't paying them any attention: head down, hands folded in her lap. Freddy thought maybe their music had put her to sleep.

"Fellas, take it easy," Freddy said. "I just haven't found the groove yet. It's not all that easy to do when Red decides in the middle of 'Blue Ribbon' to take it back to the edge."

Red Simmons, the tenor sax, said, "It's called timing, Freddy." He leaned in close. Two of Red's lower incisors had been capped with silver. "You just get into the groove too late."

Bobby laid his drumsticks carefully on the beat-up snare. The nickel rim glittered in the stage lights. Freddy waited for Bobby to back him up, defend him again, but he was sliding the sticks onto the edge of the drum as if he were barely listening.

"The point is," Eli went on, "this isn't working. I don't know if you just don't get it or if you just don't care."

"Of course I care." Freddy's suspenders felt way too tight. His shirt constricted his chest. He so desperately wanted respect from these three talented men. He was afraid they'd see that he cared too much. "Fellas, look, I know I made a few mistakes, but you have to admit, we're really getting better. I thought 'Burndown' went as well as we've ever rehearsed it. Think about it," Freddy went on. "The crowd was bigger this week than the past two weeks combined. We must be doing something right. Maybe they'll move us to Friday or Saturday night."

His words sparkled like motes in the club's glow. Eli's mouth had dropped open slightly. Then he burst into laughter, and Red and Bobby joined in.

Freddy kept his smile tight against his lips. Why were these lights so bright? The heat was in his hair, in his temples. Sweat slithered down his cheeks. How could he make his bandmates like him, make them understand how important this was to him?

"See, when you say stuff like that, it's hard to take you seriously,"

Eli said, shaking his head and wiping his eyes. "The only reason the crowd looks bigger is because they took out all the tables in the back. Don't you see that?"

"Fellas," Freddy said again—somehow calling them "fellas" made him feel like he belonged—"I really think we can do it." He knew he wasn't a bad musician. Compared to some, he was downright good. He played the clarinet and the piano, even mucked about making up his own jingles. He'd taken lessons for years back in Indiana. How was it that these three Black musicians with no formal training could be this good? Did they just work hard? Was their talent God-given? As soon as he'd heard each of them, he'd known they'd be incredible as a group, and he was right. They were all on the verge of discovery. "Okay, look, I know it's not been great, but I'll fix it. I could've sworn I was playing it right."

Had they been positioned onstage slightly differently—with Red on the other side, perhaps—no one would have noticed. But as it was, Eli, Bobby, and Freddy all saw the woman suddenly shake her head as if to say, *No, you didn't play it correctly.*

Eli laughed again. "See! Lookee there. Even Crazy Jo knows you missed the change."

Her face tilted up toward them. "Late," she said, very clearly this time, the word crisp and round in her mouth. "It was too late." She was surprisingly beautiful, with a medium-brown complexion and full lips. Thick lashes framed wide-set eyes; her eyebrows arched up perfectly. But something seemed off—something about the way she looked at them, as if seeing through them or beyond them, not quite connecting.

"What are you talking about?" Freddy said.

"You were late," she said, voice low and even, utterly confident. "Two bars late. The green with the star came in two beats after it should have."

The green with the star?

"See?" Bobby said. "She said it, man. The green star. Come here, Jo."

"What—" Freddy started, but Eli chimed in.

"Yeah, Jo. Come up here and show him how it's done." And then to Freddy: "Even Crazy Jo can play better than you."

She had jumped up, desperate to get onstage, hauling with her a thick leather handbag.

"Whoa, fellas, come on," Freddy said. "You aren't trying to prove a point by letting this—um—this vagrant play my piano, are you?" Freddy kept the smile fixed on his lips.

Her ankle-length dress had once been light green, but now its hem was dark with grime, the neckline and arms dark with perspiration stains. The heel of one shoe had come off, so she limped as she made her way up to the stage, set down her handbag next to the piano bench. She was small, maybe a shade over five feet tall; her feet barely reached the piano's pedals. From up close, Freddy could see leaves, a few still green, in her shoulder-length hair.

No music in front of her, eyes fixed on the keys: and then she started to play. Easily, ridiculously, Freddy's musical chart poured from her fingers and, in a moment, the combo, as if powerless against her, joined in as her right hand echoed the melody that Red lifted into and her left complemented Eli's rhythm.

"Yeah! That's it, that's how you do it," Red said, silver teeth flashing.

"That *is* what I did," Freddy said.

The woman, still staring at her hands, which magically continued to skip across the keys, said, "You were late. Two bars behind."

"Did you memorize this?" Freddy said, inching closer to see if there was somehow music written on the piano itself.

The woman turned her head slightly. Freddy caught a glimpse of her high cheekbone. "You did this," she said to him, and began to play the changes differently, perhaps as Freddy had, complete with mistakes. "You were late," she said. "See? The green with the star is supposed to come in here. Not here."

To his shame and consternation, he heard what she meant. Not the green star bit, but he heard the difference. Thank goodness she wasn't a man, or he knew they would have replaced him on the spot. "Okay, fellas, you made your point," he said, talking over the music. "The bottom line is, we need more work—okay, okay, *I* need more work. Give me a couple weeks. There'll be a whole cheering section just for me."

Did they believe him?

The song ended. Her fingers were still raised lightly on the keys, as if she were waiting for a cue to begin again.

Eli said, "Look, this is serious. You've got to make time to practice or make a wish or make a deal with the devil. No more chances. Our next gig's in—when? Two weeks? That's all the time you've got."

Freddy's smile never wavered. "It's gonna be great. You'll see. You guys want to get a drink? My treat."

Eli looked over at the other two, but not at Freddy. "Naw. We got us some other business to attend to. We'll catch you later. In the meantime, why don't you see if you can take a few lessons from Crazy Jo here?"

The three combo members let out a collective laugh, but Freddy didn't.

After they'd packed up and left—what kind of "other business" were the three of them doing at this hour?—Freddy made his way to the back of the club, where a makeshift bar served a couple of varieties of giggle water. Rotgut, mostly; bitter and oily. Freddy ordered a double.

After a big gulp of the foul stuff—his eyes watered and he couldn't stop coughing—he'd all but convinced himself that his position in the combo was iron-clad. No way those guys would dare try to replace him. After all, Freddy was the reason they were all together in the first place.

The woman—Crazy Jo—had returned to her seat, back against the wall, head down. No way in hell would they even—

Tom Magnus, the Alibi Club manager, was giving Freddy the evil eye. Time to go. All the patrons had left, except the crazy lady. She either didn't notice or didn't care as he sauntered over.

He stood well back from her. "Hey, um, I'm Freddy. Uh, Freddy Delaney."

Head still bent, staring down at her curled hands, the woman said, "Hello, Freddy Delaney."

"Um, can I sit down?" he said, and when she didn't reply either way he pulled out the chair across from her, sat. "Do you know those guys? Eli, Bobby? Red? Are they friends of yours? Relatives?"

"No," she said, eyes on her hands. It was disconcerting not to have her make eye contact. She said, "The teal is always vibrant. When you come around the beige takes over."

"Yeah," Freddy said. "That beige. Hate how it does that."

She didn't reply.

"So, where did you learn to play changes like that? I thought maybe one of the guys knew you from—"

"It was easy. Orange and teal go together."

He had absolutely no idea how to respond to this. "Orange and teal, huh?"

"Sometimes there's yellow, too. More of an ochre."

"An ochre," he said. "Of course." A pause. He wasn't even sure what color ochre was. "So, look, would you be willing to show me? How to do the changes like that, I mean."

Her head came up, and she peered at him as if through a fog: those huge dark eyes, really looking at him this time, burrowing into his skull. He wanted to look away but didn't. She was very pretty, but he could tell that there was something—well—*off*, somehow. She didn't regularly look him in the eyes, for one thing: she stared at his chin or at his shoulder. He checked to make sure he didn't have a spot on it (he didn't). Plus the weird stuff she said so confidently, as if Freddy would understand and be able to respond in kind. Crazy Jo indeed.

"I'm guessing that's a yes?"

"No," she said flatly. "I don't have a piano."

Freddy smiled. "I have a piano. It's no Steinway, but it works." He'd bought it on time, but she didn't have to know that.

From the back, Tom Magnus called out, "Hey, Freddy, I'm closing up here. You hear that, Jo? That means you, too."

"Okay," Freddy said to him, and then to Jo, "You obviously have talent. I haven't taken lessons in a long time and I could use a refresher. I'd pay you, of course."

A beat. Now her eyes never left his face. "You would?"

"Of course I would. What kind of gentleman would I be to take advantage of a talented young woman?"

She smiled for the first time, and it was as if some powerful light switched on. She really was very pretty.

The lights flashed. "I'm locking up now," Tom warned.

"I'd love to start tomorrow, if you have time," Freddy said, standing. "It's Jo, right? I'm down on Seventy-Fourth. Between Amsterdam and Columbus. Here. I'll write down my address for you." He groped in his pockets for a pencil and paper, wrote down his name and address.

The lights went out, and a light by the back door turned on. "Coming, you two?" Tom said. "I ain't waiting around."

Freddy and Jo threaded their way between the tables to the door. "So I'll see you tomorrow," Freddy said outside. "I get off work at five. Come anytime after six." He would have shaken her hand, but she had already slipped into the darkness. "Goodbye," he called after her. He didn't expect a reply, and didn't get one.

13

White Torrent

Freddy

THE NEXT EVENING, at six p.m. precisely, Freddy's buzzer rang and he ran across the hall—he had a ground-level apartment because of the piano—to let Jo in. She was wearing the same stained light green dress as yesterday, but he didn't see leaves in her hair. She had a small leather handbag tucked under her arm, and in both hands she held a large maroon carpetbag, bulging and unwieldy.

"Jo, so glad you could come," he said, and meant it—even if the carpetbag took him aback. All day long he'd been wondering if she would actually show up. "I don't even know your last name. Is Jo short for anything?"

"Josephine," she said, looking past him, and then down at her shoes. "I go by Josephine, not Jo. Josephine Reed." With stained white gloves she clutched her leather handbag. She hadn't worn gloves the night before.

"Great to meet you," he said, and meant it. "This way."

A quick check up the hall: no neighbors. Good. He didn't need them to see him ushering a colored woman into his room.

He led her up the three entrance steps, across the landing, and into the tiny studio apartment furnished with a narrow bed on one wall, an upright piano on another, and a tiny kitchenette—a hot plate, a sink, and a few shelves—on a third. A yellow-and-blue threadbare rug he'd found at a secondhand store covered the cheap wooden floor.

"Here it is," he said unnecessarily, gesturing to the thirdhand piano that he'd gotten from a failed music plugger who was leaving the city. Somehow he wanted her to applaud or to acknowledge his luck. Not a lot of young men had their own studio apartments and their own pianos—most times the fellows were crammed three or four to a room, all fighting for time with a borrowed piano.

Josephine Reed didn't applaud. Instead she sat down on the bench, leather handbag tucked neatly at her feet, and immediately kicked off "Burndown," a jazzy in-your-face tune with a lot of syncopations and block chords. Freddy had always thought of the song as a bit lame and repetitive, but this time it sounded fun. Her changes flowed effortlessly.

"How did you—" Freddy started, but Josephine shushed him, saying, "Listen very carefully here. This sapphire chord is the one you're always late on. Always two bars late. You can't be late. The change happens here, not here."

She moved over on the bench, gestured for him to sit next to her. He'd barely touched the keyboard and tapped out the first measure when she stopped him. "No. If you blur the white you'll be late. Your position is faded. Try it again. Don't fight the falling knobs."

He had no idea what "blur the white" or "falling knobs" meant, but he tried to play each note clearer, more individually. She stopped him again. He tried again.

This went on for a good twenty minutes before Jo must have decided that Freddy wasn't going to make the changes on time and tried a different approach.

"Stand up," she told him.

Freddy stood.

"Now, sit like a white torrent."

Freddy shook his head. "'Torrent'? 'White torrent'? I don't—"

"You sit like a trickle. To play this correctly, you need to sit like a torrent. Right where it boils up."

No wonder she was called Crazy Jo. What had Freddy gotten himself into? He looked around as if hoping someone would leap out and explain.

She was staring impatiently up at him. He sat down, back straight, and started again on the first six measures. He was three bars in before she laid one hand on his, stopping him. "This is a bit better but you're still coming late. And your torrent's fading." She brushed his hands off the keyboard, again playing the first six bars of "Burndown." "White torrent," she told him, leaning into the piano as if overexaggerating. "The falling knob went with me."

Josephine's wrists were very high. He remembered fourth grade, sitting in his piano teacher's parlor, his knuckles bright red as Mrs. Maloney smacked them with a ruler whenever he bent his wrists. "No broken wrists!" she'd shout at him. "Curve them! Now!" *Smack.*

He curved his wrists, started in with the opening bars of "Burndown."

"Sit like a white torrent and don't fight the knobs."

He raised his wrists, dropped his shoulders, started again. It sounded more robust.

"Good. The sapphire was almost there. Again."

Freddy went through the motion of standing, sitting, leaning over the keys, raising his wrists. This time he meant it, snapping down his fingers and focusing on each note.

"Good. Now the sapphire is singing. Again."

He tightened his shoulder blades even further, started from the top.

"There," she said. "Now the white torrent is flowing. You stopped fighting. The knobs are all in place. Very good. Now you must flow evenly."

"I won't even ask," he said. "Just show me."

She attacked the keyboard with ferocity and an incredible accuracy that could have rivaled Willie "The Lion" Smith. Then she made the chord changes—deftly, cleanly, instantly, so smoothly that he almost missed them.

"Easy flowing blue," he said. "I think I get it. You see, I was thinking that the A-flat chord came right before the recap so I—"

"No, no, no. The magenta comes earlier. Watch." Josephine played the changes again. "See? Magenta, then blue. Try it."

Twenty minutes later, the groove of "Burndown" was unspooling around him, each change elegant and precise. Josephine drilled him again and again. After more than a dozen times, he felt confident enough to embellish and add a ninth, dominant and augmented chord right before each change. He could feel Josephine nodding.

After almost two hours, Freddy leaned back, flexed his fingers, rolled his neck to alleviate the stiffness. He glanced at the alarm clock next to his bed. "Goodness, I can't keep taking advantage of your kindness. I was thinking only an hour-long lesson—you've already gone beyond that."

"That's fine," she said. "You still have to get the turnaround."

"Are you hungry? I haven't had dinner yet."

Her eyes flickered to his face.

"You haven't either," he guessed.

"No."

"Well, it's my treat, then," he said. "I don't have much but I make good flapjacks. They're good any time of day, I always say. I'd be happy to make you some." They were filling, the ingredients cost pennies, and could be cooked in a saucepan on his heating plate. Freddy ate them almost daily, either with jam or plain.

As soon as he stood from the piano she took over the keyboard, her fingers sweeping majestically into "Burndown," but now he was aware of how the richness of her tone reverberated: how she pulled such extraordinary depth and resonance out of only eighty-eight keys.

Could she teach him to do that? He'd rule the world if she could.

He bustled around the kitchenette, adding flour, baking powder, and the little milk he'd saved from breakfast, pouring in some water to make it go further. "So where do you live?" he asked her, more by way of conversation. "I hope it wasn't too inconvenient to come up here."

She played on, modifying the melody with a major third on top, then abandoning "Burndown" altogether, modulating until the tune became recognizable as "I'm Always Chasing Rainbows," the old Harry Carroll song.

"I asked where you live," Freddy repeated, wondering if she hadn't heard over the piano. "Am I being too forward? I'm just worried about inconveniencing you."

She shrugged. "Here and there. It's fine to be here. I'm going up to the Showstopper tonight but not for a few more hours." Freddy had been only once to the jazz club tucked into the basement of a Harlem brownstone. Its tiny stage was not much bigger than the handful of tables that surrounded it.

"Who's playing?" he asked.

"Barry's Black Cats." Her hands hurled into a snappy piano rhythm with boogie-woogie bass lines and machine-gun right-hand melodies.

"Yes, well," he said. She kept playing as he worked on the flapjacks, stacking two plates. "You ready to eat?" he said.

"Oh yes," she said. By now she was deep into Chopin's Piano Sonata no. 2.

"I hate to do this, but I need you to stop playing," he said. "I use the piano as a table. Just be careful not to spill on it. I always put glasses on the floor."

She eyed the full plate. He could almost feel her fingers resist parting from the keyboard, but hunger won out. He closed the keyboard cover and set a plate in front of her, along with a knife, fork, and jam.

She ate quickly, economically, smearing the jam over each flapjack before folding and tucking it into her mouth. He was only halfway finished by the time she was done and had rinsed her plate in the tiny sink in the corner.

"Thank you for dinner," she said, standing, putting on her coat. "It was nice."

"Wait, where are you going?" he asked. "I thought you said you were just going up to the Showstopper."

"It opens at nine. I like to be there early." She pulled on her gloves and turned the doorknob, which didn't open; he'd thrown the dead bolt. She fumbled, trying to figure out how to get out.

"But I haven't paid you," he said. "I owe you."

"Owe me for what?" She looked at him, clearly mystified. "I played your piano."

"Of course you did." He grinned at her. "And you were great. But I can't have you spend all this time and do all this and not pay you for the lessons. Remember I promised to pay you?"

"Oh," she said, thinking. "Okay."

"How much do you charge?"

She looked panicked now, staring at the floor and at the piano as if expecting them to chime in with a price. White people would have charged fifty cents for a lesson, Freddy knew. Negroes, despite often being thought of as more talented teachers, would charge twenty-five cents.

"Here," he said, coming over and putting two quarters in her hand. "This is fifty cents. That's the going rate. Will that work? I don't want you to feel like I'm taking advantage of you."

She shook her head, confused. "But I played the piano," she repeated, as if she'd expected that *he'd* charge *her* for it, that she was the one who'd been rewarded, not him.

He reached past her and unlocked the dead bolt. In a moment, without a goodbye, she'd slipped out, shutting the apartment door before he had a chance to speak.

"Wait," he said, opening the door again and leaning in the doorway. She was on the landing, almost to the front entrance.

He looked up the hallway. No one there. "Can we set up another lesson? How can I find you?"

"When?" she asked.

"When are you free?"

"Tomorrow," she said.

"Okay. Same time? And I'll pay you fifty cents again. Promise."

"Yes," she said, struggling slightly to open the exterior front door—its hinges were bent, and it often stuck—

And she was gone.

14

Azure & Birch

Freddy

THE NEXT MORNING, Freddy couldn't wait to play the piano. He picked up his day's assignment from the Ditmars & Ross offices on Twenty-Eighth Street. The moment he said hello to Eunice, the perky redheaded receptionist who'd started a few weeks back, his boss, John Ditmars, yelled from upstairs, "Freddy! Get in here."

How Ditmars could know Freddy was there was always a mystery. Somehow he could sense his voice, Freddy guessed, despite the racket: piano playing rang out from several closed doors. His coworkers were always cranking out new songs to meet Ditmars's approval, and to hopefully be a hit the next season.

Now he poked his head into Ditmars's office. Although it was barely nine o'clock, John Ditmars was already at his desk, already gnawing his way through the first of many cigars, already wreathed in a thick plume of cigar smoke. "Shoe sale today at Altman's," Ditmars told him. "Here's the lineup. We're changing things up today. I want you to really push 'When You're Married' and 'You're My Baby,' you hear me?"

Right by the Empire State Building, B. Altman & Company department store always had the best chicken à la king. Maybe he could score a free lunch off that curly-haired waitress. He'd flirt with the cute salesgirl in cosmetics, too, right near where the piano was stationed. "Sounds good," he said.

"You're pushing the ballads, you hear me?" Ditmars said. "This house is known for its ballads. Not that comic claptrap."

"Yes, sir," Freddy said. For the past couple of weeks he'd been plugging half a dozen songs: "When You're Married," a comedy song; "You're My Baby," a rag; "I Want a Little Lovin', Sometimes," a coon song; the ballads that Ditmars was wanting; and several others: "Moonlight Bay," "Waltz Me Around the Old Ballroom," and "Fairy Moon."

His job was to sit in the mezzanine of department stores and play whichever song the customers wanted to hear—and if the customers had no requests, then Freddy would play from the lineup. The important thing was to play the music *as it's written*, Ditmars always told him. He wasn't supposed to embellish it "the way the coons do up in Harlem, you hear me?"

Well, Freddy would play the music *as it's written*, since the customer needed to hear what she was buying. No worries on that score. But he'd put his heart and soul into it. He'd play with a white torrent. His knobs would fall everywhere. He couldn't wait to impress all the shoe shoppers.

He couldn't wait to play. He lived for music—plugging songs by day, scrounging up a jazz band at night. Now he felt that, after just one lesson, Josephine Reed had already made him a better player. He couldn't wait to play for her again.

Luckily Altman's was about a fifteen-minute walk—no bus fare (Ditmars didn't reimburse him for travel costs). Signs with SHOES!

SALE! fluttered on the limestone facade. The little salesgirl wasn't in sight as he took his place at the piano on the mezzanine.

He started with "Waltz Me Around the Old Ballroom," a lush piece appropriate for the matrons in their longer gowns. He played it through twice and then moved into the other ballads until a scrawny-faced elderly woman with bushy eyebrows and enormous wrinkled earlobes asked him to play "You're My Baby."

After an hour, it was hard to remember stuff about white torrents—let alone falling knobs. Such slow, safe ballads didn't require too much practice for the music to be recognizable. He kept trying to imagine Josephine playing these thin, average tunes—and failed.

After a fifteen-minute break—he hunted for the salesgirl, but she was nowhere to be found—he was back at it. He did the rag and the comedy song, "When You're Married." He didn't like playing the coon song, so skipped it.

Then he had a thought. What if, rather than play a coon song appropriate for a minstrel show, Freddy played a real song that real colored people listened to?

He played "Burndown." Played it the right way, the way Josephine had taught him. Several of the younger ladies were tapping their feet. People actually stopped shopping. They were actually listening to him. He was having a blast.

At the end of the song, a round-bellied older man approached him. "That's a swell tune, young man. Which is it?"

Freddy was supposed to hand him the sheet music so he could pay for it downstairs. Instead, Freddy said, "It's called 'Burndown.' It isn't for sale here, but you can come to the Alibi Club and hear my jazz combo perform it."

"It's not for sale?" The man looked mystified. "Alibi Club?"

Freddy would lose his job if this got back to Ditmars. "We're there every Tuesday," he said, and started in again on "Waltz Me Around the Old Ballroom." As he played, a frazzled-looking woman towing two children came up. "What was that song you were just playing?" she asked. "Can I buy it?"

"It's called 'Burndown,'" he said. "It's new. No sheet music yet."

He couldn't stop grinning. He felt really good. Fifty cents was too cheap for Josephine! He'd pay her a dollar if he could feel this way every day! The entire day at Altman's went on like this. He didn't bother to keep track of his sales. For some reason it didn't matter. He even paid the curly-haired waitress for the chicken à la king instead of trying to charm a free lunch out of her.

As he finally left the building at just after four, he couldn't stop thinking about Josephine. She had done this for him. Made this possible. And she'd be at his place at six. Just a couple of hours away.

That evening she arrived right on time and drilled him mercilessly. She returned the next night, too.

Each time, Freddy met her at the door to head off any neighbors. The second night, his landlady, Mrs. Overberg, was out in the hall, so Freddy met Josephine on the street and lingered with her on the stoop until Mrs. Overberg had headed back inside.

On both nights Josephine Reed worked with him for exactly an hour and a half, and in exchange he paid her fifty cents and fed her dinner: boiled potatoes and peas one night, macaroni and hot dogs the next. (He'd gone shopping beforehand for the hot dogs.) She wore the same green dress and carried the same leather handbag, and rarely spoke except to instruct him.

By the end of the second lesson, as he handed over the two quarters, he was feeling guilty that he couldn't pay her more. Sure, that was the going rate; but she'd improved his playing astronomically! He couldn't even begin to thank her for what she was doing for him. He hoped that by feeding her dinner he was showing his gratitude.

She stuck the quarters in her purse without even looking at them. He could have put in two nickels and she wouldn't have noticed. His heart opened to this fragile, odd being. How was she able to survive in the rough-and-tumble chaos of New York City?

That third night, as they finished the lesson and Freddy started preparing dinner, they tried to set up his next lesson: it was a Friday, and he had plans after work. He wasn't sure about Saturday, either, but thought that perhaps Sunday might work if she was free earlier. But how could he reach her?

"You still haven't given me your address," he said, although he suspected he knew the answer. "I'll write a note and drop it off on Sunday morning for when I'll be free."

"Just tell me a time," she repeated. "I'll be there. If it doesn't work for you, I'll go away."

"That's not fair to you," he said, and then, so gently that he could barely form the words, "Where do you stay?"

"Here and there," she said.

"You don't have a room at a boardinghouse or an apartment, do you? Do you sleep on the street?"

"No," she said, "sometimes on the grass."

"We can't have you sleeping outdoors," he said. And then voiced the offer he'd been mulling over all week. "You're more than welcome to stay with me for a while, in exchange for lessons. I know it sounds a bit forward, but I'm asking for very selfish reasons. My music really benefits from your teaching."

She was on the piano bench and he was in the corner of the kitchenette. "We could fix up a bed for you over here," he said, trying to convince her. He gestured to where the armoire held his clothes. "It wouldn't be the most comfortable, but it might be better than where you're sleeping now."

She looked at him for a long moment and then nodded. "Yes. Thank you, that would be fine."

"I have plenty of quilts, so it will be padded," he said, chest expanding with her gratitude. "That should make it a bit more comfortable."

"That's okay."

A pause. "Fantastic, then. Let me reassure you that I'll be a perfect gentleman. I'd never try to take advantage of you. This is strictly a business arrangement."

She nodded, looking down.

"My landlady, Mrs. Overberg, is a doll. It's a pretty quiet building, but she probably wouldn't be keen on your kind of people living here, so you're going to have to be discreet."

"Discreet?"

"Make sure nobody's in the hallway. Nobody sees you coming and going. If they do, you're my cleaning lady, okay?"

She said nothing, staring down now at her feet.

"It's just for a little while," Freddy said. "Just till you save up some money for your own place. And it's really a pretty small deception, isn't it?"

She still said nothing, so after a pause he said, gingerly, his tongue light on his teeth, "Would you like to clean up a bit now? Do you have any other clothes?"

She leaned over, finding the leather handbag at her feet. "Yes, I do."

"Splendid," he said. "Why don't you lay out what you want to wear and in the meantime I'll run you a bath? The tub's just down the hall. Let me see if it's free." He knew it would be, but out of delicacy, and to make sure nobody was nearby, he left her hunting in her handbag. He was sure that all the clothes within it were just as soiled as the green dress she wore.

He returned to his room. "Your bathwater is running. Here's a towel. You go wash up. It's macaroni and hot dogs tonight."

Josephine said, "You are very kind."

"Oh, don't feel too special. I'm this nice to everyone," he said modestly, looking around the room as if expecting other homeless musicians to pop out of the plaster.

Josephine took her handbag and her carpetbag with her, as if afraid Freddy would root around inside them. Almost an hour later, when she returned, hair damp and skin shining, the meal was ready. Freddy slipped down the hall to check the bathroom; it, too, was clean and shining. She'd somehow scrubbed it.

"What are your plans for the night?" he asked as they ate. Every night—and, for all he knew, most of the day—she would be at some musical venue: an open-air band, a vaudeville show, a dance hall, or anywhere else she could talk, or sneak, her way inside. He thought he had it bad, but he'd never seen anyone so invested, so desperate for music; it was as if she couldn't breathe without it, as if she were a fish swimming in melodies—and the melody itself didn't matter, only that it surrounded her.

"There's a new act in Hattie's Dance Hall uptown," she said. "A tenor I'd like to hear." Hattie's Dance Hall, despite its regular name, was known to be a burlesque theater, featuring sexually suggestive acts interspersed with comedians and bands strumming sentimental ballads. Some burlesque theaters even had striptease dancers.

"Really? Are those your bags?" he said. "I wouldn't have thought so." He thought a moment. "So I don't have plans tonight. Could I come with you?"

"To Hattie's?"

"Yes. Can I come?"

She ducked her head in a way he'd come to learn meant *yes*.

That night they rode the A train up to Harlem, to a shabby burlesque theater with the word HATTIE outlined in electric light bulbs. A few colored patrons stood smoking on the sidewalk. Freddy had never been to the place; his tastes ran more toward jazz and some of the new music that colored people were bringing up from the South. Besides, white people didn't usually come here.

Still, he was curious to see the striptease and the nudity, and also to watch Josephine. He could feel her—actually feel her—vibrating next to him as they waited their turn to go in.

They made their way inside, and the theater was just as shabby as the Alibi, although slightly larger. The walls held framed photographs, which lent the space a somehow more respectable air, but it was too dark for him to recognize any of the snapshots. They found seats at a small table far to one side. Josephine clearly liked to have her back against the wall. Freddy was the only white person in the room.

Although he played gigs with colored people, it was very different now to be sitting in the audience—especially with a colored woman. He felt at first like everyone was looking at him, but within ten minutes he realized that nobody was paying him any attention.

They'd arrived as a comedian was trotting out jokes that had to be nearly a hundred years old—reworked, renamed, but still the same jokes. Freddy laughed a few times. Josephine, however, seemed less interested. She fiddled with her gloves, looked around the vast seating area, admired the orchestra set up on one side.

"What do you think of him?" he whispered to Josephine. "He's pretty funny, huh?"

She shrugged.

One act followed another, and Josephine digested them all. Finally the tenor she'd been waiting for took the stage wearing a pale blue suit with silver lapels.

When he began to sing "Carillion," Josephine rocked back and forth, eyes clenched.

Why was she so emotional? The singer, whose skin glowed walnut under the stage lights, had a rich, smooth voice, but it didn't seem that exceptional. And the lyrics were rather racy—about a man chasing his lover and ending up in a bathtub. But something caught Josephine, something held her thin, trembling shoulders; he had never seen anyone listen so intently before. It was as if she were soaking up the voice through her skin.

After it ended, he heard her whisper, "Silt. Violet. Periwinkle. Yellow and copper," repeating this over and over, and rocking back and forth slightly.

"Is that good?" Freddy asked her.

She shook her head, unable or unwilling to answer.

15

Following the Trail

Freddy

THE NEXT DAY was Saturday. They'd gotten home a little after two in the morning, Freddy tumbling into his bed and Josephine slipping into her pile of quilts on the floor. Yet a few hours later, long before he was ready, a gentle tune poured out of the piano—softly but inarguably. It was "Carillion." He forced his eyes open. Yes, Josephine was at the piano, playing the song they'd heard last night. It was a little after 7:30 a.m.

"Well, that certainly is a pleasant way to start the day," Freddy said as he sat up, yawning.

Her tone was deft but zealous; she kept her fingers light, the melody quiet—in deference, Freddy hoped, to the early hour. He knew his landlady, Mrs. Overberg, was a gentle soul, but he didn't want her knocking on his door just then.

But no one pounded on the walls, the door, or the ceiling, and Josephine segued into the saucy "Darktown Strutters' Ball," and then into the lyrical "Just a Baby's Prayer at Twilight," another big hit that summer. All from memory. And all apparently flawless—he couldn't detect any mistakes in her playing, and he was listening for them.

She shifted into "Killin' Time with Wine," which he'd played with the combo a few weeks ago, but she modified his part.

"What did you just do?" he said. "What made you choose a seventh chord? Where did you learn that?"

"It's not difficult," she said, continuing to play. "You simply follow the trail."

"Trail, huh?" Freddy said. "I know it's way too early for a lesson, but I have a hankering to see the trail."

Josephine turned toward him, still playing. "I can show you where it is, but you have to follow it when you get there."

It's too early for this, Freddy thought as he pulled his dressing gown around his shoulders and sat down next to her, conscious of his unwashed breath. He wished he could rinse out his mouth.

In the meantime, Josephine went back to playing "Darktown Strutters' Ball." But in the middle section, where she should have played a G chord, followed by a C, a D, and then back to G, Josephine stopped. "Here's where the trail begins."

She switched to B-flat.

Freddy almost said out loud, *That's the wrong chord*, but he knew better. Josephine didn't seem capable of playing a wrong chord. Her right hand stayed in the key of G as her left hand played wild and imaginative augmented and dominant scales and chords. Going from B-flat to A-flat to F minor to D-flat major then landing on C, the process growing more complex as she went on. He never would have thought to use those chord combinations.

"I'm on the trail," she told him. "Listen."

There it was. She'd completely transformed "Darktown Strutters' Ball" by using an unanticipated series of scales and chords. "So by following the trail, you come up with something new?"

"Yes," she said. "It's here for the taking."

"Okay, okay. Let me ask it another way. You went to B-flat, then

A-flat, F minor, then to D-flat major, all to end up in the key of C. That was genius. I've never heard anything like it. So by choosing specific notes in any given scale, you bring out the options for the leading tone?"

She shrugged.

"Incredible, Josephine. You're really incredible."

Monday it was back to song plugging: this time pushing the Ditmars ballads in Siegel-Cooper Dry Goods. Freddy's musicality was definitely improving—his lessons with Josephine made even these tunes feel gorgeous and evocative. When he got home that evening, the tiny studio was meticulously clean. Even the thin curtains above his bed looked as if they had been ironed. But even more delicious was the smell of roast beef and Franconia potatoes, both simmering on his hot plate. How had she cooked roast beef and potatoes on a hot plate? A half loaf of fresh rye bread sat next to a pitcher of cold tea. Freddy felt like he had just won first prize for something.

And Josephine herself looked terrific. Her hair was pulled back into something resembling a chignon, and her face was unobstructed and clear of any smudges or loose hairs. "I hope you like roast beef and potatoes," she said.

"Wow, you did all this? The cleaning must have taken hours. Where did you get the money for roast beef? You didn't rob Mrs. Overberg, did you? Old Man Jones on the second floor has a lot more money than she does."

Josephine was carving the meat, laying it on plates. "You paid for this. I've been saving my money from your lessons."

Freddy washed his face and hands in the sink. "You're just the bee's knees, you know?"

Josephine let out a very unladylike belly laugh. For the first time since he had met her, she seemed genuinely happy. He had seen her excited, enraptured, when she listened to music, but this was different. She was just—simply—happy. So was he.

16

Gainful Employment

Freddy

ONLY TWO WEEKS had passed since Freddy had been in the Alibi Club, but the place seemed very different. The lights were still too bright, the tables still rickety, and the chairs seemed lashed together with bailing twine. But now he noticed where the walls glowed, pearly and open; how the ceiling threw the sound of his footsteps back at him. This would be a place that would hold his music; oddly, it seemed almost sacred.

The rest of the combo was already setting up onstage. "Well, lookee here," Bobby said. "You got a pep in your step." He flipped a toothpick from the left side of his mouth to the right.

Josephine slid into the seat she'd had a couple of weeks ago. A few more patrons than usual sat at tables near the front.

"Looks like you've made a friend," Eli said, gesturing with his chin toward Josephine.

"I took your advice," Freddy said. "Miss Reed gave me a couple lessons. I asked her to come tonight to see if her teaching pays off."

"Well, good for you," Bobby said.

Eli looked Freddy up and down. "Okay" was all he said, but Freddy read a lot into those two syllables: *You better be good, Mr. Delaney, or else.*

Freddy seated himself at the piano, eager to show the fellows what he could do. He looked over at Josephine.

"Ah-one, ah-two, you know what to do." Bobby counted them into "Ja-Da," the new piece that the guys loved and Freddy had always loathed performing: it had a huge piano part where the guys encouraged him to improvise. He rarely did, always keeping it straight so he didn't mess up. The guys meant business, he knew.

The jazzy bright tune snapped out of the piano. He was thinking of white torrents and falling knobs. He wouldn't look at Bobby, Red, or Eli. He concentrated on his playing. Shoulders over the keys, wrists arched high. Focus on the change. Stay in the groove. Let the emerald turn to sapphire. Whatever that meant.

At the end of his solo, the light sprinkling of audience members applauded. This was the first time that Freddy had ever gotten any applause during a solo, and he loved it.

Later, when the band got to "Burndown," Freddy didn't even wait for Bobby to count them in. He jumped right in. The others scrambled to follow. He played "Burndown" like a fiend.

At the end of the first set, Eli came up to him. "Here's what we're going to do for the next set," he told Freddy. "What do you think?"

Freddy had, without question, passed the test. He was staying in the combo.

The next morning was a Wednesday, and Freddy hoofed it to Ditmars & Ross before anyone. He had to slouch on the stoop until Mr. Ditmars himself, keys jingling, showed up at eight fifty to let him in.

"What are you doing here at this hour?" Ditmars asked him, chomping the end of an unlit cigar. Freddy knew that Mr. Ditmars lived just over on the next street; rumor had it that often he came to work in the middle of the night, testing new music and doing his paperwork. Freddy didn't think he'd like to be a boss: too much pressure and not enough fun.

"Just wanted to get a jump on things," Freddy told him casually, following him inside, trying not to let his nervousness show.

"It'll take me a minute to get your assignment."

"Okay," Freddy told him. "I can wait." He made a great production of slumping into one of the chairs in the tiny reception area, the place where the independent songwriters hung out, waiting for Mr. Ditmars to deign to listen to their jingles. Ditmars rarely bought songs from the freelancers—he liked to work with his own people.

Ditmars stomped up the stairs, floorboards creaking under his weight. Freddy checked his watch: the others would be arriving momentarily. He decided the casual approach wouldn't cut it. He followed his boss up the stairs.

"I said I'd get it," Ditmars said from the other room.

"Yes, I know," Freddy said. "But, hey, Mr. Ditmars, I had a thought and I wanted to run it by you." He was standing in the doorway. Ditmars's back was to him as he bent over a credenza, probably getting the music lineup for the day. "So there's this girl," Freddy began.

Ditmars stopped his shuffling. "Is this about your sheba? Is that what this is about? Aren't you too young to get involved with a dame?"

"She's not my sheba," Freddy told him, feeling himself flush. "She's looking for a job, and I was thinking about how you really need someone else to help with the filing since Tina left."

"I don't have time to train anyone. Plus Louise does all the filing."

"Boss, you fired Louise two weeks ago, remember?" Freddy's words tumbled out almost faster than he could think them. "She always filed everything wrong. That's why I was thinking of the woman I know. Her name's Josephine. She's extremely meticulous and organized and always on time. She also loves music. And she's not my sheba. What do you think?"

Ditmars turned around, chewing his cigar thoughtfully. A little crease had appeared between his thick eyebrows. "Eunice runs clerical. I really don't have time to . . ."

Freddy took a few steps into the room. "Eunice has her hands full keeping us straight. Not to mention keeping your meetings straight, all the writers and all. My friend, she's very smart. She likely wouldn't need much training. She's a real doll, sir. She knows all her letters and the alphabet. She loves music. I mean, really loves it. I can personally vouch for her."

A long pause. Freddy wanted to look away but didn't, stared straight back at Ditmars, determined.

"It's a good thing sales are up," Ditmars said at last. "Bring her in tomorrow. Let's give her a shot."

That night Freddy hurried home to tell Josephine. He could hear the piano from the foyer but didn't stop to identify the tune. "Hey, I have a surprise for you," he said as soon as he unlocked the door.

Josephine was playing something intricate—Liszt, maybe? Freddy didn't really know those old-timey composers—and her head was bent low over the keyboard, inches from her fingers.

She sat up when he came in. "I don't like surprises," she told him warily. "I don't want it."

"You'll like this one," he said. "I got you a job. A real job. Working with me."

"You don't want me to teach you anymore?"

"Oh, no. I definitely want to continue lessons. You're a swell teacher. I just thought it would be a great way for you to make a little more money."

She didn't respond right away; stood up from the piano bench and went over to the hot plate, where Freddy realized their dinner awaited. Ham and fried cauliflower, sizzling gently in a skillet. "What would I be doing?"

"Well, you'd be doing some clerical work. Mainly filing. The place is completely disorganized. The last file clerk that worked at Ditmars & Ross was about as bright as an unlit match."

"You'll be there? Aren't you out playing?"

"We can go there together. I have to go out and play. But you'll have music all around you, and there's a lot you can do to help."

"Okay," she said slowly, as if trying out the idea in her head. "You got me a job." Josephine was pulling out the dinner plates. As Freddy was washing his hands in the sink, he noticed many more papers than usual in Josephine's corner—a pile on the rolled-up blankets she used as a mattress, and more peeking out from underneath. "What's this?" He leaned over, hands dripping, to get a better look.

Josephine dropped a plate on the floor, and they both jumped. Luckily, it didn't break. She barely noticed, bounding over to her pile of papers, stuffing them under her bedroll. "These are mine. They aren't for you to see. For anyone to see."

"Whoa, I'm sorry. I didn't mean to—"

"Please don't disturb them." She was very agitated.

"I won't. I won't. I'm very sorry. It won't happen again," he told her, mystified and a little affronted. After all, he'd just gotten her a job and she was already yelling at him. And she'd almost broken one of his few dinner plates. Then she was back in the kitchenette, spooning ham and cauliflower on the unbroken plate and handing it to him. He decided to just let it go, and told her about the day's song plugging, instead.

The next morning they took the subway together down to Thirty-Fourth Street. Josephine was wearing what Freddy thought of as her "other dress"—a loose-fitting blue blouse with a ruffled lighter blue skirt. She'd cleaned her shoes, but one was missing a heel. He vowed to get her new shoes, and kicked himself for not thinking of it sooner.

Down Broadway and over to Sixth Avenue they walked, her limping unevenly next to him. They turned onto Twenty-Eighth Street—

Tin Pan Alley, home to many of the music publishers, although many more were now moving uptown toward Times Square. Signs with legendary names lined the street: ENTERPRISE MUSIC SUPPLY CO., HUGO V. SCHLAM, YORK MUSIC, JEROME H. REMICK & CO., and the famous composer and publisher HARRY VON TILZER, among dozens of others.

At least she was clean and neat. And it was just filing, after all, right?

He led her up the steps of the brownstone with DITMARS & ROSS emblazoned across the entablature, opened the door, and grandly gestured for her to go inside first. Eunice, the redheaded receptionist, was at her desk in the back of the small reception area, busily typing. When she caught sight of Josephine, her mouth hung open a little. "This is Josephine Reed," Freddy said to Eunice. "Josephine, this is Eunice. She's great. She's just great."

Eunice closed her mouth.

"Very nice to meet you," Josephine said evenly, ducking her head a little.

"The boss in yet?" Freddy asked and almost immediately, before Eunice had even said "Nice to meet you, Josephine," he could hear Ditmars roaring, "Freddy, that you? Get up here." He led the way upstairs. "Come on," he said.

On the first floor he poked his head into Ditmars's office. "Hey, boss? Mr. Ditmars? Sir?"

Ditmars looked up from his pile of papers. "Okay," he told him, "today you're going to Constable's for the morning, and then I'm going to put you in Broadway for the afternoon."

"Boss? Remember you told me to bring the woman I told you about? For the filing job?"

Ditmars paused, clearly confused. "Oh, right."

"To replace Louise," Freddy prompted. "I brought her like you asked me to. This is her. Josephine Reed."

Freddy took a few steps into the office, Josephine on his heels. He wondered if Ditmars would be able to tell about her shoe from just a couple of steps.

"Very nice to meet you, sir," she said to Ditmars.

Ditmars stared blankly at Josephine, then at Freddy, and then at Josephine again. He chewed his cigar. Looked again at Freddy. "She's a colored," he said. "You want me to hire a colored woman? To work here?"

Freddy of course knew that Josephine was a colored woman. It wasn't like she was hiding it, trying to pass as white, the way he knew some Negroes did. So how had he completely, totally . . . totally what? Forgotten? Ignored it? What an idiot he was. "Er, yeah," he stammered. "She wanted to be a teacher and reads real good. She's great with music. Real organized."

Josephine's eyes were darting around the room, taking it all in, never looking at Ditmars. From down the hall a piano started up—a few bars of a lyrical ballad—and then stopped. Freddy finally saw Josephine as Ditmars and Eunice probably saw her: those eyes that didn't quite fix on you; the posture, ramrod straight but somehow loose and boneless; the way she blinked at or her shoulders jerked at an unusual sound. He'd gotten so used to it that he didn't notice. Like he didn't notice the color of her skin.

"Have you gone screwy?" Ditmars was saying, and Freddy found himself agreeing: he *had* gone screwy. "What do you mean, bringing a colored woman in here? To work instead of a white woman? Is that it?"

Freddy could feel the weight of Josephine's gaze on the side of his cheek, like sunburn. It wasn't that he'd failed; it was that he'd set her up for this humiliation.

"Boss, I know what you must be thinking—" Freddy started.

"Do you? Do you? Tell me, Freddy." Ditmars swore like a sailor. Josephine was listening to all this. "No, let me tell you what I'm thinking," Ditmars was saying. "I'm thinking that there is about to be an opening for a new song plugger. What the hell were you thinking, bringing that coon in here? Did anyone see you come in?"

"Sir, some colored folks are really capable people. This one in particular. Josephine's extremely intelligent. She loves music and is a swell musician. You should hear her play. She actually wanted to be a teacher and—"

"You can't just bring a colored in here and expect me to give her a job. Do you know what would happen? Do you? This isn't a mixed-race establishment. We don't do that kind of thing, do we, Freddy?"

"Sir," Freddy said, somehow walking closer to Ditmars's desk—why was he going *closer*? He really was screwy. "You know as well as I do that you need help around here. This place has been disorganized ever since Louise left. Just think of how many more pieces of music you'd sell if you could actually find them."

Ditmars, surprisingly, was listening. Or seeming to. Well, Freddy had come this far. "Does it really matter if she's colored or not?" he said. "It's not like she'll be the face of Ditmars & Ross. She's going to be on the inside helping you make everything run smoothly and efficiently."

"She's—a—colored—woman," Ditmars said, as if by speaking more slowly, Freddy would at last understand. "Colored. She can't be working with the rest of us. We don't sell music to coloreds."

"She'd just be in a back office," Freddy said, but by now even he could see how hopeless this was. "And, besides, we do sell music to coloreds. What about the coon songs?"

Ditmars was ignoring him, turning to Josephine with a fake smile wrapped around his cigar. "Thank you for coming in, Miss—"

Freddy pushed harder. "You were just saying the other day that you wanted us to be plugging coon songs more and—"

"Go chase yourself," Ditmars said. "Now you want her to be plugging the coon songs? Have you lost your mother-loving mind?"

"Not plug. But she knows them all. And the rags. She knows every rag ever written." Ragtime had started in the Negro community and now was a large percentage of what Freddy plugged every day. "She could help us get a handle on the Negro market. You know there are more Negroes than ever moving in and—"

"Negroes don't shop at Constable's or Altman's," Ditmars told him. "They have their own shopping stores."

"But regular people are buying coon songs, and I bet she could help—"

Josephine spoke up next to him, and both Freddy and Ditmars jumped: it was as if they'd forgotten she was there, and human, and able to hear them. "I do know the coon songs, sir," she said quietly. "I've heard them for years. And minstrel songs. I know you don't sell jazz, but I'm familiar with jazz, as well. And there's a new music coming up from the Deep South called the blues, which is just starting to catch on."

"See?" Freddy said. "She knows her music."

"I'm sure she does," Ditmars said to him, "but we don't sell music to coloreds." He repeated to Josephine, "We don't sell music to coloreds."

"More and more white folks are listening than ever," she said. "Lot of clubs playing Negro music and not even letting Negroes inside. Alamo Club uptown and Minsky's. Donovan's and Short Stack and—"

"See?" Freddy interrupted. "She knows her music. She could be a real asset around here, I'm telling you, boss. And we need the help. Nobody has to know."

There was that moment when Freddy realized that he'd gotten through: he watched as the color shifted in Ditmars's eyes, his cheeks relaxed. Freddy went on, eager, "The only people who would ever see her would be the people in this office. She could come in through the back and leave the same way. It could increase productivity around here. She's smart as a whip. For a colored."

A pause that stretched on. "Okay, this is what I'll do," Ditmars said, gnawing again on his cigar. "I'll give you a chance, Miss—"

"Reed, sir," Josephine said. "Josephine Reed."

"Miss Reed. One week. If you're as good as Freddy says you are, well then, well and good. If not, you're out of here."

Josephine nodded.

"You've gotta come through the back door. I can only pay you half of a file clerk's wages. One mess-up and you've gotta scram. You got me? I'm taking a giant risk with both of you."

Freddy didn't allow himself to relax. "You won't be sorry, boss. You won't."

"Yeah, well," Ditmars said. "Okay. Josephine is it? You'll be filing all this sheet music that's been taken out and sampled. You can start right now. Go down and meet Eunice and she'll explain the system. I trust we won't have any problems?"

"No, sir," Josephine said. "Thank you for the opportunity, sir."

Ditmars looked at Freddy, who explained, "She thinks this place is the bee's knees, sir."

"I don't want any funny talk around here," Ditmars said. "You hear?"

"She hears you, sir," Freddy said, and then muttered to Josephine, "Go down and get Eunice to show you the ropes." As Josephine left, Freddy said loudly, "Now where do you want me today, sir?"

"What?" Ditmars stared at his desk, then back up at Freddy. "Yes. I want you at Constable's this morning, then I have a new plan that I want you to try." Ditmars outlined Freddy's assignment and, moments later, sheet music under his arm, Freddy was thundering down the steps. He caught sight of Josephine in the back room beyond Eunice, head bent over a filing cabinet.

He sure hoped he hadn't made a colossal mistake.

17

The Orange in the Black & Green

Freddy

BUT THAT AFTERNOON, when Freddy returned after a day's plugging, he immediately sensed a difference in the office: the magazines and sheet music in the reception area had been sorted and stacked. Upstairs, the piles of paper on Ditmars's desk and credenza had all but disappeared, and the Music Room—the storage area where they kept all the sheet music—had been organized and swept. Josephine was in one of the niches, sorting through a pile of half-written compositions that a composer had left on the floor.

"Hey," Freddy said, "you do okay?"

She nodded.

"I'm heading out of here," he said, and then more quietly, "I'll meet you back home later."

She nodded again, understanding.

Surprisingly, the next few days went well. Freddy bought her new shoes to celebrate. Josephine worked tirelessly, filing, stacking, organizing, and sweeping, all the while soaking in the sounds of the pianos and singing that resonated from behind closed doors. She didn't really say much, but Freddy could tell that she loved every moment of it. Ditmars would never give him any accolades for bringing Josephine in, but her continued day-to-day existence in the office was proof that she was a success.

Each evening, when she returned—they traveled separately back and forth—Josephine would carefully place her new shoes in a corner and set about making dinner for them both. Freddy had never had it so good: applesauce, beef stew, mashed potatoes, and even—wonder of wonders!—fried chicken and greens. Freddy paid for much of the food, and Josephine cooked it. The arrangement seemed to work for her. He kept paying for piano lessons, and she paid him a dollar a week for her corner of the studio apartment.

Josephine had encountered several tenants—including Mrs. Overberg—but, following the script that Freddy had laid out for her, had explained that he'd hired her to clean his room and do his laundry. The neighbors didn't complain or pursue it further, but Freddy didn't know how long that would last. He wondered if people were enjoying the music pouring out of his apartment these days: a far cry from Freddy clunking around on the piano.

Soon, it seemed like Josephine had always been working at Ditmars & Ross. No more shouting to Eunice nor stomping around hunting for sheet music on bookshelves and under desks. No loose sheets, no misfiled songs, nothing out of place. Josephine even dusted and swept. Freddy was going to ask Ditmars about expanding the publisher's repertoire with more coon songs and some of the music he'd been hearing at night in the clubs, but he wanted to give everyone a chance to get used to Josephine before he asked. She was a colored woman, after all, and none of them had ever worked with a colored woman before.

In the meantime, Freddy could feel that, thanks to lessons with Josephine, his own musical abilities were improving astronomically. He felt he was on his way to being a top-notch musician, and that was a dream come true. Truth be told, he was starting to love the applause almost as much as the music. Loved being part of the jazz combo, feeling the rush of playing with musicians who already were extraordinary performers, getting caught up in the sound and the camaraderie and the melodies swirling around him.

So he was feeling confident and cocky one Wednesday afternoon, coming back to the office from plugging over at Altman's. When he opened the front door, Eunice wasn't in her usual spot at her desk, and the pianos—which should have been thrumming through the walls—were silent. A murmur of voices came from upstairs, so he bounded up to see what was what.

A crowd clustered at one end of the hall, all focused on one of the piano rooms. "Hey, fellas," Freddy said to Calvin Broadwell and Miles Turpin, two songwriters who were standing on the outskirts. "What's going on?"

Calvin glanced at him and called out, "He's here, Mr. Ditmars. Freddy's here."

"Freddy!" came the well-known roar. "Get the hell over here."

Freddy's heart was sinking into his shoes, his worn two-tone oxfords. "What is it?" he said, wedging himself past Josh Roberts and Ernest Greene.

"Josephine," Eunice said. "She's hiding under the piano and was yelling something fierce a few minutes ago."

"Josephine?" Freddy asked her. "Yelling? You sure?"

By now he was face-to-face with Ditmars, whose eyes were bulging furiously. No cigar in sight. This couldn't be good. "Your darkie is having some kind of fit," he said. "What kind of spook lunatic did you bring in here?"

"'Fit'?" Freddy said. It felt like all he was doing was repeating what other people told him.

"She was yelling fit to beat the band," someone said.

"Screaming her head off."

"Get her out of here," Ditmars told him.

"She's not yelling now," Freddy said, trying to think what to do, craning around the people blocking the door to the piano room.

As if in answer came a loud yelp—not quite a scream, but hoarse and more ragged than a yell. Freddy hadn't ever heard a noise like that before. It didn't sound human and certainly didn't sound like Josephine.

Josephine was curled into a ball in a corner, hands over her ears, shaking and mumbling, repeating something over and over. Again she let out that high-pitched, deep-throated growl. This time—perhaps because he was closer—he could somehow hear words in it.

"Hey, what's going on?" Freddy said, trying to sound casual and easygoing. "Josephine? You okay?" He leaned over and lightly touched her shoulder—he didn't think he'd ever touched her before—and she flinched, not even looking at him, shuddering, mumbling quietly but so quickly that he couldn't parse it into English.

"Jo?" he tried again. "Josephine? What is it?"

The rocking back and forth and the mumbling continued, and slowly Freddy deciphered, ". . . isintheblackandgreenandtheorange-isintheblackandgreenandtheorangeisintheblack—"

"Orange?" Freddy asked her. "Green?"

She just rocked faster, weeping, shrieking, "Black and green," and then whispering, "Orange, orange, orange."

Freddy could feel the weight of the others looking at him. He had no idea what to do. "What's black?" he asked her. "Is there something wrong with the green?"

No response.

Should he just wait for it to end? She'd have to stop sometime, wouldn't she? She couldn't just sit there forever, wailing and yelling about black, green, and orange.

Then he remembered her piles of drawings in her corner of the studio. How she'd hidden them away as soon as she'd seen him. Well, there was one thing he could try. "Can someone get me some paper," he asked the room, "and a pencil? Maybe a bunch of sheets?"

Paper—music-lined—appeared, and a pencil. He leaned down, put it in front of Josephine. "Here's some paper," he said loudly. "You want the paper?"

"—green and the orange is in the black and green and the orange—"

He was afraid to touch her, afraid she'd scream again, but he picked up the pencil and gently tried to brush it against the clenched fists covering her ears as she oscillated back and forth like a pendulum. Back and forth, and again he held out the pencil to her. Finally, he somehow slipped it into the tight wad of her closed fist, and it hung there, swinging in her hand.

She stopped rocking, unfurled slightly from her ball, tucked the pencil into her palm, and he could now see that her eyes had unclenched. Tears dripped from her lashes. She groped for the paper. Slowly she quieted and, although her torso still swung back and forth, it was less now. She pulled the paper into the arc of her body, and he could see her writing, or drawing, or whatever she was doing, furiously on the paper. She turned away from him, her shoulder blocking his view, whispering now, "The orange is in the black and green, the orange is in the black and green, the orange is in the black and green."

Freddy stood up. "Okay, show's over," he told the crowd. "Let's give her a minute, can we?"

"I want that monkey out of here," Ditmars told him.

"Give her just a minute," Freddy said.

"What did you do?" Eunice said. "What's she writing?"

He shrugged. "I don't know, honestly. She just writes stuff sometimes. She's never shown it to me."

"Well, it worked," Ditmars said, and then to the crowd, "Okay, people, get your butts back to work. Show's over, you hear?"

Freddy gently shut the door to the piano room and left Josephine in peace. He went into Mr. Ditmars's office. "I'll take her home, sir," he said. "Just give her a minute to calm down, okay?"

"I can't have a crazy coon in here," Ditmars said. "How could you bring in a nut like that? Seriously, Freddy? I gave you a chance and, Christ, did you blow it."

"She's been great," Freddy said. "The office has never looked so good. I never saw her like this. I swear."

"Well, I can't have a loon working here." Ditmars was fumbling in his desk drawer for a fresh cigar, unwrapping it, clipping the end. "A loony coon. Christ, Freddy."

"I bet if she has her paper she'll be fine. Can you give her one more chance?"

"One more chance?" Ditmars blinked up at him. "Are you out of your mind?"

"She didn't do anything. She just—well, she just had a breakdown, is all. I bet if she has her papers and she knows she can write on her papers she'll be just fine."

Ditmars shook his head. "I seriously can't believe you're asking me this."

Behind him another voice chimed in. Eunice, leaning in from the hall. "Come on, boss, the kid's right," she said. "Josephine's been wonderful. She's an odd duck to be sure, but I agree with him."

Ditmars looked from one to the other. He shook his head, sighed, lit his cigar. "Christ almighty. I'm a patsy like there's never been a patsy. One more chance," he told Freddy. "That is, if you get her out of my sight right now, and if she's okay tomorrow. Any more of this and she's out, you hear? Out."

"Thanks, boss," Freddy said. "Thanks a million." He ducked out of the office before Ditmars could change his mind. In the corridor, out of Ditmars's sight, he mouthed *Thank you* to Eunice.

She winked at him. "You're a good egg, you know that? You did a good thing, helping her. Those people really have it rough."

Ten minutes later, when Freddy knocked and opened the door to the piano room, he found Josephine sitting up, papers on her knees, drawing madly. She looked up at him. Although her face was still wet with tears, she seemed her usual distant and detached self.

"Hey," Freddy said. "You all right in here?"

She nodded. He couldn't tell if she was embarrassed or shy or just disconnected—he wished he could read her expressions.

"You wanna go home? I thought I'd splurge and get us a cab uptown." A cab would cost the entire day's worth of Freddy's wages.

She thought about it, nodded, got to her feet.

That night Josephine sat in her corner and drew her drawings. She didn't cook. Freddy made flapjacks. He could see she was fragile and left her alone. No lesson that night, and no outing to a club. But the next morning she was awake before he was, dressed for work, and playing the piano as if nothing untoward had occurred.

No other incidents happened that day. Eunice told him that Josephine would sometimes stop what she was doing, tuck herself into a corner, and scribble madly for a few minutes before returning to the task at hand. But nobody else seemed to remark upon it, and the office sparkled.

As long as Josephine was never far from her papers.

18

Amber in the Speedway

Freddy

EARLY ONE SATURDAY MORNING, about three months after Josephine moved in, Freddy was sound asleep when the piano started up. More days than not, especially after a scintillating time at a club or a dance hall the night before, she would skulk to the piano as soon after daybreak as she thought feasible, press down the damper pedal, and play. Sometimes he heard melodies from the night before, other times songs that Freddy was plugging. Sometimes she'd tell him that these were tunes that she'd heard a week or a month or ten years previously. Her memory was vast.

This morning, as usual, Freddy recognized most of the melodies—he'd heard her play them before, and, with a deftness that dazzled him, she'd slide from one tune into another.

Then she played a melody that he'd never heard: evocative and haunting, memorable and fresh. Unerringly, she played it through, and then segued into a bright jazz theme that was making its way around much of New York.

"What was that?" Freddy asked her.

"This?" she said, shifting her hands on the keys, and the music poured back to that haunting melody.

"Yes. What is it?"

"It's a long flash of amber in the speedway," she said.

By now he was used to her crazy talk. "Yeah," he said. "But what's it called? Where did you hear it? Who played it?" He was sitting up now.

She shrugged. Her hands seemed detached from the rest of her body, effortlessly dancing over the keys. "I listened for years to the flash. The songs my grandpa played. These songs from the blue fire my mother sang when I was young. Some were sad. I made them happy. Sometimes when I hear the anchor lines in the clubs, I feel them. So I wanted to bring them to the amber speedway."

He tried again, although he suspected he was wasting his time. "You said 'the flash.' You said you listened to the flash for years? Was that in North Carolina? Was this a work song that you heard back then?"

"Yes," Josephine said. A pause. "And no."

"What do you mean?"

"Some of the notes are from my grandpa. But the work song goes like this." The melody shifted into a Negro spiritual that Freddy had heard dozens of times. But now, every few bars, he caught a glimmer of the new song that Josephine had played.

"Now play the other one again," he said. "The amber one."

The tune morphed back to that original beguiling melody.

"Did you write this?" he asked.

She looked over at him, but he couldn't read her expression. She didn't have facial expressions like other people.

"Josephine, did you think of this yourself? This song?"

She nodded, kept playing. "It's one I wanted to hear."

He closed his eyes, trying to figure out what the song was. It wasn't the usual jazz or even the minstrel songs she'd play most mornings;

not quite a work song, nor a field song. He'd heard some of the blues music that was coming up from the Deep South, played in a minor key with a series of major thirds and fifths. Many people thought it sounded lazy because of the repeated bars and repetitious lyrics, especially in the chorus. This new song, however, wasn't the blues. It somehow seemed both an amalgamation of them all and entirely its own.

The melody finished, and Josephine rose from the piano, closed the lid. "I put the oatmeal on," she said. "Do you want it now?"

He opened his mouth to speak, closed it again.

She was at the kitchenette, pulling down two bowls. "Do you want cinnamon in it?"

Cinnamon? "Josephine, what were you playing?"

"I told you. It was a long flash of amber in the speedway. I'm going to have cinnamon," she said, pouring a dollop of oatmeal into a bowl.

"Yes, the amber speedway. Can you show me? Wait, hold on." He launched out of bed, pulling his dressing gown around his shoulders, and dashed to the bathroom. When he returned a few minutes later, Josephine was eating calmly at the piano bench. Freddy grabbed a few sheets of paper and a pen, sat down next to her, moved the bowl to the floor. He lifted the piano cover. "Play it again. The amber song. Just keep playing it. When you get to the end, start again, okay?"

Josephine nodded, started, and continued to play. Shoulders hunched, wrists arched.

For the next forty-five minutes, Freddy transcribed "Amber." She replayed it one last time as Freddy followed along on his manuscript. To his credit, he'd missed only a handful of notes, which he scratched through and corrected. "Okay," he said finally. "I got it. So here's what I think we should do. I think we sell it to Ditmars and split the money. What do you think?"

"Sell it?" she repeated, turning toward him.

"Sure! It's the beans! I bet we could get five dollars for it. Let me take it into Ditmars and see if he can turn it into a hit."

She considered.

"It needs some lyrics, though," Freddy went on. "And a better title than 'Amber in the Speedway.' Let me see what I can put together. I bet I can come up with something. If he takes it, we'll split the money. Fifty-fifty. What do you say? Sometimes the guys make as much as ten dollars for a song. That would be five dollars for each of us. We can eat like kings. You could buy a new dress. It definitely needs lyrics, though."

She shrugged. He took that for a yes.

Most of Saturday he stayed home, and he didn't go uptown that evening with Josephine as she checked out the Quincy's Social Dance Room in Midtown. She was excited to hear a saxophone quartet there. Instead he worked on the lyrics: What was the best word to rhyme with *staying*?

The following Monday, Freddy and Josephine took the subway as usual down to Thirty-Fourth Street, parted in Penn Station, and made their separate ways to Ditmars & Ross. Freddy went in the front door and Josephine, a few minutes later, took the service door from the back alley.

He whizzed past Eunice, straight into Ditmars's office. "Boss," he said, "this is it! I'm holding the next big thing right here!"

Ditmars looked up. "I'm putting you in Lord & Taylor today. You'll be there all week. They're getting ready for a big autumn white sale. Here's what you're going to do—"

"No, wait." Freddy handed him a page. "I have a song you've got to hear. It's great. You're gonna love it."

"Freddy, don't make me say this again. Quit wasting my time, you hear?"

"I swear to you, if you don't like this one, I'll resign right here on the spot. Honest."

Ditmars smiled around his cigar. "Be careful what you wish for. You've been a real pain in my ass. Don't tempt me."

"Boss, this is the real McCoy! I guarantee it!"

"You know what? Fine. Don't say I didn't warn you."

"You won't regret it."

Freddy led Ditmars down the hall, past Chuck Keats banging his way through a version of "Simply Lovely," and into the next room. He sat down on the bench, ostentatiously arranged the handwritten music, although by now he knew it by heart. He played the first verse:

It's gone dark and the trees are swaying
You're gone and the clouds are always staying
It seems like yesterday I could find a better way
But you left me and our love one afternoon
Somewhere anywhere
Bring back the moon, bring back the moon

"What's it called?" Ditmars said.

" 'Bring Back the Moon.' "

"I'll give you eight dollars for it."

"Twelve," Freddy said. "You can tell it's going to be a hit. We can sell this sheet music like crazy."

"Ten, and you should be grateful," Ditmars said.

That night Freddy and Josephine celebrated: ten whole dollars for the song! Five dollars each! This was almost a week's wages for Josephine. She would get a new dress.

Two weeks later, Freddy returned from a day plugging music at Lord & Taylor late one afternoon. He'd no sooner crossed the threshold of Ditmars & Ross when he heard the lyrical melody of "Bring Back the Moon" pouring down from an upper floor. He took the stairs two at a time and opened the hallway door without knocking.

Miles Turpin was halfway through the chorus and looked up when the door opened. "This is yours, right?" Miles said, continuing to play.

"Sure is," Freddy told him. "What do you think?"

"It's darb, pal. Darb, plain and simple." Miles, a tall skinny guy who rarely smiled, met Freddy's eyes as his fingers roamed the keyboard. "I didn't know you had it in you. Frankly, I'm jealous I didn't write it."

"It's pretty good, isn't it," Freddy said.

"It's darb, I tell you."

Ditmars was yelling from the front office. "Freddy! Get in here."

Freddy rolled his eyes at Miles. "Well, you keep practicing. Let's sell lots of copies."

When Freddy poked his head into Ditmars's office, Ditmars waved him in. "Your song came in today. Five hundred sheets." He handed a sheaf of paper to Freddy, and there it was, in black-and-white, real printing and on real paper: *Bring Back the Moon" by Frederick Delaney.* "You're a songwriter now," Ditmars said. "Tomorrow we're going to start selling copies."

"Now you're on the trolley," Freddy told him. "This is the best song ever."

Ditmars shook his head. "We're taking a risk with you, young man, but let's see if this will sell." He shook Freddy's hand, and Freddy pumped back enthusiastically.

As soon as he was out of sight of Ditmars he went in search of Josephine. She was in one of the composer's playing rooms, sweeping up a pile of cigarette butts from an ashtray that someone had knocked over.

"Hey, kiddo! Take a look at this!" He brandished a sheet, twenty of them. "You know what this is?"

She stared at it blankly a moment, but even as recognition dawned, he told her, "That's the sheet music to the song you wrote! Your amber song. And you know what? I just know it's gonna be a big hit. You did such a swell job and nobody's ever heard a tune like it before! Ditmars is over the moon, you hear me? We're gonna have to bring him back from the moon when this is done!"

She examined the pages, scanned the notes. A smile touched her lips, then her eyes. He didn't think he'd ever seen her radiate joy like that before, and his heart flipped.

"Freddy," she said, looking back down, looking at her notes.

"This is just the beginning! I can see it now. All your songs filling the department stores! Selling like hotcakes! I'm gonna plug it nonstop tomorrow and I'm gonna get the other fellas to plug it, too."

He imagined what she must be feeling; that, for the first time, a melody that had been only in her head was now printed in black-and-white, so the world could finally hear what she heard. And he, Freddy, had done this for her. What a gift—just a small token of what he owed her for teaching him, for opening up a whole world of music to him. How elated she must be!

"This is 'Amber in the Speedway,'" she said, turning the paper around.

"Yeah," he said. "Remember I wrote the lyrics? It's 'Bring Back the Moon' now. But that's your music—your terrific music."

"I don't think this is mine," she said, puzzled. "My name is Josephine Reed. This says 'Frederick Delaney.' Is this the right music? Did Mr. Ditmars make a mistake?"

"It's only because Mr. Ditmars is a very conscientious businessman. We'd all have a difficult time selling the music if people knew it was written by a colored woman. You know what Ditmars thinks about you people. I thought it would be better not to tell him that you wrote the music because I wanted you to have the best chance of success. Plus if I told him it was written by a white man he'd pay more for it. This is the best thing for you. I promise. This is going to be great! Have I ever steered you wrong?"

She shook her head, her eyes distant and unfocused. "No, you haven't."

That night they celebrated. He arrived home before her. When she came in, he opened the tiny refrigerator, removed a bottle of champagne. From the shelf he pulled down two juice glasses—he didn't have the fancy crystal, but just you wait. "Bring Back the Moon" was going to be a bestseller. A chart-topper. The first of many. He'd chosen the most expensive-looking bottle he could find. He'd tried to impress the other shoppers by reading the label carefully and holding the bottle up to the light, slowly twisting it as if to inspect each bubble.

The champagne opened with a very loud pop that felt very alien. Freddy wondered if the room had ever heard that sound before. He poured them each a glass, handed her one.

"A toast," he said.

She seemed unsure what to do with her glass. He gestured for her to pick it up, touch its lip to hers.

He met her eyes and realized almost belatedly that she was looking directly at him, and smiling. He'd seen her smile, and he'd seen her look at people, but never the two at the same time. This was different. It was as if she were seeing him, Freddy Delaney.

She was beautiful, wasn't she? Odd, to be sure, but beautiful nonetheless. Those cheekbones, those huge eyes, those eyelashes.

"Um," Freddy said. "Well. I propose a toast. To us! To Josephine and Freddy! You're the best thing that's happened to me in—well, ever."

He expected her to look down, turn away as she always did. This time, she didn't. She met his gaze as they clinked glasses and she said, "To us. For riding the white torrent."

Freddy smiled. "Yes," he said. "The white torrent. Now what's for dinner?"

The next day "Bring Back the Moon" had been included in the song-plugger rotation. Freddy had taken seventy-five sheets—a very solid number—to Altman's, and had sold them out before he'd even managed to take a lunch break. This wasn't so unusual: a lot of regular shoppers frequented Altman's, and they all wanted the latest music, but it was still gratifying to think that people would be playing Freddy's song, and singing it, and dancing to it, later today and in the weeks to come.

Every day Freddy plugged "Bring Back the Moon," playing it almost every other song. Pretty soon he was hearing it from other department stores, dance halls, and vaudeville houses as he wandered the city. Even the fellows in the office were humming it. One afternoon Miles Turpin collared Freddy outside the building. "Hey, Delaney," Miles asked. "Did Ditmars buy your song off you outright?"

"Yeah, of course," Freddy said. "Why?"

"Because he's making a killing off it," Miles said. "And you sold away your rights to it, I bet. How much did he pay you?"

Freddy shrugged.

"Let me guess, twenty dollars," Miles said.

Freddy shrugged again.

"You know how much Ditmars is making off this? Mucho mazuma, pal. Mucho."

Freddy shrugged yet again. "I have to start somewhere, you know?"

"Well, if you have another golden nugget like that sitting around in a drawer, don't sell it to him so cheap next time, you hear? Sell it to me instead."

Freddy laughed, but he had been thinking that he'd let Ditmars off too easy.

The past week, except for the jazz combo, he'd let Josephine go out to her clubs without him. The other evenings he'd spent with the piano and his music sheets to write a few more songs, emulating the style of "Bring Back the Moon." His first song, "Cyrillian Nights," took three nights to create. Then he penned two more tunes—"Lemon Shines the Wick" and "Apples & Stardust."

The next morning, Freddy knocked on Ditmars's open door. "Boss, you're gonna love these. Talk about a follow-up! Any one of these songs could be the next big hit!"

Ditmars shifted his cigar, stood up immediately. "You got more?"

he said. "Let's hear them." He followed Freddy to the first open piano room.

Twenty measures in, Ditmars said, "Next."

Freddy paused, surprised. He was sure "Cyrillian Nights" was a surefire hit. Well, okay. He had a few more.

On "Apples & Stardust," Ditmars took even less time to say, "Next."

Freddy hesitated. "Okay," he said. "I know you're gonna think this one is swell." He began the introduction to "Lemon Shines the Wick," and seconds later Ditmars cut him off.

"Look, Freddy, I don't know if this is your idea of a practical joke or not, but it ain't funny. What are you tryin' to pull here?"

Failure was cold on Freddy's back. "Boss, I—"

"Don't come in here wasting my time. I got a business to run."

"What don't you like about them? They—"

"This, and this"—Ditmars held up the sheet music Freddy had played—"this is trash. I'd have to pay people to listen to this garbage. I'm not sure what you're trying to pull, but this ain't no 'Bring Back the Moon.' Stick to what you know. This sure ain't it. Get back to work."

Freddy couldn't believe Ditmars was saying this. Wasn't everyone playing "Bring Back the Moon"? Only yesterday he'd heard someone humming it on the subway. On the subway! Maybe Ditmars was trying to pull a fast one. Maybe Ditmars would return to the practice room, let Freddy know that he was just giving him a good old-fashioned ribbing.

The door stayed half-ajar, as Ditmars had left it. He did not return.

ACT 3

Bern & Freddy

19

In the Crash & the Dissonance

Scherzo: Josephine

MONDAY MORNING, long before Freddy was awake, she rose from the bedroll (Bedroll! She was still impossibly grateful to Freddy to have been given this bedroll, to not be tucking herself under a bush or against the walls of the St. John Cathedral at night. Back in Oxford she'd had a bed, and she'd had one in Mrs. McMurtry's boarding-house when she and her brother Howard had first come to the city, but still it felt odd after so many months to now be sleeping on something so padded), neatly tucked in the sheets, tucked in a few errant pieces of the Compendium that had wriggled out overnight, and put oatmeal on to cook.

Freddy was asleep still, from the hitch and pause of his breath (F-sharp sliding to a D-flat, three beats, and again F-sharp), and the click of the gas didn't wake him. She crept out, the G click of the doorknob barely cutting the darkness, and padded down the hall to the bathroom. The water came out of the spigot in a roar that reminded her of the ring of a kettledrum just after a drummer lifts their sticks from the skin.

She dressed in the bathroom in the Monday Blue Dress, peeked out to make sure no one was in the hall (Freddy had made it clear what would happen if his landlady caught her living in the room with him), and padded back down the hall, let herself in quietly, although Freddy was awake now, half-dressed, turned away from her, his bare shoulders so pale in the dimness of the room, somehow fragile, as if made of paper or wax. She wanted to cover him, he looked so delicate, so unprotected, but instead she closed the door more loudly (B, but the force of closing it pulled it up into E-flat) and he turned.

"Hey, kiddo," he said, and he grinned at her, and she tried to remember how long it had been since someone had smiled at her like this, so welcoming, so impossibly glad to see her, and her chest tightened and loosened all at once and she was afraid, right then and there, that she'd start to cry: it all seemed too much, the F-sharp and the kettledrum spigot and the pale wings of his shoulders, all welcoming, all accepting, all comfortable and familiar. Her index finger and thumb itched for her pencil, the side of her palm yearning for contact with the Compendium. She wanted to memorialize this feeling—there was a C chord begging to be played, and an A would run into an E and then a G chord and—

"The bathroom is free," she said instead, moving to the stove, where the oatmeal was boiling slowly, thick unsteady-but-rhythmic bursts of bubbles popping, and she stirred it. A pause, caesura, and then the rhythm started again. She needed to write this down, told herself to remember the pause, the unsteadiness of the oatmeal's breaths.

He left to use the bathroom and she prepared her Monday Lunch Sandwich, knife cutting through the ham with a sizzle that felt almost umber. The Compendium called to her, and she was just about to Transcribe when Freddy returned.

By then the oatmeal was ready and they ate, she barely tasting, because she was thinking that it was already eight thirty and she needed to walk the two blocks to the subway station. But then Freddy told her that it was only eight ten (his watch, the tiny ticks eating away at the world, how grateful she was to it, too), so she discovered these twenty minutes and felt even more blessed.

Because the piano (not the piano at home, in Oxford, the one that her mother had forbidden her to play, had put a lock on to keep her out of because she'd sit before it with her hands arching like bridges, connecting this instrument that created music to Josephine herself; not that piano, this one was Freddy's, and he never locked it away from her) called to her in a voice that brooked no argument, she left the oatmeal and sat on the piano bench and her fingers were vines growing into the keys and the piano's gilded energy shot through to her fingertips and she fell into the bright shadow: Brahms felt right, his Waltz in A minor, so rich and melancholy, with a longing that pulled her back to the North Carolina farmland of her birth. Which reminded her of a phrase from the bluegrass song "Bill Cheatham," and that led her inexorably to the vaudeville minstrel song she'd heard last week, "Broke Fiddle Blues."

She could have played forever, but Freddy was saying, "Hey, kiddo, get your hat, we need to hit the road," and although the piano continued to call to her, she left it there, promised she would return, and she knew that it would wait, eager, and remain there, faithful.

She wrapped her sandwich in paper (the crinkle like gravel under horses' hooves or like muffled bells, B-flat up to D-flat; she would write this in the Compendium), and Freddy ushered her before him and closed the door and locked it (the door G, the lock C-sharp).

In the subway car she brought forth her Compendium and jotted down the Brahms and the stairwell's F-sharp and the sound of the lock clicking into place. The tick and the rhythm of the subway kept calling for a C and then an E and then a G. She had a melody, neat and orderly, completed before the train reached Penn Station.

"How wonderful," Freddy said when she showed him, looking at her with his blue eyes so admiring.

At Ditmars & Ross, Josephine said hello to Eunice and created a new sheet of the Compendium on a ripped gas-bill envelope, scanning in the sizzle of the knife through the ham, the *tink* of the spoon on the bowl. She was going to place it with the rest of the Compendium in her maroon carpetbag, but the piano tunes were leaking down from upstairs, the cacophony of all the pianos playing several different tunes at once—she picked out four separate melodies, although three of the pianos were playing the same tunes, just in different sections.

The music was so powerful, filling her so full of joy that she was tapping her foot before she realized she was doing it.

There was something here, she realized, in the crash and dissonance, in the syncopated chords briefly rising together into the day, and then trundling apart again, like trains sliding side by side on parallel tracks and then veering off.

She had taken such a train when she and Howard had come from North Carolina—Howard to find work and she because she'd had no choice, because Mrs. Johnson over on West Elm, in Oxford, hosted the visiting teacher, Miss Ames, from Harlem, who played ragtime and jazz, melodies that Josephine had never imagined could exist, and that was it, there was no going back, no staying in Oxford once she knew that such harmonies existed in the world.

Oh, the music she wanted to hear!

And this—*this*—was why she'd made Howard take her up to New York City, why she'd stood in the back of the train all through Virginia and Maryland and part of Delaware—and then endured the chaos and the cries of the city when the train pulled into Penn Station with her Compendium: *this music* that she was hearing or wanting to hear right now, right this moment, and she realized that she had never, ever, been as happy as she was right this moment, here on Twenty-Eighth Street in the back filing room of a music publisher, and she stood in the middle of the room and breathed it all in, and breathed it in again, and again.

"Josephine," Eunice called to her, and she went to work filing the *A* correspondence under *A*, the *H* under *H*, and so on. It was orderly and clean, and the music in the walls flowed into her skin and allowed her to breathe.

Miles Turpin asked her for a stack of "Bluebell Poppy" and she found it for him, thinking that his *L*s sounded guttural, like the creek churning down beyond the house in Oxford, and she handed "Bluebell Poppy" to him. His shoes gleamed.

He didn't thank her but she didn't care, she was Transcribing the way he said "Bluebell," the guttural creek noise of him, and the way his shiny shoes cracked a C-sharp on the second stair as he ascended into the piano rooms. She'd have to change out the ashtrays, but not yet. Because Miles Turpin's phrasing of "Bluebell" hit a note that came from the third piano down the hall upstairs, the way the pianist (Calvin Broadwell, she thought; his fingerings were always clumsier than the others) hit the D-major chord, and that led her into another melody, she used some of the bass phrasings of the third movement of Schubert's Ninth Symphony and the way the woodwinds leaped upon a branch for a version of "Tiger Rag" she'd heard when she'd first come to New York City.

Within minutes she had another song she would have liked to hear and it really was time to empty the ashtrays, sweep the upstairs, and tidy Mr. Ditmars's office. So she stuffed the latest piece of the Compendium into its resting place, in her maroon reticule, and climbed the stairs to the second floor, thinking again how lucky she was, how grateful she was—

And it was all—*all*—because of Freddy Delaney.

20

Decoding a Treasure Map

Bern

GIVEN ALL THE TRAVEL and distractions, Bern found that he was working on the *RED* score until very late at night, sleeping sometimes only three or four hours before his phone blared its morning alarm. Each morning it played another Delaney piece, and he'd lie there, eyes closed, just letting the music wash over him.

He would have thought, since he was breathing and sleeping Delaney's music all day, that he'd be growing tired of it, but that was never the case—and he thought it made his understanding and appreciation for *RED* grow only more profound.

Each time he listened to a Delaney composition, no matter how many times he'd heard it or played it or studied it, he found something new. A short melody might, surprisingly, remind him of a phrase from Chopin or echo a folk song. For the more complicated pieces—the symphonies, concertos, and of course the *Rings Quintet*—the orchestrations were so rich and full that often Bern felt like he hadn't properly heard the piece before, when he listened to it the next time. The overture to "Ravenswalk," for instance, had that brilliant bass clarinet solo in the allegro section. He'd heard the flutter of bird wings, had picked out the faint oboe and piccolo obbligato that sounded like a raven hopping along a fence; but then the subtleties of the bass and violas were the wind whispering in the grass—grass so real that he could actually imagine it, pale yellow in the gleaming late autumn sun.

He decided, the more he listened to RED, the more he wanted to surround himself with Delaney's music. Even Schubert and Vivaldi seemed to pale in comparison. He bathed in Delaney's harmonics. Whenever he wasn't actively working on the RED analysis—walking to the Foundation, going to Eboni's, on the way to a pizzeria—he'd play another Delaney composition. There were hundreds, so the hardest choice was just picking something. Then he'd listen to it over and over. This was the beauty and the curse of music in general—and, for him, Delaney's music in particular.

For instance: on the first loop, he could focus on the cello line and wonder how the London Symphony Orchestra could play the lower notes so perfectly clear at such a fast tempo. The next time around, he'd sigh when the trumpet fanfares came through. Three times after, he was shocked that he hadn't noticed the trumpets playing triplets, using two different notes. Man, this was double good.

Over the next few weeks, he spent less time at the Foundation offices, and worked from Eboni's. She had RED on her very-secure server, and he was able to tunnel into the Delaney archive remotely. The Foundation didn't seem to mind that he wasn't actively in the office, since he was cranking through RED: finished pages were piling up. He was halfway through act 2 now.

But he could only really focus and analyze the RED scores for five or six hours a day. More than that and he'd lose concentration and make mistakes. He had to clear his head. Instead of going for a bike ride or a run to rejuvenate, though, he worked with Eboni to decipher the 147 separate pages of Delaney Doodles from Josephine Reed's trunk.

But only more questions surfaced. Had Delaney given them to Josephine to hide? Had he sent the trunk down to North Carolina for safekeeping? Had she stolen them? Were there other trunks somewhere full of Delaney's stolen musical notations?

They had no answers. So they focused on trying to decode the actual pages: Was it a code? Some kind of language? On one old envelope from L. Davis's Printing, which had gone out of business in 1921, tiny symbols spiraled down to what looked like a quiver of five arrows, one arrow more prominent than the others. "It's not just what you were telling me about annotations," Eboni said. "It's not just saying 'speed up' or 'slow down' or 'play this louder.' There's a whole language going on here."

"Maybe the Delaney people know more than they're letting on," Bern said. "Maybe we should ask them."

"That Mallory seems like the type to hold on to information and dangle little bits in front of you to keep you interested. Like how she wouldn't let you see the original pages." She stared at her monitor, where a page glowed enigmatically. "We need a real-life cryptographer. Know any?"

"Nope. Apart from Lomax Cuellar. And he's more of a linguist. What are you thinking?"

"A mathematician," Eboni said. "Maybe someone from the CIA? There's got to be an algorithm for this that would break it wide open. Let me ask around." And then, seeing Bern's expression, she grinned and told him, "Don't worry, Sherman. I ain't gonna broadcast it or mention your precious Foundation. Nobody will ever know."

She reached out to a cryptographer at MIT, but in the meantime she developed and ran programs, figuring out which Doodles appeared how many times in all the Delaney oeuvre. She scrutinized each symbol, each page. If Bern was sleeping three or four hours a night, he knew that she was sleeping even less. Her cornrows grew fuzzy with neglect, and he got used to seeing her in sweatpants.

He and Eboni were spending a lot of time together, and Bern really enjoyed it. The relationship was purely platonic, but he did learn that she didn't have a boyfriend. Not that he'd ever be applying for the position, he told himself quickly.

But there were times—splitting a sandwich at the conference table, pouring her a cup of coffee, opening her office door—when they'd catch each other's eye and a connection, bright and instant, would flame between them. Neither acted on it. Bern knew that she never would; and he was glad to avoid the complications that this would bring to their relationship. Despite how the Doodle mystery obsessed him, he still felt lonely here in the city. He had friends from Columbia but rarely saw them, and dating seemed too complicated right then. He tried not to think about it, however. RED, and the Doodles, absorbed him almost all the time anyway.

He spent every spare moment trying to figure out what had actually happened to Josephine Reed. Eboni did the same. When she got frustrated with the Doodles, she blew off steam by searching all the online databases she could find. Bern scanned the state census, which was performed every ten years, checking for misspellings and any variation of "Josephine" and "Reed"; reviewed obituaries for all the local papers. Many of New York City's records had been digitized and were searchable online, but other databases, especially older genealogical records, were still available only locally in hard copy, and others were on microfiche.

"We need a professional to do this. Let's hire a detective," he finally told Eboni after they'd exhausted all the online resources.

"Good idea," she said, clearly relieved. "Make sure they check hospital records, too. For births. Oh, and orphanages."

"You gotta get off the baby thing."

"I'm tellin' you," Eboni said. "There has got to be something going on with our girl Josie and Delaney. There's a secret baby somewhere. His career would've been wrecked if people found out that she had his baby. I say they did the deed in 1923, and she got pregnant. And he either sent her away, or sent the baby away, or both."

"And she stole his trunk to sell his music? To provide for the baby? I wish I understood the relationship between them."

Eboni thought for a moment, then said, "It's obvious. He had his secret Black family stashed somewhere. Maybe the baby died and she couldn't handle it, and she died, too."

"Okay, *Murder, She Wrote*, don't you think you're jumping to conclusions?"

"I'm just saying you should check hospital records," Eboni repeated. "And adoption records."

"She couldn't just disappear, could she?"

"I tell you, he had a secret love nest for her somewhere."

"Maybe," Bern said. "Or she could have left the city. Headed out west. Sailed around the world. Who knows."

"And never had any contact with any of her family again? I don't think so," Eboni said. "Women don't just leave their kids. Especially a Black woman with a mixed-race child in the 1920s."

"Would you stop it? There's no evidence of a baby."

"Mmm-hmm," she said, rolling her eyes dismissively. "Whatever. No baby. Sure." She pulled out one of Josephine's photos. "Look at this face. She's 1920s cute. No way he didn't hit that. And that means only one thing: a baby. Maybe more than one."

He shrugged. "You're probably right. A single woman, alone in the city, and they're sharing an apartment. Or at least in the same building. But that doesn't explain why she never talked to her family again. Or what that trunk was doing with her name on it."

Finally they hired a forensic detective to search every database throughout the five boroughs of New York City, tracking down crime reports, medical records, tax records, property records. Two weeks later the detective came back: 12,483 Black or mixed-race children had been born between 1918 and 1937 (Bern added nine months from Delaney's death, just in case). But what to do with that information? None listed a questionable Reed or Delaney in birth certificates. Josephine could have used a false name.

Similarly, 881 unnamed Black women died between December 1923 (the latest date they could find with a photograph of Reed) and 1937. Sometimes, mostly in the 1930s, the medical examiner had taken a photo of the deceased, but the photos—when there were photos— were usually blurry and the features difficult to decipher. In any case, the information in the files was scant and hard to make use of. Besides, who knew if Josephine Reed had even died? She could have moved away to Kansas or India for all they knew. They could find no record—of her life nor of her death—anywhere.

If they hadn't seen her face in the photographs, if they hadn't found her trunk, Bern and Eboni would have doubted that she'd even existed.

One morning he showed up at Eboni's office. She had arrived before him. The three large monitors that took up most of one wall were, as usual, filled with pages of Delaney Doodles.

She looked shaken.

"What?" he said. "What is it?"

"BOOM!" she told him, grinning from ear to ear. "Your girl did it. We 'bout to get paid!"

"Did what?"

She sighed dramatically, her eyes dancing. "So it turns out that there's a lot more to our girl Josephine than we thought. She was a genius, for one thing."

"What are you talking about? Would you please start making some sense?"

"What would you say if I told you that Josephine didn't steal Delaney's Doodles? She didn't follow him around like a puppy. She wasn't just his baby mama."

"What the hell are you getting at?" Bern kept studying the monitors, trying to figure out what she saw that he didn't. Two pages looked like typical full sheets of Doodles. The center one was a receipt from the Club Car Diner, where symbols and pictograms crept down the margins of a yellowed sheet memorializing that someone had bought a cup of coffee and a roast-beef sandwich for twenty-seven cents.

"They're hers," Eboni said. "I've confirmed that these Doodles are hers, not Delaney's. I bet this was a secret way for them to communicate. A code. A language."

"That's not possible. These are his. No question. Every scholar from here to Kandahar, including me, has gone over every Doodle ever discovered."

"Yeah, but they didn't have Miss Earlene's trunk, did they?" She pointed to her center monitor. "Look at the address. Look at the date." She zoomed in on the faded print.

The Club Car Diner
162 W. 66th Street
New York City
April 22, 1923

"Okay," he said. "So someone likes roast beef in springtime. I don't get it."

"Don't make me hurt you. Look at the date."

"So what? I don't see how—"

"I cross-checked Delaney's schedule. His appearances, his doctor's appointments, his premieres, and when he wiped his ass. Everything I could find." Eboni tapped a few keys and an old French newspaper appeared. "So. Check this out. On April twenty-first, 1923, Delaney was in Paris for the premiere of the *Essence of Silkwood* overture."

Bern knew the *Essence of Silkwood* almost by heart. He'd played the overture in high school. It was a staple musical number for most schools around the country.

"He checked into the Hotel de Charme on April nineteenth and checked out on April twenty-seventh," Eboni went on. "I have the hotel receipt. You want to see it? And in case you think he didn't actually go to Paris, there was a huge write-up about it. Here's *Le Figaro*'s archived paper for the same date." The monitor flashed to a French newspaper clip: *Le grand compositeur Frédéric Delaney arrive à Paris.* "He was actually hanging at the Eiffel Tower when, according to this, he was eating a roast-beef sandwich around the corner from his office."

Bern compared the dates, the clips, and again looked at the Doodle-covered receipt.

"You know what this means, right?" Eboni didn't give him time to reply. "She drew these. There's even a coffee stain on it. Unless this dude could be in two places at once, Josephine drew these."

"He could have just used the sheet of paper for later Doodles," Bern argued. "There's no guarantee that he did it simultaneously."

"Yeah sure, genius, except that there are two more examples," Eboni said. She showed him a scrap from a New York City newspaper dated March 10, 1923, and a theater ticket stub for March 12, 1923. On both dates, Frederic Delaney was in Boston.

"Okay," Bern said. "Maybe. So this is a language for them. He'd write, and I guess she'd make comments in their code, in the Doodles, on his manuscripts?"

And then he realized. It was so obvious. "No," he said slowly. "It's not just a language. They're writing music. Together. It's not just Delaney who was the great composer. It was both of them. Together.

Look at this one. And this." He pulled up scanned sheets—long examples of ciphers, one after the other, zigzagging across each of the pages. There were just too many to be simple comments. This was the music itself—probably with comments interspersed.

And then his mind leaped again to Josephine. "You're right," he told Eboni. "Maybe there is a baby. I know Frederic Delaney better than anybody else out there, and I'll tell you one thing: he had to be in love with her if he shared the earliest versions of his music."

Bern's mind was jumping ahead, forging connections before his mouth could catch up. It made sense: How else could Delaney have married so deeply the Black musical traditions with the European ones he'd been taught? How else could he have written so many compositions in his all-too-short life?

Because, of course, he didn't do it alone. Josephine added her own vision to the music. It was a collaboration. They weren't just lovers. They were musical partners.

Over the next weeks, the revelation would force Bern to reexamine all Delaney's works, trying to detect the echoes of two composers, and he couldn't: the music was seamless, entire, perfect in itself. No matter how the two had collaborated, the end result seemed impossibly inevitable.

He had to reexamine how he thought about Frederic Delaney. Bern owed his life to the composer. Delaney's Foundation had gotten him out of Milwaukee, kept him away from gangs. Delaney gave him purpose, a career, a connection with something greater than himself.

But it was more than this. It wasn't just the music: it was Bern's relationship with the man, Frederic Delaney. Bern had read every biography, had made a pilgrimage to Delaney's birthplace in Bloomington, had taken flowers several times to Delaney's grave out in Westchester. He'd tried to find similarities between Delaney and himself—they both were from the Midwest; Delaney liked mint chocolate chip ice cream, too; Delaney was five feet seven inches, and Bern was five feet ten, so that was only three inches taller—and so forth. He felt so damned grateful to Frederic Delaney for creating the Foundation, for creating that beautiful music; for being such a kind, incredible genius.

Late at night, especially late at night, in those dark hours before dawn, he'd lie awake in bed, sometimes with Delaney's music washing over him, and he'd try to imagine those last broken years of Frederic Delaney's life. All that beautiful, joyous music—the show tunes and the classical tunes and the jazz tunes and the operas and all the others—all of it, snuffed out, gone. Because critics were critical. Because audiences were fickle. Because somehow making all the music was no longer enough for Frederic—he needed the adulation, the respect. Why couldn't the music itself be its own reward? Possibly, Bern acknowledged, because the music really wasn't very good. And what must that have been like, to look back, at the ripe old age of thirty-seven, and realize your glory days were well and truly behind you, to stare into the next thirty or fifty years and realize you were already a has-been to be trotted out for awards ceremonies and retrospectives?

This mix of adulation, adoration, and pity had fueled Bern through high school, through grad school, through Jacques Simon's sometimes-abusive treatment and impossible demands as they'd worked through the Quintet.

And now it felt like all those emotions that had tied Bern to Frederic were suspect, even fraudulent.

Why hadn't Delaney acknowledged Josephine's contributions? Why had he tucked her away like an embarrassment, as if he were ashamed, or frightened, of her?

Bern's new vision of Delaney trembled like a champagne glass about to overflow, about to slosh over with emotions—anger, frustration, hurt—that Bern didn't know how to grapple with. And all this made everything even more confusing, and only made more urgent their quest to figure out what had happened to Josephine Reed.

Where had she gone? Why had she taken the trunk?

What had gone so horribly wrong between them? And was there a baby—some product of their musical collaboration—possibly still alive? Possibly writing their own music?

21

Sorting Out the Noise

Freddy

AFTER MR. DITMARS had decimated Freddy's music, the rest of the day passed as if Freddy were immersed in a dull roar, as if the world's sounds didn't quite penetrate. He plugged his music, one song after the other. He didn't flirt with the salesgirl. Just clunked from one song to the next, with "Bring Back the Moon" being by far the most requested. And with every thump of the piano he kept thinking, *He didn't like any of them. He really didn't like them.* The day went by slower than any other day Freddy could remember.

When he arrived back in the apartment, Josephine was already there, making dinner. Tonight was cabbage and corned beef. The cabbage smelled like rot.

Freddy slammed the door as he came in. "He didn't like them."

Josephine said, "Didn't like what?"

"Don't act like you don't know what I'm talking about," Freddy said. "He didn't like my songs."

Josephine stopped seasoning the cabbage, looked up. "Why didn't he like them? You said they were good."

"That fat sonofabitch wouldn't know real music if it slapped him over the head."

Josephine hunched over the saucepan, stared at her feet. "They're probably good songs. Ditmars was probably not listening to the heart of them."

"You're goddamn right he wasn't." Freddy threw his satchel on the floor. It slid under the armoire. "Goddamn it," he said, scrabbling, and in the process knocking into Josephine's bedroll. The blankets had been neatly folded, but his leg dislodged them, revealing a giant mouse's nest of scrap paper.

"Why do you always have so many papers everywhere? This place is a wreck. I didn't know I paid to live in a pigsty!"

Viciously, he kicked the papers. They scattered like autumn leaves in a bonfire. Josephine shrieked, dropped the skillet with the cabbage, which clattered wetly into the sink. She dove onto the papers, frantically trying to sweep them up.

Freddy, in the meantime, had picked up a handful of the sheets closest to him. His fury was abating; he felt embarrassed. "What is this? Is it English?"

From one side of the page to the other, each paper was a bewildering tight design of dots, lines, geometric shapes. Sometimes the lines seemed to be letters, but they could easily be just arrows or a pattern of dots. None of the papers resembled the other, except for one common denominator: on one corner of each of the papers, pressed firmly into the paper, were the initials *JoR*. He'd seen Josephine sign her letters to her family the same way.

Josephine was sweeping the papers together, tucking them under her blankets.

"Josephine? I'm sorry I yelled before. It was just a rough day. I'm sorry I knocked into your bed. But what is this?"

He didn't think she would answer, but her sweeping hands slowed.

A tear splatted loudly onto an errant sheet. She said in an unfamiliar voice, "This is my assignment. I'm supposed to do this. It lets me focus. Dr. Moore said it would help me focus."

"Doctor? What are you getting on about? I can't handle any more crazy today." The instant the words left his mouth, he realized he was being unnecessarily cruel.

"He said it would help me sort the noise," she said. "I don't like the noise."

"I'm sorry. I didn't mean—"

The words were tumbling out of her in almost a monotone, almost to herself: "Dr. Moore told me to write down the sounds and that it would help me. I'm always writing down the sounds. The ones I like hearing separate from the noise. The ones I want to hear, too. I don't like the noise. He told me I'm not crazy."

"Oh." Freddy leaned down, as if to pat her on the shoulder, then reconsidered. She hated to be touched, especially when she was like this. "I'm so sorry. I know you're not crazy. I think you're just swell. Please forgive me. It was a hard day. I didn't mean to take it out on you."

Josephine had finished organizing her papers. She laid one hand lightly upon them.

"I don't think you're crazy," he said again. "I was just upset." She didn't answer, so he asked, "Your doctor told you to draw when things get too loud?"

"Yes. I should separate the noise. Separate the noise and write down what I want to hear. He called it 'Transcribing.' I should Transcribe what I hear."

Freddy pulled his satchel from under the armoire, grabbed his notepad and a pencil. He sat next to her and began to scribble.

For a long while neither of them spoke. Then Josephine said, "What are you doing?"

"I'm trying this hotsy-totsy new thing to calm myself down. I saw a good friend of mine do it a few times. I hope you don't mind."

He could feel her watching as he drew lines and circles on the page. She moved restlessly, as if she wanted to speak, but stayed silent. Then, after ten minutes or so, she pulled out her pencil and a few sheets of her own. "You're doing it wrong. Look." She drew a series of intricate dashes. "See? This is the automobile outside, the way the tires go over the road. And here's someone walking past." He could hear the footsteps, faint, retreating. A door slammed and a man shouted; sure enough, another series of slanted lines and a curved fan shape appeared.

"You really write down what you hear?"

"Yes. Dr. Moore said this is how I can process everything around me."

"How do you know what to write?"

"It makes sense." Josephine kept drawing, the ciphers expanding across the page.

"And it's the same for music? You write the music down, too? Music you hear?"

"Of course," she said.

"Where?"

She rooted around in her heap of paper and handed him another page, also labeled with *JoR*. "This is what they played a couple weeks ago at the Black Cat. See? Here are the trombones doing an evolving bass line, and here are the clarinets with an ascending melody. These are the three trumpet parts. The wall is constantly in motion."

"Oh." The symbols danced in a bewildering mass, a barrier of intricate patterns, repeating and modifying and repeating again. A barrage of sound made visible. He glimpsed what everyday life was like for her. "It looks like you have a different symbol for each instrument or sound, right?"

"Yes. Sometimes the multiple sounds take longer to write down. But I can remember it."

"I see. What's this?" He pointed to a triangle with three lines slashing through it.

"That's a flute. The lines right here show that. When it's like this, the line is soaring. When it's like this, it descends. And this is sparrows outside fighting. This is a jackhammer. This is footsteps going upstairs; here's the creak in the staircase." On and on she went, showing him how she absorbed the world.

"Wow," Freddy said, lost.

She showed him how her placement of each symbol potentially corresponded with musical notation. Josephine set the paper with the triangles on the piano and began to play, and after a few measures he recognized the tune.

The piano fell silent. Josephine was staring down at her fingers, resting on the keys. "Freddy?" she said.

"Yes?"

"Do you really think I'm crazy?"

"Hey," he said. He touched one of Josephine's hands, immediately drew away. "I think you're a lot of things, Josephine Reed. Crazy is certainly not one of them."

She looked up at him, met his eyes—something she rarely did—then began playing the jazz piece again.

Over the course of the next few weeks, she shared more about her pages. She heard thousands of sounds daily, and when they overwhelmed her she'd record them on her sheets. He couldn't believe she could keep them all straight. For instance, Old Man Jones on the second floor, arguing with Mrs. Overberg: not their words but their tones and the echoes of their voices, from banging on the door to stomping on the stairs to yelling to the slam of a door—her code memorialized the story. These jagged lines represented Old Man Jones; Mrs. Overberg was this curved line with a straight line coming out of the bottom of the curve.

He imagined a typical city street, the constant and unending onslaught of cacophony, all finding its way onto these pages. His head swam. How could Josephine do this?

One night they went to the Ivy Lounge to hear a combo from Detroit. For the first time in public in front of him, Josephine pulled her pencil and paper out of her handbag. The large sixteen-piece combo played mainly upbeat ragtime, every now and then tossing in another familiar tune that was currently popular, but their energy and enthusiasm were infectious.

When Freddy leaned over to watch the symbols unspool onto the paper, Josephine immediately and instinctively pulled them back out of his view, but he could actually see her reconsider. The paper remained on the table between them. In the middle of an alto sax solo, Josephine said, "See how his sepia rows align with the drummer's belt stop?"

He nodded, mystified.

By the end of the three-hour set, she'd packed four sheets, and didn't pause when the set drew to an end. The crowd was rowdy, the hooch was flowing, and Josephine's transcribing shifted from the rhythmic patterns to more erratic slashes and circles. He gathered she was encoding their laughter, the timbre of the voices. The symbols blurred into reality, almost too quickly for him to track before she was on to the next one. "Hey," he said at last. "You ready to go home? This crowd doesn't seem to be settling down."

Josephine, still scribbling, nodded and stopped long enough to gather her papers. Outside, she said, "The bowl contained more radiance than I've seen for a while."

"That was a radiant group. Just swell. They knew their stuff. Those Detroit guys didn't miss a beat."

"Freddy." Josephine leaned in closer to him, much closer than she normally did. "I like it here. So many sounds and not too much noise."

"I'm very glad you do," he told her.

There was a moment when they looked at each other. Freddy held his breath, wanting.

Then the sound of a door slamming down the street made Josephine's eyes jump away from his, and the moment passed.

22

Hold Up, Slick

Bern

"OF COURSE we're going to tell them," Bern said, assuming Eboni would agree.

They were in Bern's loaner apartment, a couple of blocks from the Foundation. Delaney's "Ravenswalk" was twittering on the speakers, the oboe line so delicate.

Eboni had a breakfast meeting in Midtown, and told him she wanted to go over some things with him, and that it would be helpful if he stayed at the apartment and waited for her. He'd agreed.

The Foundation had provided the apartment for him. It looked like a decorator had backed up a van to the closest Restoration Hardware store and went crazy: an oversize cream-colored leather sofa sat in front of a gargantuan beige wooden coffee table, across from taupe armchairs. It was all very comfortable, very crowded, and very bland. Bern spent as little time there as possible.

"Uh, actually, no. Are you even thinking?" Eboni was deep into her laptop, barely paying attention to Bern, who kept pacing around the apartment, peering out the windows without seeing the traffic puttering up and down Broadway.

He hadn't been sleeping much; he'd been focused on the implications of Josephine Reed in Delaney's life. "Yeah, I'm thinking. Do you know how big this is? There's probably another Delaney out there. Maybe a whole family. Musical geniuses, possibly, with two parents like them. Do you know what that means?"

"Uh, yeah. It means that they'd have to split their money again." She typed a few keys, flashed to another screen, typed again.

Bern was too wound up to see what she was doing. "I don't think you get it," Bern said. "Frederic Delaney was a genius. A genius. A one of-a-kind-like-Einstein genius. Like da Vinci. Like Mozart. If there really was a child, and the child was musical—if there's a whole family of musicians out there, maybe writing music, never getting the recognition they deserved—"

"What did your detective say?"

"That's just it," Bern said. "He hasn't found anything. But he's just one guy. If we could put the Foundation's muscle behind this, if we could have *them* tracking down Josephine and the baby—"

"Hold up, slick," Eboni said. "Do you know what would happen if we told them? Think about it. Once Mallory finds out that her precious great-grand-cousin or whatever he is got a lot of help from his Black baby mama, you really think she's going to just sit down and do an interview with ABC News about how happy she is? The Foundation probably won't even help us find Josephine. They'll probably try to bury it. And us."

Bern rolled his eyes. "Bury it? This is the biggest discovery, ever, about Frederic Delaney. We all thought he was a loner. Maybe gay. Unable to have real relationships. I've gone through all the research, and all the scholars agree on that much. Now we find out this isn't true. Now we know he had someone in his life. Someone to collaborate with, even." He paused a moment. He'd woken up thinking about this in the middle of the night, and he hadn't been able to fall back asleep. "Maybe she was the reason he killed himself. Or maybe he didn't actually kill himself—maybe something went wrong between them and she killed him."

"What is this," Eboni asked, looking up and then back down at the monitor, "*Days of Our Lives*? This ain't no soap opera. Let's just stick to what we can solve today. Your detective guy can keep hunting down Josephine, in the meantime."

"But this changes everything," Bern said. "Everything everyone knows about Delaney. His life and maybe his death."

"You're damn right it does. That's why we need to keep this to ourselves. Until we know what's what."

Bern stood up, went over to the kitchen for a glass of water. "You want one?"

"Sure," she said. "No ice."

"The thing is," he said, reaching into the refrigerator, "this is global-level stuff."

Eboni sighed, leaned back on the couch. "All right, let me stop you right there. Who's in control of the Delaney Foundation?"

"Mallory and Kurt Delaney."

"If we do tell the Foundation that there's the possibility that Frederic had a direct descendant, this could mean there's a potential power shift. It's all about their image. About their control. I wonder what the original Foundation documents say about who controls the Foundation. Who gets the Delaney fortune. Maybe it should be Josephine's kid. Or kids. In any case, you can't go to the Foundation yet. It's way too risky."

"But what if there's music—more music that Delaney created? What if Josephine has more music that the world has never seen?" He wanted to explain to her that it all went back to the music itself—pure, vibrating, able to reach people in ways that words or actions couldn't. No matter who'd written it, no matter the circumstances nor the languages, the music itself transcended all.

He returned to the couch, handed her a glass, set his down on the coffee table. The ice in his glass chimed faintly.

She drank hers down in two gulps. "What we can't do is say anything to anyone. Look. I know you get a hard-on for Delaney but now we pretty much know that everything about him is suspect. Now, as much as that means to you, imagine if you had more to lose than just credibility. More than prestige. It's their bankroll, remember? That's what we are potentially dealing with: how the Delaney Foundation makes its fortune. Do you really think these stuck-up white people are going to let somebody like us destroy all that?"

"I know what you're thinking, but it's the Delaney Foundation. Mallory—"

"Don't be naive. You can't trust her. She sure doesn't trust you."

Bern stood up again, paced to the window, which looked onto another building, most of the shades drawn against prying eyes. "Okay, but this is bigger than her. Bigger than the Foundation. This is what I've dedicated my life to. Hundreds, maybe even thousands, of us have. Think of all the DF Kids. Think what a charge it will be for little Brown and Black kids to know that someone who looks like them maybe contributed to some of Delaney's music. I can't just let all that go."

"Good idea. We run to Mallory and say, 'We discovered that you actually have a half-Black cousin and now you gotta share your money with them.' I can see that going over real well."

"I think you're wrong. The Delaney Foundation has done so much for the world—"

"Which is exactly why we can't tell them. Rich people stay rich by hanging on to their money. I know how much Delaney means to you. You've got to use your head and not follow your heart on this one. Please trust me on this." She typed a few more keys, double-checked something on the screen, and said, "Check it out."

She shifted her monitor around so he could get a better view. It was a spreadsheet. In the left column she listed what seemed like random place names, with an address. The next column clarified it: these were all places mentioned in Earlene's trunk. Out of twenty-three rows, four were highlighted in yellow. Two were green.

"What's this a list of? All the physical locations from the Doodles?" he asked.

"It's more than that," Eboni said. "It's anywhere that we know Josephine has been. So I included references to all the photos, as well."

"The Alibi Club," he said. "What are the highlighted rows?"

"The yellow means that the building seems to still be there. It wasn't torn down or turned into a skyscraper. The coffee shop where they had the roast beef is a Citibank now. The ones highlighted in green are private apartments and will be harder to get into. So I thought we could start with the yellow ones. Except the Delaney town house—we should be able to talk our way into that. You can just flash your badge."

"Got it." He studied the chart for a few minutes. "So what's the point of this? You think she carved her name on a table or in a bathroom stall?"

She stared at him, unblinking. "Don't be a dumdum," she said. "I'm wondering if one of these places might be a way into her code. Maybe some architectural detail or the layout of a room or something inspired her, and we can use that to decode some of the symbols. If I can get a place to start, I bet I can figure it out. We need an end of a thread. We tug the thread and boom, everything unravels."

"A lot of the Doodles do look like art deco," Bern said thoughtfully. "That's the angle that the Foundation was pursuing, too, talking to people at the Met."

"Well, the people at the Met don't have any of our Earlene pages," she said. "So we have a lot more options than they do. Come on, get your coat. Let's check them out."

"Now? I'm—"

"Yeah, now," she said, standing and heading around to the door. "You coming? It's cold out, so be sure you have your gloves." Her boots were black leather with heels. She pulled on her faux leopard-skin coat, which hung almost to her ankles, with a faux leopard-skin hat and gloves to match.

Bern was wearing an ironed double-creased white oxford shirt and crisp khakis. He guessed he could put on a blazer under his woolen coat. "Why don't we go tonight? I'm really trying to get through act two here."

"We need to go when they're open," she said patiently. "They might not be open at night. I googled them all—see the column on the end?—and got their hours. Let's go. You can work on act two tonight."

Five minutes later they were hailing a cab.

Of the four yellow highlighted options, they decided to start off near the Empire State Building, at the B. Altman & Company building. A department store back in Delaney's day, the white limestone structure loomed over an entire city block, and now housed the CUNY Graduate Center and several other businesses. Eboni had already printed out copies of the Doodle pages that had appeared on the Altman's stationery, with blowups of the Doodles. Once they got inside, they wandered the halls that they could access—Eboni somehow managing to talk her way past the university's security guards—holding up the sheet and on the lookout for architectural details that somehow would seem relevant.

They could find nothing. The building had been totally gutted and remodeled. Any telling design or symbol was now concealed behind drywall, dropped ceilings, and recessed lighting. A few stairwells seemed of the period, but Bern and Eboni couldn't see any connection to the Doodles.

They took the subway up to the second site: 244 West Sixty-Third Street, the original address of Delaney Music Publishing, Inc. The Delaney Foundation still owned the building, so it seemed highly probable that the Foundation had already examined every square inch, but the Foundation didn't have all the Doodles that they had, so they rode the subway with excitement and anticipation. Eboni kept leaning into Bern, playfully punched his shoulder a couple of times. If he didn't know better, he would've thought she might be flirting with him, just a little.

"I tried for years to get into this place," Bern told her as he climbed the steps two at a time from the subway station. "It's always locked up. I even asked Jacques to get me in. No dice. I sure hope this badge is the ultimate backstage pass." He fingered the Delaney Foundation employee badge that he'd gotten on his first day working on *RED*.

"Why'd you want to get in so bad?"

He looked at her like she'd grown three heads. "What do you mean, why'd I want to get in so bad? Because this was where it all started," he told her. "Frederic Delaney bought the entire building. Rented it first in 1920, purchased it outright in 1927. This was where he composed some of his best-loved pieces—*Quicksilver*, at least three of the Quintet, and so many other things. I just wanted to get in and see it. Walk where his feet walked. Put my hand on the doorknobs that he'd touched."

"Pee in the same toilet, huh?" Eboni said.

"Yeah, if I'm lucky," he said. "Absolutely."

"You're such a Delaney dork," Eboni said, and then they turned the corner. Half a block down, they realized that the Delaney town house, a modest five-story dark brick building, was under renovation. Scaffolding shrouded it. Workmen in neon yellow vests were unloading metal studs and structural supports from a truck that blocked most of the street.

"Don't tell them you work for the Foundation," Eboni said suddenly, putting her hand on his coat sleeve to stop him.

"Huh? Why not? That's how we're going to get in."

"Wouldn't they call over to the Foundation before they let you in? Your friend Mallory might hear about it."

They stared at each other. Bern said, "At least now it's open."

"Maybe we can talk our way inside," Eboni said.

He grinned wickedly at her. "Maybe we can," he said and, without hesitating, he sauntered up to a guy who was either supervising or standing there smoking, or both. "Hey man," Bern said. "Wassup? Check this out." Bern wished he were wearing threadbare jeans instead of freshly ironed khakis, but the guy was looking at Eboni more than at him, anyway. Bern couldn't blame him. He went on, "Me and my shorty used to live here back in the day. Fifth floor."

The man didn't seem too interested. He sucked deep on his cigarette, stared at the glowing end. "Oh yeah?"

"Yeah. I know it's weird, and I ain't trying to get you in trouble or anything, but would it be cool if we went in to look at the place one more time?"

"No can do," the guy said. "Construction going on. If you get hit by falling debris or step on a nail, it's my ass. Company policy."

"C'mon, man," Eboni said, sliding close. "Just for a minute. We're about to move to Connecticut. We ain't gonna be hanging out in the city too much more. We just wanted to see it one more time."

"How about if I give you fifty bucks and you never saw us go in? Right? Easy money." Bern retrieved his wallet and pulled out two twenties and a ten.

The workman looked around. "A hundred."

"Dude, you're killin' me," Bern said.

"Baby, just give it to him. I want to see it one more time," Eboni chimed in, hanging on Bern's arm.

"Here you go. We straight?" Bern handed the workman five twenties. He hoped he wouldn't have to bribe anybody else today—he had only seventeen dollars left in his wallet.

The man pocketed the money. "There are some hard hats right inside. Be sure to put one on. And no more than fifteen minutes, got it?"

Bern and Eboni slipped past him, up the short walkway, and into the building and stuck on the hard hats. To avoid the workmen hauling in the metal studs, they ducked into a room on the left. Even inside, the cold was brutal. Hammering, sawing, and drilling rang out above them.

"This is it," Bern breathed. "This is where most of the Quintet was created. Maybe all of the Quintet."

"Settle down, sweetie." She smirked. "I didn't bring you an extra pair of underwear. Let's get to work. Look for any Doodles. Especially ones from the early pages. Like the three triangles."

"And the overlapping squares with the arrows," Bern said.

They hadn't found any specific Doodle page that clearly was written in the town house—his stationery or something else that clearly referenced the place. But because Delaney—and, apparently, Josephine—had been there for years, any or all of the Doodle pages might have come from it.

Eboni and Bern walked carefully around the first room, looking at molding and paneling, many with art deco squares and patterns on them. Some designs remained, but many were thickly painted. Bern couldn't tell how original the symbols actually were. They examined the other rooms on the main floor, too, picking their way around the construction equipment. Nothing.

Back on the main level, at the end of the hall, a beat-up wooden staircase wrapped around a single tiny elevator. They decided to start at the top floor and work their way down, floor by floor.

Eboni pushed the elevator button and waited. Nothing happened. She tried again.

"It ain't workin'," said a skinny Latino guy whose beard was struggling, and failing, to come in. He carried two five-gallon buckets that looked very heavy as he started up the stairs. The wooden treads squeaked and coughed under his weight. "Hasn't worked for months. You another one of them Foundation people?"

"Us?" Eboni asked. "No. Not us."

"Oh," the man said. "Damn. I hoped you were going to get it working again. We sure would like to use it." He headed up.

"Shit," Eboni said, looking after him. "Now I gotta walk up them stairs?"

"Looks like it, princess," Bern said. "Watch your crown." They took the stairs up to the second floor, went along each wall, searching for anything that would seem evocative of a Doodle. They ducked into bathrooms and peered into closets. No luck. None of the original wooden paneling—if the building had had wooden paneling—remained; it was all drywall, and looked like the place had been extensively remodeled in the sixties. They repeated the search on the three lower floors, much of which had been utterly gutted with only metal studs separating the rooms. They found nothing. None of the workmen challenged them.

After an examination of the dusty, low-ceilinged basement, they made their way outside.

Bern said, "Well, that was a wasted hundred bucks."

"Oh, it's gonna cost you more than a hundred bucks to buy me another coat. Do you know how much this Donna Karan was?" Eboni said, trying to dust herself off.

"No, but I'm sure you'll tell me to get it from Delaney, right?" Bern rolled his eyes. "Detective work is dirty work."

"Whatever. Just get me a new one, and I mean from Donna herself, not Marshalls."

Outside, they passed the hundred-dollar workman. Bern said, "'Preciate you, bro," as they headed out to the street.

"Okay, I admit I'm impressed," Eboni said as Bern was putting the address into the Uber app for the location of the old Alibi Club, which would be opening shortly.

"Impressed with what?"

"You still got a bit of swag left. I thought Delaney may have sucked it out of you."

Bern grunted. "The Alibi is called Silvergate now."

"Good that it's still a nightclub. Maybe they have some memorabilia of the good old days." Eboni moved closer to Bern.

His phone pinged. Their Uber was a minute away.

Silvergate seemed very New York, very modern. They were the only patrons in the place: a narrow bar, a small room with a handful of tables, and a tiny stage in the back. Mirrors took up one wall. The reflected black legs of the chairs made a bewildering forest pattern.

A server approached Bern. "Can I help you with something, sir?"

"Oh no. No, thank you," he said. Eboni had disappeared into the ladies' room, searching for Doodles. She returned a moment later shaking her head.

As Bern was about to enter the men's room, she asked, "Why would Josephine go into the men's room?"

"I don't think she would. I just have to pee," Bern said.

When he came out of the bathroom, she met him on the main floor. "Find anything?"

"Just a brand-new unnamed disease," Bern said. Eboni laughed.

They talked with management and found out the building had been remodeled dozens of times since the '20s. No memorabilia remained. None of the original fixtures remained. The Alibi Club had no alibis left.

The fourth and final place, formerly Hattie's Club, was under new management. New management had turned it into a hair salon. One lonely stylist was very disappointed that neither Bern nor Eboni needed a new do. Bern and Eboni were disappointed that, in the '80s, the entire space had been gut-renovated to the original brick. Not even an old door or a window molding was left.

"Well," Bern said, back outside, "that was a bust."

"Yeah, but you got to spend the afternoon with me. You're welcome," Eboni told him.

"You're picking up the tab for the pizza," he said. "There's a place I've been wanting to try down by the public library. Supposed to be one of the best in Manhattan."

"If it's so good how come I haven't heard about it?"

"Well, I guess I've upped *the* Eboni Michelle Washington on a pizza place. Somebody write this down."

"It probably won't be that good," Eboni said.

But the three-dollar slice was that good.

"Remember when they were a dollar?" Eboni said.

"You're showing your age."

"Where're your manners? You never say that to a lady."

The crust was crispy and chewy, with bubbled and charred places from the wood-burning stove; the sauce tangy and rich and not too sweet. Just the right amount of fresh mozzarella oozed over it but didn't detract from the other flavors. They also tried a cheeseless slice—Bern was very dubious—that was absolutely delicious.

"Well, thanks to me this day wasn't a bust after all," Bern said.

Eboni rolled her eyes. "Okay, so you got one."

23

A Thousand or a Dozen Songs
I Want to Hear

Freddy

EVERY NIGHT JOSEPHINE and Freddy would hit the mixed-race clubs and dance halls. Now, everywhere they went, Josephine would pull out her papers, scribble and listen and draw.

Every day they went to work separately, and although Freddy continued to be nervous about Josephine having another breakdown, nothing of the sort occurred: having her papers nearby seemed to make it possible for her to cope in whatever situation she found herself. He heard Ditmars call her Josie a couple of times, and she and Eunice ate their sandwiches together almost every day.

One night in early October, Freddy was positively giddy after playing his final set at the Alibi Club. He wanted to ask Josephine what she thought, since she was responsible for his new playing style. They walked along companionably, Josephine silent, both of them drinking in the late night. Josephine said nothing about his music: she just said that the band had sounded "grape" and "surging," whatever that meant.

Down into the subway. Nothing from her. Waiting for the subway train to arrive. The ride downtown. Nothing.

Back in the apartment, Josephine went straight to the piano and, with damper pedal down, started in on some of the combo's riffs, then segued into other songs she'd heard that day.

He was desperate for her opinion of him as a musician, but he wanted her to bring it up first, compliment him rather than him fishing for praise. The urge to ask gnawed at him.

He tried again. "Yep, that was a great set tonight. Bobby's new tune was just swell, don't you think?"

Josephine nodded, fingers roving the keyboard.

"Man, oh man, those torrents were white-hot tonight, huh?"

"Yes. You played like a torrent. The best torrent."

His chest expanded under her praise, and he was about to say *Aw, shucks, thanks* or something self-deprecating, but Josephine went on, "It was shameful that Bobby didn't bring in the swirling tabs."

He knew better than to try to figure out what Josephine meant, but he was glowing from her appreciation and wanted it to continue. "I'm guessing you didn't like Bobby's new tune? I thought it was swell."

"It was fine. It missed the swirling tabs, but otherwise, it was fine."

"What do you mean by 'swirling tabs'?"

Josephine motioned for Freddy to sit next to her. She played Bobby's tune exactly. "This is what Bobby did," she said. "He missed all the swirling tabs. Here's where he should have let go."

"Hold on, hold on. Now, I know Bobby ain't the greatest composer in the world, but I think he put together a swell tune. I felt like I was in Brazil." The piece utilized habanera rhythms and a repeated six-bar melody. The bass line, combined with the percussion and the light, skipping piano riffs, brought the melody to life.

"I did like it," she said. "I loved listening to you. You played like the white torrent and you didn't fight the knobs."

That was all he needed to hear. "Thanks," he said. "When the melody came in again, I doubled it in octaves, did you notice? Beefed it up. Bobby never saw it coming! I thought about extending the tune by another six bars. Really catchy. But I wasn't sure if the fellas could keep up with me. C-sharp minor isn't an easy key for Red to play in. Way too many sharps."

Freddy's voice trailed off, because Josephine's hands had shifted into something different—she'd started with Bobby's tune but then she'd inverted the melody, leaving only the first two notes intact. Her left hand danced into a virtuoso rhythm, something that felt reminiscent of Beethoven but still had a habanera feel: a pulsing exotic thrum that immediately set his foot tapping.

"The tabs begin to swirl here in this section. Can you feel their pull?"

"How are you doing this?" he asked.

She shrugged, the music building under her fingertips.

"Did you write any of this down? On your sheets?"

She shrugged again.

"Did you?"

"Yes, of course. He could have used his swirling tab if he had done this." She extended the melody and inverted it, synthesized it, utterly transformed it. Because he knew what he was listening for, Freddy could still hear echoes of Bobby's original tune, but he suspected that nobody else—including Bobby—would be able to. Her fingers ran ferociously across the keys.

"I've never heard anything like this. It's—it's—I don't know what it is. It's incredible. Did you write this one down, too?" He didn't wait for an answer, shuffling through the pile of papers that Josephine had set near her bedroll. "This one. Is it this one?" He pulled a sheet out randomly.

"No, of course not. That was the subway ride yesterday morning." Josephine stopped playing, opened her handbag, flipped through her pages, and handed one to him. The ever-present JoR stood out stark in the corner. "It's this one. It has the tab that should have been swirling."

This page, like the others, was a bewildering design of curved and straight lines, geometric shapes, dots, and dashes.

"Play it again, will you?" he said, staring at the paper as if he were hoping it would light up and explain itself.

She played the song again.

"This is an amazing thing you've done. I can't believe you did this from hearing it once. This is a brand-new song, you know that? Another brand-new song, like 'Bring Back the Moon.'"

Josephine yawned, got up from the piano bench, gathered her toiletries.

"You have more of these?" he asked her.

"More of what?"

"More new songs. Not just the ones you hear. New songs."

"The songs I want to hear, you mean."

"Yes," he said. "The songs you want to hear."

"Yes, of course."

"You do? How many do you have? New songs? Just these here?"

"I don't know," she said, looking uncomfortable. "You know that I don't like numbers." One hand was on the doorknob, the other clutched toothbrush and toothpaste.

"Wait! How many more like this do you have?" He brandished the paper.

She looked back at him, blank-faced. "Probably a thousand. Or two hundred. Or maybe a dozen."

"You have a thousand new songs?"

She shrugged. "Or a dozen. I don't really count. I'm going to the bathroom, okay?" She peered out. Apparently no one was in sight so she crept out, down the hall.

While she was gone, he paced the studio. Then, too impatient to wait, he unearthed the papers from beneath and behind her bedroll, pawing through the sheets as if one would suddenly be illuminated and comprehensible.

Which is where she found him when she returned.

"What are you doing?" she said from the doorway, lunging toward him.

He stood up, clutching a handful of papers as if to ward her off. "Josephine," he said steadily, "how many new songs do you think you have right here?"

"At least twenty," she said. "Maybe forty. I don't really count."

In some places the drift of pages was easily an inch or more thick. She had thousands of pages—wrinkled, creased, folded, flattened— piled and wedged into every conceivable space imaginable.

"Oh my gosh," he said. "You have all this? There must be hundreds of— Is this all of them?" Freddy flipped through the pages.

"Yes," Josephine said, "besides the ones in my trunk."

He stopped, stared up at her, mouth open. "Your trunk? What trunk? What are you—"

"The one I left in the Pennsylvania Station," she told him patiently. "I didn't have the money to get it out. And then after Howard left I didn't know what to do with it."

"Why didn't you ever mention it before?"

"You never asked."

"Wha—what was I going to ask? If you had random luggage stuffed with your scribbles hidden around the city?"

She shrugged.

"Could we get your trunk? Could I see those sheets? The ones in the trunk?"

"It's probably not open now," she said. "And we have to be at Ditmars in a few hours."

Still he sat on his knees, staring down at her pages. "We can pick your trunk up from Penn Station after work. You should've told me about it. I would've gotten it for you."

She leaned down, kissed him lightly on the cheek. "You were wonderful tonight," she said. He looked up and his eyes met hers. The electricity jumped between them. She'd never kissed him before.

He was eight years younger than she was. Would that matter?

Probably not. Definitely not. He got to his feet, looked away. "You know something? You're pretty swell yourself." He backed away from her papers and her bedroll, busied himself getting his own toiletries for the bathroom.

When he returned, Josephine was already curled on her pallet, hair barely visible under the blankets, facing away from him.

He crept into his own bed, turned out the bedside lamp.

But sleep eluded him. How many songs—new songs, like "Bring Back the Moon"—were encoded in the pages that Josephine slept on, like a dragon on its treasure trove? And how many more were in this trunk? How big was the trunk? How many pages could a trunk hold? Ten thousand? A million?

And then there was that song she'd played tonight. Bobby's song. No, not Bobby's song—it was Josephine's now. She'd transformed it, made it her own. He would need her to play it again to transcribe it properly. Would Bobby want credit? Would Bobby even recognize his own song? Of course, if Freddy wrote great lyrics to accompany the song, then really it was more Freddy's song than Bobby's or Josephine's.

Plus there were all those songs in that trunk.

"Boss! I've done it!" A week later, Freddy bounded past Eunice's desk and up the stairs. He took them two at a time, waving the sheets of foolscap at Ditmars, who glowered at him from under heavy eyebrows. "You gotta hear these," Freddy said. "I wrote you four new songs. Four! They're all winners!"

"All four of them?" Ditmars turned back to the ledger open in front of him. "Get outta here. We've done this dance already. Come get your assignments."

"Boss, I'm telling ya, these are hits. I know you weren't too keen last time, but—"

Ditmars cut him off, even taking the cigar out of his mouth as if to be absolutely clear. "Delaney, get to work. Quit wasting everyone's time. Go pick up your assignments and get going."

Freddy stood in the hall, dazed. A couple of other fellows snickered, and Calvin Broadwell elbowed him in the ribs as he slipped past to get his assignment. Miles Turpin and Josh Roberts headed into practice rooms. Freddy couldn't believe that Ditmars had blown him off. These new songs were great.

Last Friday, he and Josephine had picked up the trunk from Penn Station. It had been an ordeal, utterly buried in the very back of the left-luggage office. The clerk—a scrawny, pockmarked young man who barely spoke English—had told them originally that it wasn't there, but Freddy wouldn't take no for an answer and made the clerk check again—and again. Finally he returned with a large beat-up steamer trunk in tow. Stripes of thick dust marked its surface.

"That's it," Josephine said, and the trunk slid beneath the counter and into Freddy's outstretched hands.

"Do you have a key?" he asked Josephine as he wrestled it out of the baggage room. It was very heavy. Josephine searched in her reticule, handed him a small golden key. He opened the lock, lifted the lid. It was filled to the very top with paper: napkins, envelopes, notepads, and anything else that would be suitable to hold Josephine's characteristic blur of ciphers. He closed the lid quickly, as if worried that someone else would rush in and grab a crumpled handful.

Back at the apartment—to take them uptown he'd had to hire another cab and pay another day's worth of wages—he dived into the trunk, handing Josephine one sheet after another.

"What's this?" he'd say, and she'd tell him it was the sound of cows back in North Carolina, or her siblings arguing, or her mother complaining, or the choir concert she'd heard when she was fifteen, or her sisters practicing piano. But every once in a while—maybe every dozen pages or so—there'd be a melody, something she "wished she heard," and he'd put that sheet into a different pile. After several hours they'd made only a small dent in the sea of paper but had forty-odd pages set aside. Plus, of course, there was all the paper underneath her bed, which Freddy had only begun culling through. His head swam.

He'd had Josephine play each of the forty-three new melodies to determine which felt the most vibrant and exciting. As a song plugger, his job was to tap into popular taste, to anticipate what kind of music his patrons wanted to hear, so this skill now stood him in good stead. All the songs were terrific, but he chose four that he thought were particularly compelling to transcribe and overlay with lyrics.

Now, at Ditmars & Ross, he marched into an empty practice room, sat down at the piano, and started off with "Walk a Mile for Your Smile." It was a bouncy, effervescent tune that should have been a rag but wasn't, should have been jazz but wasn't; it had an irrepressible beat and a melody that got stuck in your head the first time you heard it. Freddy played the whole song through, then played it through again.

You got it too
Always you
I'm headin up that aisle
I'd walk a mile
For your smile

Song pluggers, composers, and music publishers were nosy by nature, attuned to listening, always on the alert for something fresh. New songs popped out daily from music publishers, but all the songs had a commonality: ragtime songs sounded similar; the ballads all had a kinship; you knew one coon song because it resembled the one you'd played for two weeks at Altman's, three months ago. So when a new song—one that actually felt new—floated into the air, Freddy's colleagues paid attention.

First it was Josh Roberts, poking his head in, coming inside, standing over Freddy as he played. Then Chuck Keats slipped in, leaned against the wall. Miles Turpin appeared a few minutes later, joined Chuck and, after a minute, leaned into the hall. "Hey," he called, "Calvin, get in here." One by one, Freddy's coworkers peeked in, and stayed, and listened.

"Gee, that's a swell tune. What is it?"

"Whatcha playin' there, Freddy?"

He played "Walk a Mile for Your Smile" four times running, singing his heart out, and then, without missing a beat, switched it out for "Carnation Celebration," another upbeat song that had echoes of a John Philip Sousa march, but this tune combined a Texas two-step feel with the legato melody soaring above the strict rhythm. After a few rounds he started in on the lyrical "Let the Rain Come":

The wind blows from the West
And she has left me here
With one final request
Let the rain come, let the rain come, let it come

He was watching the doorway as he sang, so immediately caught sight of Ditmars behind Chuck Keats. Freddy switched into the final tune, the mid-tempo "Careful What You Give Away," which was an amalgamation of Latin rhythms mixed with a sultry soulful work song. The combination was imaginative and seemed unlikely, but worked like a dream—a clear, original take on all these disparate music styles. He reached the last note, and the little room echoed with applause. Applause wasn't really something that happened in the halls of a music publisher, but these songs were so infectious, so full of life, so absolutely fresh and charming, what else was there to do? His colleagues patted him on the back and shoulders. Miles Turpin shook his hand, saying, "You have gold there, pal." He bent down to whisper, "Don't give it away."

Freddy met his eye, nodded. He had no intention of giving any-thing away.

In the meantime, Ditmars was yelling, "All right, break it up. Eunice has the uptown assignments. The rest are on my desk. Let's get to work, fellas. These songs ain't gonna sell themselves."

Freddy joined the exodus.

"Delaney, where are you going?" Ditmars asked him.

"Just going to get my assignments for today. From Eunice."

"Hold on a minute. Those were some swell tunes you played there."

"Oh? You liked 'em, after all?"

"Who wrote 'em?"

He hesitated. Should he tell Ditmars about Josephine's involve-ment? If he did, wouldn't Ditmars be less enthusiastic? Of course he would. Coloreds weren't like regular people. And Freddy'd still pay Josephine, of course. He was looking out for her. This was better for all of them. "Those are all mine. Remember? I tried to show them to you, but you thought it was all baloney."

"Yeah, yeah, well, I'll give you fifty bucks. There's four, right?" Dit-mars shifted his cigar to the other side of his mouth.

Freddy Delaney wasn't going to be your average song plugger any-more. He was going places. Freddy Delaney had four songs in his hand and another thirty-nine back in his apartment, and another who-knew-how-many-more still waiting patiently for the sunlight and the piano to bring them to life.

"Why don't we discuss this over coffee?" Freddy said, and then yelled down the stairs, "Eunice? Could you bring us two cups of cof-fee? One for me and one for Mr. Ditmars."

The cigar almost fell out of Ditmars's mouth.

Freddy led the way to Ditmars's office, made a production of sit-ting in one of the guest chairs. "How much are you offering?" he asked as Ditmars made his own way around the desk. "Let's make it a real offer, waddya say?"

"Twelve dollars and fifty cents each. Fifty bucks total," Ditmars said. "That's more than I paid you for 'Take Back the Moon.' Take it or leave it."

"I was thinking more like forty bucks each. Plus royalties. A dollar for each sheet. And it's '*Bring* Back the Moon.' Not *Take*."

Ditmars rolled the cigar from one side of his mouth to the other, then pulled it out, stared at it like it offended him, stuck it in the ashtray. "You want what? Forty dollars per song? And royalties?"

"How much did you make on 'Bring Back the Moon'?"

"Are you out of your cotton-picking mind? It's a little early to be hittin' the sauce, don't you think? I'd never pay forty bucks for a song. Never."

Freddy swallowed. "These are hits, every one of 'em. You paid Miles twenty bucks for 'You're My Lovey Mine' and that wasn't a tenth of how good these are. Forty bucks each is fair. We both know you're going to make loads more off them. This is actually a great opportunity for you, you know that?" Freddy was surprised at himself for keeping his calm and meeting Ditmars's eyes.

"You got lucky. You're not a songwriter. I'm not sure how you pulled these tunes outta yer ass. Okay, here's what I'll do. I'll offer you fifteen dollars for each song. Each one. That's sixty bucks. That's a lot more than you normally make. A lot."

Eunice knocked, entered with two cups of coffee. She didn't look at Freddy, but he could tell by the way she set the coffee down in front of him that she was rooting for him. He met her gaze as she left.

"Thirty dollars apiece," Freddy said. "Plus royalties. That's my final offer. Take it or leave it."

"You're making a huge mistake. You should take what you can get. You're no big-time wheelin' and dealin' agent. You're a mediocre song plugger who got lucky. Take the deal."

The blood was pumping in Freddy's ears, almost deafening him. He swallowed again and did his best to make his lips curve up into a smile. Then he met Ditmars's gaze and gathered his sheet music, which he'd tossed onto the desk. "Okay, boss. I guess I'd better get to work. Those songs aren't going to sell themselves, right?"

"So that's it?" Ditmars said. "You aren't selling? You might want to think twice about this."

"I'm not selling for less than thirty," Freddy said. "I'm going to stick to what I'm halfway good at. I'll get my assignments from Eunice. Thanks."

He marched out of the room, headed down the stairs. He wasn't just a mediocre song plugger. He was great. Everyone thought so. "Bring Back the Moon" was making tons of dough, wasn't it? A great tune and even greater lyrics. That melody would have been nothing without those lyrics. The nerve of Ditmars to call him mediocre. With each stair tread he got angrier and more self-righteous. Thirty dollars a song was a steal! If Ditmars couldn't see that, he'd find someone else who could. There were music publishers up and down the block, and more up by Times Square. Maybe he'd just get a new song-plugging job somewhere else.

He was halfway down the stairwell when Ditmars's voice came booming after him. "Delaney! Get back in here."

"What for?" he called back. Lanier Publishing. He'd start with Lanier. They were a class A outfit. Not like this two-bit joint.

"Get back in here," Ditmars roared again. "I'm sure we can make this work."

Freddy paused, looked up. Ditmars was out of sight, presumably still at his desk, but it were as if Freddy could see him still sitting there, soggy cigar melting in the ashtray. Freddy called up, "If you're not going to give me thirty, there's no point."

"Will you get up here and not shout out private business where everyone can hear? Get up here."

Freddy trudged back up, stood in the doorway. "Are you giving me the thirty bucks a song?"

"I'll do seventy-five cents royalty. No more," Ditmars said.

"Thirty bucks a song and seventy-five cents royalty," Freddy repeated.

Ditmars sighed dramatically. "And not a penny more, you hear me?"

"Including mechanicals?" Mechanical royalties meant he'd get paid whenever someone bought the song to play on the phonograph, a machine that was becoming popular around town. Freddy suspected that phonographs would be the way of the future, especially since he'd heard that the technology was improving daily.

"Mechanicals too?" Ditmars said. "You trying to make me go broke?"

Freddy waited in the doorway.

Ditmars sighed. "Fine. Mechanicals too. Fifty cents. Not a penny more."

Freddy leaned in, shook Ditmars's hand. "You got a deal, boss." He handed Ditmars the sheet music. Ditmars took them, turned them around, peered down at the notations as if trying to discover something magical on each page. "One more thing," Freddy said. "I want the credit line to read 'Fred Delaney,' okay? Not Freddy. I'm gonna be Fred from now on. There are a lot more songs where this one came from."

That evening, out of sight of the music publisher, Freddy and Josephine shared a cab uptown. Because they could afford it. Josephine didn't understand about money, but Freddy assured her that they each made sixty dollars that day, which was as much as Josephine usually made in three months. He told her that the songs would be published under Fred Delaney, since he'd written the lyrics and it would be just too confusing if people knew the songs came from a colored woman. Otherwise people would think these were coon songs, or minstrel songs, or maybe jazz or the blues. Plus the songs wouldn't be worth as much, being written by a colored woman instead of a white man.

Josephine nodded as if she understood, but Freddy wasn't sure that he'd gotten through to her. No matter, he could explain it again to her if he had to.

He didn't tell her about the royalties he'd negotiated from Ditmars. He meant to, but—honestly—it had slipped his mind. He'd tell her one of these days, for sure.

They headed uptown again by cab, which in itself was unusual since they always economized and took the subway. Freddy could get used to this life.

"Not tonight," Freddy told her. "We're cabbing it. And wear your new dress."

Last week he'd dragged her up to Harlem's Seventh Avenue, the so-called Boulevard of Dreams, to pick out a new dress and shoes. Negroes, of course, couldn't shop where everyone else did, down in Midtown—they had their own shops up in Harlem, so that's where Freddy took her.

They went to three shops before he found what he wanted: what the shopgirl, eyeing Freddy, said was called a "day dress": a sleek maroon gown with a wide golden-yellow collar. "It'll match your handbag," Freddy told her. "Put it on."

Josephine had trooped obediently to the dressing room, tried it on, made her way back out, arms slightly spread, to where Freddy waited. "Ah, you look like a million bucks," he said. She did indeed look nice: the fabric hugged her form, flared out below her hips. No way anybody would think that a few months ago she'd been home-less, sleeping in public parks or down by the river. Freddy's heart expanded. He'd really been generous, taking her in and finding her a job and letting her sleep on his floor. Sure, he was getting something out of it, too—his musicianship had improved immensely, and now income from her songs were lining his pockets—but that didn't stop the basic facts of how much he'd helped her. He loved this feeling, loved the gratitude and complete trust she had in him, spinning for him and the salesgirl. He'd gotten her a maroon velvet hat, too, to match.

Now Josephine smoothed the still-new maroon fabric—Freddy wouldn't let her wear it till tonight—over her knees as she perched on the edge of the cab's seat. He wouldn't tell her where they were going but of course she recognized the place when the cab pulled up: the Shortstack. This black-and-tan club was getting a great deal of buzz from all over—colored and white. The house band wasn't an ordinary four- or five-piece band; the Shortstack's claim to fame was that they housed a genuine twenty-two-piece swing band, like the ones in St. Louis. And Freddy could tell how much Josephine loved the full-on musical immersion.

When the cab came to a halt and she moved to open the door, Freddy said, "Wait." He got out of his side, ran around, and opened her door. He held out his hand like a butler or a footman to help her out.

She stared up at him, eyes wide, not understanding.

"Come on," he said, reaching for her hand. "This is your night. This is how all the swells do it."

She laid one hand lightly in his and stood, so trusting; and he vowed, again, to take care of her.

He held her hand as they made their way inside, down a short flight of stairs, where the doors opened up into a huge subterranean room. Tables and chairs lay scattered about, and between and among and on top of them, people were dancing: white and colored, the music gyrating over them. He caught the maître d's eye and the man led them to a table, front and center, with a large RESERVED FOR PRIVATE PARTY sign tented on top.

Freddy checked his watch. When the house band started their next number, he knew they'd arrived right on time.

The band played three notes.

She stiffened, expression even blanker than usual, and he could tell she recognized the tune. He grinned at her.

"Bring Back the Moon" was pouring from the big band like water through a sieve. It was all around her. No longer in her head. He figured that she'd heard the song played, of course, but never with this many instruments, never on so large a scale. Never so full of life. Earlier that week Freddy had offered the house band the exclusive opportunity to play the new music he and Josephine had been working on, if the band would play the songs for an hour straight.

The band started with "Bring Back the Moon." Then "Walk a Mile for Your Smile" and the other tunes Ditmars had purchased. The singer was a big-voiced alto whose lips curled lovingly around each word, as if she were tasting it. Then the band played a few other popular instrumental songs—"The Last Night in Your Arms," "The Third Time Charm," "Little Green Eyes"—that Josephine had composed. She hadn't sat down at the table and now edged closer and closer to the stage, unmistakable in her new maroon dress. She wasn't scrawling madly on her paper; she just stood there, illuminated in the beam of her music, absorbing every note.

The crowd of dancing patrons had grown larger with each song. Soon everyone but Freddy, it seemed, was dancing. He leaned back in his chair, arms sprawled across the backs of the chairs next to him, and just watched. They were all so happy. He'd brought enjoyment and delight to all these people, and to Josephine Reed most of all. He, Freddy Delaney, had done this. Even the band seemed to play with more and more enthusiasm as the night went on.

He'd never seen Josephine glow like this before—yes, there was no word other than *glow*. He'd heard women described as "glowing" but had never actually seen it for himself. In her beautiful new dress with her matching shoes (he'd insisted on those, too), he could see her only in three-quarter profile: she was devouring the music coming from the dais, but her eyes were shining and her face was alight. Her smile was worth all the hours Freddy had spent plugging.

The band played the last chord of "Novelty Days" and started the opening chords to "Sublime Summer," an upbeat, danceable song that sounded like the house band was born to play. Freddy slipped through the crowd and extended his hand to Josephine. "C'mon! Dance with me!"

Josephine looked up at him, confused. For a moment her smile faded. "What?"

"C'mon, kiddo," he repeated. "Let's you and me dance to our song! Waddya say?" He inched his hand closer to Josephine's.

A glance back at the band, then down at his hand, then up to his face. Then she focused on his hand as she reached out and allowed his hand to clasp hers.

She danced effortlessly. He didn't know why that surprised him, but it did. He'd never seen her dance; off the dance floor there was something slightly uncoordinated and disengaged about her movements. Who had taught her? How had she learned? He made a note to find out. But right now her maroon dress flared as he spun her, her feet tapping in elegant rhythm. How had she even learned these steps? Arms flailing, feet kicking high, she spun and shimmied. He realized, after the third or fourth dance, that his cheeks were aching— he was smiling so much. Not just because of Josephine's happiness but from his own, too. He had done all this for her, and she was loving it.

They danced until the final note of the night. When the band finished, the applause was deafening. The band packed up their instruments and Josephine, who must have been exhausted, now sat at the edge of her seat, biting her lip slightly as if trying to remember everything.

They were the last patrons at the Short Stack. The manager had come up and shaken their hands and patted Freddy on the back, telling him what a brilliant composer he was, and Freddy had just stood there, smiling tightly, not looking at Josephine.

As the lights crashed out and the vast dance floor reduced to shadows, Freddy thought about the Alibi Club and his first late-night encounter with Josephine. How far they'd come!

At last he led her up and out into the early-morning quiet. No vehicles passed. He worried about catching a cab, but after a few moments, headlights rounded a corner and approached.

"Freddy?" Josephine said next to him.

"Yes? Everything okay?"

"Why did you do this?" she asked.

He'd been looking at the cab, holding out one arm, but now he turned to her. "Because you deserve to be happy. And I thought that would make you happy."

She was looking at the ground. Typical.

"I'll do everything I can to make you happy," he said. "I promise."

A beat, and as the cab approached, swerving toward them, she hugged him. Even though she didn't like to be touched. Even though she never reached out to anyone.

But now she reached out to him. "Thank you," he heard her whisper into his chest. "Thank you, Freddy."

24

BOOM!

Bern

"I GOT SOMETHING," Eboni announced three days later, when Bern showed up at her office that night, after spending the day working on *RED*. "It connects with 'When It Was Evergreen.'"

"What've you got?" He, of course, remembered the song: lush strings and a slightly saccharine melody that too easily stuck in your head.

I wish I could see you now
You brought me more joy than I was allowed
We thought it was evergreen
We thought our love was evergreen
Can we walk in a circle
Can we turn it around

The melody didn't make the song memorable for Bern, but the Doodles did. On the original manuscript, written in Delaney's distinctive spikey handwriting, a series of thirteen pictograms twirled down the right margin. Many of the symbols didn't seem to repeat on other Delaney manuscripts. He and Eboni had examined the sheet several times already.

"Look at this." Eboni zoomed in on the adjacent screen of one of Earlene's pages. She highlighted a section about a third of the way down.

And there they were. The same thirteen pictograms, in the same order: a tiny half circle with four lines slashing the right edge; a vertical line with two left-slanted slashes top and bottom and tiny circle below; a square balancing on its point with another square overlaid and several of the resulting pointed triangles colored in; something that looked a little like a cloud; and nine hieroglyphs more, all identical to the Delaney manuscript.

Bern said, comparing them, "They're exactly the same."

"No shit. I think this might be 'Evergreen.'"

He compared the two: the original Delaney manuscript of "Evergreen" with the page in Earlene's trunk. Could this Doodle page be the melody of "Evergreen"? The circle with the four slashes represented the descending G minor arpeggio over the course of four beats, of *We thought our love*. Then the vertical line with the slashes and the circle was a dotted combination eighth-sixteenth note—in this case, a G, which served as the root for the arpeggio and for the lyric *was evergreen*.

"He wrote the music in code," Bern said, realization sliding over him. Of course. "That's what all this is. It's not just notations on how to play the music—this *is* the music. And it's not just the notes; it's how to play them, all in one. Bring up the crossed triangles," he said. This symbol appeared fairly frequently in the margin notations: a triangle balancing on its point, with two lines intersecting. "Find the manuscript with the most uses of it."

The song "Swingin' with My Hat and Cane" popped up, and then several others. She zoomed in on the first, and now it made sense.

The triangle represented an obbligato bass line in the key of D; and when one of the lines was left out, it modulated to E-flat major. Eboni found it in several more songs.

He couldn't help it: he hugged her. She folded into him as if she'd been wanting the same thing.

He pulled away, but they held hands an instant longer than was strictly necessary.

They'd cracked the code. And the Delaney Foundation had no clue; they didn't know the code, and didn't know that Josephine had written it—or at least written some of it.

Because they had to be writing it together: Why else would every page sport a *JoR* on a corner? Every page, without fail. Bern speculated that there were—or had been—other pages in other trunks with *FBD* on them, that Delaney had written. But Bern and Eboni had found Josephine's trunk, not Delaney's.

The next week, Bern put in eighteen-hour days. He spent five or six hours transcribing and annotating *RED*, to show the Foundation he was still hard at work; and then he and Eboni spent twelve or more hours afterward comparing every Doodle from Earlene's trunk with every Doodle in Delaney's manuscripts.

Now that they knew the Doodles *were* the music, the pictograms slowly opened up. Sometimes, although rarely, the symbols referred to a specific note—a square with a corner blacked out was an *A*—but in most cases the pictogram referred not just to the note, but also to how the note was to be played: whether ascending or descending; how to modulate the key and articulate the notes; what the tempo should be; and, incredibly, the dynamic structure—how loud or how soft the notes should be played. All packed into one little symbol.

One late night while they were trying to translate page fifty-six of Earlene's Doodles—which they'd linked to Delaney's "Ice Candles in the Desert," an aria that had been briefly performed in 1923 but otherwise got little play today—Bern rubbed his eyes and looked up. "There's no question about it," he said. "Whoever wrote this—and we can assume by the *JoR* that it was Josephine—was also a brilliant composer."

"She probably wrote it for the baby," Eboni said.

Bern ignored her. "It would explain so much. This was how Delaney wrote so much music." One of the issues that had always stymied music historians about Frederic Delaney was how he could hear a piece only once and immediately be able to synthesize it and utilize it years later. But if two people had that skill—had perfect pitch and perfect recall—it was so much more possible.

A thought kept bubbling up that he tried to tamp down: What if it were all Josephine?

This was a rabbit hole that Bern really, really didn't want to fall into; but he kept picking at the scab, rubbernecking the car wreck. What if Josephine Reed had written *all* the music, not Delaney? What if she was the genius? Scholars had noted that Delaney seemed to have been an average student, an average musician, back in Bloomington; and even when he'd arrived in New York, he wasn't immediately setting the music scene on fire with his compositions. He'd been in the city for several years before it worked its magic on him and he'd started creating all those wonderful melodies.

And what if . . . what if it hadn't been the city that had worked its magic—what if it had been Josephine? And these were all Josephine's wonderful melodies?

This would mean that Delaney was a fraud. A liar. An impostor.

And that was too much for Bern to imagine.

He threw himself even deeper into his work, as if to escape. One night in early February, Bern was staring at the patterns on the screen, which were no longer a blur of disorienting symbols. They were a language, a whisper from another room, barely detectable and still only partially decipherable. Now Bern wondered if they were a cry for help. What happened to Josephine? Bern was more and more desperate to find out, if only to salvage the Frederic Delaney he thought he knew.

One February morning, Mallory stopped by Bern's office. She knocked on the door and poked her head in. "Hello," she said, black hair shining, "I was in the neighborhood and thought I'd drop by."

"Oh," Bern said. "Hi."

"I just want to thank you for all you're doing," she said. "You probably don't hear it enough, but I want you to know how much we appreciate you. The Foundation and I."

"It's my honor," Bern told her. "I can't imagine a better way to show my appreciation for everything that the Delaney Foundation has done for me."

She had crossed the room, sat in one of the armchairs across from him. "Did you find anything promising in Durham?" she said casually.

He tensed, then forced himself to relax. "Not really." He immediately felt guilty.

"I saw the plane expense report come across my desk," she said. "I didn't realize you went there."

He couldn't meet her eyes, so stared at the screen instead. Spoke quickly. "I wanted to meet with a professor down there who's done some great research on Appalachian ornamentation practices. There's a lot in this version of RED. A coloratura, too, that seemed like it might be particularly prevalent in the lowlands of South Carolina. I thought he might be able to shine some light on it and show me some examples in the library there."

"What did you find?" she said, curious.

"Delaney definitely utilized several leitmotifs from the Carolinas and adapted them significantly in act two. It's fascinating how he took the syncopation and turned it inside out. Do you want me to play it for you? I can—it'll just take a second—"

"No, no," she said with a chuckle. "I'm sure I don't have the ear for it. I just thought I'd check in and find out why you were down there. In the future, just get clearance from me first before you use the company jet."

"Oh, sure, I'm so sorry—"

"It's absolutely fine," Mallory said. "No problem at all. Just wanted to clarify."

She left a few minutes later, but Bern's guilt at deceiving her, and the Foundation, grew only more intense.

The ramifications of Josephine writing Delaney's works were far-reaching. Many of Delaney's earlier works were no longer protected under copyright laws, which meant that anyone could play them and use them. But the Delaney Foundation had, over the past ninety years, executed multiple licenses and renewals and revisions to the original melodies, and those derivative works *would* still be protected under copyright laws. Would these rights somehow be invalidated if Bern and Eboni could show that Delaney hadn't written the music? Who was entitled to the money for the music? The legal morass was daunting.

But even more important were the optics of the situation. Rich white male, appropriating—if he was appropriating—the music written by a poor Black woman? The press would have a field day, and it would likely destroy the reputation of Frederic Delaney. This could spell the end of the entire Delaney Foundation.

Well, maybe she wasn't poor, Eboni argued. Maybe there was some document somewhere that had given Delaney all the rights to Josephine's music. It was all too early, too uncertain, too stitched together with supposition and Scotch tape. "Although if there is a contract, it ain't online in their archive," Eboni said. "You've seen all the references to Josephine Reed, and that sure ain't one of them."

"This could destroy the Foundation," Bern said.

"It could. But it doesn't have to. Maybe they can spin it positively. How the rich white man didn't *really* take advantage of the poor Black homegirl. Mmm-hmm."

"Your second mother, Earlene, should be ready to lawyer up," Bern said.

Earlene had taken a liking to Eboni, so much so that Earlene had called her again a couple of weeks ago just to ask how she—"and that cute boy you came with"—was doing. Earlene was serious about visiting New York City sometime soon, and Eboni was all for it. "Damn straight," Eboni said. "Who knows how much money Josephine would have been entitled to if we could prove that she wrote all this?"

Bern just stared at the screen, thinking. He wanted Josephine to get her recognition but didn't want to do anything to jeopardize the Foundation. He knew he wouldn't sleep again tonight, thinking about it all. Whichever way it played out, he would be responsible.

25

Needing New Trousers

Fred

TWO MONTHS LATER and Christmas season was upon them. That morning, Fred was late: it was nearly nine thirty when he, slim leather attaché case in hand, marched up the steps of Ditmars & Ross. But word had already gotten out: Chuck Keats and Josh Roberts loitered in the reception area pretending to look at the music, but Fred could see right through them.

"Hiya, Freddy," Chuck said as soon as he saw him, and Fred bestowed a smile and a nod.

"Another swell song today?" Josh asked.

Fred shrugged. He swept past Eunice—tossing a small vague smile in her direction—and up the stairs. By then Ditmars had also learned of his approach. "Delaney, is that you?"

Fred didn't respond. He was halfway up the stairs already: What was the point?

Ernest Greene and Thommy Whittaker, who'd been standing on

the top landing, both disappeared into the piano rooms. They didn't start playing, though.

Fred was now in front of Ditmars's office. "Here you go," he said. "Here's my next hit." He casually tossed the attaché case on Ditmars's desk. Fred shouted for Eunice to bring in coffee.

"Same terms?" Ditmars asked.

"Fifty," Fred told him, sitting and crossing his legs. He noted that the cuff of his right pant leg was rather frayed. As soon as the first royalty check came in, Fred was going to buy a new suit. He deserved it. He also needed it, so people like Ditmars would respect him. "Plus I'm going to need those royalties upped a bit. Let's say, to a dollar."

"Fifty? Fifty dollars? For one song? Are you serious?" Ditmars said. "Let's hear it first." He clamped his teeth around the cigar.

Ditmars's office piano was rarely played and usually buried beneath stacks of paper, but Fred shifted the stacks, sat down with a flourish at the bench, and thunderously began "Blue Billy Lane":

Take a walk with me
Down Blue Billy Lane
Never missing a turn
On this pleasant terrain
The place where we fell in love
Blue Billy Lane

The music was, as usual, infinitely danceable, and singable, and memorable. In the hallway outside, Fred could see shadows of people, all listening. These past two months, Fred's songs had outsold all of Ditmars & Ross's other music. Several times Fred had been up to the accounting department—three old geezers stuck on the top floor of the brownstone, bent arthritically over their ledgers—but he still didn't have an idea of how many copies of sheet music he'd actually sold. He tried getting the printer receipts, to know how many copies of the sheet music had been printed, but the geezers shook their heads at him, as if the receipts had been magicked up to neverland. He was really glad he'd be getting royalties, though. His first payment was due at the end of the month.

Fred finished singing; the outro slid to a crescendo in a flourish of descending arpeggios. Applause wafted in from the hall. Thommy and Ernest grinned at him from the doorway. Eunice elbowed her way past them, came in and put the coffee tray on the desk.

"What did you think of it?" Ditmars asked her.

"It's divine," she said. "*Billy Blue Lane*," she sang, only slightly off-key. "I can't wait to play it tonight."

"See?" Freddy said. "So waddya think?"

Ditmars told him, "Come over here," and, to Eunice, "Close the door on your way out."

Fred returned to the chair, crossed his legs again. Yes, he definitely needed new trousers.

"You have a deal," Ditmars said quietly. "Fifty dollars for this one. And royalties. A dollar per."

"Including mechanicals?"

"Including mechanicals."

Freddy leaned over, shook Ditmars's hand.

"Now, are you planning on working today? You're back at Altman's."

"I was thinking about work today. I'm thinking that Bergdorf's would be a much better fit for me."

The left corner of Ditmars's mouth furled upward. Fred wondered how it was possible for the cigar to stay in one spot.

"You know we're on a rotation," Ditmars said. "You're due to plug at Altman's"—he riffled through a ledger—"for another three weeks. Until after Christmas. What are you trying to pull here?"

Fred chose his next words very carefully. "I'm thinking that I should be composing full-time," he said. "I don't think I should keep plugging much anymore. I'm more valuable to you as a composer."

Ditmars said, "About time you've come to your senses. You want to be a house composer? No problem. I can have you off the rotation right now. Eunice—" He started to yell through the closed door.

"No, I don't want to go on your payroll," Fred said. "I don't want to be a house composer."

Ditmars looked at him blankly. "What do you mean?"

"I don't want you owning the rights to any of my songs," Fred said. "So I don't want to work for you as an employee. I want to go free-lance. I'll keep plugging for the next couple of weeks until the first royalty check comes in, but then I want to go freelance. License the rights to you, but keep ownership."

Ditmars stared thoughtfully at him, chewing his cigar. "Remind me again. How old are you?"

"Twenty-two," Fred lied.

"You're twenty-two and you want to go freelance."

"Yes."

"That's pretty risky for a fellow your age, you know that?"

Fred shrugged. "Yeah, probably. But I have this, too." He pulled out another few sheets of foolscap from the attaché case, tossed them on the desk.

"What's this?" Ditmars asked.

"Another song I came up with. 'June in the Meadow.' You want me to play it?"

Ditmars shook his head, reading the music.

"I can bring you a couple more by the end of the week," Fred said. "I had a burst of inspiration over the weekend." He stared down at Ditmars, sitting in his chair, gnawing on his cigar, eyes greedily reading the music. *Fred's* music. "You know something, boss, I think today's going to be my last day plugging. I'm gonna start writing full-time now."

He didn't wait for Ditmars's response. He opened the door to the hall. Heads disappeared into practice rooms. He sauntered down the stairs, whistling "Blue Billy Lane," passing Josephine in the music room, where she was filing. He winked at her as he slammed the door behind him.

That night he told Josephine the big news: that he wouldn't be going into the office anymore, that he'd be writing songs for Ditmars from home. "Let's go out for dinner," he told her. There were several mixed-race restaurants up in Harlem where they could go and not attract attention.

She shook her head. "You know I don't like that." She didn't like eating in public; she didn't like the sound of people chewing.

"Ah, come on, just this once?"

"I was going to make fried chicken," she said.

He relented. Her fried chicken was spectacular.

While she was cooking, he finished recopying the latest tune they'd been working on, which he was calling, "The Way Into My Heart"—a joyous mid-tempo song that combined bouncy shifting bass lines with bluegrass-like open-fifth harmonies.

"I didn't think it was possible, but you actually outdid yourself with this one," he told her as she heated the oil on the hot plate and dusted the chicken pieces with flour and bread crumbs. "The lyrics I added really put it over the top. That's what happened today, too. The boss really wasn't sold on 'Blue Billy Lane' until I sang it for him."

"That's wonderful." Josephine said, dipping another piece of chicken in the flour mixture, turning to stir the greens. "He did like the music though, right?"

"Yeah he thought the music was fine. Just fine. But he said that my lyrics were really clever. That's what he said. 'Fred,' he said, 'those are some clever lyrics.' That's what he said, word for word."

"I heard 'Walk a Mile for Your Smile' today. Someone was humming it. On Fifty-Second Street. I heard it. Just the music. Not the words."

"Of course you did," Fred said. "The music is really catchy."

"I wondered if the person who was humming it knew that it was a song I wanted to hear. I wanted to ask her but I didn't want to talk to a stranger."

He sighed. "We've been over this. You know that I want nothing more than for the world to know that you wrote all this fantastic music that people are humming. But there's just no way. You know that, right? People wouldn't give it a chance. They'd think it was just another minstrel or coon song. I'm doing my best to protect you. Ditmars would fire you—or worse, go out of business. Is that what you want? I tell you, this is for the best. It's what's best for both of us. Don't you trust me?"

Fred said a variation of this to her at least once a week. And, as usual, she nodded, apparently mollified.

"There's my girl." He stood, planning to wash up before dinner. "I thought we'd check out that club on Thirteenth and Seventh. I think it's called the Booming Station. There's a combo that's supposed to be the real McCoy."

"It's the Blooming Station, and I can't get in," Josephine said. "It's whites only."

"Oh," he said. "Well, never mind then. Where did you want to go? We need to celebrate."

"There's that dance hall over on Twelfth that has that woolly saxo-phone," she said.

"You're on," he told her. "We'll have champagne tonight. My treat." En route to the bathroom, one hand on the doorknob, he said, "I was thinking. If things keep going the way they are, you can afford your own place, you know that?"

She looked stricken, her hand dangling a drumstick over the oil as if it were a dead rat she was dropping onto someone's head.

"You don't want to get your own place?" Freddy said, bewildered.

"I like sleeping on the floor," she said.

"That bedroll can't be very comfortable."

"I've gotten used to it. I like it."

He knew that Josephine didn't like change; she needed a routine and, whenever possible, never varied from it. She didn't even like weekends because they meant she couldn't follow her weekday schedule. But somehow he never thought she'd like sleeping in his tiny studio, listening to him snore at night. "You sure?"

"I'm sure."

"What if we could find you a room in the same building? So you'd have your own space?"

"Are you tired of me?" she asked.

"Aw, Jo, don't even think that. You're my girl. I was just trying to figure out how to make you happier."

"I'm your girl?" she said, looking at the wall behind him.

"You know you are. I'm not going anywhere without you. I just want you to be happier."

"You're making me happier," she said. There was a long pause, as if she were trying to articulate words but couldn't find them. And then she did. "You saved me."

His chest expanded, and he beamed at her. "I'm glad. I'm really glad, you know that?"

"So I can stay?"

"Sure you can stay," he promised. "As long as you want. It's swell having you here."

"Okay," she said. "Good." And she dropped the chicken leg into the hot oil.

One Saturday morning in mid-January, Fred Delaney sailed up the steps of a brand-new limestone building right off Fiftieth Street. He'd plugged there only a handful of times; usually one of the more talented musicians, like Ernest Greene or Thommy Whittaker, got that plum. But Fred had been in Bergdorf Goodman enough to vow he would be returning—the luxurious fabrics, the elegant lighting, the very smell of *money* permeated every seam and cranny.

Several days before, he'd dropped off his card—*Fred Delaney,*

Composer—and now Jeremy, the salesclerk, was ready for him. "Mr. Delaney," Jeremy said, coming forward, his pudgy face creased in what approximated a smile. "Happy Saturday. Are you having a good day?"

"Yes, thank you," Fred said. "And it looks like you're doing a good business today." The weekend crowd was boisterous, but the rooms still felt spacious and slightly empty. From upstairs came the sound of a piano plugging "I'm Forever Blowing Bubbles," the frothy tune spilling down on Fred like sunlight. Its composer, John Kellette, had whipped up a nice little ditty, but Fred didn't think it had staying power. Not like some of Fred's songs. "Blue Billy Lane" was everywhere right then. Then again, so was "Careful What You Give Away." And "June in the Meadow" was still one of the most popular tunes this month. Fred allowed himself a small smile of satisfaction.

"I understand you're looking for a suit," Jeremy was saying as he led Fred up the stairs, back into the ready-to-wear men's suit section.

"Not just a suit," Fred said. "I want something elegant. Super refined." Fred had been debating as to whether to get a fully bespoke suit, but ready-to-wear Bergdorf Goodman was the height of elegance right then. He wanted to be able to tell people he'd gotten his suit at Bergdorf's.

"Yes, of course." Jeremy assessed Fred through slightly narrowed eyes. "Thomas is just your size." He called for Thomas, a slender fellow with silvery fair hair. Both of the Bergdorf employees were older than Fred. That gave Fred some satisfaction, as well.

Jeremy led Fred around the showroom. "We have a double-breasted sack suit in worsted wool that might be just the ticket. It was popular a few years ago, but we've made some tweaks, and it's very fashionable right now. What do you think?" He pulled out a beautiful blue pinstripe, held it up. Fred nodded appreciatively, and Thomas disappeared to try it on.

After much debate, they decided the blue pinstripe did not do justice to Fred's fair complexion. The dark gray was a possibility. Then again, the dark green tailored lounge suit might be appropriate, even if it was a bit more casual. Jeremy suggested dressing it up with a few striped shirts with turned-down collars—very in, you know—accompanied by a stylish woolen homburg. "You can't go wrong with a homburg," Jeremy told him, and Fred was inclined to agree.

Two hours later, his purchases made—he'd decided on the blue pinstripe after all—Fred asked Jeremy to accompany him to the music section of the store. Fred knew where it was, since he'd played there a handful of times, but he didn't want the salesclerks to take one look at him and immediately assume he was just a run-of-the-mill song plugger without two bits to rub together. Jeremy, carrying the boxes, led the way.

But his worries were for naught. The song plugger up that day wasn't from Ditmars & Ross, and Fred didn't recognize him. Jeremy introduced Fred to the salesclerk: Miss Sophie Normil, an older matron with a pince-nez. She was new, as well. "Sophie," Jeremy said, "this is Mr. Delaney. He's a composer. He wrote 'Bring Back the Moon.'"

Sophie gaped at Fred. Her pince-nez fell off her nose. Fred would have laughed, the sight was so comical and somehow so trite, but he didn't have time; Sophie was pumping his hand, speaking breathlessly and standing a little too close.

He'd thought in the past that he just enjoyed being admired; now he realized that he craved it. Not being liked, not being respected—being adored. People idolizing him made him feel bigger and more important. They saw a better man than he saw himself, and he loved that.

"Mr. Delaney it is an honor—an honor!—to meet you. I'm such a fan—*such* a fan! 'Let the Rain Come' is one of my favorite—favorite!—songs! And 'Bring Back the Moon'! Oh! It's just divine! Divine, I tell you!" Fred could feel a fine spray of spittle on his face.

He ducked his head. He was blushing. He'd never actually met a fan before, someone who knew his name. And at Bergdorf Good-man, of all places.

"What are you working on next? Do tell! I was just telling the girls in my sewing circle—I have a little sewing circle, you see, started it during the war and we just kept it going, nothing serious of course, just gloves and scarves for the soldiers, now the veterans—anyway, I was just telling the girls that I was so hoping you'd write us a waltz—oh I know, so old-fashioned!—but I says to them, I says, 'If anyone could write a really danceable waltz, a really elegant waltz, it's Mr. Fred Delaney!' And here you are!"

"Gosh," Fred told her modestly, "maybe I'll write a waltz next. I was just thinking about it the other day."

"Oh! Would you? Would you really? Oh my goodness, wait until I tell the girls about this. That I was the inspiration for a waltz! It's too good to be true, I tell you." She waved her hand dramatically in front of her jowls as if she were about to faint.

Fred couldn't decide if she was just pulling his leg, but the way she waved her hand, eyes swimming up at him, made him believe she was serious. "Yes, well," he said. "Anyway, I'm hoping to purchase something."

"Oh! You're going to buy something here? Today? Oh goodness. What are you looking for? Do you know what you want?"

Fred eyed her again, looking for any sign that she was mocking him.

She stared back eagerly, no mischief in her eyes.

"I'd like a Victrola," he told her, already heading over to that corner of the department where the phonograph players posed like a miniature city of skyscrapers, their rosewood and mahogany cases gleaming.

"Oh my," Sophie said, hurrying to keep up. "We have a fine selection—quite fine!—so I'm happy to—"

"I'd like the Victrola the Sixteenth with the electric motor attachment," he said, cutting her off. "That one." He pointed to the Victrola No. 2. For months he'd been eyeing it: top-notch, with an improved four-spring motor and a wider tone arm. It didn't have the ornate carving of some of its brethren, and wasn't the height of beauty, but there was no question.

"Oh, good choice," Sophie said. "Its sound is far superior to the others. And so smart of you to get an electric motor. That's all the rage these days—all the rage."

"Can you have it delivered?" He handed her his card. "This afternoon?"

"Of course," she said. And—yes, Freddy was sure of it—she looked up and batted her eyelashes at him. Actually batted them. Despite the pince-nez, and despite never having been batted at before, he could tell an eye-batting as well as the next man. "Would you be willing to sign your card?" she asked him. "I'd love to show the girls."

He signed the card. *F Delaney*. His first autograph.

Fifteen minutes later he was piling his packages into a taxi and shuttling home. He didn't have much to carry: the suit and the shirts were being altered and wouldn't be ready for a few days; and the Victrola, along with a dozen brand-new phonograph records, would be delivered later that afternoon. But he enjoyed the convenience of a taxi.

Josephine was out, which was just as well. This wasn't unusual. Unless the weather was too inclement, she wandered on Saturdays. Someone usually played music in Central Park, and she could spend her afternoon in dance halls or vaudeville shows absorbing their music.

Later, when Josephine arrived home just as the March sun was setting, the studio looked different: on one wall, next to the armoire and an arm's breadth from her bedroll, an unfamiliar object sat draped in a white sheet. A large yellow bow rested uneasily on top, the ribbon's ends curling halfway down to the floor.

Josephine was wearing her new maroon dress, Fred noted with

approval. Her eyes widened and she looked at Fred, who'd leaped off his bed when he heard her unlock the door and was now standing next to the object, grinning.

"I want to show you how much I appreciate you, Josephine Reed. Your lessons, your cooking and cleaning, your talent and everything else. Go on. Open it."

She approached, slowly reached out a hand, drew back, looked at Fred.

"Go on," he said.

With agonizing hesitancy, Josephine pulled off the sheet—so slowly that Fred had to fight himself to not snatch the sheet from her and give it a good yank. She kept looking over at him as if not quite believing this was happening.

The sheet fell. She crushed a wad of it in her hand.

"What do you think?"

"Oh. Oh, my," she said.

"Does that mean you like it? Let's just say that you like it. It's electric, see? It's the latest thing. Not even a hand crank. And open the doors. Go on," he said, when she hung back, "go ahead and open them. See? I got six phonograph records, too. You can get more but I thought I'd give you these to get you started. And see?" He handed her the one on top, that had his name, Fred Delaney, on it: "Blue Billy Lane." "Our own record! Our very first one!"

Some of the Ditmars & Ross music had made its way onto phonograph discs, although not many—Mr. Ditmars had only just begun dabbling in them. So although Josephine must have seen copies of the phonograph record before now, her eyes filled with tears and she hugged it to herself.

"I love it a lot. This is swell."

"Come on, let's play it," he said. "You know how?"

He showed her how to insert the needle into the holder, position the record, flick the ON switch.

"Blue Billy Lane," sung by Madeline Ross, poured out of the brass horn on the top of the machine. She listened, eyes glistening. There was something very special about hearing it, in their room, together.

"Thank you," she said again. "I really like it. It must have cost you a lot. Especially the electric one."

"Sure, it wasn't cheap, but I wanted to show you just how great you really are." He wanted to hug her, but he knew she didn't like to be touched.

"Where did you get the money?"

"I sold 'Everyday Blues' and 'When You Saw Me Last,'" he said. "Plus I've been saving. I've been wanting to get this for you."

"Oh," she said. "I don't know what to say."

"We're a team," he said. "Your music is good, no doubt about it, but my lyrics make them great. I've got big plans for us."

They spent the evening playing the phonograph records. On Monday, when the shops opened, Josephine purchased another dozen records and played them endlessly, ears inches from the brass horn, eyes closed.

She didn't notice, or didn't remark upon, the boxes that arrived on Tuesday from Bergdorf Goodman and didn't compliment Freddy on his beautiful new suit.

26

You Can Trust Us

Bern

THE NEXT MORNING, a mild day in early February, as Bern headed toward the elevator bank, the security guard on desk duty called, "Dr. Hendricks?"

He looked up, preoccupied.

"Ms. Roberts wanted a word with you. She asked if you could stop in?"

He thanked the guard, pressed 17.

Bern hoped the conversation with Mallory wouldn't take long. He was preoccupied with Josephine, wondering about how many songs she'd been involved in, and brooding about what could have happened to her.

Mallory met him as he got out of the elevator. "Just the man I was hoping to see," she said. Her bright red blouse and off-white skirt seemed somehow joyous and summery, even though it was the middle of winter. "How are things progressing? Is the end in sight?"

"We're getting there," he said vaguely. She made no move to lead him back to her office. Why had she summoned him?

"Great to hear," she said, and it sounded forced.

Unease tingled. "Is everything okay?" he asked.

"Not really," she said. "We're just waiting on a couple more people, and then we can get started."

"Waiting on who? Get started on what?"

"My cousin Kurt wanted to have a word with you. He and a few other board members."

Kurt Delaney, the nephew of Frederic Delaney, was chairman of the board. Bern knew who he was, of course, but had never spoken to him.

"The problem is that he's in Thailand at the moment, and the logistics have been a nightmare on such short notice."

He had no idea what she was talking about, but adrenaline, cold and icy, started tingling in his fingers. "I'm sure it can wait," he said, "whatever it is, can't it? Till he's back? I have enough to keep me busy for a while."

"No, let's see if he's here," she said, looking at her watch. Maybe fifteen seconds had elapsed since the last time she'd checked.

She led him past her office, down to the door at the very end of the hall, which opened into an enormous state-of-the-art conference room that took Bern's breath away. The left wall was solid glass, with a spectacular view of Lincoln Center; behind loomed the dark mass of Central Park. An audiovisual center—an enormous television or movie screen, Bern wasn't sure what to call it—took up the entire back wall. Perhaps a dozen faces peered down from the videoconference link. A dozen or so chairs encircled the sparsely elegant jet-black table, with eight people already there, despite the fact that it was only just after nine in the morning. Ice water sweated in pitchers down the center of the table, with croissants and pastries fanning out in a decadent display. No one had eaten anything.

Bern recognized only one other person at the table: Stanford

Whitman, the lawyer he'd met the night he'd arrived. Introductions to the others followed: board members Suzanne Herz and Beth Lamb, both casually dressed in jeans and blazers; Kamae Sandgren, Whitman's legal associate, a thin blond woman with very pale blue eyes; and several others, including a heavyset dark-haired man in a beautifully tailored suit who didn't identify himself or clarify his connection with the board.

Mallory introduced Bern to the heads on the video screens: financier Momad Husseini; Michael Amoury, CFO of Orange Incorporated, one of the biggest lighting companies in the world; Thomas Alexander, the world-class conductor for Orchestra du Paravel; and Andrew Kean, the famous concert pianist, among others.

As they were making introductions, the top center video screen flickered to life. Bern recognized the chairman, Kurt Delaney, bearded and in his early eighties.

"Here you are," Mallory said to him. "Is this video link better?"

"We'll see," Kurt said. "Sure hope so." His eyes sought out Bern. "Dr. Hendricks," he said, clearly impatient and wanting to get started. "Hello. It's nice to meet you. You've certainly been an industrious young man, haven't you?"

Something about the way Delaney said *young man* made Bern want to bristle; it was overly familiar and demeaning, as if he'd called Bern *son* or *boy*.

"I've been hard at work on *RED*," Bern said, "if that's what you mean."

One of the faces on-screen—he thought it was Husseini—laughed.

Kurt was already talking. "You've certainly been hard at work," he said. "Tell us about Josephine Reed."

How did they know? Had they been monitoring his computer? Had they double-checked with the professor at Duke, who Bern had supposedly met with? He wondered if it was Stephanie. But what could she have seen?

"Who?" he said carefully.

"Come on," Kurt said. "Don't play stupid with us, Doctor. Josephine Reed. Of South Carolina. How many Josephine Reeds are there?"

Bern would give nothing away, he decided. "What do you want to know?"

"Everything you know," Stanford Whitman told him. "And Mr. Delaney meant North Carolina. Oxford, North Carolina."

Now that it was out, Bern almost welcomed what would come next. Fine. Good. They were done with the secrecy. "As I gather you've figured out, Josephine Reed is *JoR*, the initials on the Doodle page that accompanied the *RED* score."

Michael Amoury, the CFO of Orange Inc., said, "Who was she? A girlfriend? Relative? Lover?"

"I believe," Bern said, "she may have been his mistress. I also believe she may be the reason that Delaney had such a deep affinity with the Black community."

Bern's phone pinged. Eboni. He switched it to DO NOT DISTURB.

"How did she know Frederic Delaney?" someone asked.

One of the video monitors filled with the photo of Josephine Reed staring at the camera, Frederic Delaney in the foreground. "Is this her?" Kurt said.

"Yes," Bern said steadily. "I believe so."

"And you think she's *JoR*, from the Doodle?"

"It seems likely," Bern said.

"Why didn't you tell us?" Mallory said. "We would have helped, you know."

He shrugged again, kicking himself for listening to Eboni. Why hadn't he trusted his own gut? He should have gone to the Foundation weeks ago. "I wanted to have something definite to tell you first. It's all just conjecture."

"But it's *our* conjecture," Kurt said. "You should have told us."

Bern shook his head. "I wanted to figure everything out before I brought it to you."

One of the other faces spoke up. "What was in the trunk?"

How did they know about the trunk? "What do you mean?" Bern said, stalling.

"You went to North Carolina," Mallory reminded him. "You said it was to consult"—she peered at her tablet—"John Owens at Duke University. But when you came back, you came back with a black trunk. What was in it?" On the screen flashed an image of Bern and Eboni hauling the steamer trunk from the Delaney plane.

"We just picked it up," Bern said. "Eboni—she's the computer programmer I've been working with—she liked it. Brought it back with her."

"Don't lie to me, young man." Bern could hear the contempt in his voice. *Young man* sounded more and more like *boy*.

"Josephine Reed comes from Oxford, North Carolina," Kurt said. "Her descendants still live there. They told us that they sold you a trunk. That they sold the Delaney Foundation a trunk. We want to know what was in it."

Bern swallowed. Before he could reply, someone else was saying, "They said it was filled with papers. They described papers that looked like other Delaney Doodles. Where are they?"

Bern struggled to find words.

"Well?" Michael Amoury said. "What are they and where are they?"

He decided to tell the truth. "They seem to be more Doodles. We're trying to decipher them."

"Where are they?" Amoury repeated, his head large and malevolent on the television screen.

"They're in the Bronx, at Washington Visionaries," Bern said.

"They're ours," Kurt said. "Why didn't you bring them to us to begin with?"

"We wanted to find out what they were," Bern said.

"It's not your job to figure out what they were, son," Kurt said. "Your job is to prepare a definitive *RED* for performance. Not to play detective and traipse across the country."

There it was: *son*. As condescending as Bern imagined it would be. He wanted to swear at the old guy—*I have a fucking PhD from Columbia. I'm not your son*—but knew that anger never got him anywhere. He forced himself to pause, to not respond immediately. Delaney was baiting him. "Deciphering the Doodles could impact *RED*," he said after a moment. "As you probably know, this version of *RED* has a lot more Doodles on it. We thought the correlation between them would provide greater insight and accuracy into Delaney's original intent regarding *RED*. So naturally we wanted to figure it out as part of my mandate."

"I don't really care what you wanted to figure out," Kurt said. "This has nothing to do with your mandate. These papers are ours. You told the family that these documents were being purchased by the Delaney Foundation. We want them now, Dr. Hendricks. Do you understand?"

27

Open for Business

Fred

THE NEXT FEW WEEKS whizzed by. Fred's songs continued to sell. Commissions ramped up, and Ditmars tapped Fred more and more. Could Fred write a tune for this visiting dancer? A special song for a very trendy French singer? A comic melody as an introduction to a play? Fred spent most of his days in the tiny studio, transcribing songs and writing lyrics. He kept trying to get Josephine to just quit Ditmars, too, but she didn't like change. She'd gotten used to going to Ditmars and that was that.

Two or three mornings a week Fred showed up to present the latest song to the music publisher. The pieces with lyrics were selling well, but, surprisingly, the instrumentals were going through the roof. Even without Fred's lyrics, people were wanting to dance to or listen to the music that Josephine had written. This made Fred's job even easier, since then he didn't have to agonize over rhymes or new subject matter. He could just slap a title on it and license it to Ditmars for seventy-five dollars, plus a dollar and fifty cents royalties.

That Tuesday morning Fred was wearing the lounge suit he'd bought at Bergdorf's—he'd returned a few weeks after his initial visit to purchase a few more items, including a pair of handmade Italian boots with spats. His dark hair was slicked back, so shiny it seemed silver. He caught sight of Josephine sweeping out the music room but didn't acknowledge her or anyone else as he paraded up the stairs. Uninvited, he sat down across from Ditmars, crossed his legs. He hoped Ditmars noticed the new suit.

"What have you got for me today?" the older man said, eyebrows lowered. "Where you hiding it?"

Fred wasn't carrying the attaché case nor any loose sheets of music. "What I've got for you today," he said, "is a proposition."

From outside came the tinkle of pianos. When this many pianos played, it was always difficult to decipher the tune, but Fred could make out "Little Green Eyes" and "The Cow in the Clover"—both his.

"What proposition is that?"

"I'm going to allow you to make me a partner at Ditmars & Ross," Fred said.

Ditmars said nothing at first, just leaned back in his chair, looking at him steadily.

Fred continued, "I've brought you hit after hit these past few months alone. The name Ditmars & Ross is becoming synonymous with good music. Great music, even. Just think about it. With me on board, you'll be rolling in hits. I've got a million ideas that will—"

Ditmars cut him off.

"I want to make sure I fully understand you, Frederick."

Had Ditmars ever called him Frederick?

Ditmars went on, "You're going to allow me to make you a partner? Do I understand you correctly?"

Fred relaxed. Ditmars finally understood his value.

"That's right," Fred said. "As I was saying, I've got a ton of ideas about how to make this place the number one music publisher in the country. Who knows, maybe even in the entire civilized world.

My songs are selling like mad and I've got a ton more. Waddya say, partner?"

Ditmars smiled, took the cigar out of his mouth, and stood up. All this seemed to occur in slow motion. Every move seemed to be calculated. Fred instinctively stood and extended his hand.

"You've been a good plugger," Ditmars said. "A little misguided, maybe, but a good plugger. Your songs are okay but you can't be serious in thinking that you can waltz in here and demand a partnership. If you want to buy into the partnership, that's a different story. I can talk to Ross and we can figure out what we'd offer you for a junior stake—maybe two percent. Nothing more."

Fred lowered his hand. Two percent?

Ditmars went on, "Maybe in a couple years we can talk about increasing your stake. We can take the partnership equity out of your royalties."

"But—I brought in all those swell songs. Don't you think I deserve something for them?"

"And I paid you exactly what they're worth. Can't deny that, can you?"

"Yeah, but I've got dozens more songs that are just as good. Dozens. Hundreds, maybe. Better even."

"That's my final offer. You're just a kid, Freddy. You're what—twenty-three?"

Twenty-two, but Fred didn't correct him.

"Get some hair on your chest first. You've been doing this for just six months. Let's give it a year. Stick to what you know. You got really lucky with a couple dozen songs; write a couple dozen more. Then we can really talk about a partnership."

Fred decided it was better to leave with some dignity. Had he gotten too big for his britches? No. Fred was going places. Doing big things. His hit songs were just the beginning. He'd show Ditmars. He'd show everybody.

He took the stairs quietly, one at a time, his lambskin handmade

Italian shoes tapping each stair tread as if with special care. He nodded once to Eunice. He didn't see Josephine.

Outside, he walked around the corner and held on to a lamppost, trembling. Well. That hadn't gone the way he'd thought it would. What would he do now? Keep selling songs to Ditmars? He couldn't even imagine it. Take the songs to another publisher? Sure, that might be the ticket. He'd had offers, several of them, especially since he'd gone freelance, but he'd always been loyal. Well, loyalty be damned. He'd sell himself to the highest bidder, as long as the highest bidder wasn't Ditmars & Ross.

He found himself thinking about Miles Turpin, the fellow composer at Ditmars who'd gone off a few months ago to start his own music publishing business. The music industry was ridiculously corrupt—Fred knew that. He knew that music publishers swindled composers out of what was rightfully theirs all the time. Miles had gotten fed up a few months ago—especially when he'd heard how much Ditmars was paying for Fred's songs—and had struck out on his own. Maybe Fred should look up old Miles, see how he was doing. Come to think of it, he hadn't heard any of Miles's songs of late.

He headed to Penn Station, found a telephone, asked the operator for Miles's number. In a moment he was dialing it.

Miles picked up directly.

"Hey, old sport, remember me?" Fred said. "It's Delaney. Fred. How've you been?"

Miles was delighted to hear from him and had free time now. His office was right around the corner. Fred should stop by. Maybe they could grab sandwiches.

The address Miles gave him was above a wig shop on the third floor of a narrow office building off Thirty-Second. In the stairwell, the grimy linoleum treads stank of sweat and urine. Fred's toes curled inside the Italian shoes.

Miles had no secretary; he opened the door himself, pumped Fred's hand hard. Miles Turpin Publishers, Incorporated, seemed to be one room. Miles's desk took up a good third of the available space. "Freddy! Good to see you, chum! How've you been? How's ole Ditmars?"

Miles offered him a seat in a secondhand desk chair. Fred shared what little gossip he knew about the publisher and their former comrades; now that he was no longer song plugging or in the office as often, he'd begun losing touch with many of them.

Finally he shifted the topic, looking pointedly around the office. "It's really great to see you, you know? I think it's great that you went off on your own to do this. So how's business?" Fred suspected, just by the look of things, that he knew the answer.

"Well, it's not as ritzy as Ditmars, but it'll do for now." Miles shook his head, and they talked about how tough it was to get songs into rotation, how to get songs discovered. Ditmars was a master at that. "I gotta be honest," Miles said, "it's rough out there. Seems every week a new publisher pops up. It's dog-eat-dog. I'm barely hanging on. You're doing pretty good, from what I hear. 'Carnation Celebration' is everywhere. You really came up with a bunch of winners. Just between us, what's your secret?"

Fred stiffened, gave Miles a slightly puzzled look. Then decided to play it cool. "The secret, my friend, is talent. Pure talent."

"Ha, of course. Good ole Freddy."

A pause. The time had come to explain the reason for his visit. "You know when you just hit a wall and need to try something different? Well, I hit that wall. I quit. Old man Ditmars just doesn't know what he has—had, I should say. I've been thinking about new opportunities."

"You want to partner up?" Miles said. "You know, really make a go of it? We could be some real competition. With your talent combined with my connections, we could run this town."

Fred had come planning just that but, looking around the tiny grim office had changed his mind. If Miles went out on his own and this was as good as it was going to get for him, what chance did Fred have, working with him? Miles would always be a two-bit composer. Maybe it would make things easier for Fred at the get-go, but once Fred really got going, he sensed that Miles would just bring him down. Miles could never write lyrics as good as Fred's—let alone unforgettable melodies as good as Josephine's.

"Thanks. I haven't decided what I'm going to do just yet. But I'll let you know." He stood up, shook Miles's hand. "Good seeing you."

"You too, and good luck. Don't be a stranger."

Fred decided to walk home. It was forty blocks—just about two miles—but the April afternoon was cool and sunny, and he had nowhere to be. He calculated when the next royalty check would come: about six weeks from now. The checks he'd received were more than he'd ever made in his life—more than he'd made in a year song plugging—and the next check would be even bigger. The ticket to success, he decided, would be to really get into phonograph recordings. Plugging sheet music already felt antiquated. He'd been hearing, too, about someone in Pennsylvania—Pittsburgh, maybe?—broadcasting music on a crystal radio set. The phonograph business was already booming; if the radio business caught up to it, Fred's music could go national—international!—in no time. People would be beating down his door for his music.

Pretty soon he found himself near Sixtieth and Broadway. It was a colored section, with colored businesses: a few white faces were sprinkled in, but most were Brown. A woman hanging laundry on a line far above him was singing a minstrel song that Fred himself had plugged last year.

He was thinking about music and phonographs and Josephine's fat trunk of papers—he'd gone through only about a quarter of them— when he passed a worn brick building with a ROOMS TO LET sign in the window. The first floor had been some kind of shop, but now the plate glass looked onto a bare floor with only a dusty cabinet and a pile of boxes. He stared long and hard.

———

Four hours later, when he returned home in the early April twilight, Josephine was sautéing chunks of beef for soup. She glanced up, ducked her head in greeting, and turned back to the saucepan.

"Hello," he said, hands behind his back.

"Hello," she said.

"Go ahead. Ask me what I'm holding."

She didn't even turn around. "What are you holding?"

Fred whipped out a fat wad of papers printed with tiny type. "Well, for one thing, I decided to start my own music publishing company."

"What do you mean?"

"I mean that we're going to have a music publishing company, like Ditmars. Make money directly, not through him."

"Are you sure?" she asked.

"Sure as shooting. There's a lot of money to be made, what with my lyrics and your songs. We're just pissing it away, giving it to Ditmars. And besides, I'm sure you heard I quit today."

She nodded. "Why did you do that?"

"There's more," he said. "We're moving!"

"What?" Josephine now turned around, knocking a few chunks of raw beef from the counter onto the floor. She didn't seem to notice. "Moving? Where? Why? Are you kicking me out?"

"Hey, hey, calm down. Of course I'm not kicking you out. We're moving together! I just found a place that's perfect for us. Perfect!"

She stood there, uncertain.

"I did it for us, Josephine. Ditmars didn't appreciate what I was doing for him. It's time to strike out on my own. I can do it. We can do it together. I promise."

Josephine was still for a long moment. Then she said, "Okay. If you think it will work."

"Oh, I do. I know we can do it. It's not in Tin Pan Alley, but it's just ten blocks from here. The neighborhood is swell. It's that colored area around Sixtieth. There's music all around—your kind of music. I found us two rooms upstairs, each with their own bathroom. And you can have your own space. I'll be right next door. And here's the best part. The first floor is empty—I got it for a song. That can be the offices for Delaney Music Publishing. Isn't that great? So to get to work all you'll have to do is walk downstairs."

The next day he took Josephine to the building: five levels, with a creaky but functional elevator in the back. Carved wooden paneling lined the halls, and the elevator was appointed in brass filigree arranged in geometric patterns. Several rooms on the second and third floors were occupied, but several others—on the fourth and fifth floors, mostly—were vacant. Fred hired a crane to lift a piano to the fifth floor for Josephine and ensconced himself in an adjoining room.

Three weeks, a few coats of paint, some secondhand equipment, and an open moving cart later, the move was complete. Fred and Josephine spent hours transcribing new songs. Fred wanted to make sure that he would have a full set of brand-new music ready to be sold and printed for his customers.

On Monday, June 2, 1919, Delaney Music Publishing, Inc. officially opened for business.

28

Nondisclosure

Bern

AFTER HE'D BEEN DISMISSED from the board meeting, Bern pulled out his phone in the elevator heading down to his subbasement office. He needed to call Eboni.

There was one missed call and two texts from her:

Police here taking evrything
Don't give anything away. I'll be in touch

She didn't reply again. When Bern called, her phone went directly to voice mail. What had she meant, *Police here taking evrything*? He stared at her message as if it would begin scrolling into a further explanation. None came. By *police*, could she mean the Delaney Foundation? Did they come to confiscate the trunk? If so, why had they set up the elaborate meeting between the board and him?

By then he was down in the subbasement and didn't have a signal, anyway. He surrendered his phone to the security guard, charged through the body scanner. He scanned his fingerprint and opened his office door.

The office wasn't empty.

Stanford Whitman sat at his desk. How had he gotten down there so quickly? Whitman saw him, smiled a forced smile. His eyes were cold.

"Where's Eboni?" Bern asked him. "Did your goons go to her office? What's going on?"

Whitman shrugged. "We need that trunk."

"Where is she?"

Whitman didn't answer. "I just wanted to go over the NDA with you one more time." He had a file open on Bern's desk, flipped a sheet toward him. Bern leaned over. It was one of the documents he'd signed the first night he'd arrived in New York City.

"You do remember signing this, correct?" Whitman asked.

"Of course."

"And your girlfriend signed one, too?" Whitman opened another folder, slid the sheet in front of him. Eboni, Bern now remembered, hadn't signed. She'd told him to sign on her behalf, if he felt like he had to; but she'd refused. "Yes," Bern lied. "There it is."

"I just wanted to go over with you what it means if you breached this," Stanford said jovially. "You or your girlfriend. I'm sure you read it, but just in case."

"Of course," Bern said. He wanted to correct Whitman—Eboni wasn't his girlfriend—but that seemed like the least of his worries just then. He'd begun sweating again, and hoped that Whitman couldn't tell.

"You understand that the NDA applies well beyond all your work with *RED*. You'll see here that 'confidential information' includes *any* information that you obtained during your course of affiliation with the Delaney Foundation. So that goes to any and all references to Josephine Reed, as well."

"Of course," Bern echoed him.

"Just so it's clear, if you or your girlfriend did decide to breach the NDA, the damages you agreed to are pretty steep. See here? And here?" Leaning over his desk, with a fat finger he jabbed at a particularly dense paragraph, and another thick one below that. The words *ten million dollars in actual damages* and *five hundred million dollars in speculative damages* rolled up from the mist of the print. "That's the beginning of what we'd be going after if you breached the agreement."

"Got it. I read it before," he lied. He was trying very hard to appear calm. He wondered if it was too late to just dash out the door, down the hall, and somehow find himself back in Charlottesville, Virginia. He swiped at his hairline, hoping he wasn't visibly sweating.

"That's just the beginning," Whitman said. "There's also a clause about 'immediate confiscation of all documentation' right below it. See? Clause 6D."

"Yes, I see that."

"Rest assured we have no problem enforcing the terms of this NDA, professor."

"So that's your excuse for giving you permission to bust into Eboni's office and take her stuff?" Bern said.

Whitman sat back in his chair. "We all need to be playing on the same side. For the same goal."

"What kind of people are you? Do you know where Eboni is?"

"I'm sure she's safe," Whitman said.

"She better be."

ACT 4

Josephine

29

The Wrongness of G-Flat

Josephine

JOSEPHINE REED knew she had to leave. If she could just figure out how. It just wasn't right. The creak of the stairs was much sharper, like branches falling in an ice storm: and the third step's F-sharp sponged into a G-sharp, and that felt wrong, too. And the elevator: she could feel it in her ankles and in her rib cage, the press of the button and the hydraulic click (E-flat) and hum (A-flat and C together).

And where was Freddy? Fred. He didn't like to be called Freddy anymore. That was wrong, too. But he wasn't here, breathing his cream-colored breaths in the corner, the slight catch on his lips before the exhalation—that was how she knew he was truly asleep. Now she didn't know whether he was asleep or not. Now she didn't know where he was. All she knew was that he wasn't *here*. Which was the worst wrongness of all.

He'd promised her that this would be good for her, good for them, and of course she believed him. So she would move forward into the day, and she would show him that yes, she could do this. After all, he did promise.

This was not a life for her, up here on the fifth floor, alone, without Freddy living and breathing in the same room with her. Loneliness grasped at her with a pungency she almost welcomed. Freddy should be there, chattering his silver chatter, but instead he was in his own room. And now she was outside and another colored lady passed her, walking a tan poodle that yapped at Josephine as she drew abreast of it, and she cringed against a wall. If Freddy were here he would have thrown out a joke, but Josephine knew no jokes. She wondered what Howard was doing. Funny how she hadn't thought about Howard for a long while.

In the subway car she brought forth her Compendium and jotted down the Brahms and the stairwell's F-sharp and the sound of the lock clicking into place. The tick and the rhythm of the subway kept calling for a C and then an E and then a G. She had a melody, neat and orderly, completed before the train reached Penn Station.

"How wonderful," she imagined Freddy saying to her, looking at her with his blue eyes so admiring.

"Josephine?" Eunice said as Josephine entered the service door at Ditmars. Eunice sounded surprised, her red-gold voice shading slightly upward.

"Good morning, Eunice," Josephine said, just the way her mother and Mrs. Cromartie had drilled into her. *Be polite, Josephine.* "How are you today?"

"Um, I'm fine. What are you doing here? I thought you quit?"

And there was the wrongness again, blossoming up from the scarred wooden floor as if it had feathers.

"I work here," Josephine said. "Why would I quit? I like it here." She placed her paper-wrapped ham sandwich (umber! D-flat!) next to Eunice's under the outgoing-mail shelf.

"Oh dear. Well. Have you talked to Fred?"

"Not this morning," Josephine said, picking up a stack of files from Eunice's desk: accounting receipts, to their office a few floors above, she would enjoy the trek upstairs and listen to the music of the pianos and the staircase under her feet. She knew it would feel right.

"It's just that—I thought after Fred came in the other day—"

Josephine turned to make her way upstairs. Eunice was not making sense as she said, "He made it clear that you both were leaving."

"Leaving?"

The stair tread was scuffed and scarred, with a large black line under the balustrade, perhaps a heavy piece of furniture had marred the surface.

"We aren't leaving," Josephine said, but now there was a niggle of worry honeying the back of her scalp. Perhaps she should open her Compendium and begin Transcription. Dr. Moore always told her to Transcribe when the wrongness hit her.

"Oh, honey," Eunice was saying, "I'm sorry, but you'd better get out of here before Mr. Ditmars sees you. I don't think you should stay here for another minute."

Josephine could feel Eunice's footsteps in Josephine's own calves and ankles as Eunice drew close to her. Would Eunice touch her? Josephine pulled in her shoulders to avoid it.

"Josephine," Eunice said again, "I'm sorry, but you really should leave."

And that could not be right. The pianos were singing upstairs in the daylight and she was down below in the bass cave.

"Go talk to Fred," Eunice said. "Fred will explain everything."

So then, Josephine wasn't in Ditmars anymore. She was outside with her handbag and her ham sandwich. Then she was walking, walking up to Penn Station and to the subway and to the apartment, which she couldn't find because she went to the old apartment and the key didn't fit in the lock and she sat on the stoop and she Transcribed: the people going past, the woman calling to her children, the automobiles chuffing and slamming, and doors banging, and a small breeze that came out of nowhere and blew against the back of her neck.

Where would she go? Where would she live? She had no job and no money. She Transcribed and Transcribed.

Soothed by the Transcribing, she remembered the new apartment. Freddy had made her repeat the address seven times, and she repeated it now, seven times more: 244 West Sixty-Third Street. She didn't like numbers and didn't like these numbers especially. The 63 felt somehow both slimy and too leathery to her, but that was where she would go and where Freddy would be.

And so it was. Freddy was on the first floor, and moving men were there, unpacking a rolltop desk into the corner of what had once been a storefront and would now be Freddy's office. She almost wept to see him, but she kept her face blank because, after all, what had he done, changing her job and her bed on her? And not *Freddy*: Fred.

Freddy saw her and grinned. "Hey there. Where did you get off to? I was getting worried."

She would listen to music and Transcribe, that's what she would do. She would not speak to him. She would do this until the air was calm and glittered with music. She ignored him and ascended the stairs, up to her room, found the phonograph record of Chopin's Nocturne no. 2 in E-flat major and crowned the Victrola. She bent down close, her ear against the brass speaker, letting the cool wind of the nocturne blow over her, the repetitive thirty-four measures soothing in its predictability, and the waltz-like structure of the nocturne made her think of the flowers, green and pale yellow, lining the path down to the water where she and Howard and Lydia and Earnestine once played back in Oxford, and she opened the Compendium to the light.

But almost immediately, well before the air began to glitter, Freddy had opened her door and was coming toward her.

"Hey, what's wrong?" he said. "Josephine? What happened?"

She gulped in the nocturne and tried to pretend that he was not there, her Transcription unspooling before her like a lifeline.

"Josephine, what's wrong? Did something happen while you were out?"

She closed her eyes tight, but that made everything more wrong because the sounds ate up the air in her head.

"Why?" she said. "Why did you tell Eunice I quit? I liked working there. Why?"

"Let me explain. Have a seat."

"No." She meant that she would not sit, that she would crouch before the blowing nocturne and Transcribe what needed Transcription.

"I had to do it. Ditmars would have fired you soon enough. This was all for you."

"I liked working there. Why would you take that away from me? I thought you cared about me."

"This new publishing company, our company. It's going to be everything we've talked about. It's going to make us rich. You'll be able to listen to music all the time. You won't have to go into anyone's office anymore. Ditmars would never allow you to work there without me. I was the one who got you the job, remember?"

"I remember."

"This is what's best," he said. "I promise. It may take some time to get used to, but you've gotta trust me. I'm doing this for us. Do you trust me?"

She nodded. He promised. She could count on his promises. "I can still see your silver shade."

"Right, silver shade. There's my girl. I want you to know that from now on, your life is going to be filled with music. Everything you've always wanted to hear will be right at your fingertips. You'll see."

She didn't understand him when he talked like this.

"You know how hard I've been working to get the publishing company off the ground. I also landed us our first commission. Do you remember that? Isn't that just swell?"

She nodded, trying to picture a publishing company hovering a few feet from the earth. She also wasn't sure what a commission was. But Freddy was happy, and that was good, and she could count on his promises, and the nocturne blew and her fingers itched because that waltz melody was just beyond her sight, pale yellow.

"Remember we talked about this last night? The commission is for a new vaudeville act opening in three weeks. The soprano, remember? Rachel Davis? You love her voice. So we've got a lot of work to do. You need to get the music written. Remember that you promised you'd have something for me tonight?"

She was thinking of the pale golden flowers near the stream bank and how the nocturne lifted their petals, so she nodded because he seemed to expect it.

"I need that music," Freddy said, and she agreed with him; she needed music, too. What devastation would exist if there were no Chopin.

"It's for Rachel Davis. The soprano. She's singing about having way too many people in love with her. I'm going to call it, 'Long Line of Lovers.' I think the alliteration works fine. What do you think?"

The Chopin lifted into its C coda, so pure. She looked around for the yellow.

"Josephine? What do you think? Do you like it?"

"It sounds wonderful, Freddy." And then, correcting herself, "Fred."

"Thanks. And remember, you have the most important part," he said. "The music. You promised me the music today. They're expecting something tomorrow to look over. Your music is really going to open doors for us. You're going to knock 'em dead."

He paused, looked around. "Hold on a sec, let me get something."

He left the door open, and the elevator clicked its E-flat, and a moment later the A-flat-and-C-together of the hydraulic hum. While he was gone she replayed the morning's subway ride, the cluck of the subway cars and the whoosh of air blowing past. What musical note was the wind? A different wind from the Chopin. This was A wavering into C and flattening into B minor.

The elevator clicked again, and whirred, and moments later Fred returned with a stack of brand-new phonograph albums—Schubert and Jolson and Murray and Bayes, among others.

"I thought you'd want all these to listen to, for inspiration. I'm going to need your absolute best if this is going to work. Which means you'll have to concentrate, okay? I need it tonight. Tonight," he repeated.

She could feel him looking at her, his gaze rough against her skin. She was certain it would leave a mark on her cheek. "Now, you get started. You've wasted half the day already. I need Rachel Davis's melody tonight, okay? Okay, Josephine? I'll see you soon, partner." He closed the door behind him.

"Partner"? She didn't feel like a partner. She wondered how it would feel, to be a partner. The nocturne had blown away, but one of the new albums was Franz Schubert's chamber music. The C-major quintet for two violins, a viola, and two cellos. Josephine Transcribed it into the Compendium, although the second movement felt like there was another melody lurking somewhere in the bass line. By the end of the third movement, she'd added three pages to the Compendium.

That evening, Fred knocked on the door—three D-flats, *boom boom boom*. She'd listened to the Schubert, Al Jolson's "Some Beautiful Morning" and "I'll Say She Does," Nora Bayes's "How Ya Gonna Keep 'Em Down on the Farm (After They've Seen Paree)," Billy Murray's "Sahara (We'll Soon Be Dry Like You)," and several others, including the Chopin again.

She liked being able to listen to the phonograph while she made dinner for them—chicken cutlets, boiled potatoes, and carrots—and had added another sixteen pages to the Compendium. She especially enjoyed the bubbling of boiling potatoes—a ragged staccato beat with unexpected bursts that at first might seem random but weren't.

"Hey, kiddo," he called.

She was on the other side of the room, at the kitchenette. One wall was supposed to be a "living room" and the other wall was the "kitchenette," he'd told her. At his voice she brought out two plates from the built-in cabinet.

"Chicken," she said. "And potatoes."

"Oh," he said. "Oh. Hey. Oh gosh I'm sorry. Would you believe I already ate? I had something downstairs with the fellows."

She wasn't really listening to him, still thinking of that rolling boil of the potatoes.

"I ate already," he repeated. "But I'll sit with you while you eat. Now you'll have leftovers for tomorrow, isn't that good?"

That she heard. "You ate?"

"Yeah. I'm sorry." He repeated his explanation about having eaten downstairs with the fellows.

She wasn't sure who these fellows were. Why didn't he bring them up to have dinner with her?

He went on, "Is it done? The song?"

"What do you mean?"

"The new song. For Rachel Davis. Is this it?" He gestured to a piece of the Compendium, which had been stacked on top of the piano. "Gosh, you've been busy."

"New?" she repeated.

"Yes," he said. "Have you finished it?"

"Oh," she said.

"Where is it?"

She unfolded several sheets of the Compendium from where she'd tucked them in a drawer.

"Will you play it for me?"

"Can we eat first?" she said.

"Oh. Sure. You go ahead."

Onto two plates she doled chicken, potatoes, and carrots for the both of them, set the plates on the dinette table in the corner. He sat across from her while she ate, talking of his day, how he hoped he'd score a second commission, how it was trickier than he thought it would be to start the business, to figure out how to get his songs into rotations. She only half listened. She watched the steam curling up from his plate, from his uneaten chicken and potatoes, the vapor writing almost-invisible messages in the air as it disappeared. She desperately wished she could read it.

When she'd finished eating he carried their dishes—his still full and untouched—to the sink. "Okay, let's hear it," he said. "I can't wait."

"Hear what?" she said.

"What you've been working on all day. The song. Upbeat tempo. 'Long Line of Lovers.' "

"You've heard it before," she said.

He grinned at her. "No, I haven't, silly. Just try me. Let me at 'em. Let me hear this one first." He gestured to the topmost sheet of the Compendium.

She sat down and played the opening eight measures of Al Jolson's "Some Beautiful Morning."

"Wait," he said, stopping her. "That's 'Beautiful Morning,' right?"

"Yes," she said.

"I thought you were playing something new?"

She shrugged again.

He handed her the next piece of the Compendium: Murray's "Sahara" and then the Schubert quintet.

"Wait," he said. "Are you telling me that all of these—" he gestured to the Compendium—"are just what you heard from the Victrola?"

"I needed to Transcribe them," she explained.

"I thought you were writing the new song," he said. His face was getting very red. He kept putting his fingers under his collar as if it were too tight. "Josephine," he said, "I need you to write new music. New music, remember? Not the music you've already heard. The music you *want* to hear. The song for Rachel Davis. The soprano. We talked about this all weekend. The publishing house depends on your new music. You remember that, right?"

She nodded because she thought he wanted her to nod.

"Tomorrow I need you to really concentrate on new music," he said. "Not this stuff you've already heard. You need to take the old stuff and turn it into new stuff. Remember? Good. I thought you did. That's my girl."

And then Freddy left her alone again. She went to sleep, listening to the Schubert, wishing it was the quiet exhalations of Freddy's breath as he slept.

She didn't want to write Freddy's new music.

The next morning Fred was outside her door as soon as her piano started up. She always played in the mornings: back in Oxford, before they locked the piano from her, it was her special moment of the day, just her and the melody and the air fresh with the smell of birdsong. Now fewer birds sputtered and flashed here in the city, but she loved warming the air with music.

He knocked on her door during the sixth measure of the Schubert. He made her stop playing, dress, have breakfast—he cooked oatmeal for her and it was lumpy—and sat her down at the dinette table with the Compendium.

"Okay, I'll let you get started," he told her. "I'll come check on you later today, okay? Remember what I said, right? Rachel Davis, the soprano. She wants a really fun bubbly song for a darb vaudeville act. This is going to make us, Josephine. I know it! We just need a really swell melody, remember?"

He closed the door behind him.

She heard the key turn in the lock. G-flat: the sound sharp, and trailing into an F minor as he withdrew the key from the keyhole.

She went to the door, tried it.

He'd locked her in.

30

Hunting a New Ebony Handbag

Bern

HOURS HAD PASSED with no word from Eboni. He kept going in and out of the Foundation, to get his phone and check for messages from her.

Why the police? What crime had she committed?

Had Josephine's trunk with the Doodles in it been taken, and was it being pawed over by—by who? Pawed over by the Delaney Foundation? By Mallory Delaney Roberts? Why would the police care? Was the trunk nineteen floors above him? And where was Eboni? Bern couldn't think about it without his stomach churning and sweat prickling his hairline.

He tried to concentrate on *RED* but couldn't get more than a measure or two analyzed before he'd check his phone again.

What was Eboni going through? The police had taken all her equipment. It was too coincidental for them to show up randomly. It had to be Delaney. Eboni had been right all along: Delaney was playing for keeps.

By eight p.m. he still hadn't heard from her. Why had he gotten her mixed up in this to begin with? She was always right. She'd always been one step ahead. Until now.

He'd finally given up work and was heading to his apartment when his phone chimed.

UNKNOWN: Are you in a safe place to read this

BERN: Who is this

UNKNOWN: Who do you think dumbass. Go someplace you can read. No eyes on ur back.

BERN: No eyes. Are you ok?

UNKNOWN: I'm good. Get a new phone. Burner. Text this # when you get it

Half an hour later, standing under a grimy awning a block from Times Square, he texted.

BERN: Hey it's me. New phone.

UNKNOWN: Here's new #. Delete this after we R done. Throw away this phone and buy another. Just in case

Seriously? Was this some kind of spy movie? She was really over-exaggerating.

But she'd been right all along.

Fifteen minutes later:

BERN: OK, me again. Are you okay?

UNKNOWN: They took everything.

BERN: Everything? As in EVERYTHING?

UNKNOWN: Not everything. I deleted all information but saved
         the important

UNKNOWN: Trunk and papers in a safe place

BERN: You got it???? Genius. U ok?

UNKNOWN: I'm good. We need to meet. Queens.

BERN: Who took everything? Police? FBI? DF?

UNKNOWN: Will send address in 1 hr. Go back, change clothes,
         leave wallet, dont bring laptop or your regular
         phone, take subways and change trains a bunch of
         times to make sure ur not followed.

BERN: OK. Where r u now?

UNKNOWN: Not important. Safe. Be ready to meet in 1 hr

BERN: OK. Im sorry

UNKNOWN: I know. C U Soon

He flagged a cab back to the almost certainly bugged apartment.
Probably there were tracking devices slipped inside his clothes, his
laptop case, his shoes. He slid into a ratty T-shirt, sweatpants, two
sweatshirts, and his old tennis shoes, grabbed his driver's license, a
credit card, a hunk of cash, and his new phone.

Finally she texted him an address in Queens. He took six different subway trains, sometimes jumping out of one just as the doors were about to close, to assure he wasn't being followed.

The 7 train dropped him off deep in Queens, and he walked to the address that Eboni had sent. He double-checked his phone: the address was for a ladies' clothing boutique offering an ANNUAL GOING-OUT-OF-BUSINESS SALE! and LIQUIDATION TODAY!! It seemed like the kind of place where budget-conscious old ladies shopped for new teatime outfits. Perhaps Mallory had shopped there. He couldn't even imagine how Eboni knew of its existence.

Although it was after eleven p.m., fluorescent lights still glared in the back and the sign read OPEN. The liquidation sale apparently went on night and day.

The bell above the door jangled when he opened it, and immediately an elderly lady, her face lined and creased, lipstick bleeding into her lips, approached him. "May I help you find anything?" She was wearing a wig—jet-black, slightly askew. "Perhaps something for a young lady?"

"Um, no thanks. I'm waiting for a friend." This couldn't be the right place. Only in Queens would stores be open this late anyway.

"Well, we've got some nice handbags racked up in the back. Would you like to see them?"

Rack 'em up.

Bern grinned. It was the first shock of delight, no matter how ephemeral, he'd felt in hours. "I'd like that. I need a new handbag."

"Right this way." She led him through metal swinging doors, into a storage room where several blank-faced nude mannequins gestured obscenely into the shadows. Where was Eboni? He looked at his phone for a message, waited. The elderly lady held up one finger and disappeared down a narrow corridor. He started to follow her when a hand grabbed his shoulder.

"Jeez! Who the—"

"You need to chill. I'm the one runnin'." Eboni emerged from a rack of outdated pleated skirts.

He reached out to hug her.

Surprisingly, she let him, melting into him for a moment.

"Are you okay?" he asked her.

"Yeah, I'm good," she told him, but made no movement to pull away. They stayed like that for another thirty seconds, fear and comfort radiating between them. Finally she stepped back. "I need you to listen very carefully."

"What happened? What did the cops say?"

"Please don't make me bust you in the mouth. Shut up and listen." She was wearing black jogging pants and a black zip-up sweatshirt. No earrings nor makeup, and her hair was pulled into a loose ponytail.

"Sorry, sorry. It's just—"

"I know. Don't worry about it now. The cops, or whoever they were—I think it was probably Delaney thugs—had a warrant, signed by a judge. A court order because of a breach of an NDA. You remember? The bullshit NDA that I never signed."

Bern opened his mouth, closed it. That nondisclosure agreement: the Delaney Foundation was going to screw them both with it.

"So they got all the decoded Doodles, then?"

"Hell no. Miss Earlene's papers are safe. They haven't been in the trunk for a couple weeks now. I'm surprised you didn't notice."

"Why would I notice? I've been looking at the scans all this time, and I figured if I needed to see the originals, I'd just look at them. What did you do with them?"

She eyed him. "You may have paid for them, but Ms. Earlene gave those papers to *me*. And the trunk. I may turn the trunk into a coffee table someday. Maybe I'll show you where they are, but not right now. All you need to know is that they're safe."

"But the scans are on your computer," Bern said.

"Seriously? I loaded them onto a different server days ago, just in case. No way your Delaney friends will find them. And I totally wiped all the drives on my server, overwrote them with a bunch of

YouTube videos. It will take them months, if ever, to figure out what was on them."

"I'm just glad you're okay," Bern said.

"I really need you to be quiet now. It's your fault I'm out here runnin' around trying to avoid the cops, or whoever those thugs were. I can't go home."

All he could do was stand there and listen.

"We have to finish this," she said. "We don't have a choice."

"How? Delaney has all your equipment."

"I know a guy."

"Oh. Right," Bern said.

"Damn right. It's a good thing I do, or I'd be in the back of an unmarked car right now gettin' choked out."

She was so impressive. Even after she'd been raided. After all her equipment had been confiscated. She was on the run, and still so calm. "I told you. You can't trust these people."

"I know, I know," Bern said. "They must be monitoring me and probably you, too. I'm not sure how." Bern remembered how Stanford Whitman had taken his phone the first day he arrived, how they hadn't returned it to him for hours.

"We need to assume that everything is bugged," she said. "No talking on the phone, got it?"

"Yeah. I want to go through all my clothes, or just toss them and get a couple of T-shirts and jeans. New wallet. New computer bag."

"Get a bunch more burner phones, just in case."

"Already did," he said.

"I told you that these people are shady. They don't want anybody to know about Josephine."

"We don't know that, not for sure," Bern said. "What if we present it to them in a way that makes Delaney look like a rock star? That he collaborated with her—"

"You just don't get it, do you? There is no way these people can let any stain on Delaney's name be made public. I've dealt with people like this all my life. The money and the influence. They're scared. They ain't givin' up jack."

"So what do you want to do now?" Bern said. "Who's this guy? What can he do?"

"Don't you worry about it. I told you I got something for the Foundation. We're going to get everything decoded. You need to go back to Delaney and act like everything is cool."

"I don't see how I can," Bern said honestly.

"Do they want you back? Have they told you to stay away?"

"No," Bern said, thinking. "It's all business as usual to them."

"Good. Then it's business as usual for you, too."

"I don't see how I can," Bern repeated.

"I don't see how you can't," she said. "I'm sure going to be working my ass off now. I'll let you know when I get set up remotely. We can work from somewhere that they can't get to. You can't give the burner phones to the security guards. You're going to have to find a place to stash them outside the Foundation and outside your apartment."

"This is going to be impossible. I won't ever be able to reach you."

"I'll reach you," she said. "That's the only way to play this."

"Okay. You know what? I can stash them in the public library a couple blocks away. But I'll only be able to check them during business hours."

"That'll work. It'll have to."

Bern actually felt a rush: a dizzying, delirious spin of adrenaline. He was James Bond and Eboni was one of the many Bond girls, except she was much better at this than he was. Okay, so she was James Bond. He was willing to be her Bond boy.

"Hey! You listening to me?" Eboni snapped her fingers at him. "Get your ass out of here."

Bern almost went in for a hug again. He wasn't sure what stopped him, but he opted to touch Eboni's shoulder instead. A look passed between them and he wanted to offer to stay with her, but something in her body language forbade it.

A moment later the store's bell jingled behind him as the door shut, and he walked to the subway.

His footsteps echoed down Roosevelt Avenue. So late, but still people were about: an Indian woman, chiming faintly in a maroon-and-gold sari, passed him. In his heightened state of paranoia, he kept glancing over his shoulder. Was it his imagination, or were people watching him? A man talking on his phone studied Bern as he passed, and then a woman near a closed grocery store seemed to be talking to someone. To herself? Or to a microphone?

He took the 7 train toward Manhattan but jumped out at the first stop, looking to see who else was getting off: a teenage couple and an older man in a threadbare blue parka. He crossed to the opposite platform, heading deeper into Queens. Was that the same man in the parka? He couldn't tell. He got off at the next station, waited for what seemed like hours for the next train to come.

Four trains and an hour later, he noticed another man staring at him from the other end of the car. By now he was in Midtown, so he took yet another train uptown. He finally felt like he was alone. The streets were deserted, silent in the winter chill. At last he returned to his building and felt like an idiot—trying to shake off whoever might be tailing him on the way to an apartment that the Foundation had rented for him. But this was how things were: he was so rattled, so on edge, that he wasn't thinking clearly.

The silence was no comfort. As he slid through the door of the apartment building and took the elevator upstairs, he kept feeling eyes on him. Someone was watching him, tracking him, studying him. Waiting for him to drop his guard.

31

The Rightness of Falling Upward

Josephine

LATE THAT AFTERNOON Fred was back, unlocking the door. She'd spent the day playing the phonograph albums and Transcribing, and was just thinking about what to make for dinner. She'd had his chicken cutlet for lunch.

"Okay. Let's hear what you've been working on," he said, heading over to the black piano.

Josephine still Transcribed at the dinette table.

"Hey," he said, "it's time to get to work, remember? I need to get this done."

"It hasn't stopped yet," she said. "The tree falling upward hasn't stopped."

"Well, that's good, isn't it? The tree and all. Now I need to hear what you've come up with."

"It hasn't stopped," she explained. "The tree falling upward."

"Is that what you're calling the soprano song? Okay. Why don't you play the tree falling upward for me?"

"You want me to play it?" She paused the Transcription.

"I sure do."

She gathered the Compendium—dozens of sheets—and arranged them on the piano. Looked over at him. "Can we go hear the Starlight Cantina's new band tonight?"

"Sometime, sure. But not right now. I need to hear what you've written."

Only somewhat mollified, she began to play, fiendishly fast: trying to keep up from a low C to a high B-flat while somehow hitting octave Ds in the process. And that F-sharp, ringing out above the morass of the earlier notes. It was exhausting, and her fingers barely reached the stretch.

When she finished, she paused, hands spread over the keys.

Freddy didn't say anything for a minute. "What was that?"

"The trees falling upward. They're always falling upward. Unless they fall downward."

Another long pause. Outside, the elevator clicked and hummed.

"Well," Freddy said, and Josephine could hear the coldness in his voice, "that's not going to work. Let's see what else you've got."

She pulled out the next page of the Compendium: a low C to a high B-flat, and now instead of octave Ds, she played octave E-flats, and then back again to the F-sharp.

"Josephine, stop this. You know what I need. I need an up-tempo song for Rachel Davis. Not this—this—" He gestured inarticulately at the keyboard.

"You don't like the trees falling upward?" she asked him.

"It's just noise," he said. "You know that very well. Rachel can't sing that. Nobody could sing that. What else do you have?"

Josephine played through all the pieces of the Compendium she'd Transcribed that day. He stopped her a few bars into the fifth piece, stood, and paced back and forth.

"What are you trying to do to me? Are you trying to ruin me? Is that it? Are you just trying to sabotage me?" he yelled.

Each of the pieces was the same: the same low C to a high B-flat, the F-sharp. The only differences in each piece were the octaves she played in between. Sometimes D, other times G-sharp or A. Otherwise it was more or less identical. Pages and pages of the tree falling upward.

After the eleventh, Freddy said, "Stop."

He was very red in the face, and his eyes glistened. "You want to go back to being the scrap-bag lady again? Is that it? Because that's what's going to happen if I don't come through with this commission."

She looked down at her hands, long fingers resting lightly on the keys, and she remembered them dirty, clutching the Compendium as parts of it blew down the sidewalk when she would tuck herself against a wall and try to sleep. "You'd send me out?" she said. "You'd do that?"

"Of course not," he said. "Oh, gosh, I didn't mean it like that. I meant if we don't get the song written, then word will go out that Fred Delaney doesn't meet his obligations. And we won't get more commissions. This business will go under before it ever really gets off the ground. I'm trying to make this work for us. Do you understand? Please tell me you understand."

"Oh," she said, thinking.

After a moment she relented. She stood up, opened the now-unlocked door to the stairwell. She waited. Freddy watched her. After a few minutes came the creak of the front door opening five floors below, slamming, and footsteps resounding in the hall, and then the echoes bouncing in the stairwell. The footsteps hit the stairs. The fourth, fifth, ninth, and eleventh steps creaked: low C to high B-flat and octave Ds, then F-sharp. In a few minutes Ms. Schwartz, the tenant on the second floor, opened her door and slammed it with an A chord.

"There," Josephine said to Freddy. "The trees falling upward." Back at the piano she played what she had just heard: the low C to a high

B-flat, then the octave Ds, and the squeal of the F-sharp of the stair tread halfway up the second floor. "It's here."

"What? Why are you giving me the runaround? Why can't you just give me something. Something I—" Freddy stopped midsentence, staring at Josephine as if he could see the back of her skull. He looked over at the staircase and back at Josephine.

"Please tell me this is a joke," he said. "A very bad joke."

"I don't know any jokes."

"The trees falling upward. You spent all day today listening to people walk up and down stairs and writing it in your pages? Is that what you did all day today? Please tell me this is a joke."

"I don't know any jokes."

Freddy rarely touched her but now he laid his hand on her shoulder, turned her to face him on the piano bench. The weight of his hand burned her skin. She imagined a lemon-shaped scar there.

"Josephine," he said, and then he lifted her chin with his hand, and she thought she'd have a scar under her chin as well. And then she forgot the scars because she could see he was near to tears.

"Josephine," he said again, "this is going to ruin me. Ruin us. We need that song. Do you understand that? Can you understand that?"

She met his gaze, and again the electricity leaped between them. Then she looked down at his arm, slender, with golden hairs on the forearm. It was a relief to look away.

"Don't ever lock me in," she said. "Ever."

"I was just trying to get you to write—"

"Don't ever lock me in," she repeated.

"But we need that song—"

"I don't ever want to be locked up again," she said. "I'm not going to just write your music and be locked up. I won't do it. I write the music, and you put your name on it. But you can't lock me in. I want to go out. To hear the music outside in the world. I want to go to the clubs. I want to have dinner with you. I don't want to be locked in here. Can't we go back to how it used to be?"

"No," he said, and his voice was loud against her, battering at her. "No, we can't go back. I started this new business and I don't want to go back to plugging songs again. You hear me? I don't want to go back. You know how much old Ditmars makes every year? Millions, you hear me? Millions. I want that. And we can get it."

"What happened to the white torrent? We didn't go to the Alibi Club last week. You haven't even played your piano."

He shrugged. "We were busy moving. We'll go next week."

"You don't want to play anymore?"

"I'm a businessman. You need to understand that. This is our shot at making it in the big time and I don't want to jeopardize it. You have all those great songs that you always wanted to hear, remember? Now the world can hear them. Do you have anything we can use for the soprano up-tempo? Do you, or don't you? I don't want to keep asking."

"If I give you something," she said, "can we go to the Cantina tonight?"

"I don't think I can go tonight. Even if you gave me something, I'd still have to score it, arrange it, and come up with the rest of the lyrics."

"But can I go?"

"Sure you can go," he said. The rest of his sentence lay heavy and unspoken between them: *You can go if you give me the song.*

She decided she'd taught him enough of a lesson. Several pieces of the Compendium had been tucked beneath cushions of the second-hand sofa that Freddy had bought her. She dug them out, unfolded one, smoothed down its edges, handed it to him. "This?"

"You know I can't read them," he said. "Not like that."

So she sat down and played the piece, barely glancing at the ciphers: a bright up-tempo tune with arias and arpeggios and a killer unforgettable melody.

"Oh, wow, this is perfect," Freddy kept telling her.

When she'd finished, he leaned over and hugged her. This time she didn't actually mind it.

"I'm sorry," he whispered. "Really sorry. I've just been under a lot of pressure. Let's start over. Let's go back to how things used to be, okay?"

"Promise?" she asked.

"Yes, I promise."

She closed her eyes and willed herself to believe him. She was desperate to believe him. "Okay," she said. "And you won't lock me in again? Ever?"

"I won't lock you in again," he said. "I promise."

"Okay," she said. "I'm going to go to the Cantina tonight."

"Yes, you go," he said. "I'll get started on the lyrics to this, and why don't you make us dinner?"

She made fried chicken and greens, his favorite. Afterward she went to the Cantina and listened to the trio, which turned out to be a slight disappointment, but she enjoyed the bee-drenched melodics. When she returned, the light was still on under Freddy's door, adjacent to hers. He opened it when she was on the landing; he must have been waiting up for her.

"How was it?" he asked her.

She told him about it, and he nodded. "Glad you had a good time. And that song you wrote is just swell!"

"Good night, Freddy," she said.

"Good night," he said.

Ten minutes later, Josephine lay sleepless in her bed, thinking about Freddy. About how, tonight, he'd said the things he used to say. Ate with her, like he used to.

Yet, despite everything, the silver-cream of him had shifted, had transformed into something else. She didn't think he could change back. He was gray now. Fred. No longer Freddy.

32

This Is War

Bern

NEXT MORNING, at ten twenty, Bern did his best to appear as if it were just a normal beautiful day in Delaneyland. Turned out the public library a block away didn't open till ten, so he'd kicked his heels in a coffee shop, waiting. When it opened, he'd headed upstairs and hid the burner phone on a top shelf in the back of the stacks. Then he returned to the Foundation, where he swiped his pass through the turnstile. Took the elevator to the subbasement, staring straight ahead at the gleaming bronze doors. Passed through security. Trudged to his desk, sat. Opened his Delaney computer to resume work on *RED*.

Within moments, his intercom buzzed. "Doctor, Ms. Roberts needs to see you on the seventeenth floor."

"Okay," Bern said. "When?"

"Immediately," Stephanie said.

It was ten thirty-three. "Is it just her?"

"I don't know," she said.

So much for Eboni's instructions to "act like everything is cool," he thought.

On the seventeenth floor, Stanford Whitman met him at the elevator bank with a hearty "Bern, good to see you," as if he hadn't threatened Bern the night before. Stanford led the way to the conference room, where a meeting was already in progress. Most of the video screens were lit with heads, and seven people rose when Whitman gestured him in. Had they been there since last night? Danishes and croissants lay piled on the buffet, and each person had a coffee mug in front of them.

"Dr. Hendricks, let's dispense with the pleasantries." Kurt Delaney. "As you must know, we exercised our rights, per our NDA with you and Ms. Washington, to immediately demand the turning over of all documents and records relating to the Delaney Foundation."

"You took her computers, you mean," Bern said.

"We did," Kurt said. "And Ms. Washington has apparently either deleted all our materials or she's installed them behind so many firewalls that it amounts to the same thing. Our forensic technicians are working on it now."

"Okay," Bern said. "What do you want from me?"

Last night he'd been terrified, but now a slow burn was creeping from his abdomen to his chest and up to his face. They were screwing with him, and they were trying to screw with Eboni. Tightening the pressure. Jacques Simon used to do that, and all the graduate students would cower and pull all-nighters to meet his farcical and seemingly arbitrary deadlines.

"We want you to immediately turn over everything you've uncovered in your research. All the scans. All the physical evidence. We've gone through the laptop we loaned you, and it's not there. It's therefore on some other computer, and we're asking—nicely—for access."

"Ms. Washington has deleted the files from my computer, as well. And I'm not in possession of any of the physical evidence I've uncovered. I'm not altogether sure that it falls under the purview of my NDA. My attorneys—"

"Your attorneys didn't tell you shit, 'cause they don't exist," Thomas Alexander said from the other side of the table. "We don't have time for this." Spit flew from his mouth.

"Thomas, I'll handle this," Stanford Whitman said as he turned toward Bern. "Dr. Hendricks, Let's not insult each other. The NDA you signed compels you to allow us access to your research as well as prevents you from going public with any disclosures of any and everything related to Frederic Delaney. If you don't recall, I'm happy to remind you again of the eventual financial ruin you would be subjecting yourself to for failure to comply."

Bern thought about his next words carefully. "Mr. Whitman, all of you," he said, with more bass in his voice than he was accustomed to using, "like I said, I am not in possession of any of the physical proof of Delaney's collaborations. It's impossible for me to turn over to you what I don't have. Eboni's disappeared on me. She's not answering her phone—probably because you have it. But I can't reach her and don't have any of your materials anymore."

"Dammit! We are done fucking around!" Kurt Delaney shouted, and his video screen jumped as if he'd just punched the keyboard. "You think you and your girlfriend are so goddamned smart, don't you? I got news for you, boy. We own you. We want those fucking documents. They're ours."

"Respectfully," Bern said, "they're not. These documents were obtained with my own funds, and weren't a direct result of the work you commissioned me for."

Stanford Whitman spoke up. "They were obtained during your employment hours, utilizing our company plane, and it was entirely foreseeable that these types of work-product documents would have materialized. And you represented to the sellers that you were purchasing them for us. I'm sorry, Bern, but these pages belong to the Foundation, no matter who originally paid for them. And we're happy to reimburse you for the cost."

Bern took a deep breath. "I don't have them. I told you that. I don't have the originals and I don't have the scans. And I can't reach Eboni even if I wanted to," he lied.

"Well," Kurt Delaney said from the screen, "you have exactly twenty-four hours to figure out how to find her and get all that new material on my desk. If you even think about not complying, consider the alternative. I run one of the biggest foundations in the world. Are you really sure you want to take me on?"

"I can't be sure she'll reach out in time," he told them. "Unless you've managed to give her your ultimatum yourself."

"Thirty-six hours, max," Kurt Delaney said. "She'll reach out to you by then."

"Please, Bern," Mallory said, trying for a smile but not quite making it. "Nobody wants a fight. Just get us the documents and we can all make this unpleasantness go away."

Kurt Delaney said from the monitors, "And let's be very clear here. You are also to abide by the terms of the document you signed. That means you don't discuss Delaney matters with anyone—except, arguably, your lawyer, your priest, or your psychiatrist. You talk to anyone else—make one move toward the press or social media or fellow academics—and your pathetic life, as you know it, will cease to exist. You won't be Professor Bern Hendricks, who brought RED back into the public limelight, with guaranteed tenure and the world at your feet. You'll be Bern Hendricks, the worthless derelict who won't be able to get a job teaching 'Itsy-Bitsy Spider' to third graders. I will personally see to it that every university on the planet knows that you are toxic. Your dissertation will be rescinded. Your research will be discredited. You won't have a pot to piss in."

The rant seemed to have ended. All eyes were on Bern, who sat unflinching. He wanted to stand up and scream at them; simultaneously and contradictorily, he wanted to give them all the documents, show them that he wanted to play on the same team. Was trusting Eboni worth his career? Worth everything he had worked so hard for? Dedicated his life to?

"Are you finished?" Bern said.

"Kurt's finished," Mallory said smoothly. "Really, this is the worst-case scenario and none of us wants it to get that far, do we? Please, just get us the documents and we can all get back to work." She tightened her lips again.

The conversation seemed to be over. He stood.

Back on the elevator, he stared straight ahead, imagining the video cameras trained on his face. He thought about the sea of pale faces in that conference room. Were they laughing, celebrating that they had won? That Josephine would never get the recognition she deserved? That they were not going to be one-upped by some nigger with a PhD?

Instead of heading to his subbasement lair, he stopped on the ground floor, went out into a gray February morning. The sun cast no heat. He wandered the streets around Lincoln Center, barely thinking, comforted by the rhythmic pad of his feet on the cement. He ducked into the public library, retrieved the burner phone, made sure nobody was in the stacks near him. This felt safe and unanticipated. The Delaney eyes couldn't follow him here.

BERN: You were right

UNKNOWN: Told you

BERN: Theyre all assholes

UNKNOWN: You're just figuring this out? Well bettr late then
          nevr

BERN: This is WAR. We need to meet tonight. I'm going to bring a friend. With connections.

UNKNOWN: Who?

BERN: I have friends too

UNKNOWN: When?

BERN: Not sure yet. Let's say 9 PM. Where?

UNKNOWN: I'll text you an address. Give me 20

33

The Girl in the Flapper Dress

Josephine

THAT SUMMER Josephine spent most mornings wandering the city, absorbing the people sounds and strolling into Central Park to watch the ducks and listen to bird wings unfurling in the trees. She Transcribed. She sang snatches of melodies. She would return home in the high heat of the day, and Fred would have lunch waiting for her, and he'd eat with her in her room. Just like he promised.

Afternoons they would spend together, with the Compendium.

As she played the piano, Fred transcribed. They managed to rough in around eight to ten songs a day, culled from Josephine's trunk and the other places where the Compendium resided: under couch cushions, beneath the throw rug, at the back of the bookcase, lining the pantry shelves.

One day in late August, Fred surprised her as he scrutinized a page. "This figure comes up a lot. I'm guessing it's an ascending D-major scale played piano and staccato? How far off am I?"

"That's correct," she said. "But see the dot there? That means you have to play the first and third notes with a dotted eighth-sixteenth rhythm."

"Got it. And the dot makes sense. I may not be the brightest bulb in the box, but I've picked up a thing or two. Like this circle with the X. Is that a slur marking?"

"It's an accent marking," Josephine said. "If the X is this way, it means marcato. If it's this way, it's tenuto."

"Ah. Well, can't say I was close on that one. I wish you'd use normal musical terms."

"I don't like them. Mine are better. Plus they're only for me," Josephine said. She pointed to another cipher. "This is a G arpeggio ascending with a diminuendo on the last four notes."

Over the next few days she showed him more and more: her system was based not on standard musical notation, but on compositional techniques and ideas. Most composers would write articulation marks using Western symbols, such as a slur or a staccato; her pictograms went into far more detail than was standard, delineating how each note should be played, what strength and force should be brought to each sound, and how those sounds should work together as a whole. Each hieroglyph explained the articulation—the pattern, the length of note—visually and technically.

"Wow, this is definitely you, kiddo," Fred said once. "It's a little strange, but, knowing you, it all makes so much sense. I can't believe you can pack this much information on a sheet of paper. So if I do this"—he played a line from the page. "Is that correct?"

"Not quite," Josephine said. "Like this." She played the same line. Fred immediately realized what he had done incorrectly: he'd misread an eighth note triplet as four sixteenth notes, and played three notes instead of four.

"I need to make dinner," she said. "And afterward I want to go to the Grey Pony."

As they'd done in the past, she made them dinner. Then, a few nights a week, Fred would accompany her to a dance hall or club.

The rest of the time she either went alone or stayed home resting and dreaming up other songs she wished she'd heard.

Everything was as it should be, Josephine kept thinking to herself. It was as close to before as possible, and that gave her much comfort. But Fred was still gray. Something wasn't right. She didn't like the way he sometimes looked through her Compendium: possessive, gleeful. It wasn't his and yet he acted as if it were, as if he'd paid for it and now owned it.

She knew that he cared only about certain pieces of the Compendium: the sounds she wanted to hear, not the Transcriptions of the sounds she actually heard. It was simple, of course, to mark those Compendium snippets with a new cipher, and she did so—burying the symbol on each of the pages, but not telling Fred what the symbol meant. Mostly she did this with the new sections of the Compendium, but sometimes, when an older piece would call to her very loudly, she would mark that one as well.

Several of these pages of the Compendium—what she started to think of as the "Fredless Pages"—she'd tuck away in a different location than the others: folding them into a metal flour tin in the back of a kitchen cabinet. These were the melodies she loved best, that she didn't want to share with him. She didn't tell Fred that she did this. It was, after all, her Compendium, and she could do with it what she liked.

August melted into September and then October. Looking back, Josephine realized that instead of spending three or four nights out listening to music with her, Fred now spent only one night every week or so—or sometimes less. The publishing business was demanding more of his afternoons as well. Dinners with Fred was pared down to three times a week, and then twice a week. By October, she realized that they'd had dinner together only once, for Fred's birthday in late September.

He was terrifically busy, with boundless enthusiasm. The front office had already expanded to include several of the back rooms, and he'd built a small reception room in the front. Furniture blossomed on new carpeting. There were media interviews, journalists sprawled in the armchairs and stubbing out their foul-smelling cigarettes or cigars on the coffee table. He'd installed a telephone, which Josephine avoided, and it was always ringing.

"You understand, right?" he'd tell her anxiously. "It's only for a little while longer. Once I get this place up and running, we'll be right back at the clubs enjoying ourselves. Even better, we'll be able to travel and hear music from all over the country. You trust me, right? There's my girl."

Did she trust him? She didn't know. She didn't know how not to trust him.

In the meantime Fred was frantic, trying to keep up with the work. He hired four song pluggers. One of them also worked as a part-time arranger, organizing and standardizing the music and lyrics, since he no longer had time to do it.

Painters tromped in and out of the first floor, repainting the rooms; Fred had decided the original color—a dusky blue-gray—was too dark, and he wanted a clean white instead. Yet more furniture arrived, filling the first floor and oozing onto the second; among them was a gorgeous shiny rolltop desk for Fred and a beautiful couch and table for Josephine. (He hadn't told her ahead of time that he'd bought the furniture, and she'd had to scramble to remove the Compendium from the old couch cushions.)

He'd fixed up the elevator, too, polishing the brass filigree panels on its walls. Josephine liked the clear geometric patterns and would run her fingers over them on the rare occasions when she took the elevator. She much preferred the stairs.

By early February 1920, the phone seemed to always be ringing, and people were constantly interrupting their afternoon sessions with important business he had to attend to. But like clockwork, no matter what, he would spend at least an hour with her, going through the Compendium, looking at the new sheets she'd created. By now he could read much of her language—at least the language that would translate onto a musical instrument—and would sit on the new couch peering down at the music, sometimes jumping up to play a bar or two.

Josephine had never been so lonely.

And yet it was exhilarating. She had always written for herself. The music she wanted to hear: her own internal conversation, for her own delight. Now, however, she reveled in the challenge. Could she compose a ballet? What about two ballets? He'd paid for a private box so she could watch and listen to several new performances. She loved drinking in all the musical forms and stayed in the box, remembering and Transcribing, until the ushers finally pushed her out long after the other patrons had left.

Now a new musical theatrical act wanted a song to underlie the sword fight: Could she write a sword fight? Now that the sword fight was so successful, could she write the entire score beneath the whole theatrical production? On it went. One melody after another, her memory churning through the music in her head or embellishing the rattle of a cart going past on the street, and, in moments a new tune, or three, or forty blossomed forth.

At night she would haunt the cabaret halls, the dance halls, the vaudeville halls. She went wherever a colored woman could have access, even if only from backstage, down a dim and grimy corridor, listening to the white people prancing upon the stage.

One miserably rainy night in March she was up in Harlem to hear a sax trio, and in front of the Barron's Exclusive Club met Fred, tuxedoed, with a girl on his arm. Barron's Exclusive was whites only; Josephine had heard that the inside was elaborate and beautiful. Which was good, because this girl was elaborate and beautiful, encrusted in the latest flapper dress with fringe and beads, sporting a glittering headdress. The jewels on their twinkling strings swung back and forth in front of her eyes as she peered at Josephine.

Fred blanched when he saw Josephine, pretended to look away. Josephine wanted to speak, to reach out to Fred, to say something. She couldn't. Fred grabbed the bejeweled girl by her arm and seemed to drag her into the whites-only club. The door shut behind them with a booming D major. Josephine breathed deeply and got her bearings. She realized only then that she was soaking wet. She turned and headed home.

A few hours later Fred returned: even from five floors away she recognized the turn of his key in the entry-door lock. She could have performed his footsteps on any instrument at any time. The glittering elevator clicked and whirred, depositing him onto the fifth floor. His door was closer to the elevator, but her door was open. Light and her piano music—she'd played Brahms all night—spilled onto the landing. His footsteps tracked to his threshold, hesitated, and then padded toward hers. A moment later he sat down next to her on the piano bench.

"Hey. How's my girl? What did you come up with tonight?"

Josephine ignored him, continued playing.

"That's some rain out there tonight, huh?"

She stopped in the middle of her sweeping run. "Who was that woman you were with tonight? You told me you were meeting a client."

"Oh, her? She's no one. It would look strange if I showed up at Barron's without a dame, you know? You've never met Barron Wilkins, but, let me tell you, he likes to see the girls. Everybody knows it. To show up without one would be the kiss of death. She was strictly for show. To be honest, I don't even remember her name. What are you playing? Is it new?"

"It's Brahms," she told him. And then: "Why did you go without me?"

His raincoat was dripping on the piano seat next to her, but nei-ther of them moved. "You know I couldn't take you to Barron's. It's whites only."

"But why did you take someone else?"

"What are you miffed about? I told you, I couldn't show up alone. Barron's is a big-time client. You know he plays my songs regularly, and they're heard by a lot of the most important people. This was a business meeting to discuss adding to the rotation and maybe put-ting together something bigger. Barron is talking about putting on an extravaganza. I'm doing all this for you. For us."

"You are not," she said. She stood up, retreated to a corner of her room, behind the dinette table. "This isn't for us, it's for you! I want things to be like they were. I want you to be like you were. You prom-ised you would be."

Fred's face flushed. "Josephine. There's no way I could have taken you. It's whites only. If I tried to—"

"Stop it," she said, sinking into the corner and covering her ears. "I don't like this. I don't like that shiny girl. I need to feel the sounds. You promised."

"Stop being like this," he said. "You want me to get your papers for you? You need to write your stuff out?"

"No," she said. "I just need you to be here."

"You can't be like this. You know I'm working around the clock. I promised you things were going to change, and they are. I have some big plans. They're starting to happen."

"I just want the music," she said.

"I know." He knelt in front of her. "I have some really great news and I was going to tell you later this week, once things really firmed up, but I'll tell you now. We've been invited to go to Europe for a few months. France, Italy, and Austria. What do you think about that?"

"It's not the same," she said. "I don't want something different. You promised me things would be the same."

"I know, but Europe! Paris! This is great, Josephine! They'll pay our way, and we'll take the *Mauretania*. Have you ever heard of the *Mauretania*? It's the fastest ship in the world, you know that? And beautiful! So big it won't even feel like a ship, and we'll drink from crystal glasses and eat off gold plates!"

"I don't know Europe," she said. "I only know New York City and home. The sound of the automobiles and the crickets. The fire brigade and the subway. Not Europe."

"Think of all the new sounds you'll be able to hear," he said. "The sound of the sea far, far away from land. The sound of church bells! London church bells! '*Oranges and lemons / Say the bells of St. Clement's.*' Have you ever heard that? Europe is wonderful—there's music everywhere! Music on every street corner!"

"Oranges and lemons?" she said. "The bells say 'oranges and lemons'?"

"Yes," he said. "Haven't you ever heard it? The old nursery rhyme that talks about the London church bells."

He closed his eyes and recited from memory:

Oranges and lemons
Say the bells of St. Clement's
You owe me five farthings,
Say the bells of St. Martin
When will you pay me?
Say the bells at Old Bailey
When I grow rich,
Say the bells at Shoreditch

"See? The bells even talk to you. They speak a language like you do."

"Oranges and lemons," Josephine repeated.

"And there's no such thing as 'whites only' there. Everybody's welcome. You can go to all the clubs. You can listen to music—music like nothing you've ever heard before—anytime you want."

"Oranges and lemons," she said again thoughtfully.

"Think of all the new music!"

A hunger came upon her. Perhaps Europe wouldn't be so bad. Even if it was different. No "whites only." Could she really go anywhere she wanted to hear the sounds?

"Please," she said. "I miss the—"

"I know. You miss the emerald steel or something."

"Yes."

"I'll take you. You'll love it. I promise."

Promise. That word Fred kept using, open and empty like a mouth. But she desperately wanted to feel like she used to.

"I was going to tell you all this when it firmed up, but there's really no harm in telling you now. We'd leave in about six weeks. Middle of April. What do you think?"

At last, slowly, she nodded. The orange and lemon church bells were calling her.

34

#1 Best Pizza

Bern

IT WAS JUST AFTER NINE P.M., and the streetlights glared.

Deep in Brooklyn, in Crown Heights, a tiny restaurant proudly proclaiming itself #1 BEST PIZZA IN NEW YORK CITY #1! had been squeezed between a dry cleaner and a hardware store whose discarded rakes and plastic pails partially blocked the pizza place's doorway. Bern slid inside, and caught sight of Eboni devouring an enormous slice of pepperoni and mushroom, melted cheese arching between her mouth and the crust.

"Hey," Bern said, sitting down across from her. "How you doing?"

"Where's your friend?" she said, pinching off the string of cheese and popping it into her mouth.

"She's on her way," Bern said. "I told her nine fifteen."

"Good."

"How are you doing otherwise?"

"Fan-freakin'-tastic," Eboni said. She seemed brittle and tough at once. He wanted to hug her, but she gave him no opportunity. "Are you sure you weren't followed?" she asked.

"I'm sure." He kept one eye on the door but had changed subways six times on the way over. He was sporting new gear and rocking a dope-ass new laptop computer: a laptop with damaging information on it. He'd be generously donating it to Goodwill right after this meeting.

Sneaking down the sidewalk, he kept thinking that he recognized faces: that woman with earbuds, with the shiny brown hair—had she worn Beats earlier that day? Was the man in the suit talking into his cell phone the same guy in jogging shorts who'd passed him outside his apartment building? Bern couldn't be sure. One thing that he could be sure of: Eboni's paranoia was rubbing off. Eboni had been right all along. It would be foolish not to continue trusting her instincts, especially since her instincts were so much better than his.

Eboni played it calm, but she was always, always "on ready." She'd stood up to Mallory Delaney Roberts—one of the most powerful women Bern had ever encountered—and hadn't blinked.

"I'm gonna get them," she said, talking around a mouthful of pizza. "They are going to seriously wish they didn't screw with Eboni Michelle Washington. You getting a slice?" she asked him, gesturing to the pizza. "It's pretty good. Check out the thin crust. It's worth it."

He hadn't managed to eat all day, his stomach roiling with nerves, but the pizza looked tempting.

"Sure," he said, as casually as he could. "Thanks."

"Thanks nothing. You're paying for mine anyway."

He headed to the counter, ordered the baseline margherita, and then a sausage and pepperoni. When he returned, setting the paper plate on the table, Eboni asked him, "You have any trouble getting here?"

"Nope. Way too many subways and buses, though." He took a bite: the sauce exploded deliciously in his mouth. "Damn, this is good," he said. "Why haven't we tried this place already? Maybe this really is the best pizza in New York—it's even better than that place on the Upper West Side."

"My secret weapon," Eboni said.

He looked at his watch. "She should be here at any minute. Are you straight?"

"Yeah," she said. "We got us some good stuff. Oh, and speak of the devil." Eboni was looking beyond him, to where a casually dressed young woman, brown hair pulled back into a ponytail, wearing jeans and a light pink puffy jacket, had paused at the pizza counter. Her gold-rimmed spectacles glittered in the fluorescent lights, so Bern couldn't see her eyes.

"That's gotta be her," Eboni said, wiping her fingers on one of the skimpy napkins.

Bern looked over. "Yep." He stood up, and the woman came over to him, hand outstretched. "Dr. Hendricks? I'm Mona Keltner. Nice to see you again."

Bern shook her hand, introduced her to Eboni. He'd met Keltner once, briefly, when he had been a student at Columbia and she, who often covered music for the *New York Times*, wrote a profile piece on Jacques Simon. After the Delaney meeting, Bern had sent her an email from his burner phone saying he had some very damaging information about a major philanthropic entity and was ready to blow the whistle. To prove his bona fides, he included links to his faculty page on the UVA website. Out of an abundance of caution, he hadn't mentioned Eboni.

The reporter had agreed to meet, and here they were. Now Keltner eyed the pizza, its surface glistening with oil, and Bern offered to buy her something. She shook her head.

"Can't have you trying to bribe me with slices." She grinned, pony-tail bouncing, and went to order something from the counter.

When she returned—she'd ordered a coffee and a Styrofoamencased salad, which she picked at with a flimsy plastic fork—Bern said, "Everything needs to be very off the record right now."

"Of course," Keltner said, taking a sip of her coffee and pushing the wilted iceberg lettuce around. "What's this about? You said 'damaging information.' What's the philanthropic entity?"

He explained that he'd been hired by the Delaney Foundation, and she immediately sat up straighter, laid her fork down, and didn't look away from his face.

Bern went on to tell her that he was supposed to do some background research into a musical piece—he didn't tell her it was *RED* or explain that a long-lost musical score had miraculously resurfaced. Instead he told her that he and Eboni had uncovered a trunkful of the Doodles and that Eboni had managed to decode them.

Eboni jumped in, explaining the date discrepancy on the receipt for the roast-beef sandwich and how they'd discovered that the Doodles had been written by the mysterious Josephine Reed. How *JoR* seemed to have written a chunk of the music that Delaney published under his own name in 1923.

"So, here's the thing," Bern said. "We're thinking Josephine's contributions were a lot more than we first imagined. We can directly attribute forty-six musical compositions to her. But we think her contributions could be wider than that. Much, much wider."

Keltner betrayed no emotion, just listened—she had no notepad—meeting both of their eyes. Now she raised her eyebrows. "You think this Josephine Reed wrote more of Delaney's music? Why? How much?"

Bern slid a printout across the table: a scanned image of a left-luggage claim ticket:

#367
Penn Station
May 14, 1924
5 st trks

"We found this in the Delaney archive," Bern said. "We weren't sure what *5 st trks* meant, but when we found the trunk in North Carolina, a couple of things stood out to us. *5 st trks* seems to mean 'five steamer trunks.' Someone—Josephine, Delaney, we don't know—consigned five trunks to the left-luggage office. We don't know what happened to all the others, but the trunk we found had a letter from Pennsylvania Station in it." He slid a photocopy of the letter across to her.

"Here's what I think," he went on. "I think that there were five trunks left in Penn Station. Someone—probably Josephine herself—took four of them. Maybe they didn't have the claim ticket. Maybe they didn't know how many there were. But they left one behind. And that one trunk sat in the left-luggage office until 1928, until the chief porter wrote to Josephine Reed in North Carolina, and Josephine's brother went up to New York and collected it."

He slid another sheet in front of her: several photographs of the trunk they'd found in Earlene's basement, with a close-up of the top left corner of the lid's exterior, where a painted white *4* slept beneath the grime of a hundred years. "I think this was trunk number four."

Eboni said, "We don't know for sure, but it seems very likely that Josephine Reed wrote most, if not all, of Frederic Delaney's early music."

35

Oranges & Lemons

Josephine

UNTIL PARIS, everything was wonderful. After they disembarked the RMS *Mauretania* in Plymouth, England, they traveled in a motorcade up to London. Josephine shared Fred's car. Even the bumps in the roads sounded different, more free, as they roared down twisty roads in ancient villages with archaic pub signs creaking in the wind and rattled over cobblestoned London streets flanked by nearly identical Edwardian town houses.

Ensconced in their respective suites in the Charing Cross Hotel, Fred would spend the mornings with his "fellows," conducting business. Afternoons were Josephine's. She and Fred listened together to the bells of Big Ben and then St. Martin-in-the-Fields, just like the nursery rhyme that Fred had recited. He rarely dined with her—he had social obligations, after all—and often his evenings were booked, too. But he procured tickets for her to all the best music halls, theaters, and shows.

But no matter what, by eleven thirty every evening, Fred would knock politely on Josephine's door. He'd ask about her excursions as he shuffled through the latest additions to the Compendium, and there were always older pieces to sort through (he had thoughtfully brought the entire Compendium with them in five large steamer trunks, all labeled PROPERTY OF FREDERICK DELANEY). They'd play her songs on the piano—of course the suite's living room came equipped with a piano; Fred had required it—and Fred would leave her around one or two in the morning with a cheery "See you tomorrow!"

But then came Paris. A month in London swelled Fred's entourage from the four people who had accompanied him to six: a part-time song arranger, who now seemed to be full-time; a titler, who dreamed up song titles, arranged, and wrote lyrics; a secretary to manage Fred's schedule; a valet to manage Fred's clothes; a driver to manage Fred's transportation; and Josephine. Besides Fred, no one really spoke to Josephine; she was just "Josephine" to them.

The final week in England, Josephine came back late one morning from an excursion to the West End, where an impromptu jazz band had set up in a small park (the music was similar to New York's). As she passed Fred's open door, she heard her name: his secretary, James Meader, was organizing the accommodations in Milan.

"And Josephine Reed, of course," Mr. Meader was saying.

"Yes," Fred said. "Make sure you give her a nice room with a piano. She loves her piano."

Gratitude for Fred swelled in her breast.

"We already booked the Grand," Mr. Meader said. "But their renovations mean Paul and Danny will have to stay next door. If we swapped out Josephine and if Paul and Danny shared a room, we'd all be in one place."

"Except Josephine," Fred said.

"Except Josephine," Mr. Meader agreed.

"That will never do," Fred said. "She has to stay in the same hotel. I promised."

He was her Freddy, Josephine thought. He didn't show it as much—he didn't spend time with her like he used to—but he still cared for her. How lucky she was to have found him! How could she ever truly repay him for everything he had given her? She closed her eyes tightly, and that morning's music bathed her inner ears: the saxophone and trumpet solos touched the depth of her being.

"Just because you promised doesn't mean—"

"James," Fred said, "we've already gone over this."

"I just think you should see reason," Mr. Meader said.

"I promised her," Fred said.

One of the other fellows—Brian Etling, the arranger—said, "You're not treating her badly. Just differently. It would make everything much easier."

"She's a scrap-bag lady, for goodness' sake," Mr. Meader said. "She's already getting vastly more than she deserves."

"She's mine for life," Fred said. "I've told you this. No discussion."

Mr. Meader said, in a singsong voice, as if he'd repeated the words many times before, "When you rescue a dog from the street, it's yours for life. But that doesn't mean she has to stay at the Grand Hotel with you."

"Fellows, stop," Fred said in a warning voice. "Paul and Danny can stay next door. No argument or discussion."

Mr. Meader sighed. "Very well. Then here's the plan . . ."

Josephine crept away, out into the London air. She spent the rest of the day wandering the streets, trying to figure out what Mr. Meader had meant. Dog? Fred didn't have a dog. She would have liked it if Fred had a dog. She would take it for walks and feed it treats.

That night, when Fred knocked on her door, he was sunny and

warm, but disappointed that she had not Transcribed much that day. They burrowed instead into one of the Compendium's trunks.

On to Paris, where the dance halls were legendary, and Josephine was eager to listen to them with Fred. But business was becoming only more complicated and time-consuming for Fred, so he was unable to accompany her much of the time. For the first couple of days in Paris, she was alone. Not speaking the language and not knowing her way around intimidated her, and she spent several days in her suite. The melodies those days were more Transcribed from her memories in North Carolina and New York. No matter what, though, Fred would knock on her door to wish her good night, spend an hour or more sitting with her and sifting through the Compendium.

About a week after their arrival, Fred knocked and opened the door without waiting for her to tell him to come in. It was just after eleven at night. He was disheveled; his tuxedo looked ragged. His bow tie swung loosely around his neck.

He didn't even glance at Josephine, who'd been waiting for him at the piano. Instead he went straight for the pages of the Compendium piled up on a side table, began frantically flipping through it.

"What are you—" she began. He flung the pages on top of the coffee table, went for one of the Compendium trunks in Josephine's bedroom.

She tried again. "What—"

He cut her off midsentence. "Where are those songs I was playing through a couple days ago? The ones with that series of running notes at the beginning, that I told you we were going to use for the chorus number?"

"The blue willow was gritty and sandy," she said.

"Dammit, Josephine," he said, "I don't have time for this foolishness. Where's that music? I need it. Now! They'll be here soon and I need to play it." He was rifling through her trunk. "I knew I should have written it up before."

"They?" she said. "It's late, isn't it? Isn't it almost bedtime?"

"Shut up and help me find it," Fred said. "Where is it?" He was dismantling the Compendium all over the floor.

"I don't know where the azure landed," she said.

Fred continued to scan each sheet and toss it on the floor. "It is crazy you don't have a system for these! Crazy, you hear me? We need to get this organized."

"It is organized," she said coldly. "It's very organized."

"You don't understand. This is important. Please help me find that music. It was in your green notebook yesterday. The one with the zigzag on it. Did you put it somewhere?"

Josephine repeated, "I don't know where the azure landed."

Fred paused from where he knelt over the Compendium. Then, almost before she was aware of it, he was coming at her, grabbing her by the shoulders. She shrank against the doorframe, his fingers, cold and hard as bullets, pressed into her skin. "Stop talking crazy. I need that music. Right now. Do you have any idea at all who's coming over here tonight?" With each phrase he shook her slightly.

Her head wobbled, the back of it knocking against the wall. She wriggled loose. "It's mine," she said. "Let go of me. It's my music."

She didn't know where the words came from, but once the sounds of *It's my music* whispered in the room, she felt them to be true. For her, up until this moment, music had just been music: owned by no one, or owned by itself. How could someone "own" a sound? How could you hold it in your hand or stuff it in your pocket or lock it in a room? You couldn't. It would seep out, blend into the world, open to the universe.

But now, with Fred's bitter breath on her cheeks, his eyes bulging inches from hers, right then she saw the concept of ownership differently. No one could own the sounds themselves, but when the sounds took form—when they were Transcribed, transformed into regular music notation—then they held a different power. The form could be sold, bartered, traded. If you sold the paper, you could have money, and money meant freedom. Meant power. And the sounds were still, intrinsically, themselves.

"It's my music," he said. "Our music."

She didn't argue with him, not then. He was right. The papers that he was selling with her sounds on it were papers that he'd written, that he owned. But if she had her own papers? She'd have her own power. Her own freedom to do what she wanted. Hear what she wanted. Not what he wanted her to hear.

Her cheek stung with tears. Her fingers groped against the wall, her index finger Transcribing his words against the cool plaster. She refused to look at him.

"Why are you doing this to me?" Fred whispered. "Look what you made me do! I need that music."

She took a breath, the air—too warm, too foreign—filling her lungs. She met his gaze. "It's. My. Music," she told him. "Get out of here," she said.

"I—"

"Go away!" she shouted. "I don't want to see you again!"

His mouth opened and closed. His face was very white.

"Josephine. Josie. I am so sorry, I—I didn't know what I was doing. I just have to find that music. I didn't mean to hurt you."

"It's my music." She wanted to get out and run—home to New York, to North Carolina, to anywhere but here. Where would she go? How could she leave without the Compendium? Fred wouldn't let her leave with her music. She now realized what was most important to him. It wasn't her. It wasn't the time—rare now—they spent together. It wasn't the walks they took to the music halls. All he wanted was her music. All those papers and papers. He only cared about the Compendium.

"Josephine? I'm so very, very sorry."

She didn't look at him. "I think I remember where it is."

"There's my girl. Where is it? I won't hurt you again. I promise."

There it was: *I promise*. She hated him for saying it again. "I prom-ise" rang in her ears, its sting now worse than the tenderness on the back of her head.

"It's under the bed. That side." She gestured to the farther side of the bed.

Fred ran to the bed, crawled under it. While he was groping around for the Compendium, she quickly went back to the suite's living room. She'd found a shallow shelf underneath the couch where she could put the pieces she didn't want to share with Fred: the piece he was looking for was among them. Now she grabbed the sheets he wanted, slid them among the others on the piano.

Fred burst back in. "It's not there! It wasn't there!"

Josephine was in front of the piano, flipping through the music. She pulled out the sheet he wanted. "Is this one of them?"

Fred bounded over, snatched the page. "Thank god! Yes! Where are the other sheets?" he was pawing through the music. "Why couldn't I find it earlier?"

She shrugged. "I think you were in too much of a hurry."

He ran out of the room, pages in hand. "I'll talk to you tomorrow." And as the door closed behind him, almost as an afterthought, he said, "I'm sorry if I hurt you."

Hurt her? He had no idea. She wasn't a dog from the street. She made music—beautiful music. Melodies that she heard people sing. She made people as happy as she was, when they heard the songs that she had wanted to hear.

He'd promised her he would protect her, take care of her. The cool-ness of the plaster wall he'd thrown her against still burned against her skin, brighter than a memory and more terrible.

She did not sleep, Transcribing page after page of the wind blow-ing through the eaves; footsteps tapping on the sidewalk far below; doors slamming shut on quiet streets.

Next morning, almost at dawn, he knocked on her door. She'd

fallen asleep only an hour or so before—unable to close her eyes, trying to figure out where to go and how to leave France.

"Hey, kiddo," he said, opening the door—he had his own key. "I'm really, really sorry about last night."

She said nothing, just pulled the sheets up to her chin, feeling very vulnerable.

"Do you know who I met with last night? The managers for Marion Harris and Alberta Hunter. Both of them. They're doing a performance for a grand duke, and they want to sing a duet and have me write it. For the grand duke's birthday. Everyone will be there, you hear me? Everyone."

She stared blankly at him.

"Do you know what this means? Do you have any idea? It means the crowned heads of Europe—the kings and queens and princes of France and Spain and everywhere—are going to be hearing our music. Everyone!"

"You shouldn't have touched me," she said.

"I know I shouldn't. I'm super sorry. Really sorry. You should be treated like a queen yourself, and I'm an absolute heel. I just panicked, is all. I panicked, and I lashed out. Can you forgive me?"

She didn't know what to say.

"Let's celebrate by spending the day together, just you and me," he said. And then, when she still didn't speak, "You get dressed, and we'll have breakfast. I heard that there's a great little café around the corner that has the best croissants in all of Paris. How would that be?"

She found herself dressing, walking with him to the great little café, although she just pulled apart the croissant, didn't eat it. But spending all morning with him, with his infectious enthusiasm, thawed her as they walked around Paris and listened to the echoes floating in Notre Dame. She confessed to him that she'd spent the past four days in her rooms.

"Oh no, you haven't!" he said, aghast. "You haven't even gone out?

There are all the French chansons that I thought you'd love to hear! You're missing all the French music and you have to hear it! Just because I'm working doesn't mean that you shouldn't hear it!"

And that was how, two days later, Clarice joined them: a twenty-year-old Parisian woman who spoke broken English, some Italian, and German and who desperately needed a job because her parents had both been killed in the war. Fred hired her to be Josephine's companion: to accompany her to the theater, to the vaudeville shows, anywhere Josephine wished to go. Fred's promise that all of Paris would be open to Josephine turned out to be true. Josephine was never turned away for the color of her skin, and Fred pulled strings and bought the best tickets to the most-talked-about performances. Clarice proved a competent companion, even if she rarely spoke. She had thick eyebrows and lips that often turned down but she was nice enough, and could maneuver Josephine through a crowd. Fred's party had grown to eight.

From Paris it was on to Nice, then Rome, Milan, Antwerp, and Vienna. Europe in the summer of 1920 was still broken under the weight of the war and gripped by the Spanish flu. Too often, from a train or a motor carriage, they would catch sight of bombed-out buildings, wood like matchsticks splintering up from a blackened hole. There were bread lines and strikes. Josephine, in her wanderings off the main tourist areas of the cities they visited, often found starving children and homeless men roaming the streets. Sometimes she scuttled away from them and other times she and Clarice would give them all the money they had in their purses. The street people reminded Josephine too much of her own peripatetic wanderings.

As the summer wore on, the specter of the war lessened; more cafés and dance halls opened. Josephine was enthralled. Sounds she might not ever have heard were now hers: French ballads, Viennese operas, Italian street singers. Into the Compendium she Transcribed the sounds of the Thames, Seine, Tiber, Rhine, and Danube.

Although Antwerp hadn't been on the original itinerary, in late August Fred impulsively decided to go. The international Olympic Games were being held that summer, and were still continuing for a few more weeks, until mid-September. Fred wanted to see the athletes perform. It was easy to get tickets: few locals could afford them. Fred told Josephine that he followed a troop of schoolchildren into the stadium—the schools were admitted free, just to swell the crowd.

Sporting games did not hold much interest for Josephine, so she and Clarice wandered the bombed-out city, which had hastily been readied for the Olympic Games. Buildings often had whitewash only on their fronts, a thin veneer of paint; while on the sides, blackened plaster outlines defined now-disappeared structures; and in the back, rubble still lay in broken heaps. Once, passing a scorched jumble of brick and ancient stone, she saw what she thought was a doll's hand, buried in the wreckage, reaching up toward the sky. The image haunted her. She wasn't sure if she saw it as a symbol of Antwerp or of herself. The melodies that emerged for the Compendium were often in minor chords, with wistful, plaintive melodies that drifted away into silence.

The Olympic Games would be concluding on Sunday, September 12; Fred's entourage would depart for Vienna midweek. Josephine had only seen Fred in his late-night visits to the Compendium, but that Saturday he'd begged her to come with him to the games—there would be a Flemish cantata performed by an enormous choir and musicians.

"It's not to be missed," he told her. "I thought you wanted to hear more Flemish music?"

So that Sunday, Josephine was a part of Frederick Delaney's entourage at the closing ceremony of the Olympic Games. Above the stadium flew a flag that caught Josephine's attention. Clarice caught her watching it and asked one of the people sitting near them if they knew anything about it. It was the new Olympic flag, debuted especially for the occasion: five interlocking colored rings—blue, yellow, black, green, and red—symbolizing the five continents on a white field.

As row upon row of musicians and vocalists trooped into the stadium, Josephine watched the flag, pouring its endless dance out into the wind, and as the cantata's harmonics twined high in the air, enrapturing her, she closed her eyes to freeze this moment, these rhythms and vocalizations. Her fingers itched to Transcribe.

After, at the end of the evening, as the trumpets sounded the Olympic anthem, the five-ringed flag was lowered. They were close enough to see one dignitary hand the flag over to another.

"It means it's going from one city to the next," their helpful neighbor told them as the musicians broke into "La Marseillaise."

That night, when Fred came to her room to rob the Compendium, she said to him, "The five rings were singing to the countries."

He ignored her, as he often did. He was clearly tired and out of sorts.

"I want to write a song for the countries," she said. "Five songs. One for each country. Blue yellow black green red. The Olympics."

His head turned slowly, as if it were on a string being pulled unwillingly toward her. "What? What did you say?"

"I've started writing the music I want to hear for each of the countries. Green is for the island countries." She showed him a sheet of the Compendium: water music, cool and sweet, but triumphant, with echoes of Japanese and Chinese instruments, and also the exuberant swagger of the Olympic theme.

"I'm going to write each of the rings," she said.

She played the piece on the piano. It was longer than many of her melodies, expanding already onto three sheets of foolscap.

"How long is this going to be?" he asked.

She shrugged. "As long as it needs to be."

"It's beautiful," he said. "Gosh, Josephine, it's really beautiful. I wonder if they'd want to perform this at the next Olympic Games? Do you think you can write all five? What are you envisioning them as?"

"A symphony," she said. "Something very grand."

"How about an opera?" he said. "Five operas. Like Wagner. *The Rings of Olympia.*"

She nodded thoughtfully. After a pause she said, "That might be music I would want to hear."

36

A Sorry-Ass Apology

Bern

A DAY PASSED. No word from the *New York Times*. The Delaney Foundation's deadline came and went, and Bern spent it working on *RED*.

The next morning, though, Bern was again summoned to the seventeenth floor. He hadn't heard back from the reporter yet, and anxiety gnawed at him. Had Mona Keltner or her bosses at the *New York Times* gone directly to the Delaney Foundation? He tried to take a breath and couldn't, and his legs felt not quite able to bear his weight.

Stephanie met him at the elevator bank, escorted him back to the conference room. This time the video monitors were off, and only four people sat at the table: the chairman of the board, Kurt Delaney; Mallory Roberts; Stanford Whitman; and the heavyset well-dressed guy who'd never given his name.

None of them stood as Bern appeared in the doorway, and he didn't fully enter the room.

"Dr. Hendricks," Kurt Delaney said. "So glad you could join us."

Bern said nothing. The black table stretched out smooth as a shadow, and he kept his eyes fixed at the center of it. One-one-thousand, two-one-thousand, three . . .

Bern had hit eight before Kurt Delaney went on, "You'll remember that we requested you provide the documents and the trunk to us, as of last night."

What, he wondered, did the Foundation use to keep the table so smoothly polished? This shine had to come from something more than Pledge.

Kurt Delaney spoke again: "I take it by your silence that you are not going to be providing the materials to us. Where did you go last night? How is your girlfriend?"

This time Bern counted to fourteen.

"You understand the civil penalties in front of you? You understand that we are certainly in our rights to terminate your association with us? And destroy any chance of your working in the music or academic industries again?"

Now Bern spoke, thinking about how Eboni had been so vocal about the Foundation's baked-in racism. "You understand how it would look? Your all-white board firing a Black man?"

"A Black man who refused to turn over documents—"

"You're firing a Black man," Bern said overconfidently, wondering if the board would buy the bluff. But he had nothing to lose. "That's all the media will hear." What the hell was going on with Mona Keltner? Had the board gotten wind of it?

"Bern," Mallory said, helmet hair glittering like fresh shoe polish. "It doesn't have to be like this. We're on your side." Did she have stock in Aqua Net?

This time the silence stretched and stretched. Finally, after twenty seconds, Bern said, "Is there anything else?"

"No," Mallory said.

"Are you firing me? I just want to make sure I'm absolutely clear that you aren't."

"We're not," Mallory said. "We really think we can come to some arrangement. If you—"

"Okay," Bern said. "Have a nice day."

He swung around and marched back to the elevator bank, where Stephanie was hovering. Bern could hear Mallory say something else, probably to him, but he was already out of earshot.

He went down to his subbasement dungeon and got back to work on *RED*.

And then, for the next week, nothing further happened. Eboni stayed out of sight, texting him only briefly as she tried to cobble together her business, working remotely via a complicated system of OpenVPN and anonymous servers. Bern spent his days working on *RED*, whose music was more and more remarkable. He wondered if it was because he knew of Josephine's involvement, or if it was just so double good on its own; he was not an unbiased academic anymore.

The early sections of the original *RED* score had been fairly clean of Doodles—just a scattering in the first 150 pages or so. Deeper in, however, the Doodles began to multiply so that now, in act 3, the hieroglyphs blanketed many of the pages; not just the margins, but within each of the musical lines, as well.

He thought again about his original hypothesis that the Doodles were a language. What if they were also a means of revising? Of taking the transcribed musical notation and tweaking it slightly, so the new version would be enhanced? What if this was Josephine Reed reading the transcribed material and honing it still further?

Perhaps something had happened, during the writing of *RED*, which meant that the later portion of the manuscript wasn't as developed as the earlier portion.

He needed to see the original: Was there a difference in the paper, in the ink? Was there a specific page where Frederic Delaney had bound together the early draft with the later?

He wrote to Mallory to again to request access to the original. He didn't hear back.

He hadn't heard from Mona Keltner, either. After a week, he emailed her on his burner phone. Last time, she'd responded within an hour. This time, like Mallory, she didn't respond at all.

He emailed Keltner the next day as well.

Again, no response. Now he was getting worried. Had the Foundation gotten to her, too?

So he called, left a message.

She didn't call him back.

The next day, however, her number flashed on his phone. As soon as he answered, she began speaking quickly and, he soon realized, uncomfortably—as if someone were listening in on her end of the conversation.

"Hi, Dr. Hendricks, this is Mona Keltner here. I'm afraid I won't be able to pursue the story you shared with us. It's fascinating, but our editor has decided not to sanction looking into it any further."

"What? Wait—why?"

She hesitated. "You signed an NDA."

"I know," he said. "I told you I did. I showed it to you."

"I took your story up the chain and we've decided that it's not a story we're going to pursue. The NDA makes the situation too difficult. We didn't want to spend the next several years tied up in court litigating your breach of it."

"You're kidding me," Bern said, tendrils of hopelessness wrapping around his neck.

"I'm afraid not."

He didn't know what to say. "What about Josephine Reed? Did you find anything?"

When they'd first talked, Keltner had offered to research what had happened to Reed in the *New York Times*'s archive, which were deep and extensive. Now she repeated, "I'm afraid not."

"Nothing? Nothing at all?"

"Nothing," she said. "Nice speaking to you. Sorry it didn't work out."

She hung up.

Later that night, when he told Eboni, she slumped back in her chair. They were in a food court in the basement of the New World Mall in Flushing. Neither of them had the stomach or enthusiasm for pizza anymore; but they didn't have the appetite for anything else, either. Neither of them was eating.

"She had everything she needed to take Delaney down. It was basically a Pulitzer waiting for her to accept." Eboni exhaled, closed her eyes, rubbed her temples. Her nails were chipped. She wasn't showing it, but Bern knew she must be scared, too. Her business was being destroyed. Her life was ruined.

"You know what?" she said with her eyes still closed, "if we are going down, I say we do it on our own terms."

"What do you mean?"

"I say we blow their entire operation up. Blast it all on social media. Facebook, Instagram, Twitter, TikTok. Hell, even Pinterest. All of it. Just go nuclear."

"Are you psycho?" Bern said. "We couldn't even get a reputable reporter to do a story with every bit of evidence she needed. Putting this on social media will turn me into a nutjob. A conspiracy lunatic. My academic credibility will be totally shot. This would destroy me."

"Fuck them," Eboni said. "They've already destroyed me, remember?"

"I know. But there has to be another solution."

"Don't tell me you're scared of these people. We can't just let them get away with this."

"I want to get the info out as much as you do, but—"

"But nothing. There's a way to get back at them. We just need to find it."

"I know, but doing a social media blast ain't it. We have to lie low for a while. Think our way through this. Don't you know a guy?" Bern said, only half joking.

Eboni gave him a swift side-eye. "I'll tell you what I do know. When bullies come at you like this, you need to come at them the exact same way. I called in all my favors, but I think I may have one last card to play."

"What's that? Please don't say you want to blow up the place."

"Not literally." Eboni grinned, and he realized with a pang how long it had been since he'd seen her really smile.

37

Honesty & Cooperation

Josephine

IF JOSEPHINE THOUGHT that she could reconnect with Fred in Europe in order to return to those early, happy days in the studio, she was wrong. When they returned to New York, the situation only worsened. Fred was very busy and moved his bedroom down to the second floor of the building, one flight of stairs from the rooms he'd converted into his offices. She was alone on the fifth floor; the other tenant, who'd lived in Fred's old rooms for a few months, had moved out. Josephine eventually started piling the steamer trunks of the Compendium in the unit.

But every evening—or, more and more often, after midnight, so it was early in the morning—she would sense Fred's tread on the landing, and the D-major knock of his knuckles would rattle the door before he came in to peruse the Compendium for what she'd done that day. By now Fred could transcribe some of the Compendium on his own, although he often made mistakes and couldn't grasp its subtleties.

At least she was back in New York, with its comfortable sounds, familiar clubs, and favorite dance halls. Josephine made it a point to go to as many clubs and music events as possible, both to immerse herself in the music as well as to stay away from Fred. He was different and she didn't like it. Almost every night, as he sat at her piano and transcribed, he would promise her that soon—"Soon, kiddo!"— everything would go back to the way it had been. Josephine didn't think Fred even remembered how things used to be. It didn't matter. The more he promised, the less likely he was to deliver on his promises.

She was hard at work on the songs for the operas, and they were a delight and a ravishment. He worked with her on the story lines, pulling up myths and legends and plots from who knows where, getting her musical samples to hear and assimilate.

It was how it had been before Paris, before she'd been called "a dog from the street." The operas required additional input from him, so for the two or so months he was home every evening, his thigh brushing hers as they sat at the piano. She even made dinner for him again, twice, and he ate with her at the dining room table.

She wrote *BLUE*, and he told her later that people really loved it. She heard the music on the street and in the department stores, listened to it being bastardized and parodied in the vaudeville shows. She couldn't wait to work on *YELLOW* and *BLACK*.

The years spooled by; 1920 blended into 1921, then 1922. Fred bought her a new Victrola, and then a brand-new radio.

"Stay home and listen to the world," he told her, and he tuned the radio dial to different stations with such music as she had never heard before. She finished *YELLOW* and *BLACK*, was hard at work on *GREEN*. Every night Fred would appear for a couple of hours to go through what she'd created, and she was so desperately happy that he was paying attention to her again.

They'd work together on a piece of music, and a few weeks or months later she'd hear the melodies on the street or plugged in a department store or—more and more frequently—on the radio.

One cool November evening in 1923, Josephine came home from watching a traveling ensemble specializing in New Orleans jazz. Her handbag was bursting with the Compendium: several dozen pages, tightly scrawled. The lights were out in Fred's office—no surprise there—and she peeked up the landing to where sometimes lights glowed from under Fred's door in his rooms on the second floor. It was dark. He was, as usual, out. She hummed the final tune the jazz combo had played and wondered if she could lift a few of the bass melodies, invert them into a different key, and perhaps use them in the ritual sacrifice she was working on for *GREEN*. Josephine was happier than she had been in months.

Her door was unlocked. She didn't quite register it at first—her key turned and the lock closed, and then she turned the key the other way and it opened again. She pushed the door open: Lights were on. Fred was sitting at the piano. A stack of pages in a red folder lay open next to him on the piano bench.

"Hello," she said, taking off her coat and hanging it in the tiny front closet.

"Josephine," he said in just above a whisper, "we need to talk."

"Okay. What would you like to talk about?"

"I'd like to talk about something very important. Honesty and cooperation."

Fred didn't seem angry or upset, just friendly and a little tired. "Okay," she said.

"This business, my publishing company, is very important to me. It's what keeps the lights on. It buys us food. It allows you all the luxuries I've given to you. Do you like that dress?"

Fred pointed to the dress hanging from a hanger over the wardrobe: a blue-and-green silk. He'd given it to her last year, and she often wore it on Thursdays.

"It's a beautiful dress." She began to extract the Compendium from her handbag.

Fred hadn't moved from the piano bench. "Do you know how I bought that dress for you?"

"Yes, Fred. I do." She unfolded the pages of the Compendium on the dinette table. The jazz tune was strong in her head. In GREEN there was a scene called Dreamtime, where the Aboriginal Australians are dancing with their supernatural ancestors. The music was wild and discordant: Surely the bass melody line she'd heard tonight could hold the drumbeats? Perhaps it called for clarinets and flutes, too.

"I sell music. If I don't sell music, you don't have a fancy new dress. There's no more good food. No nice place to live and certainly no more going out to listen to all the songs you like to hear. It all goes away if I don't sell music."

He paused. After a long while it seemed that he expected a response, so she said, "I know."

She looked quickly up at him, then down at the pages. Yes, clarinets. No flutes. Oboes. Definitely oboes.

Fred sat down next to her. Josephine couldn't remember the last time they'd eaten together. Was he hungry? Should she offer to make him a ham sandwich?

"I've noticed your notebooks have been looking a little thin lately. Why is that?"

"I don't think so. I put the walking pages in trunk four. To make room for the magenta mound. You know that everything has been GREEN this month."

"Right," Fred said. "Green. And the magenta mound. Only thing is, I checked your magenta mound and couldn't find any extra pages. Isn't that odd?"

Josephine stiffened, glanced at the wardrobe. "That is odd," she said, realizing that she had just made a mistake—she'd hidden some Fredless Pages inside.

Besides *GREEN*, she was still writing music she wanted to hear. She was writing more than ever, as if the setting down of one song somehow engendered the writing down of three more. But many of those new songs were Fredless, and she was hiding them where he couldn't have them.

"I'm going to guess that you were tired and accidentally put those sheets in your wardrobe rather than giving them to me, like you were supposed to. Would that be correct?"

"I must have been tired," she said eagerly. "It was a late night. The rows were numb."

"Right. Numb." Sheets of paper were spread out before him: she'd thought they were sheets from the Compendium that she'd left on the piano for him. Now he fanned them past his face and she realized that these were the Fredless Pages that she'd squirreled away in the wardrobe.

He must have found them. He must be going through her things, looking for more of the Compendium.

He spoke just above a whisper, which made Josephine's skin crawl.

"We've got to make sure that you're giving me everything you're writing," he said. "You can't misplace this music. We—you and me— we have so many obligations these days. So much music to write. We're a team, remember? That means you share the music with me. That's what teamwork is."

"Yes," she said. "I'll be more careful."

The Compendium lay flattened before her. The jazz tune she'd been humming had disappeared from her mind. The Aborigines stopped dancing.

"Good. I'm glad we both understand how important keeping things in their proper place is," Fred said, standing up. Why had she ever thought he would eat with her again? He couldn't get away from her quickly enough.

At the doorway he said, still in that quiet voice, "Do me a favor.

Don't you ever think about hiding anything from me ever again. There's more than just this business at stake here."

Fred carried her sheets out the door, closed it solidly behind him. She was too distracted to even hear what note the door made as it shut.

She did not sleep much that night. She knew Fred was under a great deal of pressure. He didn't know—how could he?—of all the Fredless Pages that she'd secreted all over the apartment: under floorboards that she'd carefully pried up, cut into the sides of doorframes where the wood met the plaster, tucked into bins, and slid into the cracks between cabinets, taped to the undersides of drawers. The Fredless Pages he'd found in the wardrobe were from a few months ago—she'd just put them in with her hose and underthings. She'd meant to find a better place for them.

She wondered what Fred would do if he found all the other hiding places she'd created.

ACT 5

Ensemble

38

Person of Interest

Bern

THE DELANEY FOUNDATION moved against them before Bern or Eboni was ready. The night after he and Eboni had talked about posting their findings online and he'd, at least temporarily, dissuaded her, someone knocked on his apartment door. He didn't know how they'd gotten into the building without buzzing.

It was almost one a.m., and he'd just gotten out of the shower. He'd worked on *RED* for a couple of hours, until his eyes started crossing, and had sat down on the edge of the bed, still damp, his head in his hands, trying not to think about what tomorrow would be.

Then came three firm, clear beats on the apartment's door.

He wrapped the towel around his waist, padded over to the foyer. Through the peephole he saw a wall of very official blue uniforms: three police officers.

"Kevin Bernard Hendricks? Please open the door. We know you're in there."

What do you do when the police come calling? Bern had no idea. But he opened the door.

"Um, can I help you? Any or all of you?" Bern said, trying to lighten the mood. The towel slipped slightly down his hips, and he readjusted it. He never went out without ironing his shirt—he even ironed his T-shirt. He ironed the creases in his jeans. Now he'd never felt so naked, so exposed. He'd even wear jeans without a crease. "Can you give me a minute to get some clothes on?"

The policemen were not amused. The skinny officer on the left seemed to be taking the lead. His thin mustache drooped like wilted parentheses on either side of his mouth. "Mr. Hendricks, we need to ask you a few questions. Can we come inside?"

"What's this regarding?" he asked.

"We'd prefer to come inside and discuss this," said Mustache.

"I'd prefer to discuss it here," Bern said. Once inside, could they search his room? There was nothing to find, but he still didn't want them searching. What could this possibly be about?

"Fine," Mustache said. "It's regarding stolen property belonging to the Delaney Foundation."

Of course it was. Because what else did the Delaney Foundation have to do, except get the cops to torment him in the middle of the night? For an instant Bern wanted to laugh, then thought better of it. Three cops wouldn't be at his door at one in the morning if it weren't somehow legitimate, would they?

"Stolen property? If it's about the pens I took from my desk, I was going to return them," Bern said.

"Can we come in?"

Bern couldn't see standing there any longer with a towel sliding off his ass, so he backed away and the three men brushed past him. He could smell stale coffee on their breath. His jeans were in the bedroom. If he could just get to them and—

"Mr. Hendricks, I'm Officer Fields," said Mustache, once the door was closed. "This is Officer Fry and Officer Dickson." Although Bern didn't often think about race and racial differences, right now their faces looked very white and he felt very Black. He readjusted the towel yet again, feeling very naked.

Officer Fields was saying, "Do you work for the Delaney Foundation?"

"Yes. Why? What's this about?" He took a step back.

"We have reason to believe that you're in possession of property reported stolen by the Delaney Foundation."

"Stolen property," Bern said repeated. "What are they saying I stole?" Indignantly he leaned forward, and two of the officers—Fields and Dickson—put their hands on their holsters.

"Whoa, fellas," Bern said, holding up his hands, "can we take it down a notch?" He could feel the towel slipping and grabbed it before it slithered off.

"We'll ask the questions, chief," Fields said.

"You gotta be kidding me," Bern said. "What do you guys want? Am I under arrest? Do you have a warrant?"

Dickson took a step forward. "You need to keep your mouth shut and answer the questions."

"What is this about? Do I need to call my attorney?"

"Mr. Hendricks," Officer Dickson said, fumbling with a blue-backed, stapled sheaf of paper and scanning it, "we understand that you may have in your possession a very expensive laptop computer. One that contains extremely sensitive company information. We understand that you were not to take this laptop off the premises. The Foundation has tried repeatedly to reach you and has now filed an emergency court order compelling you to return the device."

Bern looked from one white face to the other as Dickson paraphrased the document. He was almost sure that at one point he saw Officer Fry roll his eyes.

Bern felt like rolling his eyes, too. "What the hell are you talking about? I have my work computer and my personal computer. They gave me a computer to use for my research. If you call Stephanie—"

"Sir," Mustache said, "is this computer in your possession? It was reported stolen. We have the serial number. Can you produce it?"

Surely the Foundation wouldn't trot out policemen in the middle of the night to harass him for having their computer. He'd been using his personal laptop for the past several weeks, so the research on Josephine stayed between him and Eboni. Would they go this far? Of course they would. "Yes, I have my Delaney laptop. Do I have permission to show you and maybe put on some pants, please?"

"Where is it?" Fields's hand was still on his holster, as if he expected the half-naked Black dude to rush him and body-slam him to the floor.

"It's in my room. Right this way."

He led them to the bedroom, where the Delaney laptop rested regally on his nightstand. Officer Dickson turned it over and compared serial numbers.

"Everything good?" Bern said as he slipped on a pair of gym shorts.

Dickson looked up, nodded to Fields. "This is it."

"Good," Mustache said. "Mr. Hendricks, you are under arrest for possession of stolen property. You have the right to remain silent." Officer Dickson was pulling out handcuffs.

"What?" Bern said. "Is this a joke?" He knew better than to resist at all, but he stiffened when Fields grabbed his arm to cuff him.

That was all it took.

"Sir," Fields said, "you need to calm down. Put your hands behind your back. I'm restraining you for our safety."

"Can one of you please tell me what's going on?" Bern said.

"They gave me this laptop to work from. The Foundation contracted me to—"

"Tell it to the judge, chief," Dickson said, hauling him out of the room.

"Can I at least put a shirt on? Shoes?"

They ignored him. He couldn't imagine going outside like this, unclothed, let alone to a police station. "Wait, please let me put on some clothes!"

As Dickson guided him toward the front door, Fry picked up the laptop and Fields radioed the station. "Stolen property recovered," he said into his walkie-talkie.

When Bern heard *stolen property* again, he stopped mid-stride, turned around, and said, "Stolen property? I work for the Delaney Foundation. You—"

He felt, rather than saw, Dickson fumbling with his holster, and then a bizarre and terrible sensation poured through him, jolting him and flattening him on the ground.

He'd been tased.

He could feel himself losing consciousness. As he was lifted up by two cops and dragged out of his apartment, Bern could have sworn he heard one of them say, "Delaney had this one all wrong. They said he wouldn't put up much of a fight. He's stronger than he looks."

He was slipping in and out of consciousness. He heard laughter. What kind of cops would treat him this way? Before he passed out, he was sure he heard Officer Fry shouting at the other two, "Settle down, guys, just settle down. He's not resisting. He's out."

The next thing he knew, he was in the back of a police car, hand-cuffed, barefoot, wearing only gym shorts. The vinyl seat was warm and sticky against his back. If this weren't so unbelievably terrible he would have laughed. It felt utterly alien and impossible.

"What's going on?" he said. "Am I under arrest? I want a lawyer. Where are my clothes? Where's my phone?"

"Shut the fuck up," Dickson said.

Bern was trying to think. He couldn't. The inside of his head was mush.

A few minutes later, the car pulled up in front of a police station. He was about to be paraded through the police station in a pair of gym shorts in the wee hours of the morning for apparently taking his work laptop home without signing it out.

"What is going on?" Bern shouted. "Why are you doing this to me?"

Looking back, almost embarrassed, Fry said, "We're bringing you down to the station for questioning about your possession of stolen property."

"I need to speak to an attorney."

Fry replied before Fields, who was driving, could. "Just go with it, man. If it's a mistake, you'll be out soon. I'm sure it will be cleared up in no time."

He didn't want to get out of the squad car. He was more angry than embarrassed. He remembered the times he'd seen people who look like him get hauled off to jail. Never in a million years would he have imagined himself in the same situation. He was a professor. He was on a tenure track at the University of Virginia. He had a fuck-ing PhD.

"Let's go, chief," Fields said.

"Can I at least get some clothes?" Bern said, unmoving.

"I said get your ass up." Fields yanked Bern out.

"Hey, take it easy, Jerry!" Fry said.

All Bern could say was, "Doctor Hendricks. My name is Dr. Hendricks."

Dickson, who'd parked his squad car behind them and had come strolling up, snickered. "We got us a smart one, don't we. United Negro College Fund must be real proud."

"I hope you have an idea of the lawsuit I'll be filing against you tomorrow," Bern said.

Both Fields and Dickson looked at each other and laughed out loud. Fry kept his head down.

"These people are insane," Dickson said.

"Yeah, I guess the smart ones got more balls than the rest of 'em," Fields said, still dragging Bern out of the car. He managed to hold his head up as they led him, barefoot, inside.

39

Mrs. Carney Moved Out

Josephine

ONE EARLY MAY evening in 1924, Josephine returned from a street festival. Fred was in his office. She was surprised to see him there this late, and even more surprised that he was alone. She didn't know how many people worked for him now. He never introduced her. Some of the faces were familiar but most weren't. Not wishing to disturb him—he was feverishly writing something at his desk—she hurried past, head down.

She was waiting for the elevator when Fred called out, "Josie? Is that you? You have that new section of *RED* done? I'll be up to take a look at it when I finish this."

He'd recently taken to calling her Josie. *Josephine*, she wanted to tell him. *My name is Josephine. Not Josie or Jo or kiddo. Josephine.* She nodded as if he could see her, pressed the elevator button again. *Click, whir.* The brass of the elevator panel flickered, and somehow seemed menacing.

In her room she dropped her coat over the sofa and went immediately to the bathroom with her purse. Months ago, under a thick orange-and-white-striped rug, she'd worked a floorboard loose. Now she pried it up with a metal hair comb. From her purse she extracted more than half of the Fredless Pages from the Compendium and shoved them inside the open space beneath the floorboards.

She returned the planks and rug back into position, then slid over to the piano, arranged the remaining sheets of the Compendium on the music sheet holder. She'd just set them in place when Fred knocked his D-major knocks, popped open the door without waiting.

"Okay, Josie," he said. "What do you have tonight? Where are you with the *RED* revisions? You were gone a long time today."

She spread the pages in front of him. "I have the next scene but the arrows felt lean by the wire."

He leaned over the pages, sight-reading. "This is great," he said after a minute. "Really great. Just what I was hoping you'd do. Thanks! It's perfect!"

It had been so long since Fred had praised her, and now she could feel her shoulders slumping as tension seeped out of her.

"You keep outdoing yourself, you know that? This is one of the best things I've seen you write in months. You got your mojo back."

Mojo. He'd learned the word when he'd gone on a tour of the Southern states for a few weeks, but she'd heard it before. Back when she was a child, whenever she and her siblings had gotten the flu, her mother had made her *mojo stew* to heal them. Now just the use of the word made it feel as if something inside of Josephine were healing, binding together, reconnecting. "I was just writing what I wanted to hear. And what I thought you'd want to hear, too."

"And I do want to hear it, Josie. I really do." He looked at her, so sincere, and for a moment he was Freddy, silver bright and glossy, and that gave her the courage to say what she'd been mulling for weeks.

"You spend so much money," she said. "Where does it come from?" She knew the answer, of course: from the paper where he wrote down the music, where he translated it into musical notes that other people could read. But lately she'd been wanting to know more. Wanted to understand how it went from the musical notations to the cash that he used to buy the new loafers twinkling on his feet.

"Really? Again?" He gave an exaggerated sigh. "We've been over this. I sell my songs, our songs, and—"

She cut him off midsentence. "And they pay you. You give me half. But you don't give me as much money as you're spending. I can't buy all the things you buy. Is it because your name is on the music? Because it's your name and not mine?"

"I don't know why you keep harping on this," he said. "I told you we split the money. And that people who love music give us these things. They're grateful."

"Who are these people? Why don't they give these things to me?"

"They don't know you. They know me."

"That's because your name is on the paper. If my name were on the paper, they'd know me."

"Josie. We've been through this. You know people wouldn't want your music if they knew you were colored."

I don't believe you, she thought hotly. *They love music because it has all colors.* But she felt like she couldn't deny it. She could not go to so many of the places where whites could go. So many doors had "no coloreds" signs posted out front. But what about Louis Armstrong and Duke Ellington? And all the other colored musicians?

"Can you just trust me, please? We don't have time to waste on this kind of nonsense. We have over a dozen commissions that we have to get done this month alone, let alone finishing *RED,* and there's going to be a rehearsal of *BLACK* soon. Do you want to come hear it?"

She did want to hear *BLACK.* She'd poured all the memories of her childhood into it, as well as the rhythmic beats and exotic melodies that Fred had found for her in Europe.

Now he was flipping through the Compendium on the music

stand. "Where's the *RED* stuff? Is this it? You were supposed to go over my draft and fix it. Did you?"

"It's right there," she said.

"Where's the rest of it? Cripes, you've been gone all day. There must be more."

"It's all there," she said, thinking instead of the thick wad of the Compendium nestled safe in the bathroom floor. Let the colored music hide in the dark, away from him.

"Damn it," he said, pounding his fist on the piano top. It reverberated: A, C, G, D thrumming into the air like hornets. "Where. Is. The. Music?" With every word he punched the piano.

She stood up, moved away from him, putting the sofa between them. "It's my music," she told him. "I can do with it what I like."

"You can't act like this." He'd stood up, too, on the other side of the sofa. "You can't be serious," he said.

Spinning so quickly that she almost didn't realize it, he flung the table lamp into the wall. It crashed and splintered in a chaos of broken chords, glass spinning crazily in a legato B-flat across the hardwood.

There was no one else on the fifth floor. But people—Mrs. Carney, directly below her—would hear this and come running.

No, Mrs. Carney had moved out months ago. Who was on the fourth floor now? Josephine couldn't remember. Was the fourth floor empty, too?

She was suddenly aware that she'd been alone—for months, probably—on the top floor of the apartment building. All the empty apartments breathed silently around and below her. Her only neighbor was the Compendium, stacked in five steamer trunks in Freddy's room next door.

Meanwhile, Fred was shouting, "Why do you do this to me? I work so hard to make sure you are taken care of and this is how you treat me? Do you have any idea how much pressure I'm under?"

She was alone. No one would hear her if she called out. No one had come running when the lamp shattered. No one.

He paused, visibly trying to calm himself, continued in a quieter voice, "You know this isn't right. Just tell me where the new music is. You'll be okay. I promise."

I promise. Those words again. *Rescue a dog from the street, it's yours for life.* That had been a promise, too, of sorts, hadn't it?

"It's mine!" she screamed at him, hands clenched. "It's my music. I wrote it. It's mine!"

Fred flung the entire table into the wall, on top of the remains of the shattered lamp. His face was very red. One carefully pomaded lock of hair fell over his left eye and he brushed it away as if he wanted to rip it off.

"You're trying to ruin me, aren't you? You've got to have written more. I know it's here somewhere."

She couldn't help looking at the shattered table. There, in the wreckage, lay sheets of the Compendium, which once had been taped to the table's underside; and other Compendium pages had been tacked carefully on the bottom of the pull-out drawer. He hadn't noticed. He was pulling up the dark rose cushions of the sofa, searching. No Compendium. He flipped the couch on its back.

Tacked across the entire underbelly of the couch were more Compendium pages.

"Here we are," he crooned. "I told you there was more. Where else are you hiding it?" He caught sight of the pages from the broken table. "And there, too, eh? This is how you betray me, is it? This is how, is it?"

For the next hour he methodically worked his way around her apartment, unearthing the Fredless Pages from the kitchen cabinets, from under the sink, from beneath the throw rug in the living room. Hundreds of Fredless Pages: when the pile grew too thick, he stacked it on the piano top.

Josephine wept in the corner, hands over her head, wishing only to Transcribe, to disappear into the music. Freddy exhumed more and more of the Fredless Pages, not looking at her, muttering like a crazy man. When at last he seemed satisfied that he'd retrieved all of the Compendium that she'd hidden away, he took the sheets and left, not even glancing at her. As he slammed the door behind him, he said, "Don't think of hiding anything from me again. Ever."

Ironically, he hadn't found the bathroom floorboard. He hadn't found the Fredless Pages in the closet ceiling, either—nor the ones folded and stuffed carefully in the crack behind the bedroom radiator, nor in many of the other hiding places she'd created. All in all, he'd found only about half of what she'd secreted over the years.

She vowed that he'd never find the rest.

40

Here's Your Jumpsuit

Bern

BERN HAD GROWN UP in a lower middle class family. He'd always had to push, to fight for what he achieved: that French horn in middle school, that chemistry exam, or begging Jacques Simon to let him work on *The Rings of Olympia*. Embedded in his DNA was the feeling that if he strove, he would accomplish; if he pushed, the other side would give.

No more.

Despair and inertia swallowed him whole.

As he walked almost naked into the police station, Bern felt as if he were a tiny grain in a vast churning machine that would grind him to dust and there was nothing—nothing—he could do about it.

Whatever was going to happen would happen. No point in putting up a struggle. He kept his head up and trudged with the officers into the police station. He focused on keeping his gym shorts from sliding down his hips, focused on any small anything that crossed his path: the crack in the cool linoleum tile, the slight sheen on the door's bronze kickplate. Anything to take his mind away from this humiliating reality. To think, he used to get upset when he had a wrinkle in his khakis. Now if he only had khakis—wrinkles and all.

They led him to the back of the station, and he found himself trying to hum a tune to drown out the comments and laughter that were following him. He hummed "Radioactive" by Imagine Dragons and even Delaney's "Evergreen."

But no sooner had the first well-known bars of "Evergreen" unspooled in his inner ear than he forced himself away, on to J.O Blanco's "Flex on Me." Delaney's music had become too difficult for him to listen to. If it hadn't been for Frederic Delaney, Bern wouldn't be in this police station with his professional and personal life in tatters. Eboni would be chatting it up with Tim Cook or Jeff Bezos; or upgrading the security for Instagram or Nike.

Even more important, his idolization of Delaney—the core that had held Bern up for so many years—was disintegrating. Was Delaney just a fraud? Just "unbelievably forgettable, a pastiche of worn-out hackneyed tunes that never unite into a cohesive whole," as that memorable *Life* review in 1935 had called his music?

How, now, could Bern give his heart, his loyalty, his imagination to an unknown woman who was just a name and a few photographs? Someone he knew virtually nothing about?

Delaney had rescued him. Now Bern wished that Delaney hadn't. Working at Walmart in Milwaukee seemed like a much better option than what lay ahead of him now.

He fought to keep his mind blank. Not to focus on what he was going through. He tried not to imagine Eboni. He just concentrated on his feet hitting the cool, gritty floor. He had done nothing wrong. They would see that, too, soon enough.

Because of the Delaney Foundation, Bern was being made a fool of. Someone snapped a picture. The laughter continued. He tried to hum "Paid in Lies" by Geppetto's Wüd, but he could hear nothing but the blood pumping through his ears, loud enough to drown out everything else.

One thought crept in. This would be the last time the Foundation—any Delaney, Mallory or Frederic or Kurt—would take advantage of him, ever again.

Bern found himself sitting at a desk being fingerprinted by a woman who refused to look him in the face. Bern couldn't tell if she was embarrassed or just didn't care. She just said, "Name."

Then he was sitting handcuffed to a bench, waiting to be interviewed. He was in possession of stolen property: his Delaney laptop. He hadn't signed out his laptop properly, and they were now "holding" him.

They held him for three hours. Half-naked. Shamed. But not broken. He got himself together enough to ask one of the many officers for a phone call. He was ignored. It was probably a good thing. He had no idea who to call. He didn't have Eboni's burner phone number. The only number he knew by heart was his mother's. That was not an option.

"Hendricks?" a man said from across the station: middle-aged, overweight, with a clipboard and a slight frown, like Bern was inconveniencing him.

"Right here, Detective," said Officer Dickson. The heavyset guy went around the officer, chuckling as he uncuffed Bern from the bench and led him to a tiny interrogation room that smelled very strongly of body odor. There was a table and a laptop computer, which the fat officer sat in front of.

"Have a seat. I'm Detective Kirdahi. We just need to ask you some questions."

"I want to call my lawyer," Bern said, wondering who he could call. He didn't have a lawyer on standby, the way they did on *Law & Order*.

"You're not under arrest. We're just wanting to ask you some questions."

"Can I get some clothes, please?" Bern said.

"Name."

"Bern. Hendricks. Uh—Kevin Hendricks. Doctor."

"Which is it? Don't fuck with me. It's been a long night. This can go easy or rough. Your choice." Kirdahi didn't look up as he typed on the laptop. He wore at least six rings buried in the pink folds of his fingers: diamond and topaz winked at Bern.

Bern took a breath. "Kevin Bernard Hendricks."

"Address." That was awful nice jewelry for a cop.

Bern gave his New York address along with a host of other information. After what seemed like hours, Kirdahi slid back his chair, got up, and walked out. Bern found he was trembling, and he couldn't catch a breath. No clothes, no phone, no sleep, no food, no water. He yanked on the handcuffs, tried to extricate his hands. The cuffs were warm from his body heat and very solid: their weight both comforted and sickened him.

"Hey, hey, hey, calm the fuck down," Kirdahi said, returning with an orange jumpsuit. He threw it at Bern, who couldn't put it on, in the cuffs, but held it in front of his chest like a shield. Kirdahi said, "I'm not gonna tell you again to calm the fuck down."

"What do you want from me?" Bern asked.

Kirdahi pointed to the laptop. "Where did you get this?"

"It was given to me by the Delaney Foundation."

"We understand that," Kirdahi said. "We also understand that you're not authorized to remove Delaney property from the premises. This laptop was reported as stolen."

"That's crazy! Just call the Foundation. Mallory Delaney Roberts—or my assistant, Stephanie!"

"Sure. We'll call them as soon as they get into the office. Are you sure you don't want to save me a lot of paperwork and just confess to receiving stolen property?"

"I can't believe this. Who called you guys on me anyway? This is a huge misunderstanding."

"Okay, maybe, but if we receive a credible report that property has been stolen, we are obligated to investigate. We did. You have the property in question. Right down to the serial number." Kirdahi said it proudly, as if he'd just arrested a big-time drug dealer.

"Who called you? Who reported it missing?" Bern persisted.

Kirdahi ignored him. "I'm going to take you back to a cell and let you think about anything further that you might be able to tell us about the stolen laptop. You can search your soul and see if you think of something."

"I want a lawyer," Bern repeated.

Kirdahi looked at Bern and said, "Right. They said you wouldn't put up a fight. Let's go."

"'They'? Who's 'they'? Where are you taking me? What are you doing?"

Kirdhai had gone behind Bern, uncuffing him and yanking him up roughly by one arm.

Instinctively, without any conscious thought whatsoever, Bern yanked his arm away.

His latest boneheaded mistake.

Kirdahi let him go, swatting the back of Bern's head with a blow that jolted Bern's teeth together as he collapsed back into the chair and partially onto the table.

Dimly he heard "Officer in need of assistance" from Kirdahi.

"Wait," Bern said muzzily, "hold on. Wait a minute."

He tried to sit up and get his bearings, but before he could clear his head, three more officers—he recognized Officer Fields—burst in. One tackled him, smashing his head onto the linoleum tile. An elbow thrust into his jaw, and, dimly, he could feel blows to his eyes and mouth as someone held him down. Someone else stomped on his legs. He kept hearing different voices shouting, "Watch his hands! Stop resisting!"

He lay limp, not believing this could even be occurring, almost detached from his body, almost floating above or next to himself. A near-naked Black guy surrounded by four white officers in uniform. He had never felt so utterly alone, so completely vulnerable. And who would believe him, afterward? All it took was for one of the officers to say "He did it," and it instantly became fact.

Then, he was being dragged down corridors—dazed and confused—and tossed into a holding cell. Someone threw the orange jumpsuit on top of him. As the cell door slammed, he could have sworn he heard one of the police officers say, "Why do they want him so bad?"

Another man replied, "Fuck if I know. Don't care. The money's good."

Bern lay on the floor for a long time. No one else was in the cell with him. He felt his face with his fingertips, trying to assess if bones were fractured. He was broken and embarrassed and felt like so much less than a man.

And the whole time he kept thinking, *Delaney. A laptop was the best they could do.*

That was his last thought before he passed out on the floor.

Two hours later, the sound of the heavy steel door opening woke him. He tried to sit up and fresh pain shot across his shoulders and right hip. "Hendricks? Kevin Bernard Hendricks?"

"Yeah," he said, this time leveraging himself up onto the floor.

"You're free to go. Leave the jumpsuit. That's station property. Here are your keys." A man he hadn't seen before—thin, well-built, a thick blond mustache—was staring disinterestedly at the wall across from him, as if Bern weren't even worth looking at.

Fine. Free to go. He tottered up to a standing position and, holding on to the wall, he again pulled his gym shorts up. Of course it was Delaney. They didn't have the balls to confront him themselves. They used the low-life losers posing as New York City's finest to intimidate him. No doubt to show him that he was solidly under their thumb.

It was working.

But if they were doing this to Bern over a laptop, what would they do to Eboni, if they could find her?

Bern trudged out of the police station, found he was only two blocks from his apartment. Still barefoot, wearing only gym shorts in the bitter January morning, he slogged home. His feet burned with cold, but at least there was no snow. Nobody seemed to notice him, and he couldn't care less if they did.

He needed to get back to his apartment. Get to his phone. Get clothes.

Most importantly, he needed to make sure the world knew what these people were. He needed to do it for himself and for Eboni.

And for Josephine Reed, who was so much more—to the world, to music, to Eboni, and to Bern—than a few photographs and a trunk-ful of old documents.

41

Coming Back Tomorrow

Josephine

THURSDAY MORNING, Josephine Reed hesitated only an instant before she rang the buzzer. She knew the risk she was taking. Her underarms were damp and clammy from fear, and she clutched her purse tightly to her abdomen. Could she actually go through with this? She couldn't imagine what would happen if *he*—she couldn't think of him by name anymore—found out. *When* he found out. What, though, was her alternative?

No. Especially not now. Everything was in motion.

She pressed the buzzer hard: a solid C. Silence for a moment. Then: "Yes?"

Deep breath. She wanted to say, *The pink goes on top of the vine,* but instead she said, "I'm here to see Mr. Turpin."

"What about?"

Place the violet between the lavender. "It's a private matter. Tell him Josephine Reed is here. I used to work with him at Ditmars and Ross."

Silence. Then the door buzzed, and she was in.

Up a narrow rickety flight of stairs and into a small reception area, where a young woman presided. Josephine again explained who she was. The receptionist disappeared. Josephine would have sat in one of the two small wooden armchairs but she wasn't sure if colored people were allowed to sit, so she stood, sweating, her fingers digging into her purse.

Miles's voice, before she saw him: "Can I help you—Josephine? It is you!"

Miles Turpin appeared in the doorway. Tall and in need of a haircut, wearing a threadbare dark suit. He was skinnier than she remembered, his chest more concave and shoulders more hunched. He'd grown a potbelly. "What are you doing here? Come into my office."

She followed him. He sat behind a desk that was half the size of the dinette table in her room and perhaps a quarter the size of Freddy's desk. Again, she wasn't sure if she should sit, so she stood until he gestured for her to take the chair opposite him.

"How have you been? What a surprise to see you," Miles was saying. "You were one of the few good things about Ditmars and Ross. I knew exactly where to find things. You did a nice job organizing the place. Are you still working there?"

"No."

"Oh, well. That's too bad. Their loss, right? So what brings you here? Are you looking for work? I'm afraid that I don't really have any job openings, but as soon as I do—"

She told herself that if she could just speak the words, she could make it happen. "I have music," she said. "I want to sell it."

Miles sat back in his chair. "You have music? To sell?"

"Yes."

"Well, that's nice, but I don't think your kind of music would sell very well."

"My music is good. People like it. From everywhere. My melodies have all the colors in them. Not just a few."

Miles looked at her blankly. "Yes, well, be that as it may, I don't think your kind of music would sell too well. Maybe if you come back in a few months I may be able to hire you as a helper for Rita. How does that sound?"

Josephine moved to the piano against the back wall, sat at the bench. Miles was getting up, coming toward her with a fake smile stretched across his lips, and she began to play: the first few bars opened like a dance-hall tune but then morphed almost immediately into an upbeat rag; and, then, somehow, impossibly melded jazz into its own unique, unforgettable melodic style.

When she finished, she told him, "That was 'When It Was Evergreen.' I wrote it four days ago."

Sometime during the song, Miles had carefully closed the door. Now he leaned over to look at the foolscap.

She'd printed WHEN IT WAS EVERGREEN in careful block lettering and had transcribed the music into passable notation. She could, of course, read and write music. She'd been able to do that from her earliest days, from the locked piano in Oxford, before she'd developed her own system. But Fred had never asked her to write in regular notation, and she'd never offered to do it for him. Before, it had been an excuse to see him every night; and then, later, she thought he would be angry that she hadn't told him.

"Did you write this?" Miles asked, as if he hadn't heard her.

"Yes, four days ago."

"Uh-huh. I see. What inspired you to write the music?"

"Is there something wrong with it?"

"No, nothing at all. As a matter of fact, it's quite good. It sounds familiar. Almost like something I've— You say you wrote this?"

"Yes, I did."

"How much do you want for it?"

"Twelve dollars."

"Twelve dollars, huh? Well, I may be able to work something out.

I'll need a copy so I can play through it, see if it can be arranged. Do you have another copy?"

"No," Josephine said. She hadn't thought of that.

"I can buy the original, then," he said.

"I want my name on it. I want it to say, *Music by Josephine Reed*."

"You do, do you?"

"Yes," she said. "Twelve dollars, and I want my name on it. If you don't want it because I'm colored, I'll take it somewhere else." She knew from Fred that people didn't like music written by colored people.

"Because you're colored," he echoed. "You don't have to worry about that with this song. It's a good song. It's not just a coon song that only colored people would like. I don't think people will care who wrote it if they can sing it and dance to it."

She was so surprised, she looked right at him, could feel a gong go off in her chest, a full-on F chord, and tried to catch her breath. After everything Fred had said. All the promises he'd made. No one would care if she was colored?

She tried to gather her thoughts. Tried again. "Do you want it? You have to tell me now."

She could go to Ditmars next. All she knew was that it had to be today. She was leaving tonight. Last night, while Fred was out, the Compendium had been loaded into two taxis, and she paid the porter in Penn Station to haul all five steamer trunks into the left-luggage office—the same room where she'd stashed her single trunk of the Compendium all those years ago. The train to North Carolina would leave at 10:15 tonight, and she and the Compendium would be on it.

"Really?" Miles said. "What's the hurry?"

She looked down at her hands on the keyboard. How many pianos had she touched over the years? Most of them uprights: beat-up, damaged things, few of them really in tune, none of them the kinds of instruments that she'd heard in concert halls. She'd imagined, when she first came to New York, that everyone would play on baby grands.

"I want the twelve dollars now," she said. "And a letter that says I wrote the music and that I'm selling it to you."

"Now you want a letter?" Miles sounded amused. "Before it was just twelve dollars. Now it's your name and a letter."

She was silent, still marveling over his words, how being a Negro didn't matter to the music.

"Okay," Miles said at last. "I'll do it, Miss Josephine Reed."

He went over to a file cabinet, thumbed through some files, pulled out a form. "This form says that I'm buying all rights, title, and interest to your music from you. In exchange I'll give you twelve dollars and give you a credit line for the music. See?" He handed her a single sheet of legal-size paper with tiny lettering and several blanks to be filled in. "Will this do?"

She pretended to look it over, but the words swam. "Yes," she said at last. "I have four other songs, too."

"You do? Four more? Like that one?"

"Yes," she said. "Can you pay me sixty dollars for all five?"

"If they're as good as that one, I can," Miles said.

She played the other four for him.

"I have other songs, too," she said. "If these work out, I'll bring you others."

"You will?" Miles rubbed the side of his face. "I'm happy to pay for music like this. They're swell. Just swell. I'll buy them, but can you come back tomorrow? There're forms and signatures I'll need to have prepared. And I don't have that much cash on me."

Josephine stared at her fingers on the keyboard. She said at last, "But then my name will be on them? The papers will show my name?"

"Absolutely. That's what this set of forms is for. I always write my own songs, so I don't buy music directly from other people. That's why I need a lawyer to approve it first. Standard procedure."

"Can you get it today?" Her train left tonight at ten fifteen.

"I'm afraid not," Miles said. "Could you be here tomorrow morning at ten o'clock sharp?"

She sat, thinking. She supposed that she could have one more night in the apartment on Sixty-Third Street, come back here tomorrow and then head immediately to Penn Station. She could take her already-packed suitcases to Penn Station today, leave them with the Compendium.

The trick would be tonight: when *he* stopped by for the music. She'd have to pretend everything was as it had been. That the Compendium still hunkered in Freddy's old rooms. She'd have a few tunes ready for him. He would knock his D-major knocks, open the door, take the music, and leave, and not stay long enough to notice any difference.

It was a risk, but now Miles Turpin promised that she'd have her own name on her own songs, and an income stream for the future.

Yes, she told Miles, she could be there tomorrow. Ten sharp. She gathered her handbag, nodded her thanks.

Tomorrow morning it would finally be done. These were her songs, after all. She could do with them what she liked. The world would know that Josephine Reed wrote this music.

Moments later she found herself outside in the May sunshine, breathing in the smell of Tin Pan Alley and New York in the spring: heat, flowers, metal, and the distant smell of sewage.

42

Dear Members of the Board

Bern

Dear Members of the Board and Executive Director of the Delaney Foundation,

The past several days have shown me exactly who you are and what you stand for. You have lied, cheated, manipulated, threatened, and humiliated me for the last time.

I dedicated my life to making the world a better place, partially by following the lead of Frederic Delaney and the Delaney Foundation. Now it's become apparent that your organization, like its founder, is riddled with disease and disinformation.

If you hoped to intimidate me with your clumsy and brutal police tactics, please know your plan has backfired spectacularly. In your attempts to destroy me, you've left me no choice except to destroy you. And I absolutely intend to do so.

Please be advised that I hereby terminate all affiliation

with you and my employment by you. Rest assured, however, that you, and the rest of the world, will be hearing from me and my attorney in the very near future with a full account of the activities of your founder and of yourselves.

Sincerely,
K. Bernard Hendricks, PhD

"What do you think?" Bern asked Eboni.

She was sitting across from him, balancing a laptop on her lap. They were holed up in a shady fourth-floor walkup deep inside the Bronx: one of Eboni's friends had a friend who had a friend who was out of town for the month. It had a great view of a fire escape and laundry draped over a matching fire escape on the other side of a narrow exterior shaft.

"I think it's way too nice," she told him. "You need to go for the jugular. Show 'em how we do it in the hood."

He tried to smile, but he was too tired. He had no doubt that the Foundation would poison every institution against him. He wouldn't work in academia again. He wouldn't work with music again. What options did he have? He imagined a career delivering pizza. Driving a cab in Manhattan: he'd heard of plenty of PhDs who did exactly that. Could people even earn a living driving cabs these days?

He'd lost everything—and for what? For a half-baked, half-formed, half-believable story about a now-long-dead woman no one had ever heard of?

He'd left everything behind in the tiny Upper West Side apartment, except his driver's license. Now—using a burner phone, paying with cash, wearing faded clothes from a local thrift store—he wasn't even sure he was himself. Eboni, on the other hand, seemed right at home. Somehow her cornrows had been re-braided, her nails were done, her clothing trim and tailored.

"I don't think we should give away the game plan to them," he said.

"No effing way we will," she told him. "But this'll be a lot more fun if they're running scared. If they're worried about what we'll do. Because we're gonna go big."

"I'm worried about contacting the media organizations. The Foundation seems to have everyone in their back pocket."

She nodded. "Yeah, and as soon as we expose them, there's a very real possibility that they will come after us extra hard. I mean, really come after us."

They'd gone around and around about the nondisclosure agreements. Had consulted a lawyer—yeah, Eboni knew a guy—who said that courts sometimes didn't uphold nondisclosure provisions if they were too broad, and perhaps whistleblower protection programs might shield them, but of course it wasn't cut-and-dried.

"What about that I didn't sign the paperwork?" Eboni demanded. That didn't seem to matter since she knew about it and had assented to its signing. Of course they would make the argument in front of the court that she'd known about the document, and the technicality of a forged signature wouldn't get her off the hook.

"It has to work," Bern said now. "Don't ask me why, but I have a feeling that they think I'm bluffing. They think they broke me."

"Why do you think that?"

"Because they almost did. I almost gave up. I was embarrassed and devastated. When I was in that cell, I wanted to tell them that I'd do whatever they asked. Then I thought about you. And, honestly, about Josephine. It's time we stood up to them. Time we held them accountable."

She stood up and gave him a fist bump. He hugged her tight, and she hugged him back.

Somehow he found her lips with his own. The kiss was somehow surprising, but familiar, as if they'd recognized something that they'd forgotten. Her arms were around him, and his were around her, holding her tight, so tight.

Bern closed his eyes and lost himself in her lips, the touch of her tongue on his own. Time stopped. Neither of them spoke. He kissed her again and then they were moving together to the bed and he was unzipping her dress and she was fumbling with his belt buckle.

What seemed like hours later, they lay together on top of the covers. He held her, feeling her breathe against him. Her warmth felt delicious. Neither spoke. He hoped she felt the way he did: regardless of what was happening with Delaney, this moment was untouchable.

He was drifting off into a light doze when Eboni said near his ear, "These people only understand power. You know me. I don't like to get ugly unless I have to."

He opened his eyes. The peace was ebbing, sliding like a wave into the corners of the room, disappearing into the crevices. He pulled her closer to him. "What are you thinking?" he said.

She slipped away, and the space where she'd been was cool and felt very empty. A moment later she was back, carrying the two laptops. She tossed one onto his belly, slid back next to him, then leaned her shoulders against the headboard. "We just have to dig deep. Here. Start looking up names."

She opened the laptop, gave Bern the password to his.

"Let me give you a lesson," she said. "You should never, ever screw around with someone who does cybersecurity for a living. Number one rule of life. Get it tattooed on your chest."

"That's the number one rule, huh?" he said.

"Damn right. Here's what we're going to do. We're going to get a list of the board of directors and all the officers. We're going to research them and their immediate families, and we're going to hunt through any recent public business dealings. We're going to look for any announcements and figure out what lawyers represent them."

"Seriously?" Bern said, "How are we supposed to find out all that?"

"These are public figures. They're rich white people. They're all the same. They like to put their business out there. They like to see themselves in print. They also don't think anybody will ever touch them. No matter how many times rich people get busted, their neighbor is always convinced that it can't happen to them. I'm sure at least one of them—or maybe all of them—has some skeletons in their closet. Trust me."

She pulled up a site, showed him how to maneuver through it.

"Just get started. Remember, only board members and officers. None of those low-level jerks. Leave Mallory to me. One thing I guarantee you: there will be dirt, and we will find it. That's how we get even. That's how Josephine and her family get what they're owed."

"I'm going after those NYPD officers, too," Bern said. "The one that tased me. That took me to jail."

"Damn right you are," she said.

Over the next eight hours—Bern couldn't believe the minutiae, the following of one buried lead into another—Bern learned that Suzanne Herz was a majority owner in fourteen corporations—some well-known, many unknown—around the United States, Hungary, and Germany.

"Get a list of them and all their websites, and then I'll see if we can hit their servers," she said. She was busy making lists of her own. "And zero in on the ones who don't have too much information or who look like they aren't doing too well."

"What are you digging for?"

"Trust me. Those are areas where we'll want to focus. He's probably up to something shady. If it were legit, he would've cut ties—he'd have sold it if it's not making him any money. He's probably laundering money or doing something rotten. The easiest way is the way that they think no one will suspect."

Bern wanted to ask how the hell Eboni knew all this but thought better of it. Regardless of how she knew, she was right. After Bern had compiled nine corporations around the United States and three in Hungary that had all reported losses for fourteen straight months,

Eboni worked her magic. Bern watched in awe as she hacked into several servers. Thousands of keystrokes later, she discovered that his dealings went through shell corporations in Russia, and then she traced the money for them.

She was single-minded; hours went by. He dug into the backgrounds of more board members, and she pulled out all her resources to research all their companies—from whom they bought land to where they'd bought the blinds in their offices.

They worked through the next two days, sleeping a few hours at a time, and then getting back to it. On a credit card owned by one of the shell companies, under the name Kurt Fredericks, which seemed to be an alias that Kurt Delaney used from time to time, Bern came across a large purchase to the Good Tidings Company. There were dozens of corporations with that name, but Eboni hunted systematically through each of them.

Finally, four hours later, she choked on her coffee. "Holy shit. That's it. Look."

He tried to follow her keystrokes, but she'd already spun out of that web page and into another. Now she was searching hospital records and clinic files.

"Boom. Just a nasty old man," Eboni said as she turned her screen around.

Bern looked. "Ew. Just ew," he said.

43

Stealing Your Songs

Fred

EVERYONE SAID they wanted to be like Fred Delaney—the wunder-kind, they called him! Only twenty-eight, and the top composer in the country! Dining in Europe with heads of state! His music featured throughout not only America but the world! Fred's staff of twenty could barely keep up with the workload—the requests, the commissions, the adaptations—and Fred had to manage them and seek out new business and write new music and new lyrics! No wonder Fred was under such pressure. No wonder he wasn't sleeping and his hair had started to thin. "Wunderkind" was all well and good, but all those admirers should try walking around in Fred's shoes for a day; they'd see it wasn't all sunshine and starlight and graceful melodies wafting upon the breeze. It was work. Hard work.

He was knee-deep in an argument on the telephone with a concert hall in San Francisco: they wanted to adapt *The Wanderers*—one of Fred's musical theater shows—and had the temerity to request culling a couple of the characters, removing a few parts, and cutting

four songs. Fred was having none of it and was telling Mr. Randolph
Martin of the San Francisco Players what he thought of Mr. Martin's
ideas when the receptionist buzzed him, saying a Miles Turpin was
outside and that it was urgent he speak with Fred.

Miles Turpin. Fred remembered visiting Miles in a run-down
office after parting ways with Ditmars. Fred knew all the composers and music publishers, of course—he had to stay abreast of the
competition!—but Miles, with his lackluster melodies and tepid show-
manship, had never presented much competition.

"Tell him to come back later," Fred told the receptionist. He
returned to Mr. Martin, telling Mr. Martin that it was crucial that
the character of Libby be kept exactly as written, that cutting Libby
completely would undermine—

"Excuse me, Mr. Delaney," came the receptionist's voice again,
timid but resolute. "I've told him to come back or to leave a message,
but he wants to speak directly with you. He says it's very important."

"I'm busy," Fred told the intercom. He really needed bigger offices.
And a better receptionist, come to think of it. What he had to deal
with on a daily basis! "Have him come back. Have him make an
appointment like everybody else." He turned back to Mr. Martin.

Eventually, after another ten minutes—and this was a long-
distance telephone call! His bill would be astronomical!—Mr. Martin
saw the error of his ways and agreed to keep Libby intact and to pay
the full performance rate for *The Wanderers*. Now why did Fred have
to deal with that? Isn't that why he'd hired lawyers, so he could focus
on the creative? He shook his head, laid the phone down in its cradle.

No sooner had he hung up when the receptionist—what was her
name? Fred really couldn't keep them all straight—knocked on the
door. "Mr. Delaney, I hate to disturb you, but Mr. Turpin refused to
leave. He gave me this to give to you." She handed him an envelope,
sealed. It was one of Freddy's own, labeled DELANEY MUSIC PUBLISH-
ERS, INC. in blue lettering embossed on heavy stock.

Fred tore it open with a thumbnail. One sentence: *Someone is stealing your songs.*

A pause. Fred glanced up at the receptionist, down at the page. *Stealing.* "Send him in, would you?"

A moment later Miles Turpin was in the room, shaking Fred's hand, looking as seedy as he'd looked several years ago. The shine on Miles's suit was positively pathetic. Fred's suits were now, of course, bespoke silk and wool.

They shook hands, exchanged brief pleasantries. "Sorry, Miles, it's a busy day for me," Fred said. "What's this about someone stealing songs?"

Miles was in an indolent mood, casual and expansive. He took his time settling himself in one of the leather chairs across from Fred's desk. He was holding a manila envelope and laid it lightly on the desktop. Not that there was much room to put it down; Fred's desk was piled with music, contracts, notes, fan letters, and dozens of other papers.

"I had a visitor this morning," Miles said at last. "Just a couple hours ago."

"Oh yes?"

"You remember that pretty colored girl, Josephine, from the office?" Miles said. He leaned forward, touching the manila envelope.

Fred looked at Miles, face blank. He blinked once. "Sure, I remember her. Had a few screws loose." He stood up abruptly, went over to the wet bar to make himself a drink. It was almost lunchtime, after all. "You want one?" he asked Miles.

"Sure," Miles said. "Is that whiskey, this early? Aren't you a bad boy. I'll have what you're having. Guess you've got yourself a supplier these days. Good for you."

"So what about Josephine? She came by, you say?" Fred said, his back to Miles as he poured out two glasses. Lead crystal. Waterford. Fred's hand shook.

"She did. She did indeed. Damnedest thing," Miles said.

The two glasses, each a quarter-full of whiskey, stared back at Fred. He took a breath, and then another, set the whiskey bottle back in place, and said, "Don't tell me you're going after darkies now."

"Oh no. Nothing of the sort. She came by to sell me a song. Five songs, actually. And promised me more. A whole lot more, she said."

Fred counted to three and then, careful, picked up both glasses with fingers that were suddenly slippery with sweat. It wouldn't do to drop the Waterford crystal. He imagined a rainbow-colored explosion, shards sparkling on the carpet. After handing a glass to Miles, Fred went around to his desk, sat down, the whiskey untouched in front of him. "A song?" Fred repeated. His voice sounded odd to him: strangled, too high. "I didn't know you were selling colored songs now. Is business that bad?"

"Well, I'm not sure if it's a colored song or not. See, she comes in with this song, she plays it and it's just swell. I mean, it's *swell*. She tells me she writes it. I don't believe her, of course, because the coloreds can barely write, let alone write a masterpiece like this. The best part is, she asks for twelve dollars for it. Can you believe that? Twelve dollars."

Fred took a sip of his drink and somehow found himself swallowing the entire three fingers of whiskey. "That's quite a story there," he said at last. "So what is it that I can do for you?"

"Here's the thing, Freddy. I think Josephine may have stolen this music."

"From me?"

"Yes, I believe so. It's definitely one of your songs. It's trademark Freddy Delaney. I'd know it anywhere. The one thing that all your songs have in common is how singable they are. Memorable, right? No matter what you've written, they all have that characteristic I've-heard-this-before angle to them. This was exactly like it. Exactly."

Fred could hear his voice, bruised, coming from a distant place. "Interesting," he heard himself say.

"No way anybody else could have written a song like that," Miles said. "It was way too sophisticated, especially for a Negro. She played it pretty good, though."

"Did you tell anyone? The police?"

"Of course not. I came straight to you. Here." Miles pushed the envelope across the desk. "Take a look."

As Fred pulled the sheets from the envelope, Miles said, "She called the first song 'When It Was Evergreen.' Said she wrote it a week ago. But check out the one called 'Sapphire in the Morning.' That one is the berries."

Each of the twenty-odd pages was in regular musical notation, each bearing the initials *JoR* in the top right corner. "So you say she brought this to you this morning?"

"Yeah. This morning. You recognize them? I bet she stole them from you while she was at Ditmars. You can't trust these coloreds."

"You're right, this is mine," Fred said. "I'd hate to lose out on a great song because some colored bitch stole it from me."

"It is yours," Miles said triumphantly. "I thought so. I said to myself, *This is a Freddy Delaney song if I ever heard one.*"

"I'm going to have to go to the authorities," Fred said, trying out the words, nerves and rage simmering through him. "I tried to be nice to her, but she's a loon, you know? Who knows when she stole it. Niggers shouldn't be allowed to work with white folks, that's really what it boils down to, doesn't it?"

"Glad I could help," Miles said. "Glad I could do a good turn for a chum." He looked around exaggeratedly. "You've sure made something of yourself. I'm proud of you."

"Thanks," Fred said. "Can I reimburse you for the song? How much are you out of pocket?"

"Sixty bucks. But if you want to find her, she's coming back to my office tomorrow morning. I told her to come back at ten a.m. But, honestly, it's okay. You don't have to repay me. Although I was kinda hoping you could do me a favor in exchange."

Again Freddy's voice seemed to be coming from far away. "Favor?"

"Come on, pal. You own one of the fastest-growing publishing houses in New York. Your music is all over the place. You're printing money these days."

Fred said nothing.

"I was hoping you'd throw some work my way. You've got enough going around, you know? And I can handle some of it. I hired a couple of people. Two song pluggers. We're mostly doing rags and ballads, nothing big-time. Nothing like you. So just some of the projects you're going to turn down. Things that are out of your wheelhouse."

Fred breathed again. "Of course. I'd love to." His lips made a smile. He wiped his hands repeatedly on his silk-and-wool trousers. "Let me reimburse you for the song, too. And yes, of course I'd be glad to throw some business your way. Why don't you meet me for dinner tonight so we can talk about it? Can you meet me at The Little Restaurant, that basement place on Forty-Fourth? Tonight, maybe at eight? We can talk about some of that business I'll be throwing your way."

Fred stood, held out his hand to shake. He wondered if Miles noticed how sweaty Fred's palm was.

Miles didn't seem to.

"Actually, make it nine," Fred said easily. "Is that too late for you?"

Nine was swell, Miles told him.

"Great," Fred said. Surely Miles, pumping his hand, didn't notice anything amiss.

But Fred could not be sure.

44

Coffee & Toilet Paper

Bern

BERN WAS MAKING SIMPLE MISTAKES. Stupid stuff, like forgetting to turn off the oven, or hearing directions to turn left and turning right even though he was thinking left. Eboni often had to tell him the same thing three or four times before he understood what she was saying, and until then he just stared at her like she wasn't even speaking English. He knew why it was happening: he was battered by the constant realization of how the Delaney Foundation was sabotaging his life—he'd probably never work again in academia; he'd be lumped in with cranks and conspiracy theorists, a joke; as one of the leading scholars on all things Delaney, he'd never again study Delaney's music. The music that had once saved his life now was ruining it.

He didn't know anymore what he thought about Frederic Delaney, or about Josephine Reed, or about the music they'd written. He felt betrayed by everyone, except Eboni. Now all the pathetic stores of energy he had left were focused on bringing down the Foundation.

So he slept as much as possible, when he wasn't researching the Delaney Board, and when he wasn't with Eboni.

The new place she'd found seemed safe enough. It was deep in the ass-end of Queens, in a cul-de-sac, so few pedestrians passed; and only a handful of cars, looking for elusive parking spots, turned down the street. From the window Bern could see who was out front. Out back, the building butted onto a small trash-strewn park, empty except for a handful of homeless people and drug dealers who prowled their turf more relentlessly than rottweilers. Eboni really had found a perfect spot. When he told her so, she rolled her eyes.

"You think I didn't realize it when Marissa rented this place? I told her then it would be the place to hang if I were ever on the run from the law. How would I know it wasn't just the police that would be after me but a bunch of musicians with harps and trumpets?"

That had made him laugh, and he'd kissed her again, and then they didn't talk for quite a while afterward.

They had no idea what was going on with the Foundation, and he hadn't logged on to emails or texts. He reached out to no one, in case the Foundation had already reached out to them. He'd gone underground, not contacting his family or any other friends. In the back of his head he worried about what the Foundation was doing to take him down: how they were discrediting him. Had they told UVA some mash-up of lies and half-truths? The FBI? Was all the good work he'd done on *RED* discredited as well?

The Foundation must have gone after Eboni, too. Nosy-ass Colleen must have told them everything she knew, and everything she thought she knew. Had the Foundation reached out to Eboni's clients, spewed their vitriol to them, too? He had no idea.

Nights had blurred into days, burrowing into hidden dark paths on the internet. Now, although it was only after two in the afternoon, Eboni had fallen asleep, her fingers still in place on her laptop's keyboard.

She'd lost everything for him. If that wasn't love, what was?

He was determined to make things right. He'd gotten her in this mess and he would fix it. In the meantime, they were running low on basic supplies. They could do without most of the luxuries they were accustomed to, but toilet paper and coffee were nonnegotiable. A drugstore was just four blocks away.

He knew the drill. He wasn't to leave unless it was necessary (it was). They were to give each other exact information and details about where they were going, and check in every twenty minutes. They had to be back within an hour.

He penned a quick note that he was going to Duane Reade for coffee and toilet paper. She didn't stir as he slipped out the door.

He kept his head down, baseball cap covering his face and the cheap red puffy coat pulled tight around him.

One block down. He passed a woman pushing a toddler; two young Latinas laughing and talking in Spanish; a small group of young Latino men smoking weed, passing the joint back and forth.

Two blocks down. He thought he could see the pharmacy's red lettering.

He wanted to look behind him but knew that might give him away. He took a chance and glanced back. Four men, one carrying a black duffel bag, had appeared several blocks down and were heading his way.

Two more blocks. A smoke shop glittered bright with bongs, pipes, and vape pens in the window. He went inside, ducked to the left to see if the guys would follow him. They wouldn't try anything in a public store, with video cameras everywhere, but would they once he was outside? Should he call Eboni?

The four men continued past the smoke shop. He could barely make out their laughter, one guy saying, "Why the fuck would you do that, man, that shit for brains—"

They sauntered down the block, and he decided he wasn't going to get coffee and toilet paper after all. He could get it delivered. It wasn't safe to be out on the streets. He wanted to get back to Eboni. Vaguely, he thought that he should get back to protect her, in case anything happened. He could barely protect himself, but he wouldn't let that stop him.

He slipped outside again, but instead of turning right, toward the apartment, he turned left. He'd go around the block, make sure those guys weren't following him back to Eboni. Was he being paranoid? How could the Foundation have found him so quickly? It didn't seem possible.

He checked his phone. There was a bodega on the next block, around the corner. He was walking faster, glancing into each storefront to see if anyone was inside, lying in wait for him. He rounded the corner, waited. Contemplated whether or not to call Eboni. Maybe he should call the police? That wasn't an option; a lot of crooked cops were in the Delaneys' back pocket, and would just a phone call draw attention to them, put them on the Delaney Foundation's radar?

He turned; the four men were farther down the block. A couple of them were really big, with muscles that swelled their shoulders. One carried a duffel bag. Two eyed him. They strolled in his direction.

He turned and fled back the way he'd come, not running but certainly walking briskly. He cut across against the light. Horns blared. He turned randomly up another side street, and wished he hadn't: it was deserted.

He walked as quickly as he could, but then two men appeared from in between parked cars, and Bern thought he recognized the duffel bag. He was pretty sure these two guys were part of the same group he'd seen a moment ago. They must have split up.

He fumbled in his pocket for his phone, worried that he'd somehow drop it as he went. He reached the end of the side street, blindly turned right, broke into a light jog. Halfway down the block he took off into a full-on sprint. He didn't know the area, so he kept running straight, dodging people and cars, paying no attention to the crosswalk signs.

Now it was more crowded, which made navigating through the

pedestrians difficult. The men behind him were surprisingly nimble and managed to keep up. He knew he was in trouble. No weapons, nowhere to go for safety. They were getting close now. No breakfast, no energy; Eboni had worn him out. Maybe he could lose them, double back? But now he couldn't go home—that would lead them to her.

Bern was terrified. Blood roared in his ears. He turned another corner and caught sight of a man texting near a parked car. He wore sweatpants, a gray hoodie, and a leather jacket, and he wasn't part of the other group. Could he help Bern? Bern couldn't gather his breath enough to call out before the man sauntered through the door of his apartment building. By the time Bern reached the guy's door, he was out of sight. Bern was gasping for air. He didn't know where he was, being chased by goons who might do who knows what to him.

He was out of options. He had to face these men. At least he'd go down fighting. Where the fuck was he, and how far was he from Eboni? He looked around for a weapon. No luck. Why did this neighborhood have to be so tidy? Even if there was something lying around that he could use as a weapon, what could he possibly do against two big dudes? What would they do to him? Beat him up as a warning? Kill him? Stuff him into the back of a van and haul him off to the Foundation?

The two men approached. Bern was breathing hard, but so were they. He tried to muster up as much bass in his voice as he could. "I don't know what they told you, but you better back the fuck up."

"Hey man," said the one on the left, who was taller and skinny and not carrying the duffel bag. "It's cool. Just be cool." His face was cavernous, with sharp cheekbones and pale brown eyes. His beard was a few scant hairs curling in on themselves.

"I'm not staying cool," Bern said. "Stay the fuck back."

"You got some property that we need to collect," the duffel bag guy said. He was a walking gorilla in need of a haircut: a square jaw and deep-set brown eyes. His shoulders were so broad that his arms hung far out from his waist.

"Property? What property?" Bern said. "Who sent you?"

"Just give us the stuff and we're out of your hair, man," the skinny guy said.

"I don't know what stuff you're talking about," Bern said. "You need to leave me alone. I'm going to call the police."

"Yeah, you go ahead and do that," the gorilla guy said. One of his ears was messed up—a cauliflower ear. Bern wondered if he was a wrestler or a boxer. Maybe he was on steroids. The guy was antsy, on edge, his eyes flickering to, and past, Bern. Bern itched to turn around but didn't dare; he slid over to put his back against the building.

"Just give us the stuff and you can be on your way," the skinny guy repeated.

Bern started, "I don't know what—"

Gorilla rushed him, barreled into him with his shoulder. Bern felt himself scraped off the wall and thrown into a beat-up gray Pontiac parked on the street. The car alarm immediately went off.

Now Gorilla was standing over him, laughing over the blaring horn. "I love it when they put up a fight." He turned toward the skinny guy behind him.

Skinny was laughing, too.

Bern was on the ground, sucking air. He was getting his ass kicked. This was really happening. Were these guys going to kill him?

All Bern wanted was coffee and toilet paper. All he'd wanted before that was to do the right thing. All he'd ever really wanted was to teach and listen to great music, to share the music with students. What the hell was he doing, ass out, lying in a peed-in gutter in the middle of a broken street in Queens?

And now they were laughing at him. These hired Delaney animals, laughing at him.

Bern would give them something to laugh at. Rage boiled up, and he tightened his fists. He didn't know if it was in his head or if he

actually made a noise, but he imagined himself growling. He struggled to rise, wanting to take a swing at these monsters.

And then he saw it.

Just on the other side of the Pontiac's tire, an empty bottle of Mad
Dog 20/20 lay on its side. Bern backed toward the Pontiac, grabbed
the bottle. In one motion, he smashed it against the concrete and
lunged up at Gorilla, broken bottle outstretched.

Nobody had expected this. Gorilla started to back up but was an
instant too late, and Bern was pouncing. The bottle seemed to fly
forward all on its own, slicing through khaki pants and shredding
the meat of the big man's thigh. The sharp glass had gone in and out
almost before Bern knew it.

The guy had dropped the duffel bag and let out a high-pitched
scream. "What the—" He collapsed.

Skinny said, "What the fuck, Joey?" and just stood there, watching
the blood pump from the big man's leg.

"Yeah," Bern said, "your boy's gonna bleed out. You want some
of this?" It surprised him, how good it felt, this striking back.
Finally—finally—he was getting even. He'd always been under someone else's boot, but now he was the giant and this 'roided-up asshole
was the ant.

"Hey man, just calm down, we can talk this over—"

"Good luck with that." Bern took a step toward Skinny. Bern had
no idea if he'd actually hit Gorilla's femoral artery, but, damn, it felt
great to say it. He hadn't known that he even knew the word *femoral*,
but apparently he did. Did the skinny guy have a gun? A knife? Bern
kept one eye on Gorilla, who was rolling around with both hands on
the wound. Blood oozed from between his fingers. The khakis were
turning a very bright red.

"Your friend here doesn't have long," Bern said, now feeling a little
sick. Had he just killed a man? He wanted to call 9-1-1 and get an
ambulance. But he wouldn't let these guys know that. "You and I can

go at it, or you can get him to the hospital. I hope you do the right thing. Make the wrong choice and he's dead in ten minutes. And the cops may be here by then, too."

Skinny pulled out a knife. "You just fucked up, son. All you had to do was give us the shit. Man, you didn't want to do that," he told Bern.

"Man, get me to a fuckin' hospital!" the gorilla—Joey—screamed. "Fuck him! I'm bleeding out. Holy shit, I'm bleeding out! Get me to a hospital. You can go after them later. You know where they fucking live."

"We know where you fucking live," Skinny told Bern. He took two steps back, away from Bern's outstretched broken bottle.

"Yeah," Bern said, "You might want to make a tourniquet out of those shoelaces, chief. Just a thought." He bucked at Skinny, who flinched. *Fuck yeah.* Bern felt great. Delaney fought dirty, and Bern could fight dirtier.

"Bitch," he told the guys, and, sucking wind, still out of breath from the gorilla's tackle, he limped around the corner as quickly as he could. Where were the other goons? They could show up at any minute.

When he was well away, he tossed the broken bottle in a trash can.

Then he was on the phone to Eboni.

She answered immediately. "Where in the—"

"They found us. Get ready. We need to get out of here right now. I just tangled with two of them and sliced one guy's leg wide open. There are at least two more, and they know where we live." He kept looking for the other two men he'd seen earlier.

"I'll be downstairs in two minutes. Meet me outside. I'm getting an Uber."

Ten minutes later they were in an Uber heading toward the subway. They carried nothing. Eboni had destroyed their laptops in the car: she'd had the Uber pull over, and she'd tossed them in a garbage bin on a side street. She'd saved everything to her online servers.

The Uber driver let them out in the chaos of Jackson Heights: hundreds of languages and ethnicities, and a half dozen subway and bus lines spiderwebbing in all directions.

"Let's go toward Brooklyn," Eboni said when they were out on the street and climbing the stairs to the elevated trains.

"Where do you want to go?" Bern said.

"No fucking clue," she told him. "I don't have a bunch of safe houses stashed away just in case. Marissa was my best shot. I guess I can call up nosy-ass Colleen, but all our business would be all over the Bronx before midnight. Maybe I can hit up Chandra or Larissa and see if we can crash on their couch for a couple of days. Bet Delaney has a list of my friends. Phone records or social media. Hell, Colleen's probably on the payroll by now."

"We need help. We need to call someone."

"Let me think," she said.

"Or we could go to a hotel for a couple of days." Then he answered himself: "Naw, too easy to find us, even if we do pay cash. Should we get out of town?"

"And come back in if we have to?" Eboni said. "We could rent a car."

"Not without a credit card," he said.

For lack of any better plan they took a subway all the way through Brooklyn, down to Coney Island. There, in the dead of winter, the streets were emptier, plastic bags blowing like ghosts along the boardwalk. This area was predominantly Russian, with signs both in English and with Cyrillic characters. As they wandered down a side street off Neptune Avenue, they passed rows of small, detached houses.

A small deli was open on the corner, and Eboni went in to get them both coffee. As they were leaving, Bern noticed a handwritten sign, barely legible: ROOM FOR RENT. He and Eboni exchanged a glance. They both had the same thought.

Outside, Bern dialed. A woman with a very thick Russian accent answered on the second ring. "Privet."

"Hello, I'm calling about the room you have for rent?" Bern said.

"Da, how many are you?" The woman sounded elderly.

"Um, Just me and, um"—he hesitated—"my wife."

Eboni shot Bern a side-eye but didn't argue.

"Da. You pay in cash. Four hundred dollars a week, yes?" The woman insisted, as if he were arguing.

"We only need it for one week. My wife and I." Bern turned to Eboni and mouthed the words *Four hundred*.

"Da. Yes. Okay. You want come tomorrow to see?"

"Can we come right now? We could rent it right now."

"When you come? Now? You bring cash?"

"Yes. What's the address? We have cash."

The woman gave him the address, and Eboni typed it on her phone. It was several blocks away, but an easy walk. "Okay, we'll be there in fifteen minutes."

"With the cash?"

"Yes ma'am, with the cash."

"Okay." The woman hung up.

In a few minutes they found the address. Another hand-lettered sign hung from twist ties to a chain-link fence. Inside, scruffy grass surrounded an empty concrete birdbath. "Well, we have a room for a week. At least we can crash for a while and regroup. Damn. I forgot to ask her about internet." Bern took the sign off of the fence.

"For four hundred a week, I hope she has cable, too," Eboni said, only half joking. "I wonder what kind of pizza is out here?"

"You ever have borscht pizza? This might be our chance." Bern opened the gate, and they went up the steps and knocked on the door. Eventually an old woman answered, cracking the door barely wide enough for them to glimpse part of her face, one bleary eye.

As soon as she saw them, she started to close the door in their faces.

"Hi, ma'am," Bern said. "I just called about the room for rent?"

"No, no room to rent." She began to close the door.

"Ma'am, we just spoke. I have cash. Four hundred, you said. I need a room for my wife and me. We have cash." He tried not to sound desperate.

The woman used her one good eye to look Bern and Eboni up and down. Bern forced a smile while Eboni looked the woman up and down just as hard as she did them.

"No. No room." The woman started to close the door again.

"Ma'am, the room was available to us fifteen minutes ago. What's the problem?" Bern brandished a wad of cash, and that stopped the door from closing.

"I'll tell you what the problem is," Eboni chimed in, "Boris and Natasha's great-great-grandma over here don't want to rent to us because we are too dark. Ain't that right, Black Widow Senior?"

"No. No room," the woman was saying.

"Five hundred dollars," Eboni said loudly. "Hear that, Natasha? We'll give you five hundred dollars for the week."

"No. No room for you." But the door stayed open. She peered up at his face and down at his fist. She was wearing slippers, very worn in the toes.

"Dammit, six hundred dollars. We'll give you six hundred dollars to stay in this fleabag for a week. You'd be crazy to pass that up." Bern tried to a form a friendly smile, but he knew that all she saw was the type of person she did not want in her home: Black.

"You steal. You come from jail. No room for you. You go."

"Eight hundred dollars," Bern said, worried that Eboni was going to snatch this woman through the crack in the door and drag her bodily onto the sidewalk. "We'll give your racist ass eight hundred dollars to stay in this dump. You don't want our money, your neighbor will."

That caught the old bat's eye. "You have money? You have eight hundred?"

"Yeah we got eight hundred dollars," Eboni said.

"Let me see."

Bern counted out eight one-hundred-dollar bills. "Can we see the place?"

The door opened. "You pay now. One week, then you go."

"We couldn't afford to stay more than a week at this rate," Bern said.

They went inside.

45

Steak Dinner & Two Bottles of Wine

Fred

THAT EVENING, Fred wiped his mouth with the napkin, laid it across his plate. "So, I'll have my secretary prepare the files of the accounts I won't be taking. That should do you for at least a year."

"You aren't going to eat any more? That's more than half a steak left," Miles said.

Fred shrugged.

"You're a good egg. I can't tell ya how much this is going to help me out. Who would have thought that me and ole Freddy Delaney would be in a fancy restaurant talking business? Ain't life something?"

"It sure is." Fred finished his wine, poured the rest of the bottle into his glass, and finished that, too. "So after she left, you didn't say anything to anyone else? What about the people who work for you?"

Miles shook his head. "I told you I wasn't going to spread gossip."

"Not the police? No one at all?"

"No sirree. I came straight to you, chum. We gotta stick together."

"Sure," Fred said.

"Right." Miles took another gulp. Fred ordered another bottle, which they consumed with a perfectly symmetrical pineapple upside-down cake.

"You sure you don't want any more?" Miles kept saying, gesturing to the bottle. "It's delicious."

Fred picked at the cake instead. By the time he paid the check, Miles was drunk, stumbling as they stood up to leave.

"Whoa there, pal," Fred said, "you'd better walk off some of that vino or you'll pass out in the cab."

"Yeah, I suppose I should. Good thinking." Miles stood carefully tall, and with the slightly swaying gait of the truly inebriated, tottered up the stairs and out onto the sidewalk, down Forty-Fourth Street. He lived far to the west, in Hell's Kitchen. Once out of sight of the Broadway lights, the streets were dark and sparsely populated. It was after eleven p.m. Fred had involuntarily volunteered his shoulder for Miles to latch on to as they walked, and it was pretty clear that Fred was the only thing keeping Miles upright.

"Yes sirree," Miles repeated for probably the twentieth time, "my pal Freddy is a big-time publisher now. How'd ya do it, Freddy?"

"Hard work, Miles."

"Aw c'mon. We both know there's gotta be more to it than hard work. Let me guess, you had some dirt on Ditmars, right? That's gotta be it."

They were past Ninth Avenue now, nearing Tenth. The Hudson River was another two blocks away. "Say, where are we going?" Miles asked. "I thought we were gonna take a cab home?"

Fred led Miles down an alley whose only inhabitants were several rats—and a cat who had just scored one of them for its dinner. "Oh, cab's coming soon. I figured you might want to take a piss. Go ahead. Do your business."

"Thank goodness. I really hadda pee."

Miles put one hand on the brick wall to steady himself, unbuttoned his fly. Fumbling in his pants, he looked down at the ground, saying, "I wanna thank you again, Freddy. This is the nicest thing anyone has . . ."

The back of Miles's head seemed so fragile as he watched where he was aiming. Even in the faded light, Fred could see that the hair above his collar was uneven and rough, as if Miles had tried clipping his hair himself, in the dark. And the collar of his shirt: so worn, one spot rubbed all the way through. Poor Miles.

Well, Fred was doing what had to be done. He groped in his jacket for the revolver that rested like a second heart against his chest. Pulled it out, aimed at Miles's back, hesitated, then lifted it to the space right above Miles's ragged collar.

He shot Miles in the back of the head with a single bullet. The shot rang out, echoing against the brick, and died away immediately. Miles's body collapsed against the wall. Fred returned the .22 to his breast pocket, took the wallet from Miles's inner jacket. He slipped smoothly back out of the alleyway, back onto Forty-Fourth Street. No one was nearby. He zigzagged up to Eighth Avenue and hailed a cab.

Now that Fred had neutralized the threat of Miles, it was time to teach Josephine a lesson. She needed to understand, very clearly, that Fred—and only Fred—was her lifeline. That the music she was writing was Fred's and no one else's.

46

Sincerely Yours

Bern

Dear Members of the Board and Executive Director of the Delaney Foundation,

Please be advised that as of 9:00 a.m. on Monday, March 4, 2024, the following shall occur:

To Kurt Delaney:
   Documents (see Attachments A–F) detailing a money-laundering scheme between Biolumens, a wholly-owned subsidiary of the Delaney Foundation, and various other entities and affiliated corporations shall be forwarded to the offices of the U.S. Attorney General, the Federal Bureau of Investigation, the *New York Times*, the *Wall Street Journal*, the *Washington Post*, and the *Economist*.
The documents shall also be posted in their entirety on www.fredericdelaneyisafraud.com ("the Website").

The documentation makes clear that you are the sole shareholder of many of these entities, but further penetration of the corporate veil will no doubt determine the level of involvement from other board members and/or shareholders.

In addition, we have obtained photographs and text messages (see Attachments G–O) belonging to you and several young men from rent.men. We will be forwarding these materials to Mrs. Delaney for her edification. We shall also post these materials on the Website. (Please note that images of genitalia will be redacted for your privacy.)

To Thomas Alexander:

Your personal and business tax returns for the years 2016–2021 failed to report approximately $3,247,998 of income derived from various non-U.S. sources (see Attachments P–Y). We shall alert the Internal Revenue Service of this deficit and post all records of such income, including the all-cash payments delineated in Attachments I and J, on the Website. (Please be assured that, in order to protect your privacy, all sensitive Social Security and Employment Identification numbers will be redacted.)

We note also that, since 2007, you have hired a series of undocumented illegal workers (see Attachments Z–FF). We have alerted the undocumented workers, who were, until this week, in your employment, so no doubt you have already noticed their absence. Be advised that we are collaborating with local charities to find the workers lawful employment and a path to citizenship. In the meantime, however, we shall utilize the Homeland Security Investigations Tip Form on ice.gov, which helpfully includes "Employment/Exploitation of Unlawful Workers" in its list of optional violations (see ICE Tip Form Section II, "Suspected Violation"). Please prepare to be contacted by Homeland Security, the Internal Revenue

Service, and several other governmental entities regarding this matter. In addition, we are including all relevant information, including photographs of your three homes (the Hamptons "cottage" should fetch top dollar if you decide to declare bankruptcy) and the living conditions of the undocumented workers in your employment. All this shall, as you can imagine, be included on the Website.

Further, for all other board members and employees of the Delaney Foundation, we have created 20+ websites whose contents shall be identical to that of the Website (see Attachments GG–YY). Note that the Website contains the following information:

• A full and as complete as possible portrayal of the collaboration and/or appropriation of materials written by Josephine Reed and subsequently appropriated by Frederick Delaney.

• A discussion of the five trunks of coded music, and our subsequent belief that Josephine wrote all of Delaney's music. After Reed disappeared or left Delaney, Delaney spent the next ten years trying to write Reed's music himself, and failed.

• A full and accurate list of all intimidation tactics employed by the Delaney Foundation to silence Ms. Washington and Dr. Hendricks, including photographs of the abuse Dr. Hendricks suffered at the Foundation's behest by the New York Police Department. Full records and detailed payments by the Foundation to the NYPD officers listed in the Attachments are also included (see Attachments ZZ–JJJ).

This information shall be released at the aforementioned time on March 4. These 20+ websites, which may be as many as 50, shall go live, and URLs shall be sent to all major media outlets (television, newspaper, radio, and internet sources) with accompanying posts and/or URLs on all major social media platforms. Instructions for screen capturing and data storage shall be provided.

In the alternative, we suggest that all board members shall, with their legal representatives, appear at The Pierre Hotel, Ballroom #3, at 12:00 p.m. on Friday, March 1. Ms. Washington, Dr. Hendricks, and respective attorneys shall be in attendance and shall provide clear instructions on working out a full and final settlement of this matter. Any further efforts by the Foundation at intimidation or coercion will be met with a swift and fully public release of all the above materials.

Finally, please be advised that Ms. Washington and Dr. Hendricks are checking in every few hours with third parties who have clear instructions to publish all this information if they fail to receive ongoing communication regularly at the appointed time(s), so we suggest the Foundation refrain from further attempts at intimidation until the meeting.

Very sincerely and seriously yours,
Eboni Michelle Washington & K. Bernard Hendricks, PhD

47

Save a Dog from the Street

Josephine

THE MUSIC of her last night in New York bloomed around Josephine as she waited for *him* to come. She'd intended to be gone by now. The train to North Carolina had left three hours ago, and she imagined herself on it: the click of the wheels, the bass thrum of momentum as they barreled southward.

She'd originally booked a sleeper car. Second class because she was colored, but that train did have a few second-class sleepers available. The train she'd had to rebook for today had none. She'd have to sit on a bench the whole ride down. It would take almost an entire day to arrive in Oxford.

It would be worth it. She was done with Fred Delaney. She was done with New York City. The music that she wanted to hear would be whatever she, Josephine Reed, wanted to hear. No one else.

The old apartment building on Sixty-Third Street breathed and creaked and she pictured herself, a tiny speck of warmth alone in the cool empty darkness. She felt unmoored without the comforting weight of the Compendium nearby: untethered, floating above the city. From far down the street blew the sound of laughter and—she was almost sure of it—the tender hook of a saxophone—E-flat—a running G-major chord suddenly cut short. The music probably from Jessie's, the colored speakeasy a block away.

She should have gone out tonight, she should have revisited her favorite haunts, she should have walked with the sound of her footsteps tapping out "Goodbye" to Harlem, to the Village, over to Tin Pan Alley and up Madison to where the new department stores stretched vast. *Goodbye, goodbye, goodbye.*

But she'd been unable to leave her room. She wanted to get it over with: for *him* to rifle through the Compendium she'd left for him on the piano, to nod at her, to go. What if he asked to see the score for *RED*?

RED. That reminded her. She groped in her leather handbag for the tiny brass jeweler's screwdriver she'd used to pry open the place where she kept *RED* from *his* grasp—*he* had hunted through the bag, tossed it across the room, but none of the contents had fallen out. Now the brass smiled up at her, the crosshatched handle fitting comfortably in her palm.

Then she'd cleaned up the damage he'd done so her room looked as it had before. Without the lamp and end table. She'd put those in Freddy's room, where the Compendium had rested until earlier today.

The breezes would be quieter in North Carolina. The cicadas would be humming in the sunshine; and every night, as the shadows flowered, the crickets would spiral out their F-sharp to B-minor rhythmic progression. A train would roar its weight from the top of the hill, and below, before dawn, the roosters would call to each other. The finches would sing by the creek, where nasturtiums would still be nodding their pale heads. The mornings would smell of honeysuckle, fresh eggs, and ham sizzling in the pan. She was so close.

Tomorrow she would collect RED, she would go to the station right after she signed the papers from Miles Turpin. The train wouldn't leave until early afternoon, but she would wait in the echoing vastness of Pennsylvania Station, the steamer trunks of the Compendium spread around her like trunk-size bean pods: she thought of *trunk*, as in *tree trunk*, as something vast and living, a conduit carrying musical sap up and out into the world. She had painted her name in white on all five trunks, plus the one she still had in her bedroom, white paint proclaiming that the Compendium belonged to *Josephine Reed, Regina Street, Oxford, NC*, with the cicadas and the roosters and the finches.

Evening passed slowly. Just after midnight, the front door boomed and his footsteps tapped through the landing far below. The *click, whir* of the elevator. And then the familiar footsteps beat their familiar tattoo to her door and that knock, that so-familiar knock, D major, three beats, and the door opened.

He didn't look at her. Which was good, because she didn't look at him, either. She listened as his feet found their way to the piano, as paper rustled, as he thumbed through the pages. She heard them being folded, the sound of cloth rustling. She supposed he'd inserted them into his jacket pocket.

She waited for his footsteps to start up again, to beat their way back across the room, for the door to open and to close behind him, for the footsteps to pad their way down the hall and out of her life.

Instead: the creak of the piano bench, E minor. He sat. The room yawned between them. She felt him looking at her.

"Why?" he said. Just the one word. When she didn't answer, he repeated, a little louder, "Why, Josie?"

Her name was Josephine, but that didn't matter anymore. If she answered his question, he would stay longer. She longed for him to go.

"Why would you do this to me?" he said. The piano bench creaked again, the E minor squealing out into F-sharp; he was standing, striding four strides over to her, towering above her as she stared down into her hands.

"All I've done since the day I met you was try to help," he told her. "I took you in. I fed you. I gave you experiences people like you only dream of. Why, Josie?"

If you rescue a dog from the street.

She said, "I don't—"

He was leaning over her. She could feel him coiled above her, his lips inches from her ear. "The next thing out of your mouth had better be a good reason for why you stole from me."

She tried to struggle to her feet but he shoved her shoulder back into the armchair. "I never stole anything from you," she said.

"Liar!" He slapped her across the face. "I know you tried to sell my songs to Miles Turpin."

She fell back, reflexively looking up at him, her eyes swimming.

He knew about Miles Turpin.

He no longer was the shining young man who had rescued her. His cheeks were distorted, eyes bloodshot, lips wrinkled back in a snarl. This was how he would look in another fifty years, she thought.

"You stole my music," he said. "You're trying to ruin me. After all I've given you."

"It's mine," she said. "It's always been mine. You're the one who stole from me. I tried to help—"

He pulled her up, hands under her armpits, lifting her so they were face-to-face. He smelled of wine and shame, and something else—something smokier, burnt. What was it? The scent was familiar but unusual.

"Your music?" he was saying. "Your music was nothing until I made it work."

"That's not true," she said. "It was mine. It worked just fine."

"Why would you go to Miles? Why would you take my music and try selling it to him? After all I've done for you?"

"It's my music," she said. "I wrote it. I heard it first." What was that smell? He was inches from her, but she would not look at him. "I can do with it what I like."

"Well, Miles won't be buying any of it," he said with a short laugh. "He won't be buying anything anymore."

"What do you mean?" she asked. She had never understood other people, how their words and the timbre of their voices never quite matched.

"Your pal Miles won't be buying anything ever again," he said, and he reached in his pocket and slid out a tiny revolver, barely the size of his hand, and he slid it back into his pocket again, and she realized what that smell was: gunpowder. Her father had smelled like that, and Howard, when they'd returned from a day hunting.

Now she looked up at him, looming over her, too close. "Did you do something to Miles? Did you kill him?"

"Stop your stupid talk! Just stop it!" he said, his face creasing up, and she looked away, down at her hands. And then he was screaming, howling. "Why did you make me do it? I don't want to do any of this, Josie, but you keep making me!"

"Miles is dead?" she said again, not quite understanding.

"You can't sell the music to other people," he said. "It's mine. You have to promise me that you won't ever do it again. You just can't go to other people with it. I'll take care of you forever, I promise. But you just can't betray me."

And there it was: his *promise.*

"It's not yours," she said.

"It is too! Can't you see that? We just have to have things the way they were, okay? Just promise me, okay? We're a team. We can do this. Just don't ever try selling it to anyone else ever again."

"It's not yours," she repeated. "It's mine. What did you do to Miles?"

"It was your fault," Fred told her, holding her by the shoulders, shaking her. "You betrayed me. You need to understand that the music is mine, you hear me? It's mine. I took you out of the gutter, I gave you a roof over your head, the music is—"

How did he know about Miles? She could feel her plans disintegrating, falling from her like broken autumn leaves.

"Stop it," she said. "Just stop. You're the one who's taken everything from me. My music is all I have. You promised me things would be the way they were. You lied again and again. It's gone." She pushed herself back, trying to shake free, but his hands tightened around her shoulders. "Let go," she said. "You're hurting me."

"The clothes, Josie. The trips. The money. I gave you everything."

"Liar," she said, breathing in the smell of him, charred and rank, almost welcoming it. "You have more money than me. You put the music on the paper and that gave you the money. And you have more. You said we would be partners and split everything. We'd both get the same, you promised. It all came from my music. You need me. Without me, you're nothing."

He stared at her, and she stared back, defiant.

"You piece of garbage," he whispered. "*You* are nothing. You're just a crazy scrap-bag lady. You were on the street living like a dog before I took you in."

"I was happy before I met you," she said, trying to wriggle away.

And then oddly, impossibly, holding her tight, he began to cry. "I'm sorry," he said, sniffling. "Josie, I'm so sorry. I failed you."

She froze.

"I thought I could make you understand what this was for," he said. "Why I worked so hard for you. I only wanted to make you happy, because you made me happy. Why you would do this to me,

I just don't understand. Why you'd you want to sell the songs to Miles—"

His grip loosened on her and he shuddered, great heaving gasps blowing over her as if belched from a train. In that brief instant, she felt sorry for him. He seemed genuinely grief-stricken for ignoring her, for striking her.

But not for stealing her music.

He hugged her tightly to him. She could feel the choice lying before her: she could forgive or she could speak her truth.

Why did she think she had a choice? She had no choice.

"It's my music," she told him. "It's always been mine."

He shook her so hard that she became dizzy. He put both hands on her face and squeezed.

"It's mine," he said. "I'm the one who made it great. Why can't you understand that?"

She struggled to free herself. His fingers dug into her cheeks, forcing her eyes up to meet his. He said, "You did this. You did all of this. It didn't have to be this way, but you made it like this."

His hands went from her face to her neck. She gasped for air.

"You won't take it away from me," he said. "It's mine. I worked too hard to let you or anyone else destroy what I've worked so hard for."

He was still weeping: his face so close to hers, tears oozing, a splash onto her jaw and onto her ear as he pressed his thumbs deeper into her windpipe. "Oh, Josie," he kept repeating, over and over. "Josie, we have to make music together. It's together, Josie. We're a team, remember? We're a team, Josie. You and me."

Squeezing, hands around her throat.

She couldn't breathe.

She tried to pry loose his grip, but her fingers could find no purchase.

She looked up at him, his silver-black hair flopping in his face, his lips contorted and trembling, his blue eyes leaking tears, and then she wouldn't look at him anymore, and refused to hear her name on his lips.

"It was mine," she told him in her mind. *Mine.*

And then, somehow, it didn't matter anymore whose it was.

She closed her eyes and listened: listened so very intently, with every molecule in her body and every drop of blood that moved sluggishly in her veins.

Listened: for the distant echo of a saxophone: for the upward lilt of a piano: for the ragged slide of a trombone lifting up across a city block, or a mountaintop, or an eternity, far away.

48

Ormolu & Lawyers

Bern

THEY FILED IN, all fifteen board members, plus Mallory and the Foundation's other officers; and each had at least one, if not two, lawyers in tow. All told, thirty-eight people, all in business suits and many with briefcases, sat on narrow hotel chairs arranged loosely in the ballroom in three rows, balancing legal pads and laptops on their knees. They also carried loose-leaf notebooks that Bern and Eboni had prepared and had left at the back of the ballroom: dark blue three-ring binders with tabbed pages, photocopied documents, and about two hundred densely typed pages of pure legalese, courtesy of the firm they'd hired to make sure everything was buttoned up properly.

Despite the ormolu and rococo of the ballroom, despite the glittering chandeliers and the polished parquet floor, the Delaney Foundation contingent all seemed somehow undignified.

Facing them were Bern, Eboni, and one of their attorneys—Lauren Weber, a smooth-faced woman with deceptively blank gray-blue eyes and an omnipresent faint smile, as if she'd just heard a terrific joke and couldn't quite shake her mirth.

While the board members took their seats, Bern turned on the PowerPoint presentation on the screen behind them: *Delaney Foundation Settlement.*

"Thank you all for coming," he said, loud over the murmur of voices, which instantly quieted. "Let's discuss what we're going to cover today. We'll go over each of these points in detail. I'd appreciate your full attention."

He introduced Eboni and Lauren Weber; then asked the room, "Ready?" and clicked to the next slide: *FINISHING <u>RED</u>.*

Before he could continue, Stanford Whitman spoke up from the seat next to Mallory Delaney Roberts. "You understand that you're both in full violation of the nondisclosure agreements you both signed, don't you? This charade is a complete waste of time."

Lauren Weber smoothed her gray skirt over her knees as she said, "You're absolutely right, Mr. . . . . ?"

"Whitman," Stanford Whitman said. "Stanford Whitman. In-house counsel."

"Yes, of course," she said, her cheeks dimpling as she smiled. "Nice to meet you in person. We'll let a court determine whether the NDAs that my clients allegedly signed are actually binding, and whether whistleblowing provisions might apply. As you know, the court system generally takes at least eight months, if not well over a year, for you to pursue your claim. Since my clients are prepared to go very, very public with their own claims in a matter of hours, the damage to your clients may be significantly more problematic to them, even if you could get a temporary emergency injunction. But of course that's for you to advise your clients. Shall we proceed or do you want to adjourn and pursue whatever remedies you want to pursue?"

"I don't understand why we had to meet in person," Thomas Alexander said. "Isn't this what lawyers are for? Emails?"

"We appreciate your willingness to show up," Weber said. "Your presence here speaks to the gravity of the situation. We wanted to have one chance to resolve this in person, before everything goes public and the suits and countersuits begin."

"Let's get started," Kurt Delaney snarled from a seat near the back, so loudly that the others swiveled to look at him, then faced forward. There was a very pointed clear space around him, as if no one else wanted to sit too close.

"Are we all in agreement?" Eboni asked. "We can just go on home, if you prefer. Oh, and I love that outfit, Mallory. My grandmother had one just like it."

Mallory Delaney Roberts, in a bright red dress with a white lace collar, smiled with her lips.

"No takers?" Eboni said. "Okay, then. So here are the terms:

"First order of business. Dr. Hendricks will continue to work, unimpeded, on the score to *RED*."

A rustle from the seats, but no one said anything.

"I have every intention of completing this historic work. The *right* way," Bern said. "And you'll include all—*all*—the updated information that we've uncovered. If you turn to the first tab in your binders, you'll see incontrovertible proof that Josephine Reed wrote most, if not all, of *RED*. And she's going to get proper credit for it."

"This is fucking ridiculous," Kurt Delaney shouted. His face looked extra red against his white beard. "You have this outrageous list of threats and demands that will never come to fruition and you think we are stupid enough to believe that you won't release this obviously falsified information out of spite?"

"You started this," Bern said. "This is a game that you and your fellow board members decided to play. You lost. Deal with it."

One of the board members spoke up from the back. "I do want to say that much of what you're alleging was done without the board's permission or authorization. Kurt and Mallory seemed to have acted without our approval. We're concerned about how they've dragged our name in the mud."

"Good," Eboni said. "Hopefully, you can take some steps to deal with Mr. Delaney yourselves."

Lauren Weber interrupted, "Can we stay on track, please? If you'll open your binders to section two, we've spelled out clearly how we believe the works previously listed as having been written by Frederic Delaney will now be listed as 'by Josephine Reed and Frederic Delaney.' There's a list of the music that my clients are certain was written primarily by Josephine Reed—see pages eighty-six to ninety-one."

"You're getting off easy," Eboni said. "We know she wrote all Delaney's music. All the good stuff, anyway. All the *Ring* operas. All the musicals that all the high schools perform. Plus the overtures, the symphonies, and 'Bring Back the Moon,' and the *Spider-Man Waltz*—"

"Eboni means *Spider Web*," Bern interrupted. "Not *Spider-Man*. In any case, we think Josephine Reed wrote most of Delaney's music, but we're only going after the ones that we can prove, with academic rigor, that she wrote. If you look at appendix two, we've provided notes and translations of the annotated pages."

Most of the people in the ballroom chairs flipped to the end, stared blankly at Josephine's hieroglyphs; but Thomas Alexander, the conductor; Andrew Kean, the concert pianist; and a few others studied the pages carefully, eyebrows furrowed.

Lauren Weber said, "Let's move on, now, shall we? Let's get down to brass tacks and discuss the financial settlement. If you'll turn to sections three through six, we've delineated the financial terms to the Reed family that we think are fair. This is all based on a clear and full audit of the Delaney properties, of course. And our financials will have to be evaluated once that happens."

"Josephine Reed has three nieces and nephews, fourteen grand-

nieces and grandnephews, and eight great-grands," Eboni chimed in.
"You're going to give her family a very nice sum of money for all the
royalties that the Foundation has received for the past hundred years.
You're gonna make those people *whole*."

Bern said, "The Foundation always tells everyone how much you
care about the community and want to help people. I have to believe
that, deep down, you all want to do what's right. The Delaney Foundation has always stood for hope. Maybe somewhere along the line
some of you forgot that. There are millions of people across the world
who rely on this Foundation's support, for what it is you stand for."
Bern stared back and forth between the two surviving relatives of
Frederic Delaney, Kurt and Mallory. "Or stood for at one time. It's
not too late to go back to the Foundation's roots of helping those in
need through the power of music. I believed in you all. I'd like to be
able to again."

There was silence, and then whispering, but no one spoke.

Weber continued, "The next tab delineates a sizable and fair mon-
etary compensatory package for both Ms. Washington and Dr. Hendricks as a result of lost revenue, services performed, damaged
equipment, and pain and suffering."

Apparently, many of the board members hadn't gotten to that tab
yet, so when they turned to those pages, a few audible gasps circu-
lated the room. Mallory Delaney Roberts shifted uncomfortably.

"There is no way that—" Momad Husseini began, when his attorney, a portly man with a gray ponytail, put a hand on his shoulder to
quiet him.

Bern said, "Your little stunt—locking me up for taking home my
work computer—having me beaten and tased and paraded almost
naked through the police station in the middle of the night—for
what? To keep your precious family secret? It's a funny thing about
secrets. They only stay secret if nobody tells. Can you imagine what
happens when I go public about how you treated me?"

Eboni said, "You're getting off easy. I think he deserves twice this."

"What are you talking about?" Kamae Sandgren asked. "'Police station'?"

Several others looked bewildered.

Bern asked Mallory, "Did you authorize it and not tell the board?"

She had the decency to look down.

"Authorize what?" Thomas Alexander said, turning toward Kurt. "What the hell are they talking about?"

Briefly, Bern explained his experience at the police station. "As soon as I got back, I wrote it all down, with all the names of the officers. I took pictures of the bruises."

"Appendix four," Eboni supplied helpfully.

"These numbers are going to cripple the Foundation," said someone at the back of the room. "We don't have these kinds of assets."

"Everybody, out!" Kurt screamed at the board members. "Mal, stay here. Everyone else, get out until I send for you."

"We're not leaving," Thomas Alexander said. "This involves all of us." Several heads nodded.

Lauren Weber looked at Bern and Eboni, said, "Everybody stays. This meeting involves all of you. You're all board members, and you need to know what's going on."

"If you turn to section five," Bern said, "you'll see some additional information that we uncovered that we think will actually break the Foundation if it gets out. You'll see compelling evidence showing Frederic Delaney was not only a thief.

"He was a murderer."

49

The Long Arm of Justice

Bern

THE BANKERS BOXES containing the Ditmars & Ross archive would perhaps be of interest to a handful of academics researching minor music publishers in the 1910s and 1920s. Few scholars, if any, would care about the company's employment records. Eboni and Bern, however, had dug right in.

"If this is where they met, maybe there's more here," Eboni had told him. So when they'd hired detectives to track down Josephine Reed, they'd also hired a forensic detective to comb through the Ditmars & Ross papers, tracing each employee who worked at the company from 1918 to 1924 in the hopes that someone would have had some affiliation with Josephine Reed.

In the process, the detectives discovered an interesting fact: a former song plugger turned composer had been murdered on May 23, 1924, in what police believed to be a robbery gone wrong. Miles Turpin had been shot once, at close range, and his wallet stolen. His murderer had never been found.

Most interestingly, the night he died, Miles had dined with the famous Frederic Delaney. Although the police must have questioned Delaney, the remaining police records were very thin: apparently Delaney said they'd dined together and he'd gone home. He didn't know where Miles had gone. That was the end of Delaney's involvement. As a major celebrity, Delaney wasn't questioned further. The case went cold.

On the fourth floor of the Delaney Foundation, Frederic's personal property was proudly on display in the museum. Among the collection were specially commissioned pens that he was purported to have used to create his music, several custom-made Victrolas, a beautiful leather letter opener, a collection of wine and champagne stoppers, and several small handguns.

The New York City police detectives determined that Miles Turpin was killed by a single small-caliber bullet to the back of the head and cataloged the forensics of the bullet. They never found the matching gun.

Bern's detectives, however, were able to determine that the same type of bullet perfectly matched one gun in Frederic Delaney's collection. Delaney, no doubt, had never supplied the handgun to the police for a ballistics test, and there was no way now of finding that bullet.

In the meantime, Bern's detectives tracked down Miles Turpin's grandson, Dan Rosenbaum. Rosenbaum had never met his grandfather, but his mother—Miles's daughter—had saved all Miles's correspondence and paperwork.

And there, among the paperwork, lay the equivalent to a smoking gun.

The melodies of five songs, never published, never performed: "When It Was Evergreen," "Chartreuse Limelight," "Shades of Warriors Past," "Blackfold," and "Racer's Crimson Tears."

On the top right corner of each page, in clear and familiar handwriting: *Music written by Josephine Reed.*

And an unsigned contract between Miss Josephine Reed and Mr. Miles Turpin for the sale of those five songs to Turpin Music Publishing.

The contract was dated May 24, 1924: the day after Miles Turpin died.

After he died.

The pieces fell into place. Why would Josephine Reed have sold those songs to Miles Turpin? Why was the contract never signed?

Because Miles was dead.

If Miles was dead, where was Josephine?

And why did Josephine want to sell the songs to Miles?

Because something went wrong between Josephine and Frederic Delaney.

Frederic Delaney had killed Miles Turpin to keep his secret.

"Boom," Eboni had whispered.

Now, in the gold-encrusted ballroom of The Pierre Hotel, Bern and Eboni walked the Delaney Foundation board through all their findings and suppositions, delineated clearly in section 7 of the binders. When they'd finished, the room was silent for a long time.

"There's still no proof," Kurt Delaney pointed out. "It's all just conjecture. A spiderweb of conjecture."

"It's not like you have the bullet that killed Miles," someone else said.

"Do you really want all this to get out there?" Bern said to Kurt. "If all the information we have gets out—the stealing and the murder—Frederic Delaney's reputation is ruined. Permanently. How do you think it'll go over for your licensing deals and your merchandising arrangements, let alone all the corporate sponsorships and partnerships? This plus your fucked-up tactics of hounding Eboni and me? It's gonna destroy you, buddy. Your Foundation and you, personally."

"Enough!" Kurt Delaney roared. "You two think you're the smartest people in the room. Do you honestly believe I would allow a pair of mooks like you to come in and threaten my family? We are the

Delaney Foundation. *The* Delaney Foundation." He pounded the back of the chair in front of him. "With power comes reach. I know you thought you were going to hold these outrageous items over my head, but you need to know that well before you were hired, Professor, I had some research done on you and your friend here."

"Mr. Delaney, you're embarrassing yourself," Eboni said. "You should sit down and take your meds before you have a—"

"I've tolerated this charade as much as I'm willing to. My patience has its limit, and you two just reached it. The Delaney Foundation has always been a pillar of hope and stability for the world. Your idle threats are meaningless. You are in the presence of some of the most powerful people in the world. You dare threaten us with innuendo and falsified information? We—"

"Kurt, shut up," Andrew Kean said. "Just stop talking. Right now."

"I—" Kurt started.

"You need to stop talking," Mallory Delaney Roberts agreed.

Bern could feel the tide shifting.

Except for Kurt Delaney, the board was firmly on his side.

Justice was really happening. Justice. For Bern. For Eboni.

For Josephine.

"Boom," Eboni whispered.

CURTAIN CALL

50

Sliding into the Corner

Frederic

LATE THAT NIGHT, he wrapped her in her coat as if she were asleep, propped her against him, and took the elevator down. As they descended, her body kept sliding into the corner, her sleeve catching on the filigree of the back wall, as if reluctant to leave. The elevator whined as it sank. He wondered what note it was. She would have known instantly.

He carried her down four blocks, the longest four blocks of his life, her head resting on his shoulder, her legs dragging uselessly along the sidewalk, and then down into the subway. The station was empty, a train idling on the platform. After it pulled away, he hefted her body onto the tracks at the far end.

As the body fell, he thought that he heard the tiny *tink* and spin of a metal object whirling out into the dark: a pocketknife, perhaps, or an errant nail. He would never know. For the rest of his life, for those next twelve appalling years, that sound would haunt him. He'd curse himself for not checking her pockets before letting go of her forever.

When he returned from the subway station, he knew he wouldn't sleep—couldn't imagine ever sleeping again—and went up to her room. He almost knocked on her door, which he'd left ajar, and he stood in the emptiness. Stood there as if waiting for her to reappear. As if she'd gone to the bathroom or down the hall to his old room to hunt for a page in her trunks. He stood, waiting. The world echoed dimly around him and he'd never felt so deeply alone.

The city stopped. The automobiles no longer drove outside, the wind died away, no one sang drunkenly from the bar. Was this— this aching, crippling loneliness—was this his, now, forever? Until tonight, these last years of his life had been defined by melodies, and now the melodies had gone silent. He had stopped them. He looked down at his hands and they were alien to him. Could these have done that? Killed her? Killed Miles? No. Of course not. He wouldn't do such a thing. The arms that would do this were not his arms. The tears that were, bizarrely, pouring down his cheeks, were not his tears. In hor- rified amazement he watched them spatter on the scuffed wooden floor, next to the piano bench, where only hours or minutes before she had sat with her wrists arched and fingers splayed.

Oh, those white torrents.

How had he silenced her music? All that extraordinary, extraor- dinary, beautiful music? He couldn't believe, it didn't seem possible, that she wouldn't be there tomorrow making more of it, weaving gos- samer and silk out of a puff of smoke. Of course she was here. Of course this terrible night hadn't happened. He'd just wanted to scare her, threaten her, that's all. Nothing more.

The horror built slowly: terror sparkling with self-revulsion and a grief so wide that he never glimpsed the other shore. He could barely read some of her notations, had never understood the subtleties of her ciphers: How would he survive? How could he make more music, make her music his own? He'd just killed the one person who had made everything, all of his life, possible. None of this seemed imag- inable, starting with the words *he'd killed*. He was shaking, suddenly, with something more chilling than cold. He wondered if he would ever get warm again.

Perhaps he'd retire. Rest on his laurels. He'd hand over RED and that could be his final, greatest, achievement. He'd bow out at the peak of his fame.

Which reminded him: Where was RED? He should retrieve it; he usually left the first drafts of manuscripts with her so she could correct or tweak what he'd transcribed. Sometimes he made errors, and she rectified them; and other times she discovered melodies that she "should have heard" more than the melodies she'd originally written. She'd been working on this draft of RED for several weeks. She should have been done with it by now, thank goodness.

Almost casually, the tears still pouring down his face, moaning softly to himself like an animal that had been hit by a bus, he started his search for RED. It wasn't in the usual places, nor in the steamer trunk that was sitting primly near the door, as if asking to be let out. Perhaps she'd stashed it in one of the other trunks in his old room?

In his old room, the trunks—all of them—were gone. The space echoed. And now he was frantic, tears forgotten, as he dashed back to her room and upended the furniture, tearing it apart as he went. He found cavities in the wardrobe where, perhaps, manuscript scores had once been hidden; loose floorboards in the bathroom, with a space between the joists; false backs to kitchen cabinets and even a cleverly concealed niche in the overhead light. But no RED, and no other pages, anywhere.

He spent the next day prowling the building and the street, trying to figure out what she had done with those steamer trunks. There had to be half a dozen or so. He'd never counted. She didn't have any friends, but he'd asked the local theater people who knew her if she'd been in lately, if she'd left anything with them; and she hadn't, and he grew more frantic, and he did not sleep the next night, either.

(And what had been that clinking sound, that metal *tink* in the subway tunnel? He returned to the station after the police had done their work, but he found nothing. He wanted to visit the morgue, duck into the police station, ask if they had found anything when they retrieved the woman's body, but he did not dare.)

Instead, he presented himself to Penn Station's left-luggage office, explaining that he had lost his ticket but had dropped off around half a dozen steamer trunks. He was wearing a full-length mink coat and sporting a gold pinkie ring, and of course they believed him. They handed over the trunks, and he had them hauled back uptown, up again to the fifth floor, noted how each had been neatly painted with her address in North Carolina, each numbered one through five. Number four was missing, but he assumed that the trunk in her room, the one she'd left by the door, was number four, and thought no more about it.

RED was in none of them. *RED* was nowhere.

For that whole summer, he barely slept. He would close his burning eyes and an image would flash across his eyelids: the curve of her hands on the piano keys, or her pencil on the music score; fried chicken on a plate; the glitter of stage lights on a trombone, lifted in song. Each time these images flashed, he'd force his eyes open, stare unseeing at the bedroom ceiling. There would be no new music. There would be no redemption for him. Drinking did not help, nor did sex, nor did food. And *RED* was still, impossibly, gone.

He hired workmen to demolish each vacant room in the building, dig up the back garden, excavate the basement. He checked everywhere he thought she might have hidden it, all the while haunted by that tiny sound of spinning metal, which grew in significance in his mind as the years crawled past. A key, perhaps? He hunted for a lock, found none.

Everyone wanted *RED*, and he didn't know how to magic *RED* out of nothing. He still had scraps of some of the melodies in his office—early drafts that he hadn't gotten around to destroying yet—and those became the basis of the opera that he would work on for a few days before the opium claimed him once more for the rest of the week, or for a month.

In a narcotic daze, he sifted through her trunks, laboriously deciphering all the ciphers he knew. And published her music as his own: *Frederic* Delaney. He decided his birth name, Frederick, was too gauche, too raw, too Midwestern. Perhaps if his name were more European, more elegant, then the melodies he wrote would flow out more smoothly, more assuredly, more believably?

The resulting music was less revered than the earlier material had been, but for a while he got by. She'd left enough half-completed melodies that he was able to round out the unfinished portions, and if the critics complained and the audience was less enthusiastic, so what?

But as time went by and the music dwindled, all that was left were pages or phrases that remained incomprehensible to him.

Around 1930 he'd deciphered the wind, decoded the rattle of a bus over cobblestones, drilled into each of the five trunks that she'd left behind. Desperately he swanned around with Duke Ellington, with Count Basie, with Irving Berlin, hoping their proximity would be enough to light up his own melodies with her magic. It was not enough.

"Tired and overwritten," the critics called his new music; and then "trite and overly familiar" and, soon, "ludicrous and embarrassing."

But music? Critics? They barely touched the ache in him. His loneliness was a spear in his chest. He never became accustomed to her absence. Never. Surely, after three or four years, he wouldn't look to find her scrolling out her patterns in a nightclub, but each night he searched for a woman with her eyes downcast, her fingers gripping the stub of a pencil as her hieroglyphs danced across the page and forever out of his life. He braced himself for her to round a corner or descend the stairs, and she never, ever, did.

She had haunted his memories, but around 1930 he began to think that she actually haunted *him*, as if by wanting so desperately to see her he had actually manifested her back into existence. At three in the morning he'd talk to her, call her kiddo and plead with her, bargain with her, try to bribe her. Even as the ghost of her melodies faded, her presence strengthened. He should have taken her to more shows so that she could have heard her music played; and so, on opening nights, he pretended she was there, rattling along behind him like an unseen, empty subway car. He thought, superstitiously, that if they drank a toast together before the start of a performance, the music would be wonderful, the applause heartfelt, the critics effusive. It never happened, but still he persisted.

He wanted the audience to love him because, he realized, he had lost the only person who really *had* loved him.

Soon it became a ritual: the pouring out of two glasses, his toasting to her photograph, corking the bottle, and, at the end of the performance, finishing it as if with her. He began to believe that she was with him in those quiet moments of the before and the after; that she would, if the stars aligned just so, part unseen curtains and her unseen hand would scroll out the new melodies that he desperately needed to sell.

He tried partnering with other composers but was terrified that they'd find out the truth about him and terminated the associations before they got very far. Through webs of lawyers he tried anonymously hiring others, but their music never reached the level he needed. He tried "retiring" and living on his laurels. Nothing helped.

And then there was *RED*, her greatest creation, his greatest hope. Drunk and dazed, he wrote out the musical notation, trying to drag the melodies out of his subconscious. The lyrics came more easily, but the music was a painful rasp in his throat.

In the meantime, as if to appease the gods, he created the Delaney Foundation to do some good in the world. As if by doing some penance—as if by opening his wallet to other poor musicians in the way he'd opened his door to Josephine, so long ago—he would be redeemed. The shadow of Josephine would forgive him if it saw he was trying, at the height of this Great Depression, to make amends. And if her shadow forgave him, perhaps he'd find RED or rewrite it in its full glory.

He really did have the best of intentions, he told himself. He just wanted the best for everyone—for Josephine, for himself. He didn't think about Miles Turpin.

But this new Foundation was not enough. Nothing was enough.

Only finishing RED, he came to believe, would suffice: If it were a success; if it were, indeed, his triumph, perhaps that might atone? Perhaps that might, for one moment, make her live again? Was this so much to ask? He deserved it. Yes, he'd made mistakes, but he'd spent the past dozen years making up for those mistakes. Hadn't he done enough penance? He had suffered and repented. He needed to rediscover RED as if to rediscover the crimson heart of himself.

At the beginning he'd been a good guy, he told himself. He'd wanted the best for everyone. He'd gotten Josephine that job. He'd given her stability, a place to sleep, a world where she could compose her music. He'd made her happy, and he looked back now at those joyous moments, as she cooked for him on that hot plate, and he longed for that moment again. He would pay any price and the Foundation was, in part, the price he was trying to pay. This was Frederic trying to do everything over, and do it the right way. The way he should have done it from the beginning. This next time, he would do it with her. He'd even give her top billing: *Music by Josephine Reed, Lyrics by Freddy Delaney.*

That last night of his life, when he had only a handful of hours left, just before the curtain rose on what would be, he was sure, his triumphant return, Frederic took his seat in his box to the left of the stage: his music had been performed so many times over the years that the Met had designated this box as his. Once—it seemed like long ago—he had envisioned standing onstage for this inaugural night, introducing *RED* to the crowd, telling them what the opera meant to him: it was the fire that burned in him, the ruby light on his closed eyelids, the scarlet cacophony of the city and of what his life had become.

But he would not address this audience. *Doing a Delaney,* he'd heard people say when someone did something particularly stupid. Oh, they were nice enough to his face—obsequious, really—but he knew they snickered. Until they heard his new great *RED* for themselves, he was afraid that this crowd would burst into laughter at his very presumption to stand before them.

Instead, he lurked in his box, the champagne wet on his lips. The curtain rose on *The Triumph of the Americas: The Red Ring of Olympia.*

The overture and act 1 seemed to go well. The audience was silent, eyes on the stage. Rapt. He watched them more than he watched the show: loving the feeling of all these pale faces, eyes reflecting his glittering music, all caught like fish in a net, tied up in this single moment, twisting and dancing and breathing together. He had them, and his music was keeping them.

He began to hope.

After the first intermission, act 2 commenced. He'd been worried about this section of the show—he'd rewritten it the most because he couldn't remember these melodies very clearly. But it was fine: better than fine. It was glorious. Besides, once they reached act 3 he knew the audience would be enchanted once more.

From the audience came a restless shifting of legs. A bubble of conversation bloated up from the opera seats. From the mezzanines a tiny ripple of laughter faded and bounced off the ceiling. Feet shuffled.

The singers sang. Mouths open as if gasping for air, they poured everything out on the stage, and mentally he applauded them. Such power! Such control! Such performances!

The audience seemed to disagree. Just before the end of act 2, a man and a woman stood up from aisle seats about ten rows from the stage, making their way slowly—why so slowly?—up the aisle. Perhaps they had a prior engagement. Perhaps the wife needed to use the facilities. There were dozens—hundreds—of reasons why an audience member might leave in the middle of a performance.

A minute later, four people on the other side of the auditorium stomped up and out.

Just in time, the curtain came down on act 3 and the lights came up for the second intermission.

He was afraid to leave his box.

So he stayed, and those of his public who wished to make obeisance made their way to him, and he shook their hands and bathed in their compliments, and he noted with no small satisfaction that the line to meet him was at least four or five people deep. He couldn't see beyond the curtains to know how much farther his flatterers went.

The lights flashed. The toadies disappeared. His public took their seats.

As the lights went down to begin act 4, he thought, at first, that he was misunderstanding. Were the doors locked from the lobby? Were the lines for the lavatories ridiculously long?

Why were a third or more of the seats empty?

Where was his public?

The lights dimmed. With a flourish, act 4 commenced.

The seats stayed vacant.

His audience had not returned.

The tops of his ears felt hot and then cold—and then it was all of him, flashing into a sweating, panting mass, and then the heat faded and he began to shake with chill. He saw his breath in the air, a frigid mist dancing like a ghost between him and the stage and the empty seats below.

Act 4 stuttered to a close, and then the curtain rose on act 5, which dragged on like a body that he carried in his arms across city blocks in the dead of night: endless, heavy, aching with all that would come after and all that had come before.

At last it ended. He'd had a stupid, blind hope that the audience who remained would cheer him wildly, would scream ecstatically for his triumphant return to the stage; but the applause was polite, functional, ending far too quickly. He had braced himself for flowers, bouquets, too many to carry; for buckets of champagne; for toasts and roaring adulation.

There was nothing.

A few people came to seek an audience with him. He told the usher that he was not to be disturbed. Perhaps, even if the audience did not understand, perhaps the critics' reviews would be filled with praise. Surely that would be the case. They would realize how glorious this opera had been. Surely someone must love him.

Too soon, the auditorium emptied except for the ushers, picking up programs and throwing away trash, calling to one another across the empty expanse of deserted seats:

"I got this row."

"Big night tonight, Charlie?"

"Nah. I'm just going home. Early day tomorrow."

He could feel their eyes, periodically, upon him.

Still he stayed in his box. Outside, in restaurants nearby, the after-parties would have started—he'd been invited to several. In fact, he was hosting one at Sardi's. But he did not move.

There would be other parties. There would be other chances. He knew this. He knew that opportunities spooled before him, just waiting for him to reach out, to take that first step forward.

The ushers left. The lights went off in rhythmic booming crashes. Only the stage manager remained, waiting. Let him wait.

The empty theater clicked and buzzed, heat ticking into cold.

Finally, painfully, he made his way out of the box, down the stairs, backstage to the dressing room they'd converted into a makeshift office for him.

No one was there. Who had he expected, after all this time?

Resting on the table, still where he had left it: Josephine's champagne glass, gasping into the silence, a few tiny bubbles still clinging to the rim. He stood over it for a long while. Always, after a performance, he drank the second glass, toasting her again, and then he would fill up both glasses with the remains of the bottle.

But the champagne stopper had been missing. A new, fresh bottle of champagne awaited him, its sides oozing with condensation, like sweat on exhausted skin.

He was too exhausted to uncork the second bottle. Too exhausted to lift her glass, let alone drink, the liquid now flat and warm. Its pale yellow reminded him, unaccountably, of flowers: the absurd cream of nasturtiums newly opened.

He pulled out the photograph from its usual place in his breast pocket. He turned it over, groped for a pencil, wrote in his spidery, elegant handwriting:

I, Frederick Delaney, killed Josephine Reed in 1924. I strangled her and threw her body in the subway. She was a colored woman and she wrote all the music that I told the world was mine. I am a liar and a cheat and a killer and I am beyond all hope.

His pencil paused. He laid it down.

Gently, tenderly, he lifted the photograph with the message he'd just written on its back. One last look at her and he ripped it into strips, ripped the strips into shards, ripped the shards into a gruesome confetti that he sprinkled carefully onto that pale, pale liquid. For a moment the paper floated like champagne foam; and then it sank.

He left the room, left the desk, left the sodden remnants in the glass. Stepped out into the hall, which stretched cold and black before him.

Where had she hidden *RED*? She never threw away any scrap of paper with her notations on it. Never. *RED* was somewhere.

With a calm that was altogether new to him and altogether welcoming and right, he now recognized that he would never know what happened to *RED*. He welcomed the word *never*, mouthed it to himself. *Never*.

Frederic Delaney shut the door behind him and trudged out into the night.

51

Brass Filigree

Bern

"HONESTLY, I don't know why you've made such a big production about this," Mallory Delaney Roberts told them when she arrived, tottering up on heels that seemed impractically high for the light March snow still dusting the sidewalk. "I would have taken you before without so much drama." She spoke without rancor. That part of the story seemed done and behind them. Bern had to admire her for it.

"Yeah, well," Eboni said, "you didn't, did you?" She and Bern had been standing on the corner of West End Avenue and Sixty-Third Street for ten minutes, and she wasn't happy to be kept waiting.

"It's just a power play, you know?" she'd said before Mallory arrived. "Even now she can't leave it alone."

Bern had shoved his fingers deeper into his pockets, had leaned in and kissed her again. He was still so grateful she was with him. He breathed in the scent of her, held her in his lungs for a moment. "When this is over, we're going to celebrate. With pizza," he said.

She grinned. "You read my mind."

But they weren't going to a pizzeria. They'd sampled pizza all over the city, from the trendiest Brooklyn café to the grubbiest Bronx dive. They'd ventured to Staten Island, tried Costco's and 7-Eleven's plate-size slices. And finally—finally—with a cast-iron skillet and Eboni's aunt's crust recipe, they'd made their own. "There really ain't nothing better than home cooking," Eboni had told him.

"Home is wherever you are," he'd said to her. Corny, but she didn't seem to mind, and kissed him hard.

Now Bern asked her, "What kind of pizza you in the mood for?"

"As long as it's not the Delaney Daily Special, I'm good," she said.

"Yeah, I'm done eating that," he said just as Mallory reached them. He didn't say hello to her, just nodded in a way that he hoped would seem dismissive.

"Come on," Mallory said, "it's this way." She led them down Sixty-Third Street to number 244, to the small nondescript brownstone they'd talked their way into months before, a stone's throw from the Foundation offices. She could have taken him here at any time, but hadn't. He still didn't understand why. "These were the original offices of Delaney Music Publishing, as you may remember," she said. "The Foundation bought the building in the fifties, and we used it as our main office until we acquired the land where we are now. We were thinking of turning this place into a museum but never did. We rented it out to musicians, some students. It was mostly for tax purposes."

"Didn't Delaney gut the place looking for *RED*?" Bern said. "I'd always thought so."

Mallory led them up the walk, her key at the ready. "We'd always thought so, too. We have records showing a great deal of demolition in 1924. We'd always thought it was remodeling, since he said he didn't lose *RED* until 1926." The key turned in the lock; she pushed the door open into the narrow hallway that Bern remembered from months ago. The workmen didn't seem to have made much progress. Ladders and tools lay stacked in the cold. She flicked a switch and several bare lightbulbs glowed.

"He must have been lying about 1926," Bern said. "He must have lost it in 1924. She must have hidden it in 1924."

"You may be right," Mallory allowed. They followed her inside. "About eight months ago," she said, "we decided to fix the place up. Its location is terrific, of course, and we thought we could use it for visiting board members or musicians performing at the Foundation. Really make it a five-star accommodation. Plus the charm of it having been the original Delaney offices."

She led them past tool belts and sanders and saws, over to the elevator. She pulled out a key, inserted and turned it, and pressed the button. This time the doors opened.

"The elevator has been regularly in service since 1917," she said. "We have the building inspection records. The motor's been replaced several times, and there've been many service calls over the years—as you'd expect. But nobody actually replaced the elevator walls. Why would they?"

She leaned over the back panel, and they stood behind her, watching. A handful of tiny metal screws lay all but buried in the tarnished art deco brass filigree that lined the interior. Most screws had already been removed; only two remained. Mallory fished in her purse for a minuscule screwdriver, inserted it into the screwheads, and extracted them. "Workmen found this when we decided to refurbish the interior. Strip the brass, clean everything up. Of course, once we discovered what was inside, we decided to leave it intact."

The brass mesh screen fell away, revealing a space about two feet wide, three feet high, and three inches deep. "*RED* was right here. All loose paper, just squashed at the bottom. It had been riding up and down the elevator for nearly a century."

"That's my girl," Eboni said proudly.

Bern peered inside as if searching for some last sign from Josephine Reed, a final message to tell them what happened to her in 1924, why she hid the opera in its ultimate hiding place.

The space was empty.

52

Stepping into Tomorrow

THE RED RING OF OLYMPIA would be performed in New York's Metropolitan Opera House. With one of the largest auditoriums in the world, the Met could seat almost four thousand people. But it also felt right and just that here, in Lincoln Center, within spitting distance of where the score had spent the past century, it would finally sing out.

There were other considerations, too: LCD screens on the back of each audience seat to display subtitles; the Met's ability to broadcast in HD worldwide; and of course, the stunning, world-class acoustics of the auditorium itself. The space was worthy of the music that would be played tonight.

For this very special inaugural performance, seats were not sold in the usual manner, with the expensive orchestra seats going to the socialites, the celebrities, the politicians. Instead, Eboni had devised a complicated lottery system where some seats were allotted to high-paying donors, some to the media, some to diplomats representing their countries, some to opera lovers, and some to DF Kids. Bern now recognized senators and concert pianists, movie stars and financiers. Tuxedos mingled with jeans; baseball caps with ball gowns. A well-known billionaire entrepreneur stood to let a tiny woman slide past him to her center seat: she was a schoolteacher from rural Arkansas who had taught half a dozen of the best trombone players in the country—all DF Kids.

Now, in that taut moment after the chandeliers had started to rise but before the lights dimmed and darkened altogether, Bern felt like he was actually looking at a cross section of not only America but the globe: a communion of music lovers, brought together for this one night, to listen and celebrate, to bond in that magical way that only music can provide.

The lights dimmed. The curtain rose. Bern stood alone onstage, a vast video screen blooming behind him.

"Welcome," he said. "My name is Kevin Bernard Hendricks. I was a Delaney Foundation Kid, and I am the musical scholar who transcribed the music you're about to hear."

The applause roared up.

He waited, smiling, and then, "I want to thank so many people who made this possible: the Metropolitan Opera and the Delaney Foundation, to start."

Applause again. He wondered if he'd ever get through his speech, however short it was. He listed several major donors and benefactors whom the Met had stipulated must be mentioned.

And then: "I want to also thank my partner in figuring out the mystery of this most extraordinary opera: Ms. Eboni Washington, whose company, Washington Visionaries, has been critical to this whole endeavor. Eboni single-handedly deciphered the code that baffled scholars for a century. Her work has allowed us to play the original, true version of RED you are about to hear."

A spotlight on Eboni, in a box at stage right. She gave a thumbs-up. More applause rippled into the rafters.

"Now, I want to tell you a story. It's a story that was lost for a century. A story that you, along with the rest of the world, will be learning tonight."

On the screen behind Bern appeared the black-and-white photograph of a woman seated at a table: wide-eyed, beautiful, enigmatic, gazing distantly into the night.

"I'd like to introduce you to the person who made Frederic Delaney's music possible. She was born in 1891 in Oxford, North Carolina. We don't know a great deal about how she lived or how she died. What we do know is that her music changed everything we know about music today. The world is a better place because of her.

"The people sitting there"—he gestured to another box—"are her descendants, but they didn't know of her contributions, either, or the critical role she had in creating all the music we are about to hear." Spotlight on another box, stage left, where Earlene, Myrtis, Kay, Judy, Sandra, and Karl sat in new finery, smiling out over the audience and into the dozens of television cameras that clustered above the stage.

"We believe she had almost total recall of any musical phrase she heard. She was, most definitely, a genius."

He clicked on a particularly gorgeous slide of Josephine's notations: the pictographs and patterns shimmering and vibrating in the light. What would this moment have meant to her, with a worldwide audience gathered in tribute to her accomplishments? The entire world celebrating her music, broadcast live to every country, simultaneously translated into hundreds of languages and dialects?

It would have been overwhelming had he not fought so hard to make her story right. To right the terrible wrong that had been perpetuated for reasons he would probably never know. So it was not overwhelming; instead it felt just and right. He only wished he could have done more.

"Every so often, however, we discover another portion of the greater story, another section that was left out. We learn—not everything—but a little more. And because we learn more, the world is a little brighter. Our understanding is a little clearer. I'd like to think our capacity for empathy, for caring, is a little stronger, too."

The slide returned to the first photograph: a woman seated at a table, the remains of a meal to one side, wineglasses glittering in the flash. What had she been listening to when the photographer snapped this image? What music had she been composing in her head, about to jot down onto a napkin or into a notebook?

"This woman wrote much of the music that Frederic Delaney passed off as his own," Bern said. Was it just his imagination, or did she now seem to be smiling? "He wrote a different story for the world. He made it seem that the music was his. Written by him. Created by him. It wasn't. It's hers. That's the hidden story I want you to know. It's hers. All hers."

He paused, looked out over the crowd—shadows, now, in the darkness. Then he gazed beyond the faces, beyond the lights.

"This opera is her masterpiece," he said. "And her name is Josephine Reed."

The video screen lifted away, and behind him another curtain rose, revealing the opening stage set of her opera as he introduced this extraordinary woman, and the music that she wrote, to the future.

Author's Note

When my first novel, *The Violin Conspiracy*, was published in 2022, I was lucky enough to meet people I otherwise wouldn't have encountered. Readers often told me either that they were surprised to learn that the kinds of things I discuss in *The Violin Conspiracy* still occur today, or that they found their own experiences reflected in the book.

One woman, who stopped playing the violin to raise her family, was inspired to pick up the instrument again. She even bought a violin from a pawnshop and brought it to a book signing to show me.

That particular experience made me think about all the other people whose voices, for whatever reason, have been silenced. Perhaps they never had an opportunity to be heard. Perhaps they didn't have the courage to speak. Perhaps they were shut down before they could even begin.

I know that this is often how the world works, but it's something I've been mulling over more and more.

In my junior year of college, I was invited to perform the Suite for Violin and Piano by William Grant Still. When my professor, Dr. Rachel Vetter Huang, asked me if I'd ever heard of the composer, I told her I hadn't. I figured he was an obscure European or American. Then she told me he was an American composer who happened to be Black. I was dumbfounded. Sadly, I—a Black man myself— had never imagined that Black composers *even existed*. Why had I never heard of Still? It certainly isn't because Still's music is subpar; his compositions are full of passion and verve and deserve to be heard. But his music—and music by so many other musicians—is rarely played. Brilliant songs and extraordinary books or poems or paintings or speeches or—well, you name it—have been lost, thrown away, burned, or ignored. So many other artists (and their voices) were too intimidated, too shy, or too overwhelmed. Now they're lost.

The stories are endless. A single mother living in an inner city wants to be a news broadcaster, but no one takes her seriously because of where she lives and how people view her. A singer who works in a processing plant never gets the chance to showcase his talent because he doesn't fit the industry standard. And so on.

The situation can be even more precarious for people from historically marginalized communities. They often have to jump through even more hoops to get the recognition they deserve. Female composers like Fanny Mendelssohn had to pose as men to get their music played. While studying at an American academy, Mary Cassatt was not permitted to paint from live models only because she was a woman. Ellen Ochoa, the first Hispanic woman to travel to space, was repeatedly discouraged from pursuing a career in STEM.

Sometimes it's not just a question of vital voices failing to be heard. Sometimes people steal what others created. We often hear about lawsuits in which a musician lifted a melody from another musician's song—but in the early twentieth century, the situation was much more egregious. Music publishers would pay a songwriter a few bucks for a song and then own it outright. The publisher would make millions, while the songwriter got a couple of dollars and maybe no credit. (That's partly how the Copyright Act of 1909 came to be.)

I thought it would be fascinating to explore the time period of the early 1900s—when the people who were writing chart-topping songs would literally starve because the industry stole their music and their voice.

For me, Josephine Reed represents precisely that. But she also represents a great deal more. She's a woman. She's Black. And she's neurodivergent. People with differing abilities are very dear to me. My nephew lives with autism, as does my best friend's brother. I've been privileged to teach many students living with different types of neurological conditions and a wide range of learning disabilities. Two of my very best students live with autism.

As a Black man, I've often heard "You can't do that." It's a phrase so many of us hear in our everyday lives. Women "can't" run as fast, "can't" conduct a major symphony, "can't" become a CEO. Some neurodivergent people "can't" hold down a regular job or fit into society.

We all know that people *can*, if they're given the opportunity and the tools. I'm hoping this novel might be one of those tools.

All authors, like parents, have hopes for their books: that they'll toddle off into the world, touching lives, changing perspectives. When I was writing *Symphony of Secrets*, I hoped, given the unique time period we're living in, when the experiences of underrepresented communities are both celebrated and under attack (in September 2022, book banning has never been so prevalent—predominantly among books written by either LGBTQ+ people and/or people of color), this book could make a difference.

Of course, I want my book to be read, to touch lives, to change perspectives. I also hope that it encourages readers to go out and *listen.* Listen to the busker on the street; to the kindergartner unable to sit still; to the quiet woman tucked in a corner, doodling in her notebook. Listen to them. Really listen.

Who knows?—Maybe you'll be lucky enough to hear a voice, a story, that would otherwise never have been heard.

Acknowledgments

First and foremost, to the entire Anchor Books team: Thank you. I am extremely proud to be one of your authors.

Edward Kastenmeier, executive editor extraordinaire: Thank you for simply being incredible. Your thoughtful and sensitive suggestions truly expand my creativity. Every paragraph is better because of your insistence on excellence.

Suzanne Herz and Beth Lamb, the best publishers ever: Thank you both for believing in me. From the moment I met you, I knew I was in good hands. Thank you for all your support and for taking a chance.

J Funk (otherwise known as James Meader) and Julie Ertl, publicists beyond compare: I have no words. Thank you for your constant support and encouragement. And thank you for helping me with scheduling. You make it all look easy, and I cannot begin to tell you how much I appreciate all you do. Thank you.

Sophie Normil and Lauren Weber: Thank you for your overflowing creativity, your energy, your enthusiasm, and your support.

Brian Etling: Thank you for working overtime to make sure this book reached the public.

Kayla Overbey and Lisa Davis: Thank you for catching my mistakes and for making me look good.

Maddie Partner: Thank you for bringing the beautiful cover to the public.

Jenn Lynn Kerwin, you are the brightest of lights in a world that needs it. Thank you for always making me smile during rehearsal. Thank you for allowing me to share in the joy of Jake. Thank you for your honesty and caring. Thank you for being a tremendous friend. Thank you for being so incredibly open about autism. I hope I made you proud.

Dr. Hao "Howard" Huang, you continue to push me to do better. What I thought I knew about musical annotations was completely eclipsed by your expertise. Thank you so much for your willingness to share your knowledge with me, to give this story even more meaning.

Dr. Rachel Vetter Huang, I can *never* thank you enough for everything you've done for me. Thank you for introducing me to William Grant Still. Every opportunity I have to share his music, I will. Your passion and dedication to multicultural music continues to inspire me every day.

To my sister Robin, my brother Howard, and my mom, Milo: Thank you for all of your joy and support, and thank you for sharing all of your "Kevinisms" with me. He was such a character. I'd almost forgotten some of the things he said and did. I think he'd be flattered to read this. I love you all.

To Sophie Brett-Chin, indefatigable researcher: Thank you for all your insights and for enthusiastically seeking out all the information I threw at you.

To Katherine Bellando, website and social media guru: Thank you, thank you for all your help and support and ideas and enthusiasm.

Finally—last but absolutely not least—the greatest thanks to Jeff Kleinman for being here every step of the way. None of this would have been possible without you, and I'm very aware of that. Thank you. You've made a huge impact in my life, and I'll always be grateful.

ABOUT THE AUTHOR

Brendan Nicholaus Slocumb was raised in Fayetteville, North Carolina, and holds a degree in music education (with concentrations in violin and viola) from the University of North Carolina at Greensboro. For more than twenty years he has been a public and private school music educator and has performed with orchestras throughout Northern Virginia, Maryland, and Washington, DC. He lives in Washington, DC.

brendanslocumb.com

Date Due

JUL 1 4 2023		
AUG 1 0 2023		
SEP 2 1 2023		
NOV 3 0 2023		
DEC 2 0 2023		
FEB 4		